BROKEN
REIGN

AVA HARRISON

Broken Reign
Cover Design: Hang Le
Cover Image: Wong Sim
Cover Model: Lucas Garcez
Editor: Editing4Indies, Write Girl Editing
Proofreader: Jaime Ryter, Marla Esposito

The only difference between the saint and the sinner is that every saint has a past, and every sinner has a future.

—Oscar Wilde

PROLOGUE

Officer Matthews

I T'S A PERFECT DAY TO KILL SOMEONE.

Half the force is on Waverly Street, crammed inside Chief's rickety Nantucket home for his fiftieth birthday. Response time would be abysmal. Charlie and Rick are dozing at their desks, the only signs of life in a sea of empty chairs.

These days, I pack an extra pair of cuffs on my belt. But when I stare out the window from my cubicle, it's quiet out. Unusually boring.

No calls. No tears. No body bags.

The type of Sunday afternoon we used to take for granted.

The type of Sunday we used to have before things started to change.

Sure, we always had crime. But before this year, the worst criminals stayed on the other side of town. Not my jurisdiction, not my fucking headache. As long as the citizens of Reddington were safe, I was golden.

But that was then, and this is now.

These days, there isn't a single day that passes without an

overdose. The drugs are inching closer and closer to the heart of town. And if word on the street is right, the war brewing down by the docks is heading this way, too.

The district attorney ran on a campaign promise that the drugs would never get to our small, quiet community. That he would stop it.

What a fucking joke.

I glance at my watch for the fourth time in twenty minutes. Two minutes left on my shift. Just as I'm about to gather my things, my desk phone rings. A blaring sound against the silence of the day.

Ring.

Ring.

Ring.

Charlie and Rick continue to snore, unbothered by the piercing noise. I reach out to grab the phone, skimming over the mess on my desk—pens, crumbled-up paper, and even an old coffee cup cram the space.

A stack of pictures lies next to the phone. One catches my eye. It's an image of Baros, a new drug dealer in town. For the past year, we've monitored his every move, an order that came down from the top.

I push the stack aside so it doesn't topple over when I pick up the phone and grab the receiver. A booming sound interrupts me. It's the chief, accompanied by dozens of others. They enter the room in plainclothes, speaking chaotically, eyes half-crazed. A Birthday Boy pin is still attached to Chief's shirt, no doubt his wife's idea.

Loud voices echo around me. I abandon the phone, peering around the space, trying to see what's going on. A group of officers are clustered together, heads down, listening to a detective speak. It's Mark. From homicide.

Beside me, Belinda screams for someone to answer her. Across the room, Philip sprints into the hall leading to the exit. I'm not sure what's happening, but I'm instantly on edge.

Without another thought, I push back my chair so hard, the metal legs grate against the floor. The chair bounces back, probably leaving a dent against the wall. I don't care.

"What's happening?" Rick's voice comes with a yawn. He stands, stretching his arms above his head and nudging Charlie awake. His gaze darts around, trying to see if anyone knows what's going on.

I shake my head, adding another pair of cuffs to my belt's collection. "I don't know, but it's got to be something big."

My body finally catches up to my brain and reacts to the chaos. The next thing I know, I'm barreling toward Chief.

Something is wrong. His face looks unnaturally pale, and if that weren't a dead giveaway, his jaw is tight.

"Chief?"

He looks at me.

A vacant stare.

"What's going on?" I prompt.

"There is a situation . . ." he trails off, shaking his head as if he can't comprehend what he just heard.

"What type of situation?"

But he doesn't answer me. The room is in an uproar. People are shouting about the phone calls coming in.

I expect him to say something, but instead, he straightens. Standing up tall and steeling his spine, he scrubs at his eyes, which start to refocus, and then he walks away from me, making his way to the middle of the room where he stands in front of the crowd that has formed.

The room goes completely silent.

My spine locks.

I'm bracing myself for a shitshow.

"We've received dozens of reports of an explosion and screams being heard from the restaurant. Multiple eyewitnesses say it sounds like there was a hit."

The chatter begins.

Voices rise again, firing question after question at him.

We all knew this moment was coming.

It was inevitable. But as much as we've been working to rid the city of the dredges of the earth, many of us working overtime to control it before it's too late, it's still different than knowing the first strike has been fired.

My thoughts are going a million miles per hour as I wonder where. What restaurant? Was it by the docks? Maybe the café by the apartment complex that has become overrun by addicts? But then his words come out. It sounds like a hum over the beating of my heart.

Al's Diner.

Massacre.

"I need everyone to fall out. Matthews, Sterling, Bruno, and Ludlow, I need you at Al's—"

I'm taking off.

The local diner.

The local diner where people eat. Where families go to celebrate their most precious loved ones. Their friends, their partners . . . their children.

Bile coats my throat. It's not even half a mile away from the precinct.

It's not far, I remind myself. *If I leave now, maybe I can stop it. Maybe we aren't too late.*

My breath comes out in ragged bursts as I start to sprint. Voices yell at me to stop. To wait. That I need backup.

But before they can stop me, I'm already pushing open the door and am out of the building. From behind me, I hear Tom screaming that he's coming, then the rest of the men follow suit.

The chill hits my face like a vicious slap.

I never grabbed my coat.

But knowing where I'm going and what I will most likely see, I won't turn back. I can't. I don't have time.

Blood courses through my veins as I push harder.

My heart beats frantically.

Almost there.

Only a few blocks.

By the time I'm near the building, my chest rises and falls in erratic jerks. My lungs burn as I inhale deeply to calm myself.

Standing on the corner of the street, only a few feet from the entrance to the building, I whip my head around in both directions to look at the other officers who have followed me.

Most are leaning forward, their chests heaving as they try to catch their breaths. Others are on their walkie-talkies, probably trying to get orders from the chief.

I ignore them, assessing the situation. Do I wait for more men? For SWAT from the town over? Or do I go in without eyes in the building?

It's quiet. Eerily so. Like the whole town knows what's going on and decided to stay clear of the devastation.

Normally, you would expect pedestrians to be walking in a town like this. Cars driving by, friends giggling, a man and a woman strolling hand in hand.

But now, there's nothing.

The stillness around me makes my footsteps falter. Despite my reservations, I force myself to move. I press on, unsure of what I'm going to find.

Not sure what sort of horrors hide inside.

I feel like I'm in slow motion. Like I'm stuck in a slasher flick, where the world quiets before shit goes down.

The thing that scares me the most is that there is no gunfire. Not one sound comes from the building.

Tentatively, I open the door, careful when I step inside. My gun is raised, cocked and ready. Once I cross the threshold, a familiar smell of lingering gunpowder hits me.

Then the heat touches my face, infiltrating my nostrils. The shots were just fired, probably with a silencer. It only just ended, which means the threat is still out there. I keep my wits about me as I move farther into the building.

At first, it seems as if there's nothing out of place.

Except for the most important thing.

Signs of life.

Instead, only the soft hum of the jukebox can be heard. The song feels out of place in the backdrop of bright walls and party streamers. A slow, emotional melody. Goose bumps rise on my arms.

Even the lyrics feel like a warning . . .

A warning of something sinister waiting around the bend.

Normally, Al's is loud and boisterous, but now the space is empty. I clock the details. The stained wallpaper. The popped balloons. The copper scent.

As I turn the corner, the illusion lifts.

It's a massacre.

Bullet casings litter the floor like thrown confetti.

I follow them and peek into the first booth.

A bloody handprint is smeared across the bench. I look down to find wide, vacant eyes staring right at me. A bullet lodged between them.

My jaw clenches at the sight, and the muscles in my back tighten.

Gun leveled before me, my trigger finger ready, I walk to the next booth.

A streak of red coats the table. It trails along the wall, bloody handprints on the window.

Someone was trying to escape.

I look for the body . . .

That's when I see her. Tucked under the bench as if she could hide.

But death found her anyway.

I push down the bile in my throat and turn to look at the rest of the dining room.

Bodies are strewn haphazardly across the floor. There is blood. So much blood. The crimson trails across the white linoleum floors like bright-red rivulets of paint running down a pristine canvas. It'll take weeks to process this crime scene. To figure out who each splatter of blood belongs to.

Pressing my lips together, I breathe through my mouth. This is not the time to fall apart.

I push myself to take a step closer, careful not to disrupt the crime scene.

There's another body here. He's pale, wide-eyed, the horror of today permanently etched inside them. I want to run my hands down his eyelids and close them. To let him rest in peace.

I can't disturb the crime scene.

Fresh tinges of purple and gray dot his cheeks and lips. His skin hasn't become waxen yet, which means this happened sometime within the past twenty minutes.

Whoever did this can't have gotten far. And he must've used a silencer, or we would've heard the shots from the precinct.

I pull out my phone to call the station and tell them where I am and what I've seen. It's empty here, the back door hidden past the kitchen the most likely escape route. Still, I keep my gun drawn as I continue to check for any survivors.

My eyes scan the walls, windows, and tables.

That's when my eyes lock on it. A barely noticeable trail of blood. I follow it. Each step is slow and calculated as I trace where the blood leads.

A door tucked away behind the jukebox.

It's hidden.

Hell, I've lived in this town all my life, visited Al's every week, and never knew it existed.

Tucked behind the jukebox that has entertained this town for years, it's cracked open just a sliver. I move toward it, ready to pull the trigger if I need to. I hope I don't. I hope to God it's a survivor. That someone lived.

Slowly, I reach out and touch the doorknob.

The door creaks amongst the silence, amongst the stillness of the room. As soon as it opens, I dip my head to peer inside, and that's when I see it.

A hand covered in blood.

CHAPTER ONE

Twenty years later . . .

Tobias

I HAVE A SINGLE GOAL IN MY LIFE.

One goal that is always in front of me.

It's all-consuming, and it eats at me. But I need to get everything in line before attempting to conquer it.

Which brings me to the present. My right foot hits the pavement as I step out of my car and walk toward the courthouse.

There's no reason to tell my driver anything. He'll wait for me as I do what I need to do—as he always does.

I hate being driven around, but apparently, it's necessary. And today, despite my security's insistence, I am going in alone. The only one who will be here with me is Gideon, my right-hand man.

He's already here, in place and scoping out the scene, assessing any threats to be concerned with.

With fast strides, I move toward my destination.

The large courthouse flanked by pillars greets me as I climb up the massive granite steps toward the entrance.

Of course, when I make it to the top of the stairs, I have to go through security.

Fun occupational hazard is that I'm not carrying today, which puts me at a disadvantage if an enemy decides to come after me.

This is the reason Gideon has gone ahead of me. To make sure nothing gets past him.

Trained well to see a threat from a mile away, Gideon doesn't need weapons to take anyone out.

He's just as lethal with his hands as he is with a gun.

A good person to have in your pocket.

But Gideon is more than that.

Not only is he my right-hand man, he's also the man who will take over everything when I step away. There is no one else I would trust. Gideon has been my friend since we were both teenagers in Miami, which makes him perfect to hand over my keys to the castle to. Luckily for me, he has no objections, either, but until the transfer is complete, he proves his loyalty time and again.

Like now, putting my full trust in him as I walk through the metal detector with no weapon to protect myself. I'm an open target if my enemies want to kill me.

I still think it's worth it, though. I'm willing to take a calculated risk, as I need to see what I'm dealing with. See him in action.

Felix Bernard is here.

A preliminary hearing to see if probable cause of a criminal offense occurred. In this case, it's determining whether there is enough evidence to tie him to a money laundering scheme. One that would directly connect him to a large drug empire.

There is no question that Felix Bernard will get off. He's not going to jail. That much is clear to me, but I still need to see him. Look straight into the bastard's soul and see what's there. The best way to see the demons that live within is by looking into someone's eyes.

Once past security, cleared, obviously, I head toward the

courtroom where Gideon waits for me. The preliminary hearing is open to the public. Probably not a good idea.

It could be a spectacle if the case doesn't get thrown out. If I were the judge, which I am obviously not, I'd shut it down. But his dumbass decision is my gain because I get to see Felix in action. In our line of work, with security in place, Felix and I are rarely in the same building, let alone the same zip code at the same time. Precautions are taken to ensure we aren't.

I hurry my steps as I move down the corridor. The sound of my soles hitting the marble with a faint clapping rhythm marks my approach. As I weave my way through the corridor, it only takes a few seconds before I walk into the large room.

It's packed.

This is not a courthouse. This is a fucking circus. And Felix, he's the ringleader.

It's a who's who in attendance.

First, I spot the hungry newscaster from channel five. She's a pretty young thing. Perfect shoulder-length blond hair styled to perfection, with a bubble gum smile, and still wet behind the ears. I can practically see her salivating in her seat to get the story.

Little does she know, her boss probably sent her to save himself a headache. There won't be a story today.

Looking across the room, I notice Gideon. He's already waiting right where he told me he'd be.

Dressed in a suit, he acts the part of a legit businessman. But seeing him here still feels wrong. Men like him—men like *me*—spend little time in court. Normally, we are covered in blood while holding some poor bastard's insides in our hands.

Taking the seat beside him, I nod in greeting but don't speak. He probably appreciates it. Gideon is a man of few words, and when he speaks, it's often to scoff or make a snide, sarcastic comment.

A quick glance around has me taking in my surroundings, my gaze finding my target.

Bernard.

He oozes wealth.

He's not an ugly man—quite the contrary. If I were a woman, I could see the appeal. Tanned skin with salt-and-pepper hair.

Always dressed to perfection, he plays the role of a distinguished businessman to a T.

I should know. I play it just as well.

But I also know it's bullshit.

We both walk the line, lurking in the underworld in equal measures.

Felix, too, is glancing around the space as if searching for someone. Once he assesses the crowd, he looks over to where his lawyers are standing, one man and a woman.

I pay the man no mind, but it's the woman who has me curious.

From the way she's angled, I can't see her face, but what I can see, I already like. Long wavy brown hair bounces down her back as she speaks to her client.

She's dressed for court, but she'd be just as comfortable going out to dinner in her outfit. A fitted blazer over an equally fitted dress adorns her body. She moves to lift her sleeve, and an image peeks back at me. A tattoo?

Interesting. Also, surprising.

Who is your lawyer, Bernard?

That's when she turns toward the back of the room, and my actual fucking breath leaves my body.

Fuuuuck.

"Everything okay over there?" I hear Gideon say beside me, but his words sound as though he's speaking underwater. I'm transfixed, and I can't pull away.

Soft lips, that's the first thing I see. Not too large, but large enough to get the job done. She's not like the women I'm usually attracted to. She's a natural beauty, as if she doesn't wear a bit of makeup and is just gorgeous without the additional help. My gaze continues its perusal of her.

Until I land on her eyes. Eyes that look haunted. Which I can understand because I'm haunted just the same.

"Tobias." The words filter in, but I still can't break away.

A tap on my arm hits me next, but I still don't sever our connection.

She looks familiar.

Eyes I can't place.

She reminds me of a girl I once met.

Maybe it's her.

I wait to see if she recognizes me. Not only because I believe we met once, but because everyone does eventually. My face has littered many a magazine. Speculation on where my money comes from. On my bachelor status.

But there's nothing there . . .

A blank slate.

My teeth clench. She doesn't know who I am.

Maybe I'm wrong? Maybe it's not her.

No.

A flare of anger seeps into my veins as I stare her down. We're locked in a battle of wills. Who will end this first? She does, finally, after long seconds, breaking the connection to turn back to her client.

The muscles in my back tighten. Her dismissal pisses me off even more. I narrow my eyes and continue to watch her. That's when she does it. She looks back at me.

Couldn't help herself.

I wink at her and even from here, I can see her cheeks redden. Her eyes go wide. She didn't think I'd catch her.

Good.

She blinks before her head gives a little shake, and she turns back to her client.

Gideon says something else, but he could tell me the world is about to end, and it would make no difference.

The hearing commences, and I watch her for hours without pulling my gaze away. As time goes on, her arguments become more powerful and heated.

Her voice rising through the air with authority.

She's dynamic as she speaks. A force to be reckoned with.

"The prosecutor has dragged my client into this courtroom as if he is a common criminal—" But it's when her gaze meets mine, and her lip tips up into a smirk followed by a wink do I feel my breath leave my body.

Fuck.

There is a strength about her that is admirable. She's a spitfire. Time passes, but it feels as if it flies by.

The next thing I know, I'm being nudged by Gideon, alerting me that it's time to go.

The court has erupted in chatter, and Bernard's lawyers are speaking to him. The case will not proceed to trial. Not that this is a shocker. She's good.

The client can go because of this woman. I watch them shake hands. I watch him smile at her. Felix Bernard looks at her the way I did, the way every man in this room is.

With lust in his snake-like eyes, narrowing and imagining her beneath him.

My fist clenches at the way she smiles back at him. It's professional and reserved. Nevertheless, the look she gives him stirs something primitive inside me.

I'll have her. Snatch her right out from his grasp. Then, when that is said and done, parade her in front of him, all while trying to pilfer information from her on him.

Yes, that's exactly what I'll do. I make my decision. Now to make it happen.

"What's going on?" Gideon watches me intently.

"Her," I respond, inclining my chin in her direction.

"Skye Matthews?"

My curiosity is piqued. Is she the girl I think she is? She sure as fuck reminds me of her. My past batters against my brain, pushing her image into my mind.

Thrust back into the past, I see a girl. The smile she gave me. No, not a smile but a smirk, coupled with a wink . . .

It has to be her. "Details."

"She's with Stuarts, Finkel, and Williams." One of the best firms in New York City. "She's a junior associate. I'm actually surprised the senior partner is letting her take lead."

"Interesting." This could benefit me. Seth Williams is a weasel, a weasel who, for the right price, will sell Felix Bernard out to the highest bidder, and that bidder is me.

"What do you have in mind?"

My lips part into a smile. I want to hire her.

"With me retiring, I will need a lawyer to help me. . ." I trail off. A plan is settling in place. "I want to hire her."

"And how do you plan on doing that? They aren't accepting new clients."

"Let me worry about it."

"Seeing as I'm involved in your retirement plans, I think I deserve a better answer than that bullshit one."

He's right. Whatever the fallout is, he will probably have to clean up the pieces.

I incline my head and proceed to tell him my plan.

The endgame will be the same.

Skye Matthews has wandered into my path again, and this time, that's where she will stay. No matter what happens. Or what she feels about the matter.

Her future is set.

CHAPTER TWO

Skye

A S CLICHÉ AS IT SOUNDS, I FEEL HIS EYES BEFORE I SEE HIM. It feels as though the room grows quiet, and a million people are staring at me, but they all become a faint hum.

There is no need for an introduction. There's also no need for anyone to tell me who this man is. I could be a hermit who never leaves my house and still know. His reputation proceeds him.

Tobias Kosta.

Newly minted billionaire. Notorious recluse. And absolutely, positively the most handsome man I have ever seen.

The newspapers don't do him justice. Nor do the pictures that grace the internet. Dark hair. Eyes like the scales of a fish. Pale, blue, and rough. A perfect dusting of a five o'clock shadow on his sharp jaw almost completes the look, but the final piece is his tanned skin as if he was just off vacationing on a yacht somewhere.

From what I've heard, his father was a Greek millionaire, and his mother . . .

Well, that's another story.

If the rumors were true, she was from Columbia. Or, at least, someone in his family was. It's said—and again, any information on Tobias is limited, hermit and all—that his family used to have ties to Pablo Escobar.

Now, I'm not sure that's true. But seeing as it's also said half the drugs circulating this country were imported by him or his family, there might be substance to these allegations. *Pun intended.*

It doesn't matter. Regardless of who he is and what his truth is, I can't seem to pull my gaze away. I must, though, because I can see that the judge is about to enter from the corner of my eye.

I inhale deeply, calming my nerves, and then I do it. I break the hold he has on me.

I'm not one to normally lose myself. Never one to clamor over a pretty face. But jeez. He's straight out of a Greek mythology.

A deity.

I tamp down the feelings swirling inside me and turn back to my client.

I assume my client is why Tobias is here.

They are direct competition. It's rumored both businessmen run the drugs through this part of the country. I can't say for certain what Tobias's role is, but I obviously know enough about my client to know he is not on the up-and-up.

I also know I need to stop thinking about Tobias and get back to why I'm here. I am here to get this case thrown out before it even starts. Felix Bernard is too smart and employs too many lawyers for this to stick.

I won't let it stick.

I highly anticipate that the judge will throw out the case today. It will never go to trial. There is no evidence, and seeing as I'm good at what I do, I have no doubt of the outcome of today. Time goes fast from this moment on. I speak. I make a motion to dismiss. State my case to the judge. And then the room goes quiet as we wait.

I keep my eyes locked as I listen.

The moment of truth. Time drones on as I wait. And then

it happens. The case is dismissed. Not enough evidence to proceed to trial.

Once again, I did it.

I'm young and determined. I might only be a junior associate, but I have a perfect track record. My work is focused on being the best damn lawyer money can buy. I need my clients to trust me. I need my client to—

"Good job." I hear from beside me, pulling me out of my thoughts.

My lips part. It never gets old. But despite the accolades, it doesn't help the way my stomach tightens as Felix looks at me. I hate this man. How could I not? He is evil personified. But in the end, he's the key to my objective. I plaster on my fake as hell smile.

"Thank you, Mr. Bernard."

"Felix. Call me Felix. I believe we should be on a first-name basis after today. Don't you think, Skye?" The way he practically purrs my name makes me cringe, and as if it couldn't get any worse, it does. His head dips down. "We should go out to celebrate," he says as he continues his perusal. His gaze skates over me in a creepy way. Another reason I hate this man.

If he wasn't the key, I would tell him where to shove it, but unfortunately, I must play nice. Be the best lawyer for him . . . that's what I must do.

"I'm so sorry, Felix." When his name leaves my lips, it feels dirty. A desire to wash my mouth out with soap infiltrates my mind. "I have another obligation. A deposition at three. Rain check."

Sugary sweet. Let him think it's an option. That maybe he has a shot in hell. He doesn't.

"I'm going to take you up on that."

I have no doubt in my mind that he will, in fact, take me up on that. Leaning down, I grab my stuff from the table, place my things in my bag, and turn.

I look toward the back of the room, a part of me expecting a certain pair of light eyes to be watching, but nobody is watching me. He already left.

A small part of me can't help but feel disappointed. I shouldn't feel this after swimming with sharks for this long, but it doesn't seem to matter. Pushing the thoughts away, I walk out of the building. There's a lot of work to do today, and it's not going to do itself.

CHAPTER THREE

Skye

THE FAMILIAR SCENTS OF MY YOUTH PENETRATE MY NOSE AS I step farther into the space. A distinct combination of coffee, cigarettes, and the part that always makes my heart lurch . . . whiskey.

Not the good stuff, either. Not the bottles my clients consume. No pretty glasses here. No crystal with hefty price tags.

Hell, I wouldn't be surprised if the bottle is plastic, and he purchased it at the gas station. My chest squeezes tighter.

Striding through the foyer and into the living room, I don't see him, but I know he's here. Somewhere.

His usual spot in front of the small TV in the old beat-up recliner is vacant. The room is a mess regardless of it being empty. An old white throw blanket stretches across the floor. An afterthought from when he left the room.

I shake my head and continue walking. When I pass the kitchen, he's not there either.

This room doesn't fare better. If I thought the living room was a mess, this one makes it look like a sanctuary. The counter is littered with old takeout containers and empty beer cans.

The first thing I'll do as soon as I leave is call a cleaning service for him. This can't be healthy to live in.

Since he's not in here drinking, he must be taking a nap.

It's been rough for him, and it gets worse the older I get. He shouldn't even be drinking. He promised me he wouldn't anymore, not with his liver problems. If I had my way, I'd move him into a place closer to me. Someplace I can see him more often and where he'd be taken care of. He always took care of me. Now it's my turn to take care of him. For as long as I can remember, it's always been just us.

Sure, I have some memories from before, but as every year passes, they become more like a dream. Sometimes the past becomes so blurry, I wonder if I'm making it up, but I know I'm not.

Subconsciously, my hand lowers. The next thing I know, I've begun to rub the spot on my wrist. It's a nervous tic. Most of the time, I don't even realize I'm doing it. With a shake of my head, I keep walking through the hallway. My pace is slow, and I tiptoe to be quiet. That way, I won't disturb him.

If he were up, he would've already said something to me.

As I make my way into his office and straight to his desk, my gaze drifts around the space. This room is surprisingly clean. There is nothing on the floor, just an old worn-out brown shag carpet. It needs a good wash, but that's about it. Natural sunlight beams in through the drapes that are pulled open.

Taking a step closer to the desk, I realize that first appearances can be deceiving.

This room isn't clean at all.

The wood is completely overrun with files. Some open, others closed. They cover every bit of the surface.

There are sticky notes on some of them, too.

I need to go through everything, but he can't see me looking. If he catches me, he'll be upset and kick me out.

According to him, I'm supposed to leave the past where it belongs, shoved deep down where it never resurfaces, and I can never ask questions. Doesn't sound like a good idea, since it's probably the reason he drinks.

Yeah, that won't fly for me, though. I need to know the truth. Which is why I'm here.

Again.

Searching.

The house is eerily quiet around me, and as I look down at his desk, I don't even know where to begin. There are papers everywhere, thrown haphazardly around without a care in the world.

Old newspapers.

Clippings of certain articles.

Printed off emails.

Credit card receipts.

Call logs.

There is even a picture of a group of men sitting around a table with a circle around one of their heads.

There is so much here, but I won't have time to go through all of it.

But the good news is, apparently, my father and I think alike. The file I'm looking for is open on top of the mess. The pieces of paper look like they were crumpled, then uncrumpled.

Why did you do that? Why did you throw this away but then changed your mind? Or maybe I have this all wrong. Maybe he wasn't tossing it. Maybe he didn't like what it said.

As if it made him angry to read them.

This piques my interest.

Leaning forward, I flatten out the sheets, then start to thumb through the documents for pertinent information. In the corner of the first page, in familiar print, I see my father made a note in black ink: *Felix Bernard?*

My client.

"What did you find, Dad?"

I'm about to turn the page and continue my search when I hear a noise.

I still my hands, and when I hear it again, I know he's up for the day and coming in here. Closing the file, I step away from his desk.

Then I pull my phone out of my pocket, pretending to be on a call.

"Skye? Is that you?" His voice rings through the air.

"Yep . . . in your office." I take another step back as his footsteps grow closer. Just as he's about to enter the room, I lift my phone to my ear.

"What are you doing here?" he asks as his body comes into focus. His gray hair is disheveled; he looks like he needs a cup of coffee and a shower. There's also something about his complexion that's not right. His skin has a yellow tinge to it. Maybe he has a cold? "I didn't expect you to visit me so soon."

I shrug, making a great show of hanging up and placing the device back in my bag. "Can't a girl visit her dad?"

My father looks me up and down. A soft smile spreads across his face, and new lines form as he stares at me with eyes full of love. Lines that weren't there the last time I saw him. Not laugh lines. No, these pepper the skin near his temples. They make him look tired, as if the weight of the world rests on his shoulders. Which, knowing my father, it probably does.

"How are you feeling?" I move from where I'm standing by the window and step closer to him. He takes a step back, and his eyes narrow, his expression tight with strain.

"Is that why you're in my house, to spy on me?"

Yes and no.

I allow my lips to part into a smile at his question. "Yep. You know me way too well," I joke. The truth is, that's not the only reason I'm here, but I'd rather he not catch on to the other reason.

That file on his desk.

The one that has coffee stains and crumpled corners from how often he's looked at it. I wonder what he's looking for.

Proof of Felix Bernard's involvement as well?

A large part of me wants to come right out and ask him, but from past experiences, I know that if I do, he will clam right up, and then the file will go missing.

It's better to beg for forgiveness than ask for permission, and that is exactly what I plan to do, in this case. I know it's unethical, and if anyone catches me, I'll be disbarred, but I don't care.

"You don't believe I'm okay, Skye?" His voice cuts through the air, bringing tension in its wake.

Swallowing, I decide to answer truthfully. "Dad, I know you aren't. And I can smell the booze." I lift my brow at him, informing him without words that it's not okay for him to be drinking.

His arm reaches up and covers his eyes before he's dropping his hands back down to look at me. His gaze is unwavering. "Are you here to lecture me?" The bite of his voice makes me think if I don't lighten the mood, a fight will ensue.

As much as I want to harp on him to stop, I don't want to alienate him. He's all I have. I need him in my life.

"Want the real answer?" I say, keeping the tone of my voice light and airy. It does its job because he laughs. He knows I'm going to give him a talking-to. My footsteps echo around us as I make my approach. Once I'm standing beside him, I touch his shoulder, noticing right away how frail he seems under my hand. He's skin and bones. A soft gasp of concern bubbles out from my mouth, but I cover it up with a cough. "Come back to the city with me."

"I don't want to be a burden."

I cock my head, moving it slightly to look into his eyes. "You would never be a burden to me, Dad. I owe you everything."

"No. No, you don't." He shakes his head and turns away to walk out of the room. It's as if he can't look at me.

What are you hiding, Dad?

A part of me thinks it's because he's drinking again. He probably feels he's letting me down, especially after what I just said to him. My father will never understand that nothing he could do would make me feel that way.

I follow him. He's not far ahead, but I let him get his thoughts together before approaching him.

Whatever haunts him is enough to make him reluctant to share it with me, probably out of an unwarranted belief that I will judge him. That would never happen, but regardless, I give him that moment.

He heads into the living room and takes a seat on the well-weathered couch that sits adjacent to the recliner. The couch has been here for as long as I can remember. Longer than the chair, that's for sure. With countless stains and arms that are frayed, the fabric has seen better days.

Over the years, since I've become a lawyer—and since I've been able to afford it—I have tried to convince him to let me buy him a new one, but he always argues, and I don't press the issue. Truth be told, my goal is not to get him a new couch; it's to get him a new place. To move him far away from this town and the ghosts that still live here.

Ghosts that I know hover around him daily.

Standing in the doorway of the office, I look back inside. My gaze settling on the desk, it's only a few feet away. From this angle, I can see that the paper closest to me says the name *Baros*.

My fingers drift to my tattoo. Dad's eyes catch the movement, narrowing. And that's my cue to escape.

I can't handle the questions.

The memories of death.

The guilt.

Because I know, without a doubt, that if there's anything that can bring me to my knees, it's the boy who died in my place.

CHAPTER FOUR

Skye

I T's BEEN ONE WEEK SINCE I FOUND THE FILE AND ONE WEEK since it's slipped through my fingers. There is no question in my mind that something important is nestled between the clutter and mess of Dad's notes.

Shit.

I need to know what's in those files.

My restless mind will never calm until I'm able to see what he knows, and maybe, just maybe, it will lead me to get closure.

My past is fuzzy.

Only bits and pieces still linger from before my dad adopted me. I can't even remember what my mother or father look like without a picture.

It's not fair.

And although I know the gang involved with their death was caught years ago, I can't help but think there is more.

I can't help but think Felix Bernard is involved.

Which is why I have to go back through all of my father's files from the case.

I was just there, but I didn't get what I was looking for, and as much as I don't want to make the drive again, I have no choice.

Every minute that passes is another minute in which I have to work for the scum who may have had a hand in my parents' death.

I pick up the phone and dial my father's number.

He doesn't answer on the first ring, nor on the second. It isn't until I'm about to hang up on the fourth that he picks up. Which is unlike him.

"Skye?" It comes out haggard and out of breath. He sounds like how he used to when he had a bad day at work and was drinking too much. I shudder inwardly at the thought that something is wrong with him, and he's drinking more and more often. A beer here and there is one thing, but if it's more than that, I don't know how I can help him unless I get him to move to the city with me.

"Hey, Dad," I respond. "Did I wake you?" *Please say no.* He lets out a throaty laugh that is followed directly by a cough. "You, okay?" Through the phone line, I can hear him take a large sip of water.

"No. I'm up, sweetie." He might be up, but his voice certainly doesn't sound like it.

"You sound like you're in bed." I think about the best way to handle this. Should I invite myself over off the bat, see what he's up to? Or I can nonchalantly ask him about his schedule. Then I can plan to stop by when he's not there.

Yeah, that's the best plan.

If I go to his house when he's not there, I can easily go in and out without having to worry about him asking me too many questions, and then I won't have to risk him finding me.

I just need to take pictures of the file, or maybe just borrow it. Would he notice if it's gone?

I go for option one. Taking a breath, I keep my voice soft and steady.

"What are you up to today?" I ask.

"Just a few errands." His response has my shoulders dropping in relief. Depending on the errand, today could work. I don't have any meetings that I have to be at. If he's busy, I can probably make it in and out before he even realizes.

"What errands do you got going on?"

He doesn't answer at first, but then he exhales. Whatever he's about to say, he knows I'll probably ask him questions, and he doesn't want that. My back muscles tighten again.

"I have a doctor's appointment—"

"What doctor?" I interject before he can finish his sentence. My heartbeat picks up as I wait for him to answer.

"Just my yearly appointment, Skye. It's no big deal."

My father could be bleeding in the street and say this same sentence. This doesn't make me feel any less worried.

"No symptoms? Are you feeling okay?"

"No. And yes, I'm feeling fine."

"You do sound different. Your voice—"

"There is nothing wrong."

I mull over his response before pressing one more time. "Dad . . ."

"Skye. Who's the parent here?" He sounds like he's pretending to scold me. As if we traveled back in time to when I was ten years old, and I just got caught eating ice cream in my bedroom at two in the morning. He would tell me never to do it again, all while having a huge smile on his face.

"You sure? Why do I feel like you're keeping something from me? If something was wrong, you would tell me, right?"

"Yes, of course. But I promise I'm fine, just getting older. But I can't talk right now."

"Why?" I'm a dog with a bone, but I need to know how long he will be gone.

"If you must know, I'm meeting someone for lunch."

This has me perking up. "Oh? That's nice. Who are you meeting?"

"Skye . . ." he trails off, clearly not happy with my questions.

"What is this, an inquisition? I'm fine. Everything is fine, and I'm just going out to lunch. You'd think *you* were the parent." He groans, and despite my nerves over the situation, a laugh bubbles out of my mouth.

"I love you, Dad. I'm just making sure."

He lets out a sigh. "I know that, but I don't want you to worry about me."

"Well, there's nothing you can do about that. No matter what you say, I will always worry about you."

"And as much as I love that you care about me, I do need to go. Lunch is in one hour, and I'm not ready yet."

"Fine. I'll let you go. Bye, Dad."

"Bye, sweetie." And then the line is silent.

With that over, I grab my bag and head downstairs to the street. I keep a car in the city.

It isn't ideal. I have to get up early and move it often. Especially with street sweeping rules, but with my dad not living in the city, I need to have a car to visit him. I guess I could take an Uber, but I like the freedom having a car provides.

As soon as I step out of the building, I walk first to the florist, pick up my usual bouquet, and then I'm off to where I parked my car. It's only a block and a half away. The street isn't crowded, but it rarely is at this time of the day during the workweek. This street tends to be busier on the weekends because of its proximity to fabulous restaurants.

While I'm walking, my gaze scans the street, and I lock eyes with a man. He's standing by the side of my building with a hat on. I don't know him, but he seems to be staring at me.

There is something creepy about the way he watches me.

A shiver runs down my spine.

My police officer for a father has instilled one thing in my brain, it's that you can never be too careful. Mind your surroundings, and always have Mace on you.

I turn quickly and move faster toward my car. It's light out, and plenty of people are milling about, but I still rummage through my bag for my Mace, just in case.

Just like Dad would want.

When I'm standing directly next to my car, I look around but don't see anyone at all.

The breath I didn't realize I've been holding comes out in a burst from my mouth the moment the door is closed and I'm turning the ignition on and locking the doors.

It's like I know what I'm about to do isn't right, so I'm becoming paranoid.

Pulling the car out of the spot, I head toward the FDR Drive, and before long, I'm on my way to Reddington.

My overactive imagination is still playing tricks on me because I swear I see a car in my rearview mirror following me.

But that's ridiculous. It's probably not following me.

Just because it's been two cars back since the city . . .

Trust your gut. You are rarely wrong.

Before I can think better of it, I switch lanes and then switch again. I'm not usually a reckless driver, but I need to make sure they aren't following me.

Glancing back into the mirror, I notice they are no longer behind me.

I let out the breath.

Paranoia is a bitch.

An hour later, I'm pulling up to the small house I grew up in. It's only been one week since I've been here, but today, it appears more run-down than normal in the afternoon light.

It's never looked this bad before. The shingles are falling off now, and the paint is chipping on the house's siding. It used to be white, but now it almost looks yellow.

The last time I was here, I didn't notice how bad it was. But today, with the sun shining in the right locations, I can see that Dad isn't keeping up with any of the house's maintenance.

I wish he would let me help him. It's not just in need of a paint job. It also needs a landscaper to come and clean up the weeds growing through the broken concrete leading up to the front door.

I'll talk with him about it the next time I come to visit him, but seeing as I'm not here right now . . . It will have to wait.

I fish out my keys from my bag, looking around my shoulder to make sure no one is out watching me, and then I'm walking up the two steps to open the door.

He doesn't have an alarm. That's not smart for a retired detective, but this is a small town. I bet he thinks no one would dare break in.

Wrong bet, Dad.

The moment I step inside the foyer, I'm relieved. He's not here and won't be for some time. I don't have time to dally, so I head straight for the office.

When I'm inside, it's just as messy as it was the last time, so I won't be able to lift the file. I'll just scan with my phone and print them out later. I'll take pictures of the sticky notes, too. Once I'm home, I can sort it out, but for now, I need to be as quick as possible.

Biting my lip, I begin the process of copying. I start with the first piece of paper I see and take a picture. Then, once it loads, I move to the second paper in the file. My stomach churns with anxiety as I glance around. There are a lot of files filled with papers.

God, I hope he doesn't come home early and catch me in the act.

My heart pounds in my chest. No. He won't. It will be okay. He has lunch and then a doctor's appointment. A checkup, he said. He says it's nothing, but something is off. It was his voice.

Stop.

Jeez, Skye. You don't have time to micromanage your dad's voice right now.

Pushing all thoughts but copy out of my mind, I go back to the task at hand. Scouring over all his belongings.

The sounds in the house have me on edge.

The ticking of the grandfather clock in the corner of the room ominously reminds me time is of the essence.

Ticktock.

Ticktock.

My pulse thuds harder with each passing second. There are too many papers.

It's only when my fingers curl around the last document and place it back where it belongs do I let out a deep exhale.

Done.

But that's when I notice something . . .

The trash bin.

It's also filled with paper. Grabbing the bin, I take all the contents out. Most are just junk, but one has me stopping.

A bill? Lifting it up, I take a closer look. It looks like it's from an insurance company.

What type of insurance? Car? Or is it from a doctor? And if it's from a doctor, why is he going again for a checkup? And a better question is why would he have a bill from the doctor already?

He said it was his yearly.

I grab the bill, scan it, and then put everything back in the bin.

Once everything is put in place, I move to leave, heading down the foyer and then stepping out of the door. As I do, I notice a car drive by the house. It looks like the one from the highway.

But that's ridiculous . . . right?

CHAPTER FIVE

Tobias

"W HERE ARE YOU, TOBIAS?" GIDEON'S VOICE RINGS through the Bluetooth. No doubt pissed that I haven't answered his last three calls.

"That's not your concern." I scoff.

I don't answer to him. If I want to take a joyride around the city, then I'll do so without my designated fucking nanny.

Pulling my car from its parking space, I hit the accelerator, following the intel a member of my security team just sent me. She's on the move. If I head up Third Avenue, I should be able to follow.

"Tobias—" He groans, and I know a security lecture is about to ensue.

"Don't Tobias me. I'm the fucking boss, Gideon. Don't forget that," I cut him off.

Swerving in and out of traffic, I keep my eyes peeled for her car. When the black beat-up Jeep wrangler comes into focus, I know I have her in my sights.

"That may be the case, but that doesn't mean you didn't have a meeting fifteen minutes ago that you didn't show up for."

"Fuck!"

"Ah, your favorite word and activity. Not so smug now, are you?"

"Yeah, fuck is right."

I had a meeting with Cyrus Reed, my banker. He might be my friend, but when it comes to business, he doesn't care who you are. He's notoriously allergic to shit.

"Was Cyrus pissed?" Of course, he was. The man has no sense of humor. Not that I'm one to talk.

"Dude, it's Cyrus. The man is furious. He nearly tore your office to shreds."

"I had a personal matter to attend to." Personal being I'm officially a stalker, but he doesn't need to know that.

"And that would be?"

I'm not surprised by his question. If the roles were reversed, I'd ask the same one, but still . . . "None of your fucking business."

"This wouldn't have anything to do with Felix's attorney, would it?" *No one knows me like Gideon.*

"Fuck off," I respond, and I know I stepped into it this time. Gideon will call me out in three . . . two . . . one . . .

"Ah, yes. She was a fine one." He chuckles.

"I said fuck off. I'll apologize to Cyrus later. Send him a bottle of Luis Tres . . . that should hold him over."

"Sure thing, *boss.*"

I hang up the phone, done talking about Cyrus and his hot-headed bullshit. I don't want anything to distract me as I continue my pursuit. I hardly notice my surroundings, an effect of having traveled this area too many times. Out of the city. Over the bridge. Onto the highway. Same shit, different day.

I'm following two cars behind, which is one car farther back than I'd like, but I'm pretty sure she knows she's being followed. She switched lanes a bunch of times a few miles back, and her erratic swerving can't be a simple byproduct of poor driving. No, she knows I'm on her tail, but I don't give a fuck.

I find that where this woman is involved, I'm possessed.

Her car starts to head toward the right—she's exiting—and I follow as she's taking the turn toward the water.

She's heading to the small town of Reddington.

I know my way, but regardless of that, I continue to follow her, staying far enough back for her not to be spooked.

From where I lag behind, I notice she is slowing to a stop, and that's when I pick up the phone again, but this time it's to call Jaxson Price.

"Who lives at 777 Martel Road?" I don't bother with hellos. Time is money, so the faster I get the information I need, the faster I can move on with my life.

A small, pesky voice tells me I didn't need to follow her to find out all this information, but I tell that voice to shut the fuck up.

"Hold." The line goes quiet before Jax is back on. "The home is registered to Detective Matthews."

"And the relationship between Skye Matthews and the detective?"

"I have adoption papers here."

Interesting. Skye Matthews . . . you were adopted by a local hero. *You are her.*

"Send me everything. I want to know every single thing about Ms. Matthews. Her birthday. Where she went to school, her favorite color, how she takes her coffee, you understand, Jax?"

"On it."

From where I'm parked, I watch the house. "So, this is where you grew up, Skye?" I say to myself.

I'm not sure what I'm expecting, but it certainly isn't her dashing to her car fifteen minutes later.

Interesting.

Something tells me her father didn't know she came up for a visit today. What were you doing here, Ms. Matthews?

She starts to drive, and I follow her. Since I've committed to stalking, I might as well go all the way. I have to admit, this level of obsession isn't a good character trait, but I'm too curious to care.

You don't spend more than two decades searching for someone without becoming a little obsessed.

Seeing her at this house makes me think of the past. Of all those years ago when we met.

Then my hands on my steering wheel are gripping it tightly. How could you not remember me?

The thought pisses me the fuck off. I never forgot her. Not for one moment. Not after all these years later. She's always been on my mind. And me? I'm just another page in her bloodied story.

Not for long, Ms. Matthews.

Soon enough, you will become reacquainted with me.

A few minutes later, Skye is pulling up to a small cemetery. Throwing my car into park, I observe her, she's got a bouquet of flowers in her hand. She's walking up a small hill and standing in front of two tombstones.

She's not there long, but what she does next has me quirking my brow. Skye is walking toward a large oak tree.

I squint my eyes.

Why is she kneeling beside it?

That's when I notice there is something sticking out of the ground. From where I'm at, it appears like a small white stick. Maybe a cross?

It's out of place. At least twenty feet from the nearest grave. It's tucked behind a tree.

No one would see it. *Unless you knew to look for it.*

Tapping my hands on the steering wheel, I wait for her to leave. My curiosity has gotten the better of me. Five minutes later, I'm able to investigate. She's left, and despite my desire to continue my pursuit, I need to know why she was kneeling on the ground.

Shutting my car off, I head in the direction from which she came.

When I'm at the location, I see that I'm correct. There is a makeshift white cross shoved into the dirt. It looks like a child made it in an art class. It doesn't fit in here.

The edges aren't cut perfectly, and the paint is weathered and chipped. It's old. How old, though, is the question.

Despite the age of the cross, the area does look well maintained. It's clean of fallen branches and leaves. The only thing near the cross is one purple flower. It looks like it hasn't bloomed yet.

I grab it in my hand and head back to my car. Once inside, I snap a picture and send it to Gideon. The flower must be important for some reason because it didn't look anything like the larger bouquet she placed on the other graves. That has to mean something.

Me: What is this?

Gideon: A flower?

Me: No shit, dick. I know it's a flower. What kind?

Gideon: Do I look like a botanist?

Me: Make yourself one for the occasion, asshole.

Next, I text Trent. If anyone will know, it's him. His mom and sister are obsessed with flowers for some reason.

I text the same message I texted Gideon . . .

Me: What type of flower is this?

Trent: No hello? No how are you? What kind of chocolate I like? Godiva, by the way.

Me: You know where to shove it.

Trent: That attitude will not get you an answer. Or a hot date.

Why are all my friends intolerable?

Me: What is this?

Trent: Nope, still not satisfied.

Me: Please don't make me kill you.

Trent: Tell me where you got it, and maybe I'll answer you.

He is having way too much fun with this. But he's the only one who will know.

Me: I got it from a grave.

Trent: Wow, stealing from a grave. Just when I thought you couldn't get any morally more corrupt . . .

Me: I aim to please.

Trent: Nope. Okay, here is what I got. Your little flower is called a spring crocus. Aka penitent's rose. Whoever's flower you stole, is asking for forgiveness. This is low even for you, Tobias.

Penitent's rose.

Who did you hurt, Skye? She's hiding something, and I'll find out what. I know exactly how to find out.

One call is all it will take. Still parked, I text Gideon, asking for Seth Williams's number.

A minute later, my phone is chiming with an incoming text. Glancing down, I see Gideon has shared the contact information with me.

I hit the button, then lift my gaze back to the street ahead, and pull out of the parking spot. The phone rings twice before he answers.

"Seth Williams here." He even sounds like a douche.

"Seth, this is Tobias Kosta."

"Mr. Kosta," he drawls out, his voice tinged with curiosity and, dare I say, excitement. "How can I help you?"

"I want to meet with you. Tomorrow. Eight o'clock in the morning."

"To what do I owe this surprise meeting?"

"I will fill you in on all the details tomorrow." I can't show all my cards too soon.

And then, without letting him get a word in edgewise, I hang up the line.

———————

The next morning, I'm striding into the office like I own the place, heading straight for the receptionist.

"Mr. Williams is expecting me," I tell the mousy little thing behind the desk.

"O-Of course, Mr. Kosta," she stutters, and she stands abruptly, hands shaking, wobbling on her feet, clearly frazzled by my presence.

"Follow me, sir." Her right arm lifts, her hand pointing in the direction she wishes me to go. I follow her through the glass doors, down a long bright hallway, and then through another set of doors.

The office is more traditional than mine. Sure, he also has large windows that look out into the city, but where my space is minimalistic, his screams of vanity. Awards. Plaques. A constant reminder of why he should be charging the big bucks.

Seth Williams sits behind a large wooden desk that almost takes up the whole room. Gold plated, it's over the top, but I guess if you are trying to convince clients like me to give you a million-dollar retainer to secure your services, this is the look you go for.

I already fucking hate this idiot, but he's a means to an end.

He's my way in.

"Mr. Kosta." He stands, crosses the space between us, and raises his hand to shake mine. Once that's taken care of, he gestures for me to have a seat. "What can I do for you?" Making his way to his chair, he pulls it out and takes a seat. I follow suit.

Leaning back, I cross my arms in front of my chest. "I'm interested in some help with a few legal matters," I lead, dropping the bait and letting him eat that shit up.

He nods. "Luckily for you, that's our expertise."

Hook, line, and sinker.

I lean forward, cock my head, and stare at the man. "I'm particular on who works with me."

"Of course. I will make sure—" he starts to say, but I stop him in his tracks.

"I want Skye Matthews."

That's a Freudian slip if I ever heard one.

"With all due respect to Skye, who is an absolute rising star in the firm, she's a newer associate. I can find someone better suited for your needs and the scope of the work." His condescending voice has my teeth gritting together.

"Ms. Matthews. Or I walk right out that door, hire her directly, and you don't get a fucking cut."

"Mr. Kosta—"

Shaking my head, I look at him the way a parent would scold their child. Right before they sent them to their room with no dinner or, in his case, with a belt to the ass.

"Price? What's your price to get you to shut the fuck up?"

His mouth opens and closes. Good, I shocked the idiot into silence. He rights himself quickly, straightening his back and puffing out his chest. He cut the theatrics, so I still know he's scared of me. "I need to check her billable—"

"Double it."

"Tobias." He lifts his hand up. "May I call you Tobias?"

"No," I say in a deadpan. "Though if your answer is yes, I may tolerate it." Normally, I don't smile, but this time, I allow my lip to tilt up. A sardonic grin. One that tells him not to fuck with me. Not to object and just give me what I want.

"I'm sure we can work out a fair share for her to work with you. She does have other clients, so I would need to check her schedule and availability."

"I think you misunderstood me, Seth." His name drips off my lips with scorn. I reach over to his desk, pick up the pen, and scribble a number down on it, then I slide that scrap of paper that holds an ungodly dollar amount across the large wooden desk. "I want her at my disposal. Only *my* disposal."

His eyes widen. "Very well."

"Good, now that settles that." I push back the chair from the desk, then stand and head over to the far side of the room. The area of the office is perfect for what I have in mind. It's tucked away in an alcove behind the entrance. It's only partially in view, but mainly, it's strategically hidden, which works well for me. Taking a seat on the couch, I lean forward so my head is visible to Skye's prick boss.

"Call her in, and tell her the news."

CHAPTER SIX

Skye

MY OFFICE IS UPTOWN IN A BEAUTIFUL HIGH-RISE BUILDING on Park Avenue. It is pretentious and a far cry from my father's house. I grew up in a small town filled with old-world charm. Now my only view is that of the hustle and bustle of the city. Tall buildings and no trees.

I live ten blocks from where I work, and because of that fact, I never leave the Upper East Side unless it's to go to court.

All day and night, the only thing that holds my attention is work. No social life. You don't get the things you want in life unless you push. My determination, my strength, and my pigheadedness are all weaknesses and strengths, depending on who you ask. My clients only see strengths. For my soul, it's all a weakness.

Once I stand outside and the warm air slaps at my face, I lift my arm to hail a cab.

For some reason, this part of the city is busy today. I should fish out my phone and call an Uber, but I have time. It only takes a few minutes before the sea of cars has one pulling up beside me.

I should have walked, but my heels are too high, and I forgot to change into flats before I left my apartment this morning.

I step inside and sit down. As soon as I do, I'm assaulted by the smell. It's thick with a combination of smoke and a rancid odor of what I can only describe as dirty gym socks. I really should have walked. The good news is the windows are cracked, so as soon as we start to drive, clean and fresh air pours into the small space. It doesn't completely remove the lingering fragrance, but it's better than nothing.

Pulling out my phone, I begin to scroll through my emails. It seems like a good way to keep my mind off throwing up in the back seat.

One hundred emails are unread.

This should be fun.

Right off the bat, nothing screams important.

Typical annoying clients pestering me about follow ups and questions.

Lots of crap about things I have no interest in, but then an email comes through from my boss. He wants to meet today as soon as I get into the office. He probably wants to discuss the big win for Felix. Maybe I'll get a promotion. It doesn't matter since I don't do this for the money. Well, not *only* for the money. I do need to eat.

With no more emails to go through, I turn my head to face the window. The city swishes by in a sea of colors.

Yellow cabs.

Gray buildings.

The tourist with their numerous shopping bags.

On the far-right side of the street, a mother walks with her child, pink balloons in the small girl's hands.

I count them.

One, two, three, four, five.

Presumably her age.

I wonder where they are off to today to celebrate. A museum, maybe the natural history one. Or maybe they are off to Chelsea Piers. They could also be going to see the sights. Something I don't do enough and really should be better at.

I may not have grown up here, and the views are undoubtedly different from what I'm used to, but something about the chaos of New York is almost relaxing.

You can get lost in this city.

I certainly have. But at the same time, there are endless opportunities. Endless ways to figure out your goals and objectives and meet them head-on. It's cliché, but the world is my oyster here.

Lost in thought, I don't realize how fast the ride goes, and before long, we're pulling up to the familiar building. I pay on my app and head up to the top floor of the law firm via the glass elevators. I'm not a fan of enclosed spaces. Have hated it since I was a little girl, but being able to see out into the lobby while I ride up keeps me from getting in my head.

As I walk past the receptionist, she smiles at me. Head held high and shoulders pulled back, I make my way through the set of glass doors and head straight to talk to my boss.

I'm sure he has a lot to say about the other day in court.

His office is on the opposite side of the floor as mine, and his views are awe-inspiring. Mine is nice, but it's not a corner office by any means. I face the East River, where there's not much to look at other than a few small concrete warehouses and some apartment buildings. He, however, has a panoramic view of the city with the Empire State Building on one side and all of Lower Manhattan on the other.

His office door is open. As I make my approach, the sound of my heels makes my presence known long before I enter. At the large desk in front of me is Seth Williams, his chair turned slightly to face the view. He looks deep in thought.

I take a step farther inside, and as soon as I cross the threshold, I catch the familiar smell of scotch.

He's had a drink, and it was recent by the way the rich under-tones still linger in the air.

"Celebrating without me?" I ask, and at my words, the chair squeaks as Mr. Williams turns from the window to face me.

When I see his face, it's void of emotion. Maybe he's not cel-ebrating but drowning his sorrows.

The lines around his eyes are more pronounced than usual today, and his lips are set into a straight line. He gives nothing away at first glance, but I know something is wrong or something is different.

I've been working here full time for over a year, recruited straight out of law school. I started working here as an intern, and I worked summers. After graduating and taking the bar, I was scooped up for a full-time position.

It hasn't been a long time, but no one works as hard as I do. I am here all day, every day. I have no social life. Everything I do is to get ahead, and it finally paid off when I was asked to sit as co-council for Mr. Bernard.

It was exactly what I wanted. He's the goal.

Now that I've had his case thrown out, I anticipate Mr. Bernard will bring me on more. Of course, that all depends on Mr. Williams and how he feels about this. I don't want my desires to be too obvious. People are strange. I need to tread carefully on how I handle Felix and my boss. I don't want my boss to think I'm trying to leave him. Felix is *his* full-time client, and he might think I'm poaching one of his biggest clients right from under his nose.

I don't want to steal his client. I just want to be in the thick of things. In the inner circle. That's where the power is held. The knowledge. And I need those things.

"Take a seat, Skye. We have a lot to discuss." Mr. Williams gestures to the empty chair.

"Okay." It's only a few feet to where the chair sits directly in front of him. With my head held high, I pull the chair out and sit down. Then I'm waiting for him to open his mouth and tell me why he summoned me to his office.

Maybe to mention last week. To talk about Mr. Bernard. Time stretches out as I wait, and I become impatient. Absently, I look down to see that my finger has been rubbing a circle over the vein on my left wrist, right over the tattoo I had placed there when I turned eighteen. I should wear a watch. Maybe it would help with my nervous habit.

But when I do, I can't help but feel suffocated as though I can't breathe. My pulse accelerates, and it feels like—

"Skye."

Pulling myself out of my thoughts, I shake my head again, realizing that Mr. Williams is talking, and I tuned him out.

Not wanting him to know that I haven't been listening, I meet his gaze head-on as he continues to discuss all the amazing things I've accomplished, all the cases I've won, and most importantly to him, all the money I've made for the firm.

He goes on and on about the money.

For him, that's the most important thing—the billable hours. For me, that barely touches the surface of why I am here. That is not my endgame. I'm willing to take a ride down to hell, let a few criminals go free, if it means I will eventually get my revenge.

"You have done an impressive job this past year. You have risen to every challenge I have given you. This last victory proves I was right to sit you in that chair. There was speculation in the office that you would fail, I won't lie. You're young. Fresh out of law school with not a lot of cases under your belt, after all. But I do believe you proved them wrong." His smile is broad and proud as if he won in court. Like a proud parent, he prattles on.

Will he be giving me more of Mr. Bernard's business?

This could be the break I need.

"You have done such an amazing job that I know you will one hundred percent rise to this occasion."

Here it is. The moment of truth.

Are all my endless hours and selling my soul to the devil about to pay off?

"It is because of all your accomplishments that I am giving you this opportunity. It's a game changer, Skye."

He leans forward, resting his elbows on his desk. His lips turn up into a big wolf-like smile.

"From this morning on, you will be working directly for—" His eyes aren't looking at me. They are looking directly behind me. That's when I realize someone is approaching. The sound of heavy masculine footsteps comes up behind me. I swivel in my chair, my own smile starting to form.

But it stops, just like my heart, when I hear an unfamiliar voice.

"Me."

Rough.

Gravelly.

Sexy as hell voice, and certainly not the voice of Felix Bernard.

I allow myself to look up. Even though confusion and trepidation linger in my mind, I know apprehension is warranted when my gaze collides with the man behind the voice.

Because that voice belongs to Tobias Kosta.

CHAPTER SEVEN

Tobias

THE LOOK OF SHOCK ON HER FACE IS WORTH EVERY SINGLE penny it's costing me to make this happen. And trust me, it's costing me a fuck ton.

Money is not an issue, of course. But I want her, and I made sure to get her. There's no question she didn't see this coming.

Good, because I'm fucking ecstatic.

But I won't let her see how happy I am about his. I always hold my cards close to my chest.

I can't have either of them knowing how much I want this arrangement to happen. It's a done deal. I know it. Williams knows it. Even if this spitfire doesn't.

Her eyes are narrowed and her jaw set.

Confidence wafts off her like a strong perfume. Crisp and powerful, it's a heady aroma. The perfect fragrance to my needs. I want to drown in it.

Since I can't, I bask in the way her shoulders are pulled back and the way her chest heaves deeper.

She's making it clear she's not afraid of me. I can't help but enjoy how her body reacts to my presence.

The fact our previous meeting meant so little to her makes my desire to ruin her even stronger. But it's the look in her eyes that has me confused.

Does she *now* realize who I am?

I assume with the clients this firm has, she does know me. But when I saw her in the courtroom, she gave absolutely no recognition of who I am.

I start to wonder . . . but now she can't hide under false bravado. She knows, but does she remember?

The way she swallows gives her away, but then she quickly stands, back ramrod straight.

The façade that I saw in the courtroom drops back down.

It's extraordinary how quickly she can turn it on and off. I've got to hand it to her, she looks as tough as nails. Every bit the shark I'd expect and welcome from her. Standing tall and proud, she makes her way over to me.

Watching her move could be my new favorite pastime.

Fuck, as her hips sway from side to side . . . it's hard to remember why I'm here and what the game plan is.

"I don't believe we've met before?" Her question breaks through my lust-filled haze, but I can't hide my appreciation of the view as my eyes linger on her, and the right side of my lip tips up.

"Tobias Kosta."

I extend my hand, and Ms. Matthews reaches her hand out as well, but the shake she's trying to hide is still there despite her best efforts to curtail it. It makes me want to toy with her.

For now, I won't. As much as I know this is in the bag, I don't need her quitting on me. The intel she could possibly have is worth it. She might prove helpful in finding out more about Felix's business.

I saw the way he looked at her, too. For all I know, there is much more to that story, and I'm not going to let this opportunity pass me by. I need information, and she might have it. When I don't take her hand, she pulls away and then turns back to her boss.

"I think there might be a misunderstanding," she says to him.

"No misunderstanding, Skye. Effective immediately, you will be working on a retainer basis with Mr. Kosta." His voice leaves no room for objection, but the minx that she is, is about to try. I can see it in the way her mouth puckers as if she's tasted something sour. She doesn't like this, and she'll now try her best to figure out a way out of it.

Do your best, sweetheart, and I'll do mine.

"How is that possible? Isn't this a conflict of interest?" she demands. Not a good play on her part. There isn't a non-compete amongst criminals.

"And why exactly would it be a conflict of interest?" I interject, stepping forward and lifting my brow. Both their heads snap back to me, her top teeth biting into her lower lip so hard I wait for it to bleed. "Is there something you want to say?" I tease, but my voice comes out more monotone. She shakes her head back and forth, realizing the error.

She just implied that her client, *previous client*, and myself have something in common. Which, as a lawyer with confidential privilege intact, is not something she can say anything about. Two seconds in the room with me, and I already have her fucking up. By the way her face pales, she realizes it, too.

God, fucking with her over the next few weeks will be so much fun.

"With all due respect, Ms. Matthews, we allocate our associates to the assignments most suited for them. This is for best."

"The best? The best for whom? The best for you?" she says this to me, lifting an eyebrow. "Why would you want me?"

I look her up and down. My gaze basks at the way she squirms. Time draws out, and the longer it does, the more I'm enjoying myself. A million things want to come out of my mouth. I go with the answer that will piss her off the most.

No answer.

I give her no answer but watch as she grinds her teeth together. I can tell she's not happy. Hell, it wouldn't take a rocket scientist to come to this conclusion, but it's entertaining me, nonetheless.

"Skye, this is an amazing opportunity," Seth says as he leans forward and places his elbows on the desk. "An opportunity to learn, expand, and get important insight in a field you haven't had much experience with."

She looks back and forth between us like she is realizing there's not much she can do at this moment. Her boss has spoken. There's no reason to tell her why I want her. I can't tell her. Plus, I've already dealt with it in the currency that matters the most: money. The amount I am paying Williams to have her work with me . . . well, let's just say he won't be saying no.

"Now that that is settled, I will be getting out of here. Ms. Matthews, I expect you to be available to me starting tomorrow at nine o'clock."

With that, I move to step out of the room. Behind me, I can hear her voice. She's trying to keep it down, but I hear the hiss in her tone. Wanting to know what is going to happen with Bernard's cases. She's feisty, that's for sure.

I don't acknowledge anyone else as I make my way down the hall and through the glass doors. I pull my phone out of my pocket and fire off a text. By the time I pass the receptionist, everyone I employ knows I'm on the move.

The car should be in the back, and my security detail is beside me as the elevator doors open. I'm sick of this shit.

But Gideon informs me that, right now, I need the extra protection. I'm brokering a deal to step down from the dealing part of my business. To transfer all my business into a legit money source and retire. I only have one thing left before I can do that.

Take out my last enemy.

Which is another reason I need Skye on my side.

Not just for my own sick thrills but for revenge.

CHAPTER EIGHT

Skye

"YOU CAN'T BE SERIOUS," I SAY TO MY BOSS AS I HEAR TOBIAS'S footsteps fading into the surrounding sounds of the office. He doesn't blink as he responds, just drills me with a stare that dares me to object.

"I am nothing but serious, kiddo. Comes with the territory of doing what I do."

Pacing the room, I try to think of a plausible response that would warrant him turning down his request. I can't work with that man. I can't breathe around him. It's not just about the way he makes me forget my words when he looks at me with those piercing blue eyes. Nope, it's more than that.

There are reasons. Multiple reasons.

I just need to come up with a good, valid point to tell Mr. Williams, and something tells me that if I mention how handsome he is, devastatingly so, it won't sway him.

Reason one: Because he's hot.

No, that won't do.

Think, Skye.

Reasons?

You're a goddamn lawyer. Arguing should be your forte.

Okay, reason two—

"I think you misunderstand." He speaks, making my footsteps stop and putting an end to my poor attempt at a list.

"How?"

"You'll still work occasionally with other clients, but you're also taking on Tobias."

I can still get close to Mr. Bernard. Not all is lost, but my mind still reels with confusion.

"Let's cut the crap, Williams. It's a conflict of interest, and we both know that."

"Because . . . ?" he trails off, daring me to talk about the elephant in the room. We represent two drug lords now. "Both are businessmen. Neither in the same field . . ."

"Absolutely in the same field. And that field is highly illegal. What if they have overlapping so-called staff? What if they have business disputes? The man showed up in my courtroom the day I killed the case," I respond, and there is no way to hide the sarcasm dripping in my words. There is also no way Williams is not going to play dumb. "Fine. Whatever. Let's ignore the conflict for now. Revisit when it bites us in the ass. How much time will he need from me?"

Please say not much.

"Judging by his character, net worth, and scope of his business—twice your lifespan." He chuckles and, unbeknownst to him, crushes my dreams.

Scrunching my nose, I try to make sense of my boss's contrary comments. "But you just said I can still handle other clients."

Unless you were lying to me, which I wouldn't put past you since you're a prick.

"Listen, he's making changes in his life, taking a new route, and needs legal counsel for the next few months to get that done. That's where you step in."

"So, I can still work with Felix?"

His brow quirks, and I realize my mistake in referring to Mr. Bernard by his first name.

I need to take a step back and not push this. I don't need him prying into my business. He can't wonder why I'm objecting or fighting for a man like this.

"If you're available. If not, we'll assign him another associate." His eyes narrow. "But knowing you, I'm sure you will be available."

He continues to look at me as if he can read my mind. He thinks if he stares at me long enough, he can bash down the walls I've gathered around my brain. Good luck. Better men have tried. There is only one person who seems to be able to reduce me to a puddle on the floor, and it's not him. Nope, that spot is filled by a drug dealer who is way too handsome for his own good and mine, seeing as I have to work with him.

Warmth spreads over my cheeks.

"Skye, is there something I should know?"

Shit.

Here I am blushing over Tobias Kosta, and now my boss thinks I have a thing for Felix Bernard.

My heart pounds frantically in my chest. I can feel a thin layer of sweat collecting at the base of my neck. I'm happy he can't see it and, most importantly, relieved that he can't see what I'm feeling.

Play it cool.

"No, I don't know what you're talking about," I respond.

"What I'm talking about is, is there going to be a problem with you working for two of the most powerful men in the city, maybe the entire East Coast? Because having their secrets under our roof is the best thing that could happen to this firm. Do you understand?"

"Understood."

Standing in front of his desk, hand on hip, I wait for him to say more. When he doesn't speak for a few seconds and then picks up a folder in front of him, I assume he's done with me.

"If that's all, I'm going to head down to my office and get a head start on this. I have a lot to do, and I need to start prep work if I want to hit the ground running with Mr. Kosta."

"See, Skye? That's why you're the best. And now I can keep my tee time with the state attorney general. Rumors are he will be moving up and will need people outside the DOJ offices to help him accomplish his goals. With those two clients' info in our pockets and working with the US AG, things are looking very sunny for all of us."

What he's really trying to say is this is why the firm values me as much as they do.

Most people might go to lunch, have dinner, meet colleagues for a round of freaking golf, but no. I work all the damn time.

With nothing more to say, I turn on my heel and head out the door. On my way out, I don't go through the glass doors. This time, I bypass the receptionist and go the other way, through the entrance to the other section of the building. The side where my office is. When I make it, I'm breathing hard from the pace of my steps.

As soon as I'm inside, I close the door, strip off my blazer, and throw myself into my chair. Then I cradle my head in my hands and let out the biggest breath I have ever taken. What have I gotten myself into?

I don't know why he wants me, and I don't want to think about it, either. I swivel in my chair to face the East River. My office is high enough to see over the small buildings that should block the view. I stare down at those surrounding buildings, then I look out into the horizon, hoping my heart will stop pounding from my nerves that are still on edge.

This changes nothing.

I can still find out the information I want. There is no way he's going to need me that much. What could Tobias need? I turn back to my desk, touch my mouse, and allow my computer to open. The first thing I do is type his name into the search engine. Tobias Kosta.

There is a lot about him, but I find it interesting that there is no substantial evidence of his criminal practices. The news speculates, but there is no concrete proof other than to talk about his connections to the underworld.

He was raised in Miami. They mention how his father, Niko Kosta, died. He was an American drug smuggler. A major figure in the cocaine trade. He lived in Miami and transported the drugs through his private boat dock.

Nice family, Toby.

When it starts to talk about his death, I skip that part. That one makes chills form on my arms and my stomach feel hollow. And it's not like I need it to form a general picture about my new client.

Looking down, I find I'm rubbing my wrist again. This has to stop. I can't fall apart all the time. My head shakes back and forth.

Get a handle on yourself, Skye.

Death is not something I like to think about, so instead of reading how Tobias's father died, I look at who he's associated with and then check to see if there are any arrests.

Anything that gives me a better idea of what I'll be doing with him and how much time it will take. If what Mr. Williams says is true, I'll be helping him finalize the paperwork for a merger.

What does that mean? I'm not sure, but as soon as I have his file on my desk, I'll be better equipped to know how much time this will take.

After finishing my research, I feel a little out of sorts. I'm staring at a picture of him and those blue eyes that can make a woman lose her breath. Hell, they can bring anyone to cardiac arrest.

They are too deep, too intense. A world of emotion stares back at me. I don't know what to do. I don't know how I'm going to face him. Grabbing my phone, I think of who I can call and talk about this with. Besides my father, I have no one. Sure, I have a few friends here and there, but they're colleagues, not friends.

Hermit is not a big enough word for what I am. I don't have siblings. I don't have anyone.

I pick up the phone and dial, and I hear my father's voice on the line. He sounds tired. I need to insist that he come to the city, but I'm afraid of pushing too hard. Just hearing his voice is enough to help calm me right now.

"Hey, Dad."

"Hey, pumpkin, how's the city's best attorney?" He speaks clearly, so he must be having a good day so far, which is really what I needed to hear, but I still need to know how his appointment went. The fact that I haven't had time to look into the bill also weighs on me. But maybe he can put my mind at ease. I just need to figure out a way to broach the subject and not have him clam up.

"I don't know, let me get Seth Williams on the line and ask him," I joke.

He laughs. "No, but really?"

"Oh, just winning cases, getting more clients, and working my tail off," I humble-brag.

"So, a normal day, huh?"

I laugh a bit and decide not to ask too many questions today. I'm sure if there was something to tell me, he wouldn't keep it from me, right?

Plus, he sounds happy and proud, and I don't want to ruin the mood. Because of his influence, I'm as driven and confident as I am. Growing up, he did everything for me. Even working extra hours, he spent an endless amount of time researching scholarships we could apply for, and then, when we still needed more money, he took on side gigs not only to pay for my college but also to send me to law school.

This man wouldn't let me fall without getting back up. His voice reminds me I'm on a path to finding out how I fell in the first place. I can do this. I can work for Tobias and still get information on Felix. I just have to work a little harder.

CHAPTER NINE

Tobias

THAT WENT BETTER THAN I ANTICIPATED. NOW THAT I'M BACK in the car and driving toward my office, I can reflect on what went down. How perfect it all was.

Williams is a complete schmuck.

But he's an easily manipulated schmuck, which is beneficial to me. Now Skye, on the other hand . . . let's say this should be interesting and a whole lotta fun in the process.

I didn't expect her to have a steel backbone. To talk to her boss like that in front of me means she won't break easily, which has me excited. Not only will I have my fun making her life a living hell—yes, I'm holding a grudge—but it also means that she won't fall apart under pressure when I'm digging for information on Felix.

Before we get to that, I have a few loose ends to tie up, and once all is said and done, I plan on giving all my contacts over to Gideon. He will inherit the business I never really wanted.

It's always been a means to an end. My part in the underworld was never by choice, but it did have its benefits. I've amassed a bit of wealth because of my unscrupulous enterprise. Distributing drugs pays well.

A fortune, to be exact.

Speaking of that fortune, I wonder how it's doing? I pick up my phone and call Cyrus Reed.

I wonder if he's still pissed at me. The thought has my lips spreading into a smile.

He's the only person I trust with my money, besides Trent Aldridge, who helps me grow the reserve. He's the preferred banker for men like me. A vicious motherfucker who is as corrupt as he is brilliant.

I hit the button when I scroll down to his name. He doesn't make me wait long before he answers. That's the thing about Cyrus; despite his personal life and the fact he has pulled back a lot from the business, he will always answer for me.

"Tobias," he answers, his voice rough and angry, *like always*. The man never smiles and rarely jokes. He is the most serious motherfucker out there. Besides me.

My attitude could give him a run for his money. I get it. I rarely show that side of me either. You can't in our business. A moment of weakness can cost you your life.

I haven't let my guard down in over twenty years. Not since I was ten and my life changed. Too much shit has gone down in my life to show anyone that side of me. Sure, every now and then, with the right people, I might laugh. Maybe even drink a little too much. But these are men I would die for, and men who would die for me. I trust them with my life, and no, I have nothing to fear from them. Even so, I always have my wits about me.

It's probably the reason Cyrus and I get along so well. We are very similar.

"Cyrus," I offer as my own greeting.

"Never stand me up again. And yes, your money is still safe." He knows me too well. I probably call once a day to make sure I'm financially in the place I need to be in order to leave.

"Duly noted, and look at that, I didn't even have to ask this time."

"You asked fifteen hours ago," he deadpans.

"Well, I need to be sure." That's my answer every time, but when you come as close as I have, it's the only thing that matters.

"For fuck's sake. How many years have we been doing this dance? I'm not going to fuck you, Tobias."

I let out a long sigh. He's right. I'm being a dick, but I need everything to go off without a hitch.

"And Gideon. Is that ready?" I ask because that's the key point, and if it's not executed perfectly, there could be blowback.

"Yes, he's got an account all set up. When you hand over the reins, I'll be there to make sure the transition goes the way you plan. You'll have to sort some shit with Lorenzo and your other contacts, but as for the money, Gideon will be good. You sure you want to do this? It's not easy walking away." He should know. Despite trying, he hasn't fully retired.

"I never wanted to do this in the first place." My voice dips.

I don't say what I want to—that I had no choice. Cyrus only knows some of my story. He knows my parents died, but he doesn't know the dirty details. I'm sure if I did tell him my full sob story and my plan, he would understand. His is not much different than mine.

Powerful families. Ruthless fathers. Legacies forced upon us despite what we want. This world is all we know.

Raised to rule the underworld.

"And what about Felix? Have you confirmed he ordered the hit?" he asks. The hand holding my phone tightens at his question.

The hit he thinks we are talking about is that of my uncle, the man who raised me. Or at least, that's the story I told him. There's more to it. I have more skeletons in my closet than a morgue, but he doesn't need to know all the details yet.

All in good time.

"No. But that's where the next part of my plan comes into focus. I hired his lawyer."

"The fuck? I'm missing something. You think his lawyer will tell you his secrets?"

"If anyone will know, it will be her."

"Her? The plot thickens." I'm taken aback by his comment. Cyrus isn't one to press or joke, but here he is, doing both.

"Shut the fuck up. It's not like that." Sure, it is. I'd be lying if I didn't admit to myself that I wanted to fuck that smile she gave Felix right off her mouth. That ever since I saw her in court leaning over the table in that short-ass skirt, I didn't want to tip it up and take her from behind. But I'm not about to say that.

"There is something there between her and Felix. I think she is exactly who I need to get inside his organization."

"So, you want her to be your inside man."

"Pretty much." It's not necessarily a well-thought-out plan, but it fell into my lap, so I'm going with it.

"And how do you think you'll convince her?"

"I have my ways."

"I'm sure you do." He chuckles. Again, not something he usually does. I can't remember the last time I heard that sound come from his lips. "Just be careful. You're so close to being out. Do you really want to do something to derail that?"

"Let me ask you a question . . . what would you do in my situation?"

"Honestly?" he asks.

"Do I ever want less than that from you?"

"I'd gut the little shit. I would grab him, torture him, and just ask him point-blank."

I nod to myself. "Your plan certainly has merit. But unlike you, I want corroborating evidence before I kill someone."

"Him being a dick isn't enough?"

"As of right now, we have an agreement. An understanding. He doesn't dip into my territory, and I don't dip into his. I'm not going to start a war that Gideon will have to clean up without knowing the truth."

"Very well." He lets out a sigh. "What do you need from me?"

"Not a damn thing. But I can't promise that won't change."

"You know I'm here for you if it does."

"Thanks." I hang up, knowing he is on my side. That's the thing about the men I do business with, the men who have become my friends over the years. We have bled for each other. We have all gone to war for each other. No matter what, no questions asked, we would all do it again.

My shoulders uncoil. Now that I know Cyrus has my back, I can move to stage two, luring in the new bait. And while I do that, I'll enjoy every second of it.

CHAPTER TEN

Skye

WHAT'S THAT LINE FROM THE CLASSIC MOVIE? OF ALL THE gin joints . . . I am officially in the last place I want to be. Mr. Williams gave me no out when we talked after Tobias left, so here I am.

I check the address on my phone for the millionth time since I received the text. No hello. No name. Just a *"Be at this address at 9 a.m."* I only came because Mr. Williams would fire me on the spot if I didn't go. That can't happen for so many reasons.

I'm shocked by the address or, better yet, the building at the address. I'm not exactly sure where I thought I would be going today.

Yes, you do. Stop lying to yourself.

I thought I was going to a warehouse on the docks where most of the underworld seems to congregate. It never crossed my mind that I was going to an office building off Wall Street with a beautiful view of the water. This is not what the office of a drug lord is supposed to look like.

I take another step and look around. This part of the city is only busy during the workweek, and right now, it's just that. Jam-packed with traders getting ready for the day. I'm early. The market hasn't opened.

It's a quarter to nine, and though it's fun to people watch, I decide to grab a coffee before I head in to find Tobias. Across the street, I see a little shop. I have plenty of time, so I'll pop in real fast, then I'll head up. The stars align as the crosswalk signal turns in my favor, and I head to the store.

Not five minutes later, I'm holding a steaming hot cup of coffee. It warms my hands, which I don't need right now. It's hot out, much hotter than it usually is in mid-May, but I still inhale deeply as I lift the paper coffee cup. The robust and delicious smell infiltrates my nose. Pulling it away, I place it to my lips and take a sip.

It's so good, much better than I expected, and damn, I do love a good coffee. Best decision I made. I slept like crap last night with my mind going a million miles a minute. Today has been weighing on me. Not knowing how it will go had me tossing and turning all night.

Now, freshly showered, a bit more makeup than usual—I needed it to cover the swollen bags under my eyes—I'm ready to see what he wants from me. I'm dressed in a power suit and my favorite lightweight silk blouse. My clothing is my armor in meetings like this. Walking toward the address I was provided, I take a sip from my drink.

There's a doorman and even security. I smile at the man behind the desk.

"Ms. Matthews, here to see Mr. Kosta."

"You can go right up."

Something tells me he knew I was coming and expected me.

I move past the desk and make my way to the elevator banks. I need to find a place to throw this coffee cup out. I look around, not at all paying attention to where I'm walking when I hit a wall and bounce back.

My heels slip, and I fall backward, the cup in my hand toppling out of my grasp.

I hit the ground with a fierce thud. Hot coffee splatters everywhere, including on my chest.

The liquid is so warm, I frantically pull at my shirt. Buttons fly off the thin fabric and land everywhere as I peel the wet, clinging silk off me.

As soon as the material leaves my body, I instantly feel relief from the burning liquid. But I also feel something else. Cold air. Cold air from an air conditioner that is blasting in the corridor. Hitting my skin because I'm now wearing a completely trashed shirt.

Shit.

Shit. Shit. Shit. This is such a disaster.

I lift my hands to cover my chest, which is now exposed. My hands cup the damp lace of my bra. A hand reaches out, and that's when I remember I bumped into someone. My eyes close of their own accord. This can't be happening.

I'm in a torn shirt in front of whoever I bumped into. I don't want to look up. I want to curl into a ball and pretend none of this is happening. Which, of course, I can't do.

"Open your eyes, Ms. Matthews."

Not him. Please, not *him*. I would know that gruff voice anywhere.

Fuck, I want to crawl into a hole. I need a ditch that I can disappear into . . . forever.

"*Fuck me*," I mutter. I can never face this man again after today.

"Skye . . ." he drawls with a bit of a chuckle. Son of a bitch, he heard me.

No. This is not me. I'm not someone to shy away from a challenge with my tail tucked between my legs. Sure, I've embarrassed myself, but this is a momentary setback. Now I need to stop acting like a scared child. I am Skye Matthews, and I've lived through hell. I can deal with one asshole drug dealer.

My lids lift. My gaze is hazy at first, but then everything comes into focus, including the shadow of a larger-than-life man and a hand reaching out to help me. I have two choices. I can take his hand or be stubborn and get up by myself. I choose the latter. Bypassing his extended hand, I push off the ground by myself, stand tall, *a whopping five foot, two inches,* and straighten my back.

I might not be tall, but I can steel my spine until I act like I am. That's just what I do. Tall and proud, and with a tattered shirt covering me, I pick up the cup.

"Don't worry about cleaning that. I'll send someone." I don't respond. I give him a nod and then turn back toward the elevator bank, throwing the cup in the trash right outside the doors as they open.

Once they do, I step inside and am not surprised when Tobias enters the elevator with me. This day is going to suck, and it only just started. I look down at my watch: 9:02. I'm officially late.

"You're late."

"Gee, really? Thanks for letting me know," I deadpan.

"I'll let this time slide, seeing as you were . . . out for coffee."

I don't need to look up to hear the smirk on his lips. But for some reason, I do. I regret the decision the second our gazes collide. Because it's not only a smirk there. There's another look entirely, and as his eyes look down for a second and caress my skin, I can't help but shiver.

What the hell was that, Skye?

The elevator door pings open before I can ponder that thought too long. Without waiting for him to speak again, I step off, and once I'm on solid ground, I turn to face him.

Despite how warm my cheeks are, I look at him and refrain from lifting my hands to cover myself.

CHAPTER ELEVEN

Tobias

I TRY NOT TO STARE. BUT WHEN SHE SAID *FUCK ME*? I'M ONLY human. This woman will be the death of me, and we are less than five minutes into our business relationship.

She is standing in front of me, tits out. Sure, she has a bra on. But if you can call that scrap of lace holding them clothes, I call bullshit.

I try to keep a straight face.

I'm actually pissed. The anger inside me flares. Why does she have to be *her*?

The girl I've sought for most of my life. The girl I've dreamed about. Because this shit isn't me. I'm supposed to be calm. Cool. Collected at all times. I don't get a fucking hard-on in the middle of my lobby because a woman is naked.

But fuuuck.

Said that already.

I'm so annoyed with myself that I'm repeating crap in my own head. What the actual hell is wrong with me right now?

Why does she affect me like this?

This is the problem with being obsessed with someone . . . they make you crazy.

I offered to help her, and I'm damn thankful she didn't take me up on the offer. Instead, she stood all by herself. Making said tits bounce in a way that has me picturing what they would look like if I—

Nope. Do not go there. A cough escapes my throat as I step out of the elevator.

"Follow me," I say before making my way down the hall.

"You don't have to be in such a rush," she huffs.

"Believe it or not, some of us have things to do today."

"What the hell is that supposed to mean?"

"It means exactly how it sounds. I'm a busy man, Skye."

She shuts her mouth after that, and I'm happy she does without fail.

We keep moving.

It's empty in here. I'm sure she notices this. Huge office. No staff. It's a front.

The faster she realizes this, the faster we can move past speaking about my real business and get on to why she's truly here.

Skye trails behind me as I head to the other side of the room.

Her heels click in the distance, and it takes everything in my power not to stop, turn around, and watch her. Finally, I make it to my door, swing it open, and step inside.

She is right behind me.

I walk to the closet I have in here. I also have a bed behind the door in the back I would love to drop her onto, but I highly doubt she would find that tidbit of information interesting. I throw open the closet door and reach inside, grabbing a button-down. Then I turn back to her.

"Here." My voice is strained, but again, she doesn't call me out on why. Hell, at this point, I almost wish she would. The silence is deafening.

She takes it without an objection. I thought she might balk at me, but again, she surprises me.

She gives me that damn smirk, followed by a wink.

Then, there in front of me, she takes her shirt off. Her nipples press against the lace of her bra, begging to be let free and touched until she's panting and moaning for more.

"Don't have all day." My voice sounds bored when really, it's taking every bit of energy not to grab her in my arms and feast on her.

Luckily, she breaks the moment when she places my shirt over her body, buttoning only a few buttons, lifting the shirttails, and tying it so it is now cropped to fall at the waist of her skirt.

It looks good on her. Really fucking good.

"Now that you are put back together, take a seat so we can go over what I need from you."

I turn my back on her and move to sit in my chair. The chair shifts, and the sound echoes like a stampede of elephants. She pulls hers out as well, and again, the same sound. I need to get a carpet in here or something. That shit is grating on my last nerve. Or maybe it's her . . .

I'm starting to think I did not plan this out very well. Maybe Cyrus, being a smart-ass, was more intelligent than I first thought.

From across the desk, I watch as Skye stares across the room, her gaze is focused on the vase filled with flowers by the window. The vase I had filled with penitent's rose, just to fuck with her.

"You like them?" My voice must startle her because she practically jumps out of her seat before turning back to me, a scowl on her face.

"Why am I here?" She straightens her back.

"Right. Cut to the chase. I like that."

"Well, I don't really have a choice," she grits out. "Not sure what you offered Mr. Williams, but obviously, it was enough to uproot my life."

She's pissed, and rightfully so, but that's not my problem. "I made him an offer—"

"He couldn't refuse," she fires back, rolling her eyes.

"Absolutely not."

"So, here we are. Please tell me how I can be of service, and we can move this thing right along." She looks at me with cold and discerning eyes.

There is more to it than this. She fought to work with Felix, and I wonder if my initial thought is true. *Is she banging him?* I'm not sure why, but my hands fist at my side. I shake my head, clearing the thoughts I don't want right now.

"Since you're my attorney now, this is all attorney-client privilege."

"Certainly."

"Very well. I want out," I offer as my reason.

"Out?" Her eyebrows lift, clearly confused.

"Of the game," I clarify.

"And the game is?"

I tilt my head, giving her a look that says *are you kidding?* "Don't play coy, Skye—"

"Ms. Matthews," she interrupts.

"You want me to call you Ms. Matthews?"

"Yes, I think—"

I shake my head. "No."

"Um . . . excuse me?"

"Is this going to be a problem, Skye?" I lead, annoyed that she is being this difficult. "Should I call Seth and let him know this isn't going to work?" If I do that, her job is as good as gone. She knows this. I know this. There is no reason to duck behind false pretenses. "Hope your résumé is all bright and shiny. Maybe you can be a public defender. That's a good name for you . . . Sunshine."

Her eyes go wide. She doesn't like the nickname. It unnerved her.

Note to self . . . *start calling her that.*

Soon, she is righting herself, but her shock is replaced quickly with anger. The scowl that lines her face is priceless. It's also a look I have seen many times in my life: pure, unadulterated hatred. It oozes out of her pores. If looks could kill, I'd be dead. Good thing they don't, because I still have one more game to play. After that, I'd happily die by her hand.

"Yes, Skye. I want to go legitimate. Good enough for you?"

"Yes. But I don't see how I can be of service."

"I have a few loose ends I want to tie up, and I need to make sure nothing, and I mean nothing, interferes with that."

"So, what does that mean? You're talking in riddles."

"Until I get completely out, and all of my holdings are on the up-and-up, I need my new lawyer with me."

"How much time?"

"All of it. All the time. All the meetings. Every day until this is over." Her mouth drops. This isn't the first time since I have known her that she has worn this look. The shock on her face is almost laughable.

"Don't worry, Skye, Williams already knows."

"You need a high-priced babysitter?"

"I wouldn't say that."

"You want me to follow you around and make sure you don't get into trouble. That sounds like a babysitter. A nanny of sorts." She's a feisty one, and although I expected it, I didn't realize how much I would like it. That spitfire attitude is a real turn-on. And since most women don't think of talking back to me, let alone casually insulting me, I feel like a fish out of water.

What the fuck, Tobias? Get your shit together. She works for you.

"I need someone to go with me to meetings. Make sure everything I sign is legit. Make sure this transfer of power is beyond reproach."

She watches me for a second, and then she does something I don't expect. She nods without protest.

"I can do that," she says.

"Good, then let's go."

Her eyebrows pinch together. "Where are we going?"

"So many questions from one little mouth . . ." I trail off as I stand. Not giving her time to object, I start to walk. From behind me, I can hear her heels hitting the concrete as she scampers to catch up. This is going to be fun. Or it's going to be the death of me.

Either way, it's a hell of a way to go.

Skye Matthews is my obsession. My past.

My future.

My downfall.

CHAPTER TWELVE

Skye

THIS MAN IS TRYING TO KILL ME. NOT LITERALLY. Figuratively. But he will be the death of me. That's for sure.

If I could wipe the smug look off his face, I would. I would use a bleach-covered towel and hope the fumes burned his eyes out, too! Eyes that I know were checking me out.

The worst part about this whole thing is that I liked it. Every look, every glance, and every smug gesture. I should have been mortified, but I wasn't.

Sure, at first, I was. But the moment I saw his eyes dilate with lust, all thought of embarrassment went out the window. Now that I'm dressed in his shirt, it's even worse.

It smells like fresh dry cleaning and hints of his cologne. The way his fragrance wraps around me shouldn't make my belly warm.

And now my face is getting hot.

I hope he doesn't notice.

Sparing a glance at him, I see he's still looking at me. And instead of lust, I see ownership.

He likes how I look in his clothes, and fuck my life, I like how it feels. I cannot be around him for too long if this is how he makes me feel when he looks at me. As I look back at him, well— he makes me think things I shouldn't.

Like how his hands would feel on my hips. What his lips would taste like during a kiss.

I have to focus on the job at hand and not his body.

Twisting my hands on my lap beneath the table, I wring out my anxiety. I'll never let him see that he has me all worked up. I have mastered my façade, and no drop-dead gorgeous asshole is going to make me take that down.

"Now that you have me here, care to tell me what we are doing today?" I ask.

"Today, we have a meeting with Trent Aldridge."

He doesn't need to explain who that is. I'm well versed in mafia underworld bullshit. The hedge fund manager to the corrupt. This should be interesting.

Together, Tobias and I head to a car in the underground parking lot—a shiny, brand-new Range Rover—but something tells me this isn't a run-of-the-mill Range Rover. This one has all the bells and whistles.

"I bet it's even bulletproof."

"It is," Tobias responds, and that's when I realize I mumbled it under my breath, and he could hear me. I have to stop doing that, or I'll blurt out something really bad. Like what cologne is on this shirt? How do your kisses taste? *Ugh. Stop. This. Skye.*

"Nice." I grunt as a man I have never seen before swings open the door for me.

"Thank you, Leo."

"Thank you," I respond as a mimic, then shimmy into the back seat.

It's so freaking cold in here with the air on full blast, but it doesn't matter because, as he slides in next to me, Tobias Kosta steals all the oxygen from the small space between us. The car might as well be a million degrees Fahrenheit.

My face is warm. My hands are warm. My whole damn treacherous body is warm. I take a deep inhale and then push the air out of my mouth.

"You okay over there?"

"Yes."

"You sure?" I can hear the taunt in his voice. I need to rein in my emotions. Normally not one to give anything away, this man reads me like a *Skye Matthews for Dummies* book.

"I'm fine. Totally fine."

As soon as we pull out of the underground space, I turn to face out the window, trying desperately to calm myself and not pay attention to the man beside me. I do a damn good job for about four seconds. That's when he places his hand on the center console and brushes it against mine. I pull back as if burned.

Turning to look at him, I see he's reading something on his phone and has no concept of the turmoil he is causing me.

Bastard.

I turn back to look outside, and this time, I watch the road as we drive uptown. In typical New York fashion, there's traffic, and it takes way too long to make it to our destination. The morning has only just started, and I'm already exhausted by my own inner ramblings. *Will today ever end?*

I look down at my phone. Great. Just great. It's only nine twenty.

A full day ahead of me and no way to escape.

"Already planning your escape?" he says, and I pivot to look in his direction. *How does he do that?* So not fair.

"Why yes, actually. Believe it or not, my life doesn't revolve around you," I snip back.

"See, that's funny because here I thought it did." His lips part. "Or at least that's the impression Seth gave . . ." Gritting my teeth together, I refuse to fall into his trap. "No response? No funny little comeback? That's a first."

Nope. Not going to do it. The car goes quiet again. He's finally realized he won't be able to lure me into this battle. He goes back to whatever he was doing, and I go back to what I was doing.

I swear, the moment the car rolls to a stop, I'm unbuckling my seat belt and moving to open the door and escape.

"Not so fast," I hear from beside me.

"What?"

"My team needs to do a sweep."

His team. That's when I notice we aren't the only car parked in this garage. In front of us is a similar Range Rover, and there is one behind us as well.

A caravan. I'm in the middle of a freaking caravan.

Decoy vehicles.

The kind of stuff you only see in movies. For the first time in my life, I realize just how dangerous my life is.

No. Not true. I've been in more—

"All clear now. Are you coming?" Tobias's words break through my memories. I push them down.

Now is not the time to think about that. In order to get through the day, I don't think about anything from my past. That doesn't mean I don't catch myself wanting to rub at my wrist to calm the pounding in my heart. But I don't.

Instead, I take a deep breath.

Inhale.

Exhale.

Push all thoughts away other than this meeting.

I follow Tobias as he leads us to a bank of elevators. The doors open, and his men walk inside first. It's crazy that these men have been with us the whole time, yet I never noticed them.

Were they in my office building that day he came to see Seth? Were they in this morning when I grabbed my files?

I look at them with my eyes narrowed.

"You have a question?" he asks.

I turn to face him. "Were they with us the whole time?"

"They go where I go."

"That's not an answer." I roll my eyes.

"It's the only one I have."

My teeth grind at his sidestep, but I guess with the power and money, and most of all, the dangerous enemies he has, he has to have security. I'm not sure why it makes me angry.

But I do know. I have always watched my surroundings, but in the presence of this man, I'm missing things left and right.

I'm constantly being pushed back into my thoughts and making mistakes. I don't like this at all. I need to always have my wits about me, and I'm starting to understand that I might be in a little over my head where this single, solitary man is concerned.

I follow Tobias to the elevator.

Then we are stepping in and are enclosed in the space. The usual elevator music isn't present. Nope. Not here. Instead, there is a peaceful sound that makes me feel as if I'm walking into a spa instead of a business.

"Interesting choice of music."

"Trent's trying to calm his life. For some crazy reason, he says elevators are stressful."

"They are," I respond.

"Are you stressed?" he says, but his voice is a bit rougher as the elevator climbs.

I look over at him and notice the knuckles on his left hand are white.

"I don't like elevators very much."

"To be honest, me neither."

I can tell, I think, but I don't say anything because he looks uncomfortable.

"Normally, it doesn't bother me. But sometimes, like now, since we are talking about it—"

"Yeah."

"It's almost more defined if that makes sense. Like my—" I stop myself. *What am I doing?* This is going against rule number one, my biggest rule—never let your guard down. All it took was one look from him, and here I am, blowing my rules out the window.

Pressing my thumb against my pulse, I will myself to calm. Luckily, I don't have to deal with this for long because as tall as the building is and as high as we are going, the elevator travels so fast, we are already there.

As soon as the elevator stops, I swear I let out an audible sigh. I'm not normally like this. When I was going to Tobias's office, it didn't even dawn on me. Maybe because of the height of the building? Or maybe it's the size of the elevator. *Maybe it's ~~him.~~*

Tobias steps back and reaches out to signal for me to go first. I take a step and am happy to be on flat ground again. Once off the elevator, I wait for him to move forward.

"This way." He starts to move, and I follow suit. I increase my pace to keep up with him. We move down the hallway side by side. I watch as Tobias takes long, powerful strides from the corner of my eye. He looks in control as if he owns this building and everyone in it. He appears larger than life.

There is nothing this man doesn't appear to master. It's actually quite annoying. No one this attractive should be this sure of himself. Maybe that's what makes him so hot.

Nope. That's not just it.

It's the dark hair and light eyes. He looks at you like he can see everything. I wonder if he does.

Does he see everything?

The thought makes my hands feel clammy. I sure hope he doesn't. I don't need him to see the real me and know anything about who I really am. The more distance I can put between us, the better.

This office is nothing like Tobias's. There are numerous

employees. This isn't a front or pretend office. Nope. This place reminds me of my office, only higher up. Much higher up.

Tobias doesn't bother talking to anyone. He just proceeds down the hall and opens an office door. I have to assume he comes here often.

"You don't bother knocking?" I hear someone laugh.

"No."

"Good to see you are in your usual chipper mood." The voice is playful and sarcastic and pissing Tobias off. I like the voice already.

Stepping in, I scan the room. Trent Aldridge is reclined behind a large desk, wearing a broad smirk.

He is the opposite of Tobias, who looks like he's never heard nor understood the punchline to a joke.

"And who are you?" Trent lifts his brows as I step into his office.

"This is my new lawyer." Tobias's voice is stern, and I swear it sounds like a warning. *Why?* I don't know, but it's there, nonetheless.

"Does this lawyer have a name?" The smile that lines this man's face is contagious, and even though I want to smile, I have a feeling Tobias does not.

And just as predicted, my new client shows no emotion. He looks like a goddamn robot. A hot one, but still.

I step forward, hand raised. "The lawyer," I say in introduction. "But you can call me Skye."

"Skye. I like that. Nice shirt," he says, wrinkling his brow as he takes in my look.

"There was a coffee incident. I was able to borrow a shirt from Mr. Kosta's wardrobe."

"Really? Coffee. I would really love to hear the details of this one."

"How's Payton?" Tobias cuts in and asks. I don't know who Payton is, but something tells me I just entered a pissing match.

"She's fine, thanks for asking. Take a seat, guys, and we can go over everything. And before you ask . . . you still have money. I haven't Ponzi schemed your ass yet." My upper teeth bite down to refrain from laughing, but a squeak comes out. I play it off as a cough, but Tobias's scowl deepens. I'm not fooling anyone.

I can't help but watch them. The back-and-forth banter between them reminds me of a tennis match. Except Trent is playing for fun, and Tobias, well, Tobias basically is being forced to play despite hating the game.

It's pretty interesting to observe them. I can tell right off the bat that they are friends. I can also tell Tobias likes him. But even with all that, Tobias doesn't smile or smirk. He doesn't have the sound in his voice that you often hear between friends. It's not warm. There's no tinge of humor. It makes my heart clench in my chest.

Does he have anyone?

My eyes narrow as I take him in. He's not that different from me. In truth, other than our chosen careers, we are pretty similar. Both jaded and closed off with tragic pasts.

I have to stop thinking about this.

Recently, my childhood—my memories—have been haunting me again. Which is not something I can think about.

"What do you think about that, Skye?" I hear Trent Aldridge say, and I realize I have no clue what he is talking about. I had completely tuned him out, lost in my own thoughts and the similarities between Tobias and me.

"I'm sorry, I missed the question." A normal person might pretend they were paying attention. A normal person might be worried that their client is pissed that they weren't paying attention. I'm not that person.

I can give two shits what either of these men thinks of me. However, that being said, the faster I get done here, the faster I can get back to the office and see if I can get myself to work with

Mr. Bernard again. From what I *have* heard, and read in my father's files, he was involved that day . . .

"Here are the forms you need to look over." Trent reaches out and extends the paperwork to me. It's a huge pile. So much for getting anything else accomplished today.

What is all this shit?

I look down at the pile in my hand and lift the top sheet. A new account is being opened in the name of Gideon Byrne.

There are also papers for an investment tied to a corporation located in the Cayman Islands.

I see that some other things are clearly not on the up-and-up right off the bat.

"As you can see, Tobias has made quite a bit of money." Quite a bit? More like enough to start his own country. "All of this money is—"

"Clean?" I ask.

Trent laughs. "Not pulling any punches, huh?"

"I don't see a reason. I'm here to make sure everything is legal, which means at one point it wasn't. And as for Tobias, I'm his attorney. Thus, attorney-client privilege is in effect. When do you need these back?"

"Tomorrow too soon?" Trent asks, and I look over at Tobias, whose jaw is tight.

I want to say yeah, it's too soon, but it's officially my first day on the job, and that won't grant me any favors with my boss.

"Nope. I will have this couriered back to you in the morning."

"No," Tobias grits out, and I look to face him. His lips are thinned. "You'll hand-deliver it yourself."

"With all due respect, I have—"

"I do not care what the fuck you have to do. After you check them, you will have these documents delivered to me, and I will sign. And then you will traipse over here and deliver them yourself."

I take a deep breath, inhaling to calm myself.

"No problem. I will take these"—I look down at the stack—
"look them over, and then after you sign"—I look at Trent, smiling broadly—"I'll drop them off. Sound good?"

"Sounds great." Trent smiles back.

"Anything else, Trent?" Tobias really isn't one for small talk.
I can already tell that.

"Nope. You?"

"Nothing I care to talk about," Tobias responds, monotone.
He sounds bored.

"Interesting. Will you be at Cyrus's in a few weeks? Alaric
will be in town."

"Maybe."

"Oh, come on, man, give us this. Stop being a dick long
enough to just say yes. Trust me, your lady lawyer over here won't
consider that means you could be a nice guy. She knows you're a
grade A asshole, right?"

"Pretty much," I answer.

"I like this woman." Trent is like a jester hired to entertain the
king, and the king, Tobias, doesn't find him funny.

"No one asked you who you like, Trent, so shut the fuck up."

"Who pissed in his Froot Loops today?" Trent snickers.

"I think that would be me. And it was coffee-flavored." I laugh.

"Well, if you two are fucking done wasting my time, we have
another appointment."

"Dragging the poor woman around?" Trent seems highly
amused with himself as he pokes the bear. Guess he's not scared
that bear pokes back.

"Yuppers," I mutter under my breath, and Trent laughs again.

"I really like her," Trent tells him, and the look Tobias gives
Trent as he stands, well, let's just say, I'm surprised a gun isn't
drawn and Trent isn't dead. And not a normal death. Intestines
on the floor, blood splattered everywhere. Messy death.

Trent inclines his head, looks back and forth between us, and
then shakes it, letting out a sigh. "I'll see you at Cyrus's soon?"

And now it's Tobias's turn to let out his own deep breath. "Yes."

"Good. I'm sure everyone will be happy. Well, everyone except Cyrus. That man is never happy." He furrows his brow. "You kind of remind me of him," he chides.

Tobias stands. "If that's all the wisdom you have to impart today, we're done. Let's go."

Standing from my chair, I look at Trent and smile one last time before turning on my heel and following a few steps behind Tobias.

"Nice to meet you, Skye Lawyer," Trent shouts to our backs in a singsong manner.

"He seems nice," I whisper to Tobias as we walk down the hallway.

A grunt. That's all I get out of him, a grunt. So much for small talk.

This time, when the elevator opens and I step inside, I pull out my phone. Anything to distract me from not just the confined space but also the awkward silence in the air between us. I want to ask him so many questions, but I don't.

Instead, I let all the questions fill my brain, weigh heavy on my heart, and make my pulse race. As much as I want to say things and ask things, I can't. If I do, lines will be crossed, and doors will open. And once you open those doors, you can never go back.

So, no matter what my brain tells me to do, I push the thoughts down and close that door.

CHAPTER THIRTEEN

Tobias

I'M SO FUCKING THANKFUL THAT SKYE AND I HAVE PARTED WAYS for the day. After four hours of dragging her around the city, I need a break. I also need a drink. A big one. Are there Big Gulp–sized scotch glasses I can buy somewhere? This woman has me sideways. She has a way about her, and I don't like it.

At fucking all.

That doesn't stop me from wanting her around, though. It certainly doesn't stop me from going through with my plan.

A new idea pops into my head.

Seduce her. Oh, that would be so much fun. It will kill two birds with one stone.

One: Well, I get to fuck her.

Two: It will be easier for her to open up to me, and then I can also bring her into the plan.

I underestimated how tough she would be. She's much stronger than I gave her credit for. This new plan makes more sense. After watching her today, I know she's attracted to me, so it won't be that hard.

Probably shouldn't be a complete dick to her.

I shake my head. *No.* Something tells me she likes it. She's a spitfire, after all. Which would probably mean this plan would backfire on me. Knowing her, she would turn it around, and I'd end up with my dick in my hand yet no pussy.

Scratch out seduction. I don't have time for it anyway.

The car stops in the garage, and I step out. Not many people know that I live in my office building full time. It's easier for security to only have one location. Plus, this place is built like Fort Knox. Skye only saw the one empty floor. That was the only floor I permitted her to see.

I head straight for the stairs because I prefer them. The stairs are wide, open, and have clear railings.

It never feels like I'm trapped inside. I wasn't lying to Skye when I said I don't like elevators, but I didn't get into the specifics. It's not only elevators; it's all enclosed spaces. When she stopped talking in the elevator, I welcomed the silence. I didn't realize that we had that in common. But why should I?

I don't *actually* know her.

So why would I know shit about her? Despite the little time spent with her and my endless research, it doesn't ever show the real person.

Taking the steps two at a time, I head to the top floor, which is my residence. I walk straight for the bar set up in the corner of the main room. My gaze scans over my choices. Is tonight a scotch night or a tequila night?

Since I'm alone, I opt for Glenlivet 21. Grabbing a tumbler, I pour myself three fingers and then head into my bedroom to get changed. On my approach, I lift the glass and take a swig. The warm liquid coats my throat, and as I swallow, I swear it already is loosening me up. Tilting my head up, I look at the skylight I had built directly over my favorite place to sit.

I have a clear view of the night sky.

Although no stars are visible, the darkness above calms me.

Tomorrow, I have a lot more in store for her. When I said I wanted her to accompany me everywhere, I meant it. Setting my drink down, I pick up my phone to dial Gideon.

"Boss?" he answers. "Do you need me?"

"Nah. I just wanted to go over a few things for tomorrow."

"Shoot."

Technically, if I wanted Gideon here, he'd be here. He lives downstairs, along with a handful of my men. They don't necessarily live here full time, but there is a security area with rooms. That way, if something ever goes down, I have my team with me.

I won't need it for long if everything goes as planned.

"We need to go to Lorenzo and go over the logistics."

"Are you sure you want to do this? This is your legacy, Tobias."

"Yes," I grit out.

Soon, Gideon will take over my import business. Most essential is the portion I don't talk about.

The drugs.

Despite what he says, I want no part in it. It's always been a means to an end. A way to get enough power to take out my enemies and seek revenge. Now that I'm close, Gideon thinks I might regret my decision or go back on it. I won't.

All I want is to feel the life drain from the body of the man who killed my family. After that's done, I'm done with this life.

I was handed the keys to a kingdom I never wanted. It's time my reign ended.

"Yes, I'm sure. This is why we are going to meet with Lorenzo tomorrow. He needs to know the plan and that you will be taking over."

"Okay," he responds. His voice is far away, lost in thought.

"Gideon."

"Yeah, boss?"

"Is this really what you want?" If he doesn't, I'll find another way out, despite what it will cost me.

"I don't have a choice."

"There is always a choice."

"I'm the lesser of the evils. If I step up, we can control who deals, who the customer is, and make sure it's never cut."

It's true; this is the easier way. Despite my profession, I do have a conscience. Anyone who buys from me knows what will happen if it's ever cut with fentanyl. They would die just like their customers. Painfully.

"We could close up shop," I offer as a solution.

"We could, but you know as well as I do that someone will fill the void. They always do." He's not wrong.

That's the underworld. There is always a nastier, more deadly enemy waiting to strike. This way, with Gideon in charge, we can limit the damage.

"You're right." I let out a long, audible sigh. "But if you don't want this, then we just take that risk."

"I'm good, boss," he responds, and this time, I hear the conviction in his voice.

I nod to myself, happy with the outcome of this conversation. He's right. This is the only solution to the problem. There is no one I trust more than Gideon Byrne. He's the only man other than myself who will honor the principles I grew up with.

No women.

No children.

The bastard who killed my father never believed in those principles. Which is why it has always been important to honor my father and follow the rules he wanted to govern his organization with. It doesn't matter if I'm involved. My connections and contacts trust us to be better than our competition, and nothing will stop me from making sure that is exactly what happens. Consequences be damned.

The lawyer who is looking to be complete trouble?

I'll handle her, too.

CHAPTER FOURTEEN

Skye

Papers are signed, and I've cross-checked everything as I raise my hand to knock on Trent Aldridge's office door.

"Come on in, Lawyer Lady," Trent hollers through the closed door. I look up to find the camera, but I can't see one easily. Are all these guys' offices guarded like a Swiss bank?

"I brought back the signed stack for you," I practically sing-song as I walk through the door.

"Still can't believe the bastard made you schlep all the way back yourself. I mean, come on, this is the easy stuff."

"Yeah, well, I'm getting used to being dragged all over the place at Tobias's side with zero notice given. It's kind of his MO."

"Tobias's side. Never thought I'd see the day he had a woman as hard as nails next to him. We all need one, though."

"A woman lawyer?" I ask, confused by his statement.

"No, a woman to put up with us and fall in love."

"Whoa. Um. No. Trent. I can call you Trent, right? I've known Tobias for a total of five seconds, give or take. There's no love talk on the table. I barely tolerate the man, and I'm ready for him to retire so I can get back to my other clients."

"So, you talk back to him and force him to do things on Day One. Am I right?"

"Yes."

"And he didn't pull out a gun, shoot you on sight, and dump the body in the East River."

"Noooo."

"Well, in this world, that's one step away from him being in love with you, Lawyer Lady."

I huff. Genuine laughter bursts out of him.

"I gotta get back to my office. Let me know if you have anything else that needs to be reviewed for my client." I purposely over-enunciate those last two words.

"Sure. Sure, I will. Oh, and when you see him, tell him I secured the teddy bears for Lorenzo, so that's one thing off the list for 'Client Tobias,'" he air quotes.

"Teddy bears?"

"Yeah, he'll know what they are for. Let me know if you need anything else."

"Okay, have a good day. Oh, and I thought I introduced myself yesterday, but in case you forgot, my name is Skye Matthews."

"I remember your name, Skye. I think I'll stick with Lawyer Lady, though, just to piss Tobias off."

I chuckle as I walk out of his office. Just a five-minute conversation with Trent Aldridge has my head spinning again. I'm off to find out what Tobias wants and whether I can keep my wits about me with him next to me.

Time goes by fast when you're overworked. It's been almost two weeks since this man has employed me, and my nerves have yet to subside. I'm not sure what to expect today. Days keep passing, and he keeps dragging me along with him. I've gotten used to it. I've also gotten used to returning home at the end of the day bone-tired. My mind is mush.

I have worked hard before, but this is something entirely different. It is as if I am completely on edge all the time. My sensory system is on overload. I want to hate him. But really, he hasn't done anything other than tow me around to every business meeting he could have in the greater tri-state area. I've met his finance guy, security teams, brokers, and warehouse and shipping managers. I think I am missing a maid or two and possibly a gardener.

He doesn't know I need to get back to my other clients. He has no clue there is a bigger objective for me. Felix.

That's the goal.

From what I have seen and heard, Felix is responsible for a string of violent incidents. One of the incidents could very well be the one where my parents were killed.

My boss thinks I'm here to better my career, but that's not the whole story. I'm here for one reason, and that's only to fill in the blanks of my past.

My father—*adoptive* father—closes down every time I ask questions. He thinks I'm over asking about that day and the details he has patched together over the years, but I'm not. I need to know.

I feel like pieces are missing, and I want to connect the dots and understand what happened. There's no one left to ask but Felix himself. I certainly can't ask him directly, but if I have access to his computer . . . there has to be something in his files that will answer my questions.

Unfortunately, I haven't had the time to closely examine what I took from my father's house, but I believe those papers, coupled with anything I can grab from Felix, will help clear things up for me. It's not a well-thought-out plan, but it's the only one I have.

Walking into my bathroom, I stare at myself in the mirror. My hair is blown out already; I just need a little makeup before I go. A dusting of blush and mascara is enough. Once I do that, I run my hands down my skirt and make sure I look put together.

I probably shouldn't be wearing a dress. Who knows where we're going? Maybe a drug run.

Be nice.

He's trying to get out. He's not Felix.

After all the time I've spent with Felix Bernard, he has never made reference to getting out of the game. I guess not all drug lords are created equal.

Okay, enough procrastinating. It's time to go.

I leave the bathroom, grab my bag, and head out the door. I opt to take the stairs. My building is nice, but it is in no way nice enough for me to take the elevator on a daily basis. That thing breaks down at least once a week.

I also live in a relatively small building. With only five floors, I can do it. It's my cardio. My heels slap on the steps as I head down. By the time I make it to the ground level, I have worked up a small sweat on my brow.

Swiping it away, I pull out my phone, turn on the camera, and pat my hair back into place. Heading toward the subway, I make my way downtown to Tobias's office. Again, when I get there, it's the same old story. The guard waves me in, and I step into the large elevator. Now that I know how much Tobias hates enclosed spaces, this elevator makes sense. It's huge.

Even for me, who gets claustrophobic, this one doesn't make me feel like I'm suffocating.

At first, I took it because I didn't think I had a choice. Plus, I never wanted to show weakness. It only takes a second before the doors open, and once again, I'm striding into the empty office space.

Does he own the whole building?

My guess is yes.

Standing in front of the large windows in the distance, with his back toward me, is Tobias. His head is tilted up as if he's looking at the clouds, then his chin drops, and his back becomes rigid at whatever he's staring at now. He must hear me; my shoes echo in the empty space. The clicking sound rings through the air, but he doesn't turn around.

"I'm here," I say to get his attention, but he still says nothing.

Moving closer, I try to discern what he is looking at. When I'm finally close, I see he's watching a playground. I never noticed it before.

A group of kids are playing. They look to be in preschool. I stare for a minute before I hear him cough, and then he turns to face me.

"Morning," I say, and he nods, then he takes a seat at the desk. "Something on your mind?"

"I always have something on my mind."

"Since I'm your lawyer, and regardless of what you say, I have to listen, so do you want to talk about it?"

I'm not sure why I say any of this, but I want to comfort him for some reason. Which is weird because I also resent him for making me come here.

"I'm fine."

The room goes silent. I know he's lying, and I find myself wanting to know what he's thinking about.

"What made you decide to quit?" I finally ask.

"That's a long, complicated story," he mutters.

"I have time."

"Not enough time for this one," he deadpans.

"Just start talking, dammit. Our day isn't going to get better until you talk about whatever it is that's bothering you."

"Fine, but first, I have to take you with me to a few meetings."

"Duh. That's what we've been doing this whole time." I scoff playfully.

"No. This is different. I want to warn you about the first one."

"I'll be fine."

"That being said, I still want to tell you who we are going to see."

"Okay."

"We are meeting with Lorenzo Amanté."

The need to let my mouth drop open is there, but I will my body not to embarrass me, again. Lorenzo Amanté is only the rumored head of the mafia. He's supposed to be nuts, too. Real anger issues. Which doesn't surprise me, seeing the chosen occupation.

"I'll be fine," I answer before gesturing to the exit. "Ready, then?"

He nods, and after that, we walk toward the elevator. We step inside, and he turns to me.

"I want to leave this life because I never wanted to be here," he says, and I'm shocked he's broaching this story. I don't dare say anything for fear he will stop. "All of my life, I wanted something else."

"Then why did you do it for so long?" I can't help but ask as we arrive in the garage and start heading toward the Range Rover.

"Because I needed the resources and money to take out my one true enemy. And you should know the story." With a slight pause, he continues as we settle into the car.

"When I was a small boy, it was just my father and me. But even though it was just us, my father was always gone. At the time, I didn't know why. All my nanny ever said was that he was a very important man. He had very important friends who relied on him. Again, I was young and had no concept of who or what these people expected from him. We moved around a lot. He set up businesses in different locations, and once everything was in place, we got up and did it all over again. I used to resent him for it. All the moving around is hard on a boy, and I needed my father, who was never around."

Tobias stops speaking as the car slows. "Time's up for this story. We'll have to continue it later."

I'm disappointed that he has to stop his story, but I understand.

We're here to meet Lorenzo, and this is probably not a talk he wants to have in front of such a man. Looking out the window, I see that the car is parked in front of a large warehouse on the docks. The concrete building looks empty. If I'm being honest, it looks completely abandoned. I furrow my brow as I study it. I see that Tobias is looking at me from across the back seat.

"What?"

"Is anyone there? Or are we early?" I ask.

"It just looks like this from the outside. Trust me when I tell you, not only is Lorenzo here but he also has snipers on the top of the building."

At his words, I move closer to the windowpane to get a better look.

"You won't see them," he announces after I have basically squished my body as close to the glass as humanly possible. As hard as I try, there is nothing out there, yet no matter what I see, I believe him. "You getting out?"

"After you," I respond.

"It's perfectly safe, Skye. His team knows we are coming. They won't shoot at you."

A shiver runs up my spine. Despite his words, I don't feel safe. Just thinking about getting shot has my body locking up.

"Skye?"

"*Hmm*?"

"You can open the door." For some unknown reason, I'm frozen, and I'm not sure what has come over me. My head throbs, and I close my eyes to push away the feeling weaving its way inside.

Unconsciously, I touch my tattoo. I rub it once, twice, and by the third swipe of my thumb, my heart rate calms. My breath comes out in slower bursts as I move past the panic that had built inside me. The door beside me swings open, and I open my eyes to see Tobias, arm extended, eyes staring at me, waiting for me to take his hand.

"Are you okay?" he asks. I'm confused by his change in

behavior. For the time I have worked with him, he has been closed off. But now, having him ask me these questions, having him leaning down and staring at me, part of me feels as though he does genuinely care about my feelings. I don't know him. But a part of me wants to get to know him. The only thing I know so far is that he doesn't do anything legally. He makes mistakes left and right, and he needs a babysitter, but I also know he cares.

Maybe not necessarily for me, but when I get like this, he seems concerned.

His unwavering gaze does strange things to me. It feels like my face is warming. It's growing hot, and if I had to harbor a guess, I'd say my face is beet red. A shade reserved for lipsticks one would wear to a gala or fashion show.

"I'm fine." My voice comes out harsher than I want it to, but I'm already mortified. Telling him I temporarily freaked out for an unknown reason is too much to deal with right now.

He narrows his eyes. A line forms between his brow as he watches me. He's trying to size me up. There is no getting away from his assessment, but eventually, after a few seconds, he nods, pushes his hand out farther toward me, and offers it again. This time, I don't reject him. I'm still shaken by what just happened to me. That hasn't happened since forever. It's like I go off to a far-off place in my brain, then I don't know why.

I take his hand and allow him to pull me from the seat and out of the car. My heels hit the pavement; the sound of gravel smashing is in the air. The moment I step out, the first thing that hits me is the smell of seawater. It's like being on a boat when you're surrounded by the ocean. I turn to look at the water, the way it crashes against the dock. It's rough today, so a storm is probably brewing, making the day feel ominous.

I take a deep inhale, pulling the salty air into my lungs and then exhaling it out. Just this small moment does wonders to calm my nerves, and before long, I feel back to normal. I drop Tobias's hand and take a step toward the warehouse. Tobias matches my pace, and together we make our way to the door.

"Will they just let us in?" I ask, staring up at where the snipers must be.

"Again, they know we're coming. The door isn't locked."

"That doesn't sound very safe."

"Oh, it's locked right now. Here, let me show you."

The moment we make it to the front, Tobias points at the tiny camera above the door, then he looks right at it and nods his head. Only then do I hear the click.

"This place has high surveillance. No one is getting in or out without permission."

His words don't go over my head. No one is getting out. I am right to be afraid, but I won't show him. I already revealed too much of my hand in the car. I hold my head up high, then reach out and open the door, ready to see what's behind the curtain.

As I step through the entrance, the first thing I notice is that the air feels stiffer inside the warehouse. Or maybe that is just my nerves. The room is large and cavernous. A smell lingers in the air. It's almost fruity, and I can't pinpoint its origin.

My gaze drifts along the space, and on the far side of the room, I see men sitting around a table talking. There is nothing out of place. Nothing to indicate that this is a space used for illegal activity. Other than the random table, it's vacant.

A man pushes back from the table.

The metal legs scratch the concrete as he makes his way to standing and heads over to us. The first thing I notice is how handsome he is. Not as good looking as Tobias, in my opinion, but I can totally see why a woman would fall under his spell.

Well, that would be before they realize who he is.

Hell, maybe even after.

Look at me. I know full well who Tobias is, and I can't help that he makes my body warm. I have a strong desire to make him the star of my next midnight fantasy session.

Lucky for me, that hasn't happened yet because I don't know how I would ever look at him again if he starred in one.

Lorenzo crosses the space with a level of arrogance only present in a man who knows or, better yet, thinks he's better than someone.

When he's almost upon us, his stern features morph, and a wicked smirk spreads across his face. Then his gaze travels down my length, making the smile broaden.

"The lawyer," he remarks, but there is no question. It's a statement. "I can see why you hired her."

That's it. I am so sick of condescending, arrogant assholes. I step forward, meeting Lorenzo head-on.

"The lawyer has a name. She also has eyes." I lift my hand. "Up here, buddy."

A part of me expects Lorenzo to probably shoot me on the spot, and to be honest, my outburst, though warranted, might not have been one of my best ideas. Instead, Lorenzo throws his head back and laughs. "I like her already, Tobias."

"I don't need you to like her," Tobias grits out, and I turn to look at him. His jaw is set tight, and he looks pissed. Surprise, surprise. This man has worse PMS than a fourteen-year-old girl.

"Then why is she here?"

"I'm here because, apparently, I'm his babysitter, and he can't go anywhere without me," I mutter under my breath, but my voice is loud enough that again, Lorenzo's hearty laughter rings through the air.

"She's your babysitter, eh? I think I have that movie on DVD somewhere around here."

"Shut the fuck up."

Tobias is clearly frustrated by Lorenzo, and it makes me wonder why. From what I have gathered, these men are friends. *Why the attitude?*

I've seen Tobias act nicer than this. Take me, for example. Sure, he's not warm and fuzzy, but he did smirk. That one time.

Maybe he didn't laugh, but the way he looked at me, I know there is more to Tobias than meets the eye. *Why can't he let go?*

"Did I hit a nerve, Tobias?"

Tobias steps up to Lorenzo. They are around the same size, so I would clock them both close to six foot two, give or take an inch.

There is a stare down for a minute, and Lorenzo's men stand from the table.

A full second goes by, or maybe it's longer. Who knows? All I know is my heart is hammering in my chest a million times faster than normal.

The showdown continues, and I'm one hundred percent positive someone will draw a gun.

My hands are shaking at my sides, and I try desperately to ground myself. Tobias looks my way and then back at Lorenzo. Something must pass between them because Lorenzo steps in and throws an arm around his shoulders.

"I missed your broody attitude."

"And here I missed not a single fucking thing about you." This time, I can hear the bite of sarcasm he gives me.

He's not pissed. This isn't a pissing match that is about to be a war. Nope. This is the best Tobias can do. He doesn't let anyone in, and this is what Lorenzo has grown to know of him.

"Come, old friend, let's sit, drink some tequila. Tell me about the next shipment."

As if nothing just happened, the men walk toward the table. I'm stunned at first, but then I get my feet to move in their direction.

Tobias surprises me by pulling my chair out, and then I'm taking a seat with this cruel man about to discuss a shipment of drugs that I really don't want to hear about.

I don't know why I have to be here, but it's grating on my nerves. None of this has to do with my job. As if Tobias can hear my thoughts, he turns to me.

"You're here because I need to make sure that moving forward, everything I do is legal."

"I'm confused. How is it legal for me to sit here as you talk about shipping—?"

"Stuffed animals," Lorenzo cuts me off. "We have a shipment of teddy bears coming in that Aldridge arranged. As you know, Tobias is in the importing and exporting industry, and—"

"Seriously. This is low, even for you," I grit out. "Hiding—"

Lorenzo shakes his head at me, and I backpedal to say it better. "Anything that has to do with children, I'm out. Trent told me about the bears, but I never imagined this is the shit—" I move to stand.

"Stop," Tobias cuts in with a demanding tone. His voice has me halting mid-rise. "I agree. However, this has nothing to do with what you are thinking."

"Oh." I sit fully back down and look down at my hands in my lap. "Please, I don't want to hear the details of what you're up to now. The less I know about some things, the better all around."

"In the past, you might have been right about the teddy bears, you know. But your client stopped that practice years ago," Lorenzo informs me.

"Shut the fuck up, man," Tobias says.

"Fine." Lorenzo stands and walks across the room, presses on the wall, and a panel opens. I watch, transfixed, as he pulls it open and pulls out a duffel bag.

Then his shoes are pounding the concrete again as he hands the bag to Tobias.

I don't even want to know what's in the bag, but something tells me it's either money, guns, or a head. Seeing as Tobias is the distributor, it's not drugs.

Tobias places the bag on the table, but it's still far enough away that I can't see what's in it as he unzips the top. Tobias, however, has a clear view. He looks inside and nods his head.

I want to know what's in it, but then I remember what curiosity did to the cat. I have no desire to be a casualty for having too much information. It's bad enough I'm here.

After Tobias is happy with whatever he got, he rezips the bag, stands, and walks over to Lorenzo.

"Gideon will contact you about the changes."

"You sure about this, man?"

"Never been surer about anything in my life." There is no waver in his voice. It's full of conviction and truth. He wants out, and it makes me wonder why he wants it so badly.

"It won't be easy," Lorenzo says.

"Nothing in life ever is." He shrugs before he looks in my direction. He inclines his head, and I stand.

Guess he got whatever he came for because now it's time to go. I can't say I'm disappointed. The faster I can get out of here, the better. Maybe Tobias will actually let me out after this. By the way things are going, I might have to take Felix up on his offer for dinner. At this rate, that might be the only way I gain access to his files.

The idea isn't a bad one. If it didn't make me want to vomit in my mouth.

"See you soon," I hear Tobias say, and he motions at me to start walking. Instead, I walk up to Lorenzo and extend my hand. "Nice to meet you."

He gives me a wicked smile, and I notice that his gaze darts to Tobias. "Oh, believe me, the pleasure is all mine. Hope to see you again real soon."

"Let's go," Tobias's gruff voice cuts in. I drop Lorenzo's hand and start to leave.

Tobias is a few feet ahead of me. He walks up to one of his security detail and hands him the duffel.

"I want this in the third car."

His security nods, takes the bag, and heads out the door. Then Tobias leads me to the second car in the caravan.

It's kind of creepy that he travels like this. What I realized is we don't all drive together. They run two groups, and each group has two cars. It reminds me of the game you play as a kid where you hide a ball under a cup, spin them around a few times, and then try to guess where it is.

The door to the truck is opened for me, and I scoot inside. Once Tobias gets in, the car heads back to the city . . . I hope.

"Without asking—"

"Money." His one-word answer cuts me off.

"I wasn't going to ask that."

"But you wanted to find out." His voice sounds light, and I look in his direction. *Is Tobias joking with me?*

No. He doesn't joke. At least, I have never seen him joke before. If he is going to joke with anyone, I highly doubt it would be with me.

"I did."

"Why didn't you just look?"

"Because—" I stop and think of how I want to respond.

"You were scared?" And this time, I swear his lip is tipped up a little on the right. A smile.

Now I know this can't be a coincidence.

"Are you laughing at me?"

"Nope."

"I think you are," I press.

"I don't laugh . . ." he trails off.

"But if you did?" I lift my brow, and now his lips do part into the smirk I am certain has been trying to peek out this whole time.

"I definitely would be right now."

I'm not sure why, but his words make my stomach feel fuzzy. He doesn't even joke with his closest friends, but with me, he shows that side. Not a lot, but enough that I know something else is behind the menacing demeanor he portrays.

I have no doubt that he's a scary motherfucker, and no part of me is waxing poetic on what he did to warrant a duffel of money, but I can't help but feel a victory nonetheless that I got him to smile.

"Everything okay over there?"

"Just peachy." I turn to look out the window instead of at him when I answer.

There is no reason for him to know he affected me.

CHAPTER FIFTEEN

Tobias

I LET SKYE LEAVE EARLY TO WORK FROM HOME. AFTER Lorenzo's, I could tell she was itching to be far away from me, so I gave her space. I'm sure, even with her background, being with Lorenzo was a lot to take in.

Hell, I only just started working with him a few years ago, and it feels like an eternity. That's not to say he's not my friend, but his gruff, rambunctious, and loud personality is a lot.

Gideon chooses this moment to walk into the building. I hear him before I see him. He knew I went to Lorenzo's, so of course, he would have to come here and talk. I expected it. As his footsteps grow closer, I can hear that he's almost upon the desk. I put down my phone and look up to meet his stare.

"How did it go?"

"You're going to have to be more specific."

He smiles at that, then grabs the back of the chair and pulls it out. Once sitting, he leans forward and crosses his arms across his chest.

"Your meeting with Lorenzo."

"As it always goes. He gave me half the cash for the next shipment, and tonight, we'll deliver it."

"Not that. I meant the lady meeting with Lorenzo."

"Skye?"

"Yes, Skye." He laughs. "Who else would I be talking about?"

I shrug.

"Don't give me that shit. Talk."

"Talk . . . We don't do that shit."

"Well, maybe we should. Maybe we should talk about all this shit." His tone is pressing. Something tells me he's been thinking about this for a long time.

"What shit?"

"Her. Let's talk about Skye. Does she recognize you?"

I grit my teeth together but don't answer. My hands form fists by my sides.

"Well, spill it, man."

"No." My voice is too forceful, and as soon as the word is spoken, I realize how fucking pissed I am. Still. Time has not helped matters. It's only made it worse.

"No, she has no clue who you are. And you are so pissed off by it, but you don't want to talk it out."

I don't. Not without making me sound like a fucking pussy. Which, despite my relationship with this man, the man who will fill my shoes soon, I can't have. I trust Gideon . . .

But never show weakness.

"Have you thought—?"

"Shut the fuck up."

Gideon has the smarts to shut up.

"Back to business," I say. "We still need to plan a trip down South, and we need to meet with my contact in shipping."

Gideon agrees with a tilt of his head. Until this point, no one, and I mean *no one*, has known all the key players in my distribution chain. The safest way not to get caught is for no one to know the whole picture. This assures fewer loopholes for issues, and if somebody within the organization gets pinched, there's no information to get out. I ran my business the same way the cartel ran their empire years prior: old school. From this moment forward, only Gideon will know.

The first thing I handed over to Gideon was the cocaine. I no longer have any part in that operation. However, the pills are still in circulation and still running through me, but not for long.

Gideon has made a good name for himself, so I know I'm making the right decision. As crazy as it sounds, he has the same scruples as me. He also believes in a certain level of ethics, which to most would sound crazy, but not to the men I work with.

My rise to power wasn't fast. It was a carefully played chess game, all for one objective. That's what the trip down South is for. The final play. The last move. This brings me back to Skye and her role in Felix's life.

Is it more than what she has implied? I find the very notion of it disturbing. Does she not realize the type of monster Felix is?

A part of me has a desire to let her in on the information I possess. That way, she can make a decision. Another part of me—the irrational part—wants to hide her away. That option isn't on the table, and I need to decide whether I can use Skye in a way that would be beneficial to me, or if in the end, she is more of a liability.

Pulling out my phone, I fire off a text to her.

Me: What are you doing?

Skye: Working.

Me: On what?

Skye: So now I need the babysitter? I thought that was my job.

Me: Your job is to do what I say.

Skye: Yeah. . . No.

Me: Is working from home too hard. Do you need supervision?

Skye: I'm not a naive intern you can boss around, and the

diploma hanging on my wall isn't an accessory. I know how to do my job.

She sounds angry. The sick part of me wishes I were at her apartment to see what she looks like as she texts me.

Is her face red? Her fingers moving at lightning speed? Her chest heaving with anger?

Fuccckkk.

It's a visual my dick likes, and that's enough to sober me. I place my phone down before my fixation gets out of hand and glance up at Gideon, whose eyes follow me too closely for comfort.

Flicking lint off my sleeve, I go for a casual. "I want her followed."

"On it, boss." He grins. *Fucker.*

"Stop calling me boss," I respond to Gideon.

The man shakes his head at me. "Until you hand over the keys to the castle, it's still your reign."

"A soon-to-be broken reign."

The truth of those words has us both sitting in silence for a minute, and then I stand. We have a lot to plan. First, when the meeting down South will take place, and then I need to go to Cyrus's. I made him a promise, after all.

"I want every piece of information about her that we haven't already gathered. I want to know where she sleeps and who she spends her free time with. I want to know every minute of the day when she's not with me. I want to know everything."

"I'll get a few men to trail her. I'll also pull phone records. Should I speak to Jax and get eyes in her apartment?"

"No." I might not be a good man, but that was where I drew the line. "We already have Jax on this getting the info, no need to put the cameras up yet. She hasn't done anything to warrant that. She's my attorney right now, but if anything key happens, call him and get eyes on her phone and house. Got it?"

"Got it." He leans back in his chair. "Where are you off to?" he asks as I stand from my chair.

"Card game."

"Cyrus's?"

"Yep."

"Any chance I can get an invite to one of these illustrious games?"

"One day, but not this one. This one is still private."

The game Cyrus holds once a month is solely for us. Cyrus's best clients and, dare I say, friends. It's not often we are all around. Once a month is pushing it, but most of us make it work whenever possible. It's gotten harder over the years—wives and families do that. But most of the time, we are all in attendance.

"Have fun. Don't lose any of your money, or you won't be able to retire," Gideon jokes.

"Would that be so bad?"

His expression stills and grows more serious. "Nope," he answers truthfully, but that ship has sailed.

"Don't worry, man. I'm out. As soon as I kill the son of a bitch, I'm gone."

"And the lady?"

"Let me worry about that. You worry about getting me the info I need."

———

"Look what the cat dragged in," Trent says as I enter the room. "And here I thought we would never see you again."

"You still handle my money, dipshit. You're stuck with me. Well, unless . . ."

"Unless what?" His brow raises.

My lips tip up into a smirk.

"You think you can kill me?" he asks, and I shrug. Trent laughs at that.

"You two are ridiculous." Cyrus scoffs as he walks in from the opposite door.

This is the only place I can show my real personality and let loose a little. Here, we are not our titles. We are not the men who run the underworld. Here, we can relax and drop our façades. Despite this, I do refrain from showing them too much. I trust these men with my lives, but you never can tell.

"Word around town is you got yourself a lady friend." That's Alaric. Typical for that son of a bitch to focus right on the female of any subject. I haven't seen him in ages, so I stand from my chair and go to greet him.

"You heard wrong," I say as I lift my hand and take his.

"That's not what I hear." Now, it's Matteo's turn to chime in.

"I don't even want to know what that douchebag said to you." I don't need to clarify who the douchebag is. It's obviously Lorenzo.

Matteo used to run New York. He was the head of the family. Lorenzo was his cousin and right-hand man and took over for him after he retired.

"My cousin *is* a total douche." He laughs, handing me a tumbler. I take a swig. I'll need it.

"Hey fuck face, I heard that." Everyone turns to see Lorenzo striding into the room. "And Tobias might not have a woman, but he wants to."

"Fuck off, Lorenzo." I level him with my stare.

"That's not a no." He grins.

My phone vibrates in my pocket, and I see it's a text from Gideon. As I swipe the screen, I realize my mistake.

A picture of Skye pops up. She's walking down the street a block from her law firm.

"Who's the girl?" Matteo asks.

"That's the chick he's obsessed with." Lorenzo leans forward to grab my phone, but I pocket it before he can.

I tighten my grip on my whiskey, correcting, "My lawyer."

"—that he's stalking." Lorenzo has the maturity of a prepubescent boy.

"For purely business reasons—"

"If by business, you mean obsession, then, yeah."

"Maybe you're on to something. She was wearing his shirt when she came to my office," Trent adds, and I could kill him for that.

"Shut the fuck up, Trent."

Lorenzo looks me up and down with a shit-eating grin on his face. "Wearing your clothes already? Wow. Are you guys getting hitched next? Is this why you're retiring?"

"Lorenzo, leave Tobias alone." Cyrus's voice leaves no room for confrontation from a normal person, but Lorenzo is not normal. He is a sociopath.

"No can do, Cyrus. He brought her to see me under the guise of fuck knows what and then got all pissy when I started hitting on her."

"She's my lawyer," I hiss.

"And?" Lorenzo looks at me with a bewildered look. "If you aren't fucking the broad, why can't—?"

He doesn't even get the words out before I step up and brace my hands around his throat.

"Did I hit a chord with that one?" He chuckles.

I don't apply pressure. It would be so easy, but I'm only making my opinion on Lorenzo fucking my lawyer clear, which, in turn, has also made something else clear: Lorenzo is on to something. I drop my hands, and the bastard grins.

"Just admit you want her."

"No," I fire back.

"Only because you can't have her." He needs to shut the fuck up before I really do murder him. *Texas Chainsaw*–style.

"You're a real prick, Lorenzo." Alaric chuckles behind us.

"What's your deal with this chick, then?" Lorenzo presses me.

I let out a long, drawn-out sigh. This man is a dog with a bone. He won't stop until I give him something. Moving toward the table, I pull the chair out and take a seat. Lorenzo follows suit as do the rest of the men already here. We are still waiting for a few, so I might as well get this over with.

I choose my words carefully.

"Ms. Matthews and I have met before."

"And?" Lorenzo pushes.

Fuck.

Lorenzo's head bobs up and down in understanding, a smile breaking across the bastard's face. "Ahh, now I get it."

"Get what?" Trent asks him, completely ignoring my presence and, in turn, the conversation.

"It was such a bad night she didn't remember him," he clarifies, barking out a fucking laugh. I'm about ready to take back my stance from two minutes ago on not kicking the shit out of Lorenzo.

Instead of getting up, I grit my teeth together and answer him. "No, Lorenzo. It's not like that. This is from years ago, and no, she didn't remember me."

"And you want to make her life hell . . ." he trails off before looking over at Trent. "Bro, I don't think that's a good plan. Look at Trent over there." He nods at him, and Trent inclines his head in agreement. "Maybe you should just tell her who you are."

"No." My voice is rough and abrasive. They won't change my mind about this.

"Well, now that we got the gossip out of the way, can we play cards?" Cyrus huffs, probably already annoyed with us.

"You're waiting for me, mate," a familiar British voice says, and I turn to look behind my back. James approaches the table.

"What are you doing here?" I ask.

"I heard Alaric was coming in and realized the wanker gave me no choice."

"Yeah, not sorry," Alaric jokes, and then with everyone around the table, the cards are finally shuffled.

Lorenzo leans into me. "Everything good with the shipment?"

"No problems," I answer.

"And Gideon?"

"He's ready for the transition. Don't worry, Lorenzo."

"I'll kill you if he's not." His voice is serious, but I know he's full of shit. Lorenzo might be cruel, but he would never hurt one of us. He would die for us.

"I have no doubt you would try." I smirk at him, letting my guard down for a second. Lorenzo is quiet as if contemplating what else bothers him, and then he opens his mouth to speak.

"And what about Bernard? Are we going to war?"

"I need to check a few things, but it's looking that way."

I don't need to ask any of the men at this table if they are marching into battle with me. I already know the answer.

Yes.

CHAPTER SIXTEEN

Skye

I CHECK MY WATCH FOR THE FOURTEENTH TIME.
Still running late.

No matter how many times I lift my wrist and pray that time has started to go backward, it hasn't. Instead, every time I check, I'm taunted by the fact another minute has passed, and I'm still looking for my left shoe.

Last night, I came home in a huff, opened a bottle of wine, and threw my shoe . . . somewhere. Two things are clear from this. One: I need to take better care of my things. Two: I probably shouldn't drink an entire bottle of wine by myself.

My only saving grace this morning is that I'm not that hungover. That's not to say I don't have a headache, but I chalk that up to the fact I have been searching for my shoe for the past five minutes.

This is getting annoying.

Two more minutes pass before I'm on hands and knees, pushing my couch forward. Bingo. We have a winner. How in the hell my left heel got lodged behind the back of my couch is beyond me, but I really need to thank whoever advised me to drink Gatorade before bed after drinking.

Lifesaver. Moving forward, no matter how stressed I am from work, I will not be doing what I did last night.

I should join a gym and work out. The thing is, who has time to do that? Not me when I'm being dragged around the world. Speaking of, if I don't leave now, I will never make it downtown and to Tobias's office even remotely close to on time.

Bag in hand, keys locking the door, I feel my phone start to vibrate in my bag. I pull the door shut, lock it, and then fish out my phone. A new text from Tobias.

Shit.

I am not looking forward to being reamed out right now. Letting out a sigh, I swipe the screen to read the text.

Tobias: I have an obligation this morning. You don't have to come in until after lunch.

Hell, yeah! Saved by the obligation.

What obligation is this? And why am I not involved? Is this something about those damned teddy bears?

Seriously, if I find out he's lying and he is stuffing drugs into a bear, I will lose my shit. I don't have many hard limits, but this is one.

No stuffed animals. Also, no trafficking of people and no non-self-defense murder, but those seem like a given. Once I find out what I need, I'll quit and take an extended vacation alone.

Since I no longer must go with Tobias, I use this opportunity to head into my office. Instead of downtown, I head to my midtown office. It feels weird heading here. It's been forever since I took this trip, even though it's only been two weeks. The cab ride goes by fast. Lucky for me, there's little traffic.

Stepping out of the cab, I walk through the lobby. Nodding to the security behind the desk, I head toward the elevator banks. I forgot how much I hate riding the elevators here. It's funny, but in the past few weeks, since I met Tobias, I have re-membered my hatred of enclosed spaces.

For a long time, it hovered in the back of my brain, but ever since I met him, it's like a weird tickle I can't seem to scratch. A lingering memory I can't shut out.

I step out of the elevator and into the lobby of the floor, and as soon as I do, I push down my dress where the skirt rode up and fluff my hair. Then I walk toward my office. Turning the corner, I almost walk right into my boss and Mr. Bernard.

"Just the person we were talking about."

"Oh. You were talking about me?" I respond, not sure where this is going and not liking that, either.

My brain shuffles through what they could be saying. Maybe it's good. Maybe Bernard demanded I work on a file for him and wants me to move back to him.

"Yes, actually we were, my dear."

The chill of his voice makes my back go straight. In this day and age, the fact my boss hasn't stopped him from look-ing at me the way he does speaks volumes for the corruption and power this man has and what my boss won't do to keep it nearby.

"All good things, I hope?" I smile back. Maybe I can use this in my favor.

Felix steps closer, and I have to fight my desire to step back. But I can't risk looking rude or having him see the true depth of my hatred toward him.

"Felix needs your help with a sensitive matter."

Turning toward my boss, I meet his stare. "Of course. Whatever Mr. Bernard needs, it would be my pleasure to help."

"Very good answer. Then you won't have a problem attend-ing a gala with him."

"No, of course not. When is this gala?"

"Next week. It's the Fire and Ice Gala."

"I'll pick you up." Something about the way Felix says this has me not wanting him to come to my place.

"No. It's okay. I'll meet you there."

"No. I insist."

I'm about to object when my boss's hard stare meets mine. "Let the man pick you up. Can't let him not look like a gentleman," he jokes.

Nothing is funny about this, but I have no choice. I know enough about Bernard that I can't object, not without throwing up a red flag, so I nod.

"Very well." I move to step away. "If that will be all, I do have a lot of work to do."

"Yes, that's all. You can go."

I walk off to my office, not at all happy about this turn of events.

I shake my head back and forth. Stop. This is good. Everything is going exactly as planned. Hours pass, and before long, I'm looking at the clock on my desk. It's time to head over to see Tobias.

I never did eat, but I guess I'll have to do that later. Instead of lunch, I scoured over everything on the company's server on Felix. When he started his business. When he amassed his fortune. The dates ran back about twenty years.

That's when he took over. I was six years old when my parents died. He was in his thirties. The fact this man wants me makes bile form in my stomach.

There is more about him, cases from before my time. If the rumors are true, I believe he's much more than the magazines say. He's not a good man. A drug lord. Evil. He rained bullets over his competition and supposedly killed, too.

Never acquitted. Never stood trial for his crimes. Crimes that have affected the innocent. I grind my teeth together. Conflict of interest or not, I will make him suffer for the pain he inflicted. The pain he inflicted on people who mattered to me.

I shut my computer and stand, and then I'm off, ready to meet with another devil. Is this one any different? He wants out. *Or so he says.* He just needs to finalize things. Does that make him better?

Or is he also a wolf?

But the question is, behind the hard exterior, is there more? Or is he the devil like Bernard? Only time will tell. For now, I can only deal with one devil at a time. Felix Bernard must have my focus.

CHAPTER SEVENTEEN

Tobias

WHERE THE FUCK IS SHE?
I told her to be here after lunch. Not that I gave her a time, but it's now three o'clock, and she's still not here.

Each time my feet hit the concrete floors of my office, the sound echoes through the space. I'm pacing, and I don't know why. Everything is set. Gideon and I will fly down to Miami to meet with Emil. No one within my organization knows about him or the pills he distributes to me, which I sell to Lorenzo.

Just as I go to grab my phone to call her, my cell rings. It's my security detail with a text, letting me know she's here and making her approach.

The need to throw her off her game grabs me by the balls, and before I can think better of it, I'm pressing the call button for the elevator and stepping inside.

The elevator reaches the ground floor and then opens.

Skintight dress again. I let my eyes peruse her for a second before I pull my gaze away. She's stunning, and if I allow myself, I could stare at her all day. But I can't, and I won't. It pisses me the fuck off that I can't turn off the attraction. She doesn't deserve it.

Skye rolls her eyes as she makes her way inside, standing as far as way as she can in the enclosed space.

When we are between floors, I press the stop button, bringing our ascent to a halt.

I move toward her. She moves back until she's touching the wall.

"You're late."

"I thought you hate elevators."

"You have no idea what I hate . . ."

"Why don't you tell me then, it would be a lot easier to deal with your moods."

"I hate . . ." I move closer until I have her boxed in. "Being made to wait."

If I think she will cower at my tone, I'm wrong. There are no shivers or fear. Instead, she stands taller.

"I had a few things to do before I came. Plus, you didn't mention a time," she offers as if that is an acceptable excuse.

"I don't condone being fucked with, Ms. Matthews. Be here on time."

"Will there be consequences if I'm not?" she toys, and when I duck my head down to look into her eyes, she fucking winks at me, all while smiling.

Leaning down, I place my lips by her ear. "Men have died for less."

"It won't happen again." Her voice is steady, but I can feel the way her body shivers beside me.

With that settled, I step back and press the button again, allowing the elevator to move.

When it stops on the floor, we both walk out, but as we approach the doors to the office, I gesture for her to go it.

"I'll be back."

"Anything I can help you with?"

I let my lip tip up. "Not unless you want to help take care of something in the bathroom . . ." And then it's my turn to wink at her.

Five minutes later, and a hell of a lot calmer, I find Skye standing by the window in my office, taking in the view.

Her body turns abruptly at the sound of my footsteps.

"Now who's making who wait?" she chides.

"You could have come with me." My voice drips with innuendo, and her eyes go wide before dipping down to look at my pants.

I like the way her cheeks flush. I wonder if her whole body is warm . . .

But if I don't stop this line of thought, I will never get shit done today.

"You never told me why you were late," I say, not that it's any of my business, but I need something to take my mind off of imagining her naked. When she doesn't answer, I press. "It's not a difficult question."

It is. Because if she doesn't answer me, that would be within her right, but it would also be within my right to fire her ass.

It's a loss.

Her lips pucker in what I assume is annoyance. "I had to talk to my boss."

"About?" Yep, I'm an asshole who isn't going to let this go.

"Nothing. It's just, there is this gala, and I . . . forget it." She sighs in frustration. *Interesting.* The tone of her voice has me softening my own words, curious as to what has her so worked up.

"No, please go on."

She inhales and then exhales, and while she does, I watch as her chest rises and falls with each breath she takes.

"I have to go to a gala with a client." The words rush out of her lips so that I almost can't make them out. Unfortunately for her, I do. Now, I'm pissed again. So much for calm and collected.

"Which client?" I ask through gritted teeth.

She shakes her head back and forth, but I have a feeling I know the answer. It doesn't matter, I need to hear her say it.

"I can't talk about my firm's other clients."

"Which. Fucking. Client?" I demand. She places her hands on her hips like she's going to defy me. I stalk toward her. "If you say Felix, so help me."

"I didn't have a choice."

"The fuck you didn't," I bark back.

"And why the hell do you care? He was with my law firm first. If anything—"

"Careful. You don't want to say anything you might regret." My eyebrow lifts in a challenge.

"This is none of your business, and I don't want to talk about it anymore."

"Do I need to talk to Williams?"

"Don't you dare." She scoffs, her brow furrowing. "This is my job. I can't burn this bridge. And Seth is the one who is making me do this. I don't care how damn important you think you are. You're not. I have to do this. Some people have lives and need to do things they don't necessarily want to do in order to accomplish their goals."

I know a thing or two about goals. We are not that different in that respect. I will stop at nothing to have my objectives met, so I understand where she's coming from. But it's still not safe to go anywhere but court with that motherfucker. I pivot on my feet and decide to go with another tactic to break through to her.

"You can make your career goals and moves quicker if you play nice with me."

"Not this time."

She's fucking infuriating.

"He's dangerous, Skye," I say with a sigh.

"Pot, meet kettle. Didn't you take me to meet your friend Lorenzo?" She has a point. However, that is neither here nor there.

"It's different."

Her expression stills and grows serious. "How so?"

"I was there to protect you," I blurt out before I can stop myself.

Her large blue eyes look like they might pop out of her skull. "I don't need protection, goddammit! Not from you. Not from anyone. I can handle anything thrown my way."

"Don't I know it," I mutter under my breath.

"What was that?"

I ignore her and walk back to my chair, pulling it out and taking a seat. What the hell do I do about this shitty-ass situation? I fucking hate Felix. The man most certainly is the reason my dad is dead. He's been the bane of my existence for as long as I can remember. If it weren't for him, I never would have gotten into this shit to begin with. But when you plan to dance with the devil, you need money, and this was the fast way to get it.

I want to kill the man, but unlike him, I need confirmation. That's the one piece that makes me different, and I won't change that.

"Nothing."

"You said something. Just spit it out," she grits out.

"Nope."

"You drive me crazy." Her cheeks turn the color of a tomato as they puff out.

"Welcome to the club."

"Your club isn't someplace I want to be. You probably stuff drugs in your damn bears," she spits back.

I cock my head to the side and actually smile.

"Is that what you think?"

She nods. She isn't far off. Lorenzo—and Matteo, before he retired—used to take my shipment of pills and hide it in stuffed bears, but then I shut that shit down. Never sat well with me, but she doesn't know that. I can't wait to see the look on her face when I tell her what the bears are actually for.

"Are you curious about the bears?" I tease. Her eyes narrow. She's not enjoying this. But I will. "I'll make sure to take pictures."

"Pictures?" Her shocked face is comical. She reminds me of a cartoon. I almost expect her pupils to bug out of her face.

"Of the children." I deliberately talk slow and casual, just to taunt her.

"The children?"

"The children at the center for kids where they are donated at our Christmas in July party that's a few months away."

There it is, and I can't help but feel smug as her head shakes in dismay. She catches herself fast and rights the look.

"And the money?" She quirks a brow.

"Well, that's exactly for what you think the money buys." Her mouth drops, and this time, I can't help but laugh.

Full. Out loud. Laugh. Something that rarely happens. Something about this lady knocks me completely off my game. And now, I guess I'm going to a fucking gala just to keep an eye on what's mine.

CHAPTER EIGHTEEN

Skye

TEDDY BEARS FOR KIDS . . .
The man has a heart, and I don't like it one bit.

Yet I can't help but feel warm and fuzzy over that fact.

"Come on. Despite you being late, we have stuff to go over together," he says, and I welcome him speaking so I don't have to contemplate why I think the fact that the man isn't all bad. However, regardless of everything, I still feel the dig of his comment, but I don't let it get to me. Nor do I want to bring up the whys again. Tobias will go all caveman on me again. A reaction I was not expecting at all.

Then why did I like it?

Yep. That's the worst part about it.

While he was basically banging his chest with his hand and saying he has to protect me, I was imagining what it would be like if he did. And in all my thoughts . . . he was naked.

Not good, Skye. Not good at all.

Now I'm sitting across the desk from him, a vase filled with spring crocus's taunting me from across the surface, all while he's showing me files on investment properties he intends to buy in Miami.

But not the normal investment properties.

This will cost a fortune.

These are full-fledged high-rise buildings in Brickell.

The air in the room feels heavy as I flip through each document. It's way too quiet in here.

I almost want him to speak again, but at the same time, I'm not sure I can handle it if he starts spouting stuff that makes my lady bits get excited.

Why is a protective male so damn hot?

Maybe because you have daddy issues.

How cliché am I?

Apparently, very.

I shuffle in my chair to get comfortable and stop thinking about my lady bits when, of course, my leg grazes his under the table.

I try to move away, not to touch him, but dammit, it does the opposite. Now my damn foot is touching his foot.

If he notices, he doesn't let on. He's unaffected by our touching feet. Me, on the other hand . . . well, let's just say the temperature in this room has increased tenfold. It's a freaking sauna in here. My cheeks are burning, and I want to rip my blazer off because I'm so hot.

Looking up from the document in front of me, I sneak a peek at Tobias. He doesn't even notice. His eyes are trained on his phone. His fingers work to type back a message to whoever texted him. I watch as those fingers move, at the way his arms flex. His shirtsleeves are rolled up, and the veins in his forearms show. I bet those arms would feel great wrapped around me from behind.

As I watch him, my lower belly feels warm and tingly, and I know I need to stop. I have to pull my gaze away, and I certainly have to pull my foot away, too.

I do neither.

Instead, from where I'm sitting across from him, I think about what he must have done in the bathroom. How good it must have felt. The relief he must have received. And the fact that he, without a doubt, thought about me while doing it.

He must feel my stare because he lifts his gaze from his phone and catches me studying him. Now my cheeks really burn. They're on fire.

I move my foot fast.

But not before he realized what was happening. The man who doesn't smile, doesn't joke, and barely has a sense of humor is grinning like a Cheshire cat.

What the hell?

Of course, I had to make it obvious that I'm attracted to the damn man.

The way he's looking at me right now isn't helping. Tobias looks at me as though he's seeing me for the first time.

Normally, he looks at me with disdain—as if he's angry with me—which makes no sense. But it's how I feel whenever our gazes lock. There are always lines present on his brow. It's like he's studying my reaction to him and hating my reaction at the same time. But this time is different.

His gaze is trained on my face, but he's not looking into my eyes. He's staring at my lips. Out of habit, I nibble on my lower one. He swallows and then looks into my eyes. There is a hazy look in his gaze like he's lost in a dream.

He stares at me for too long, and I almost shrink under the scrutiny. If he was looking at me with hate, I probably would. But this time, it's hunger that oozes from him, and it makes me want to sit up straighter for him to see all of me.

He coughs and straightens his back, severing the moment. Now when he looks at me, there is no haze, only clarity, and the angry snarl is back. Wherever he went in his brain, he didn't hate me, but now he does again.

"Go," he commands in a voice far harder than I have ever heard him use. This is the drug dealer, the man who people fear, and I can understand why. He's scary.

"Really?" I keep my voice level, hoping not to let my feelings betray me.

"I said go. We're done here."

CHAPTER NINETEEN

Tobias

I HAD TO GET HER OUT OF HERE AS FAST AS I FUCKING COULD. Another minute with her and all my fucking walls would have come down.

The woman is fucking Kryptonite to me.

I hate that I want to fuck her. I hate that she wants to fuck me, too. And she does. I can see it each time she's near. Every time she gravitates toward me, inching closer without even realizing it.

It's her eyes. The way she looks at me.

She's the only person who looks at me like that. As if she can see the person I was. The person I was supposed to be if my life hadn't gone to shit, and I never had to become this person I am today.

For a moment, when she was staring at me, I thought she remembered, but then I realized it was wishful fucking thinking, and I kicked her the fuck out.

It would be easier if she could just remember we met before.

Then I wouldn't have to act like a little bitch because my goddamn pride is hurt.

Letting out a breath, I stand from my chair and start to pace the room. What am I going to do about this girl?

It feels like the room is getting smaller. The collar of my shirt feels tight.

I need air.

Without a second thought, I'm crossing the space and heading toward the stairs up to the roof.

It's the only place I can think.

Only when I can see the sky does my pulse calm.

All these years later and nothing has changed.

Ironic really.

All of this shit.

My feet take the steps two at a time until I'm pushing open the glass door and making my way outside.

Warm air slaps my face, but that's not enough to calm me.

Tilting my chin up, I stare up into the sky.

Despite the perfect weather, a canopy of clouds is above my head. I stare at them for a bit, and as I do, my pulse regulates, and I feel myself calming almost instantly. Looking up and seeing the vastness above is enough to make me no longer feel like I'm suffocating.

Time has no meaning when I'm out here.

I let everything go and am finally able to think.

The only problem with thinking is that I think about her.

I hear the door open, and I pull my gaze from the sky and look out into the horizon. I don't need to see Gideon to know he's striding toward me.

"Everything okay?" he asks.

"Yep."

From where I'm standing, I have a perfect view of the water, another perk to owning this building.

"You sure? Because you've been coming out here a lot." That makes me pull my gaze away from the boat I'm currently staring at and turn to look at Gideon.

He's only standing a few feet away, but I can still see the way he stares at me. His brows are knit together, and his mouth forms a straight line. The look he's giving me translates to *I think you're losing your mind.*

"I'm cool. Just needed to think."

Now his damn eyes are narrowing. Yep, he's not buying what I'm selling. This is the problem with letting people in. They get to know you and know when you are full of shit.

"About the fact that you scared Skye Matthews to run from the office."

I move from where I'm standing at the edge of the building, stepping away from the railing and stepping closer to where he is.

"That never happened," I respond, playing it cool like I have no idea what he's talking about.

"I have security footage to prove it did."

Fucker.

This time, it's me who glares at him. "Shut up."

"You're being a douche, you know?"

Pulling out my gun from behind my back, I cock it and point it at him. "Don't mistake that I won't kill you due to our friendship." I smile. The kind of smile that a crazy-ass villain from a comic book would give.

He lets out a chuckle, clearly enjoying this. "You won't."

"And how do you know that?"

"You want out too much. You kill me and—"

"I'll still be out." I smirk.

"Yes, but you wouldn't be able to live with yourself if kids start dying from 'hot shots' of coke."

I let out a sigh. "Yeah, unfortunately, you're right."

Gideon's mouth curves into a large smile. "Don't you hate that?"

Tipping my head up, I let the sun warm my face. Despite what people might think, I hate being this man. One day, I'll be out, and then I can repent for all my sins, but until that day, I just have to grin and bear it. "I really do." We both go quiet for a second, the air heavy with regrets. A cloud passes above me, bright streams of light poking through. I study it for a moment before lowering my gaze back to him.

I hadn't noticed it before, but he looks beat. Occupational hazard of working for a bastard like me. Sure, there are perks—lots of money, respect, and being able to look at my face every day, but there is also the good chance you could be shot at, a bomb could detonate when you got into your car, or a rival gang could steal your drugs. Which reminds me . . .

"Everything okay with the shipment?"

"All is as it should be," he responds.

"Good."

He nods, but it's the way he furrows his forehead that has me inclining my head. "Gideon."

"Yeah?"

"Despite what it looks like, if you have a problem . . ." I trail off, letting him fill in the blanks. I hate this sentimental shit.

"Yeah. I know." He hates it, too.

"Good. What else do we need to do so you can cut ties and kill Felix?"

"We need a plan. Any way you can get Skye to help?" he asks, and I chuckle.

"Seeing as she just stormed out of the building because of something I did, I'm going to say no."

"Hey, you never know, she might like it rough." He grins and lifts his brow.

For reasons I don't want to micromanage at this moment, my hands have formed into fists as I grit out, "Fuck off."

I shouldn't want her. Yet . . .

"I see I hit a nerve." Again with the fucking laugh. This man has a death wish.

"I said fuck off." I step into him and grab the collar of his shirt. "I can throw you off that roof."

"I thought we established it's not a good plan to kill me."

My hands tighten around his neck before dropping him. "Fine."

Gideon steps back and then walks toward the railing, looking off into the distance.

"What's going on with Florida?" he asks, still staring at the water.

"As soon as I get word from Emil that he's back in town, we'll fly in to meet him."

"You going to bring Skye?"

I fold my arms across my chest and then nod. "Yeah. But not to the meeting. I'm not sure if I can trust her yet."

His head bobs in agreement. "You still think she's in league with Felix?"

"Why else would she be working with him?"

Unless there is more to her than she lets on?

"Maybe, like you, she blames him for the destruction and death he brings to all those around him."

That's one option I've been considering, but who the fuck knows with this girl.

"One can hope. But only time will tell." I shrug.

"And if you find out she is?" He moves away from the edge of the building and starts to walk back toward where I'm standing. Once he's standing in front of me, I allow my lip to tip up.

"I'll do what I need to do." There is nothing nice about the smile I give him. This isn't a happy smile. This is menacing and evil.

"And that is?" he probes.

"Use her to take him down."

"And her?"

"What about her? I'm not a fucking animal. No women. No children."

The motto I have always lived by.

CHAPTER TWENTY

Skye

After Tobias's attitude, I don't bother to go into the office today. I didn't go in yesterday, either. Hell, I might just take off the whole week. A large smile spreads across my face at the thought of the way he must be fuming over my absence.

Or maybe he didn't even notice? I sure as hell hoped he did. Because that man can go fuck himself.

He's like a goddamn light switch, and I have no clue who turned him off. One minute, he was shining bright, and then bam, darkness.

What did I say to him to set him off? I try to scour my brain, but I've got nothing.

So instead of subjecting myself to the abuse again, I opt to say screw it and not go in.

There is no need to deal with his PMS. There are more important things in my life than a moody criminal.

For example, I still haven't figured out if I'm being overdramatic about the whole *Dad* thing.

The picture I took of the bill is now printed up and sitting on my desk in front of me. No matter how many times I look at it, I still have no clue what I'm looking at.

A sequence of numbers is all that's on this paper. At first glance, it looks like a billing sheet for insurance.

Unfortunately, my father isn't the neatest man because not only was the piece of paper crumpled, but it also had a giant coffee stain on it and a tear down the side, which means my picture sucks.

What do these numbers mean? And as for the text, only a piece of a word on the heading is clear.

St. and then there is another letter, it looks like half the letter *J*.

St. Joseph Hospital maybe? Or it could be St. Joseph Church?

Hell, this could be for the St. Joseph fundraiser held for the police force every year. Sure, my father is retired, but that doesn't mean he's not still involved.

I'm going to have to ask him, but that's not really an option.

I risk him freezing me out completely if he realizes I snuck into his house, lifted this sheet from the garbage, and, worse, made copies of his old files.

Yep, no. There will be no asking him anything.

I'll just have to use my own deductive reasoning skills to come up with a plausible means to extract the information from him or someone else.

Maybe I can call all the St. Josephs in the area and see if they can steer me in the right direction.

I'm about to pick up my office phone and call when my cell starts to vibrate on the desk.

It's Tobias.

I think about answering the phone but decide if I do, he'll probably summon me to his office. Not something I want to do right now.

No. I shake my head. I'm busy. Finding out what my dad is hiding is more important.

I hit the button. Decline.

Then get back to the matter at hand and dial the number I find for St Joseph's. I picked the hospital first. If that's a dead end, I'll call the church. I'm sure I can find a nice old lady who likes to gossip who might be willing to help me.

"St Joseph's Hospital, how may I help you?" the operator on the line answers.

"I was wondering who I can speak to about a letter I received?" I try to keep it vague in an attempt to mentally come up with a plausible reason I have for wanting this information when she asks.

I got nothing.

If my dad was there and this is a medical bill, it would be a huge HIPAA violation for her to tell me.

"I'll need more information than that." The lady practically scoffs. Something tells me if I could teleport to the hospital and see her, she would be rolling her eyes in disdain.

"All I have is a list of numbers? Will that help? It might be reference codes?"

"It sounds like a billing code."

"Oh, good. That means you can tell me what reference code 67zf means?"

"I'm sorry, I think you misunderstood. That's not something I can help you with."

"Is there someone I can speak to in billing then?"

"I'll transfer you over," she mutters.

The next thing I know, I'm being sent to the mailbox of the billing department. The good news is that I might have narrowed it down to a bill, but for what? He did say he was going for his annual checkup. Maybe they did blood earlier? That happens, right?

After the chime, indicating for me to speak, I leave a message asking for someone to call me back, but to be honest, I know it's a long shot. Even if I can get someone on the line, they won't tell me anything, certainly not what the codes are.

I'm up against a rock and a hard place. I wonder if we have a

PI on staff. I'm sure we do with the clients we have, but contacting them is a different matter.

I'm about to step out and ask Nancy, the office manager, when my door swings open and a very angry Tobias is storming toward me. He looks larger than life. Way too big for this small space.

His jaw is rigid, but it's the throbbing vein on the side of his face that gives me pause.

He is pissed. But not normal pissed.

Nope. This is next-level pissed.

I stand and make my way over to him, about to tell him where to go and gesturing to the door when he steps forward.

On reflex, I take a few steps back until my back hits the wall.

"When I call, you answer." His nostrils flare. "You don't send me to voicemail."

Crossing my arms over my chest, I roll my eyes. "I was busy."

Real mature. But I'm over being professional right now.

"Bullshit!" he bellows, and I swear it bounces off the walls like a ping-pong ball.

Paying him no mind, I give him a smile, a cheeky one. "I was."

"Doing what? Because I don't remember giving you a task I needed you to complete?"

I shake my head and tsk. "You. Are. Not. My. Boss." Overkill, maybe, but again, zero fucks given. The man is an ass. A sexy one, but an ass.

"Oh, no?" He moves in closer. *Shit.*

His arms lift to close me in.

The more distance he eats up, the fuzzier my brain gets. By the time we are mere inches away, I forget what he's saying and why I'm saying, "No." The man makes my knees wobble. What are we even talking about? Get your shit together, Skye. I give myself a little shake, knocking the fog away and remembering the conversation. I shove his shoulder. "You might be able to buy my boss, but that doesn't make you mine, nor am I for sale."

"Everyone has their price." His face is close enough that I can feel his chest expand as he speaks.

The soft fragrance of his cologne surrounds me, and I want to bask in the smell.

Crisp and fresh.

Hints of cinnamon and woods.

I'm not even sure it's his cologne. This might be all him, and it's delicious.

"Not me," I hiss. He's a planet and has a gravitational pull.

Fuck.

I need out. That way, I'm no longer under his spell. I sidestep, then duck under his arm.

Now, with a little distance put between us, I can think again. "Just because Mr. Williams says I'm going to work for you doesn't mean I'm going to drop my life for it. If you want my help, you need to back the fuck off."

"Let's go. I'm sick of having an audience."

He grabs my arm and begins to pull me out of the office. That's when his words hit me. Audience? What audience? We aren't alone? There is a group of assistants gathered and staring.

Damn glass window. I forgot to pull the blinds shut. Whoever thought having a window looking into an office was a good idea was actually an idiot.

As I follow him, I see my boss's eyes are wide.

"No other clients," Tobias snaps at him, or maybe at me, probably at both of us.

I'm too pissed to object.

Or . . .

Tobias has officially broken me.

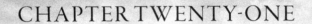

CHAPTER TWENTY-ONE

Tobias

ALL I SEE IS RED.
I'm at a boiling point.

This woman is going to be the death of me.

She fucking sent me to voicemail, and if that isn't bad enough, she gave me shit when I called her out on it.

There's no speaking as we head down to the lobby. A part of me expects her to object, yell, kick, or scream, but she is resigned to her fate.

In the lobby, she's docile, but I know this is fleeting. I'm sure once we are out of the watchful eyes of her colleagues, she will let loose, and I welcome the fire. I can't wait to be burned.

That's the fucked-up part. When I had her cornered against the wall, I have never been so fucking turned on in my life. This girl drives me crazy. We keep moving, and the doorman is quick to give us an exit.

Now outside, I'm pulling her toward the street, toward my waiting car, and for what? Fuck if I know.

I have no idea where I'm taking her, but I can't stand the

watchful eyes in the damn office. One thing has become painfully obvious to me—I have lost my mind.

I'm not even sure why I'm so pissed. Maybe it's a culmination of her not fucking remembering me and then, on top of it, dismissing me.

As soon as we are beside my car, I halt my steps and look up at the sky. The clouds above loom. A storm is brewing. I inhale deeply, begging it to calm me, and it does. It also has reality crashing down on me. The city air slaps at my face as I lower my gaze.

Fuck.

Now back in the here and now and no longer lost in my fury, I realize I might have gone a bit overboard, but *fuck*.

"Who the hell do you think you are?" Skye hisses under her breath, and now it's her turn to grab me by my arm and pull me to a small alleyway behind her building. "Your tantrum is completely unwarranted." She puffs out her chest, her face turning a red shade from the heavy breath she's letting out.

"You work for me, Skye, and I don't take kindly to being dismissed."

"You know what that sounds like?" She glares at me. "That sounds like a *you* problem. I know you think the world revolves around you, but spoiler alert, it doesn't. Believe it or not, I have a personal life."

My teeth grit together, and I want to throttle whoever she's getting personal with.

"Calling your boyfriend while on the clock—"

"Not that it's any of your business, but I don't have a boyfriend." She cuts me off, and normally, I would be pissed that she did, but hearing her words has me exhaling.

She starts to pace, her steps angry and frustrated, and for some reason, watching her, has the pent-up emotions leaving my body.

I would laugh, but something tells me if I did, she would reach into my jacket, grab my gun, and shoot me in the face.

So instead, I school my features and wait for her to calm

down. It might take a while, seeing as she's cursing under her breath. I swear, if possible, smoke would billow from her ears. That's how animated she's being.

I'm not sure how long I stand and watch her, but eventually, her steps slow. I lift my hands in a peace offering. "I might have been out of line."

"Might have been?" She scoffs.

"Let's start over."

She shuffles on her feet and appears to be considering my words. "I don't know if I can."

I step toward her, looking down at her petite form. "I was wrong to barge in—I assumed it was work."

"It wasn't. It was personal, but it doesn't matter. I wasn't getting anywhere anyway."

Cocking my head, I look into her eyes. "Can I help?"

"No."

"Skye . . ." I draw out.

"I'm good, thanks." She's being stubborn. It's cute.

"You can be like this, and sure, maybe I deserve it."

"Maybe?"

"Fine . . . " I allow myself to smirk. "I deserve it, but regardless of that fact, I have something you want."

"And what, pray tell, is that?"

"The ability to get shit done. I have a staff of ruthless men willing to do anything to get shit done. So, Skye . . . what's it going to be? You have two choices."

"And those are?" A muscle quivers in her jaw. She's worried, or at least, that's what I'm gathering from the small tremor I see.

"Put aside your hatred for me."

"I don't hate you." Her cheeks color fiercely as a stain of scarlet appears on them. Interesting. *Not the time, Tobias.*

"Be that as it may, your choice is to either take my help or not."

She nibbles at her lower lip, but that's not what has my eyes going wide. It's the way she absentmindedly starts to rub her finger over her tattoo.

The paper plane. Why a paper plane?

"What it's going to be?" I force myself to ask again rather than spend my time micromanaging her every move.

"Fine." She stops and looks down at the floor. Her brows have pulled together. I wait for her to continue. Her body stiffens before she speaks. "I need a favor."

"Okay. And what would that be?"

She peers at me, and I wonder if she is inspecting me. What is she looking for?

A tell.

A lie.

Skye Matthews acts like she's making a deal with the devil. In a way, she's not wrong.

"Before I ask, are you going to demand payment?"

"No, Skye. I won't."

She lets out a sigh. "Fine. I have a series of numbers that I need looking into."

"Any more details?"

"No. I'll just email you the paper. I made a copy. I think it's hospital tests . . . but I'm not sure. I mean, for all I know, it's Swiss bank accounts."

"Okay."

Now that she's asked, she looks down uncomfortably. Whatever Skye's asking of me is important. This is personal.

I find I want to help her with this, and the crazy part of me that wants to help her with this also doesn't have any ulterior motives. I don't want to do this for myself. I want to help her. Which should feel strange to me, but it doesn't. I find that regardless of everything, regardless of the fact that she doesn't remember, and regardless of my initial need to make her pay for that, I see the pain in her eyes, and I don't like it.

I move to walk away.

"When do you think you will have any answers?" she asks, and I stop and turn over my shoulder.

"Soon."

"Thank you, Tobias."

"Don't thank me yet." She raises her brow at my comment. "You don't know what I'll say."

Her face pales.

Sometime the fear of the unknown is easier than learning the truth.

CHAPTER TWENTY-TWO

Skye

THE SOUND OF SOMEONE KNOCKING ON THE DOOR MAKES me jump. I'm not expecting anyone.

It's the weekend—Saturday night, to be exact—and I have no plans.

A part of me thinks it's someone knocking on the wrong door, and if I stay really quiet, they will eventually go away.

Another part, the rational part, is worried about who can be coming to my door at this time of night.

In the past, if someone is at my door, it's never a good thing. It's usually a courier with work from my boss. A case I need to look over before Monday morning.

Reluctantly, I stand and make my way to answer it. Can't hide in the dark forever. When I swing the door open, I'm taken aback by who's here.

It's Tobias.

Tall.

Dark.

And standing ominously in my hallway.

What the hell is he doing here?

If he's here to yell at me again . . .

No.

It's been radio silence from him since Thursday when he yelled at me in the street.

That's not it. He's not here for round two. There's something else, another reason for his impromptu visit.

My back goes ramrod straight when I take him in. Lord, if I thought he looked good at the office, it has nothing on his weekend apparel. He's wearing jeans, a white thermal, and sneakers.

He looks so normal at first glance, but when my gaze trails up, it feels like there is a rope around my heart, and it's tightening to the point of pain.

His eyes look dark today. Not the usual blue I'm used to. No, today, the blacks of his pupils are larger than normal.

But that's not all. His jaw is set in a hard line.

Something is wrong.

Continuing my assessment, I see that he's holding something.

A bottle of whiskey.

Shit.

Something is very wrong.

"Tobias?" My voice is low. Unsure. Asking him with one word to tell me why he's here and praying I'm overthinking this.

"Can I come in?" Even his voice sounds different. Typically, it's strong and commanding, but tonight, it's softer and filled with sympathy.

"I guess," I mumble, trying not to jump to conclusions.

Moving back, I quickly scan the small living room. Luckily, it's not a mess, although my sweatshirt is on the loveseat, which reminds me—I look down and remember that I'm wearing a white camisole, my nipples clearly visible under it. Great. Just great.

When I look up to see if Tobias noticed, I see that he's not even looking at me. He seems to be lost in thought.

"Tobias?"

"Yeah . . ."

Everything about Tobias is off tonight. He's lost in his thoughts as I lead him farther into my little apartment.

"You're actually scaring me a little. Why are you here?" I ask while crossing my arms in front of me. "Why are you here?" I say again, more forcefully.

"I need to talk to you, but I think maybe—"

"Spit it out!" My voice echoes through the small apartment, bouncing off the walls. If I weren't so nervous and angry, I might care that I shouldn't be screaming when my walls are paper-thin, but I can't find it in me to care when I need to know why he's here.

"I found out what the paper was."

"And?" I croak as my heart starts to thump radically in my chest. Time stands still as he moves closer to me. It feels like my heart might burst open.

"Please just tell me, Tobias."

"Your dad's sick, Skye."

"Sick, how sick? He was just at the doctor's. He said it was routine. He said he'd be fine."

"He lied, Skye."

"How sick?" My right hand cups my left wrist as I try to calm myself. "Please tell me."

He takes my hand in his, and then his finger is on the pulse. The pulse under my tattoo.

It feels like I'm breaking apart, but with his fingers on my tattoo, I breathe.

"Your father has stage four liver failure. He's terminal."

Despite how strong I am, I can't hold back the sob that tears through my lungs.

My knees drop from beneath me, my body plunging into an abyss.

Falling.

Falling.

But I never crash.

I'm cradled in his arms.

Pulled tight to him.

His arms are around me, holding me tightly. "Shh," he coos, or at least, that's what I think he says.

It sounds like jumbled words spoken underwater. I can't make them out beneath the sound of my sobs. Before I know what's happening, I'm being lifted and carried to the couch.

Then Tobias is sitting and placing me on his lap. The small rational part of me knows this isn't right. He shouldn't be holding me. I shouldn't let him, but it feels like I have been ripped in two. I'm bleeding out all over my rug, and without him, I would surely die.

My face nuzzles into his neck. The smell of his cologne, or maybe aftershave, infiltrates my nose, keeping me tethered to the earth.

I inhale him in and will myself to stay and not escape into the crevice of my mind where I used to go. His hand is on my back. He rubs softly as I hiccup through tears.

"I have you," he tells me. I hold him tighter. "Inhale." He rubs my wrist.

For a minute, I'm transported back. To a far-off world. Long before.

Tobias isn't holding me now. No, I'm being held by a boy with crisp blue eyes.

I shake my head and push away the memories.

Tobias isn't that boy.

That boy died.

But my fucked-up brain doesn't want to believe that. It wants to worm its way into my brain and send me back in time, but I can't go back there. Not when he just told me my father is dying.

Lifting my hand, I swipe the tears under my eyes, but I'm still not strong enough to move away. I still need the protection of Tobias's arms. A thought I won't allow myself to think about now, no, that will have to wait until tomorrow. For now, I'll take comfort, even if it's from him.

CHAPTER TWENTY-THREE

Tobias

A s she cries in my arms, I hold her.
The desire to fix all her problems tightens around my chest. It feels suffocating. The need to protect her fills every inch of my body.

If only I could.

You can.

She doesn't even remember you.

Why help her?

You weren't important enough to remember.

A voice in the back of my head tells me to get over the anger and let it go. I sound like a little bitch, singing a Disney song meant for little girls dressed in princess costumes. Who the fuck cares anymore? Get over it.

I pull her closer, and her soft breath tickles my neck.

Having her in my arms feels right. Despite everything, I know I need her.

Not now, though. And not on false pretense.

Once I find out if I can trust her, she'll be mine, and I won't let her go. But how do I see if I can trust her?

It feels wrong setting her up. It feels like a betrayal. Give her information to see if she leaks it? That is the only way. Take her with you to a meeting and then set her up to see what she does.

The idea feels wrong, but before I tell her the truth, my truth, I have to see if she's worth the risk.

A part of me knows she is.

But another part still wonders why she's working with Felix or if that is a mere coincidence. I don't believe in coincidences, though.

"I can't lose him, Tobias." Her voice cuts through my inner rambling. I can give her false promises, but I read the report Jaxson provided. There's no hope. Once I found out what tests they had billed to insurance for her dad, I had Jaxson dig even deeper.

Ralph Matthews is dying.

It's not if, it's when, and by the reports, it doesn't look good. The doctors are anticipating six months, if not shorter.

I don't offer any kind words. There's nothing to say.

"He's all I have," she whimpers. My hand runs circles up her back. "H-He adopted me." Skye's voice sounds broken. She's barely holding on, falling apart at the seams. All I want to do is hold her together.

Her words have my hands stopping. I'm surprised she's offering this up to me. But as a greedy fuck, I take it.

"He did?" I ask.

I pretend not to know, but that's a lie. I know everything about Skye. From the moment I recognized her in the courtroom, I have made it my duty.

"My parents died. He took me in. He is everything to me. He took a scared, sad girl"—a sob breaks through her lips—"and taught me how not to be scared."

I feel like my throat is closing. I want to ask, but I don't.

"I don't talk about it. I don't think about it. My brain

sometimes has a hard time remembering, but he helped me. He helped me make peace. And when I couldn't remember—"

"Couldn't remember what?" I ask her, desperate to know more. Desperate to know everything.

She shakes her head, and I hear a whimper as her body starts to shake again.

What doesn't she remember from her childhood? And if she doesn't remember her childhood, is there more she doesn't remember? Am I a casualty of another story that passed through the cracks?

One day, I'll ask. One day, I will tell her my full story, but right now, I just hold her in my arms and let her cry.

Because today isn't about me.

Today isn't about my need for truth.

Today is about realizing that sometimes you put your own shit down and pick up the load for someone else.

CHAPTER TWENTY-FOUR

Skye

DAYS HAVE PASSED SINCE MY MELTDOWN. I'M BACK IN HIS office and back to work.

Despite everything, it is a bit awkward. I sit directly across from him. I'm looking over the files for the purchase in Miami he's going to make, and he's looking over his own file.

I have no idea on what, but to be honest, I don't want to know. I'm tired. My own issues are hovering over me like a black cloud.

Reaching forward, I move to grab a pen, but my hand connects with Tobias's. It seems I'm not the only one who needs one.

We both freeze.

His fingers wrap around mine.

My head tilts up, our gaze locking. He looks at me with an intensity I have never seen or felt before.

I might be the sky, but he's the sun. He's burning me up.

A nervous energy begins to course through my limbs. Neither one of us pulls our hands apart. Nor do we stop staring.

We are both stuck in quicksand. If we move, one of us can go under.

The longer we are frozen in time, the heavier the air gets. It's stifling. Filled with silent words and emotions that I can't begin to comprehend. What is happening here?

We are at a crossroads.

This moment feels important.

As the seconds pass, they turn into minutes, yet neither of us speaks.

"You never finished telling me your story," I finally say to break the silence that surrounds us.

He inhales deeply. His chest muscles expand. Leaning forward, he severs our contact. I miss the feeling instantly. He picks up the papers on his desk and pushes them aside, then he reaches for the decanter and pours himself a drink.

Interesting.

When he offers me one, I shake my head. I still have too much to do today, and seeing as I'm half his size and how heavy-handed he is with the scotch, I won't be standing if I take him up on his offer.

Tobias lifts the glass to his mouth, takes a sip, and then leans back.

"It was a normal day like today or yesterday. The weather was chilly, and I remember thinking I couldn't wait for winter to end so that I could go for a swim. It was still too early, and the water would be too cold. But it didn't matter, even if it were summer, there would be no swimming that day. My father had a surprise for me."

"What was the surprise?"

"Patience. All in good time."

I have the desire to roll my eyes at his condescending tone, but I don't. This story he's telling me feels like it will forever change me.

This is the story of how Tobias became the man he is today, and I don't know much about him. I tried to look him up, but his story comes from nowhere. He was raised in Florida, I read. His father was a successful businessman who passed away. His father's ties to the cartel are notorious. His mother was apparently a relative of the notorious family. I'm not sure why he's telling me a story about his youth, but it feels important, so I bite my tongue and let him continue.

"It was my birthday, you see. And my father had a surprise."

Questions are heavy on my tongue, but I don't speak. Instead, I wait for him to continue. As his mouth opens, his cell phone chimes. He grits his teeth, and a shadow of annoyance crosses over his features.

He looks down at his phone, and his jaw locks as his pupils scan whatever he is reading.

"Fuck," he mutters under his breath. "Time to go." He stands abruptly, pushing his chair back, the scratching of the chair against the floor severing the moment completely.

"Where are we going?" I ask, confused and clearly out of the loop.

"Miami."

CHAPTER TWENTY-FIVE

Tobias

HER MOUTH IS OPEN IN AN O SHAPE, AND HER EYES GO WIDE, blinking with bewilderment, and then staring at me intently. I like this look on her. She's cute. The only look I like better is the one she gave me when she was basically fucking me at the desk with her eyes.

I noticed.

Not only did I notice, but I also wanted to act on it. By some crazy willpower, I didn't. But fuck, did I want to bend her over my desk, hike up her skirt, and go to town. I need to fuck her out of my system. That's the only way this need will go away. Since that isn't going to happen, I'll settle for the shocked look on her face. Always professional, she tries to school her features, but I catch it regardless. It's the way her pupils dilate and her breath hitches. The average fool wouldn't notice, but I'm not average.

I notice everything about Skye Matthews.

"Say what?"

"We're going to Miami." My nonchalant answer has her scrunching her nose.

"Why?" she probes.

"To look at the buildings." I shrug as if her question is ridiculous. In fact, most people can't fathom the crazy shit I do, and hopping on a plane to look at a building with nothing but forty-five minutes' notice is not normal for them.

For me, it's a Tuesday.

She looks at the papers in front of her and then back up at me. "Are we leaving now?"

"Yep." I stand from the desk and walk toward the stairwell. No reason to pretend the elevator doesn't bother me when she's around and already knows it does. "You coming?" I ask over my shoulder.

"I didn't pack," she responds, still in the same place I left her, still staring at the mess in front of her before she starts to clean up and stand.

"You don't need to." My feet hit the steps, and then I hear hers echoing on the concrete to catch up to me.

"What do you mean, I don't need to?"

"We aren't staying overnight," I inform her.

The sound of her heels hitting the floor stops, meaning she is no longer moving. I wait for her to speak, knowing full well she will.

"I don't understand," she finally says.

"What's there not to understand? We are flying in and then flying out."

"How?"

"On a plane," I deadpan.

"Har. Har. Har. Obviously on a plane, but—"

"On my plane, Skye." I look over my shoulder. "We are flying on my private jet to Miami, and then we will fly back home."

Again, with the shocked face, mouth open, eyes wide. Yep . . . that look does it for me.

"Oh." That is all she has to say, so I turn back and start to head down to the basement level where my men are.

This is the first time she takes the stairs, and from this vantage point, you can see each floor as you pass it.

When we are down one, I can hear her gasp when she sees that this section looks nothing like the office where she usually meets me. This is where my gym is.

"You have a gym."

"Yes."

"Do you live here?"

Again, I stop and look at her. "Sometimes, but it's best that no one knows that. Do you understand?"

She nods her head. "I can't talk about anything you say to me anyway. You know that."

"I don't even want your boss knowing."

"Okay." She's quiet as we continue down another flight. Now, on the second level, she sees the security floor. Well, one of the two.

"Wow."

"Yeah."

"This is pretty insane." She sounds bewildered, and it's cute. I shrug.

It is. Jaxson Price built it for me. This shit rivals the security of the Pentagon. Actually, it's better than theirs. He hacks them weekly for fun.

When we finally make it to the basement, she asks the question I know she's been dying to ask since she saw the gym.

She's looking around like a kid in a candy store. "Where do you sleep?"

"There is another level."

"Where? Your office is the top level . . ." she trails off as I incline my head. "Ohhh, it's not. There's another floor?"

"There is. But again . . ." I give her a knowing look.

"Yep. Got it. I'm not dumb."

"We're taking the Escalade." I point at a line of cars in the garage.

This is the one we take on longer trips. It's larger, more comfortable, and, like the Range Rover, bulletproof.

"You have a lot of cars."

"I'm a collector."

"I can see that. Anything else you collect?"

"Souls."

She laughs a nervous laugh, but I'm not joking. I do. And hers, I'm still debating on.

Opening the door for her, she shuffles in. I sit beside her, and we are off. Heading out of the city and toward Teterboro Airport.

Before long, we pull up to the private hangar that I own. It's listed under one of the many private corporations, where my name is nowhere on the manifesto. Security is always present here for my plane as well.

Some might think I'm paranoid, but my father's enemy killed him. In my belief, you can never be too careful. Also, this is why I can't just kidnap Felix. He's a paranoid motherfucker as well.

The car rolls to the runway.

"You can drive on the runway?" Shock fills Skye's voice.

"I can."

"And if you have luggage? What about TSA? Security? ID?"

I shake my head. "We don't have to do that." I put the car in park and round the passenger side, opening her door. "Come on."

She's still stuck on her earlier questions as she follows me to my Gulfstream. "Wow. Really?"

"Yes, really. Come on, Skye. Believe it or not, we do have to get going."

She hesitates, blinking with bafflement, before looking at me. Really looking at me. We're close together, my body practically caging hers against the railing of the staircase leading to the plane.

Yes, I'm turned on.

And no, I shouldn't be.

She knows it, too.

A devious glint graces her eyes for half a second before she smooths it over, passing by me—but not before her eyes dip to my slacks, and she asks, "Are you sure you don't have to use the bathroom first? I know you find it hard to wait . . . "

She doesn't stay for an answer, climbing up the steps into the plane. Just as she reaches the threshold, she looks over her shoulder and throws me a wink.

I answer fast before she disappears through the entry. "I can wait. Patience is a virtue, after all. Especially when it comes to inevitable things."

A choked noise comes from her throat, but she hides it well under a cough. Then she's gone. Into the plane and out of sight.

I follow her, nodding to the pilot flanked by his co-pilot and the flight attendant along the way. We pass the couch, taking seats opposite one another, separated by a small table between us.

My team shuffles on board next before we prepare for takeoff.

"This is some plane."

She's doing her best to hide her reaction, and I bite back the laugh threatening to spill. I can't laugh in front of my men.

"It gets me from point A to point B safely. That's all I care about."

"And a bathroom."

There's that grin again. It's the second attempt at that joke, and I won't let it go unanswered.

Grabbing her arm, I lead her to the very back of the cabin.

"Where are we going?" She sounds suspicious.

Good. She should be.

"Since you were so concerned about my bathroom habit, I decided to take you." This time, I'm the one who winks, and her blue eyes go wide.

Throwing the door open, I hear her mumbling, but I don't stop until we're both inside the tight cubicle, the door shut behind us.

I stalk toward her, watching as her body edges onto the sink in her effort to back away. She's trapped, and it's doing things to me that it shouldn't.

"Allow me to offer a VIP tour of the bathroom . . . since you're so concerned."

"Concerned," she echoes, glued to my movements. "Yes. Concerned."

"This is the sink." I lean over her, wrapping my arm around her to turn the faucet on and off.

It's an excuse to brush against her, and it works. Her body arches into mine, begging to be touched.

"Nice sink," she comments.

It's hard not to laugh. She hasn't even looked at it. Hasn't looked at anything but me.

Hunger laced with fear glazes over her eyes. She wants me, and that scares her.

She severs the connection first, spinning to face the mirror. From behind her, I stare at our reflection.

The delicate curve of her neck. Her parted lips. The way her chest heaves.

If I dipped my fingers under her dress, would I find her soaked?

"Tell me, Miss Matthews. Do you often think about me in the restroom? And when you do, do your hands drift between your thighs?"

Her breath catches. "Excuse me?"

"How often do you picture it?" I step closer, gluing our bodies together. "Is it because you want to be here with me?"

In the reflection, her pupils dilate, lips dropping into a small O. She sighs, head leaning back on my shoulder. I don't think she even realizes it, but she's turned on. Craving me.

My dick is hard against her ass, ready for this. I slide my palm across her hip.

"I don't care what you do in the bathroom," she whispers.

But despite her words, she pushes back into me, grinding her ass against every inch of my hardness. She's affected by me. She wants me as much as I want her.

"If I slide my fingers inside you, what will I find, Miss Matthews?"

Kicking her legs apart, my hand drifts down the skirt of her dress, slipping under the edge of the cotton inch by inch.

"I bet . . . " Another inch. Another gasp. " . . . I'll find that pussy dripping."

Our gazes are locked through the reflection. I watch her eyes flare as I cup her pussy, our skin separated by a thin scrap of lace.

I trace my index finger over the material, circling over her clit.

Outside, we hear Gideon's raucous laughter. Skye tenses, but her hips buck forward, chasing my touch.

"Look at you, Skye. You're soaking wet." My fingers come to her nipple, pinching it through her dress. "Do you want Gideon to hear you come? I can make you scream my name."

She moans at my words. I push the lace aside, and then I collect her wetness and circle it around her clit.

Skye grinds back against me. The movement nearly sends my finger inside her greedy body.

"Tell me what you want, Skye."

She doesn't answer.

"Beg for me."

Her breathing accelerates, and I can hear the way she bites back her pleas.

"Be a good girl, and I'll give it to you. I'd give you anything. All you have to do is ask."

But she doesn't answer.

She is so headstrong—so Skye—I want to bury my head into her neck, run my tongue along the column, and make her fall apart. Instead, I wink at her through the mirror, ten seconds from pulling my hard cock out and sinking inside her.

But I don't.

I pull away, take a step back, and leave her panting in the bathroom.

It's only fair, after all.

Since it's her favorite place in the world.

Walking back to my seat, I can't help but chuckle. The guys side-eye me, but I ignore them.

It's a full five minutes before Skye returns to the seat across from me.

I lift a brow, browsing the menu without looking at her. "Do you have a problem?"

"Nope," she mutters under her breath, leans back in her chair, and buckles her seat belt, closing her eyes.

Skye Matthews thinks she can fool me, but I know better.

———•———

I was right.

She didn't sleep. At first, she had attitude, but it didn't take her long to start to talk . . . to Gideon, not me. She's still pissed at me for leaving her teetering on the edge.

Now that we are finally in the car in Miami, I tell her what's going down. I'm going to take her to look at the site for the new building after my meeting. Then we will meet with the property developers.

We pull up to my residence first. It's a newer purchase, made after I stepped into my current role in the business. However, even though I've only owned the residence since I was about eighteen, the area of Miami is where I spent half my childhood. Specifically, the land I'm considering buying. Before it was sold, it had been in my family for years.

"I need you to stay here while Gideon and I take a meeting."

It will give her time to cool off. Drop the attitude.

"What do you expect me to do?" Her voice is clipped, and I know she's still pissed.

"Go over the papers I have set up for you in my office. It has all the numbers and pricing for everything. Prepare for the meeting we have later with the realtors. I'll be back shortly."

"Okay," she says as she steps out of my car, and three members of my team escort her into the house.

"Let's go," I say to Christopher, who's driving.

Gideon turns from the passenger seat to look at me.

"Everything set?"

"Yes."

Today, I hand over the last bit of control. Today, I introduce Gideon to my supplier. As merely the distributor, I keep all access points in my drug business private. That way, I can never be cut out.

I learned from a lot of former cartel associates about how to run my empire. I watched them, saw their mistakes, and adapted my uncle's business to never make the same mistake.

The one and only mistake I ever made in this business was letting my personal vendetta lead my decisions. The road I'm about to take is dangerous. To mitigate the fallout, I'm handing over the empire to my right-hand man. That way, I only fight one battle at a time.

After today, Gideon will run this aspect of the business, and I will focus on taking Felix down for what he did so many years ago.

A while back, I stopped dealing with the cartel. All that is left of that part of the business is the pills. But after today, my legitimate business and my vengeance are all that remains.

Fifteen minutes later, we pull into the large estate of Emil Keller, the man who supplies me the MDMA he produces in his home country of Holland. Like all aspects of the business, Emil appears to be a successful business tycoon who owns a shopping mall in South Florida.

It's a front.

He's the son of the largest underground organization for ecstasy production in the EU. I know him because we went to boarding school together. That's where my plan for mass power, corruption, and payback was established.

When I met Emil, his father made pills, and my family

distributed coke. Years later, when I wanted to sever ties with the cartel, I got into business with him. However, as the opioid epidemic hit, I wasn't the only one changing focus. Bernard was already a thorn in my side. First, my father's enemy. Now mine.

But with Emil's help, I made a big enough fortune to finally go after the man responsible for my fucked-up life. It will feel good when he confesses his role in my pain, and I can rid the world of him once and for all.

CHAPTER TWENTY-SIX

Skye

A ND HERE WE ARE AGAIN, BACK IN THE CAR, DRIVING TO A location to buy.

I should think about all the paperwork I did, how everything is in order, but instead, I feel hot, achy, and needy.

My five minutes in the bathroom to calm down didn't help. Nor the hour that he left me alone to do god knows what.

Nope. I will not let myself go there.

Think about why you're here.

The land. The land. The land.

The price for the land is right, and as soon as I see the location and cross-check it against some stipulations in the contract over building rules and regulations in the area, I'll most likely advise Tobias to sign.

With his hands. Hands that only hours ago played me like a fiddle. Strumming me until—

The land is prime Florida property.

Yep. It's perfect.

Unlike how I feel right now.

Like I was left at the edge of a mountain, I'll never be able to get off . . . *pun intended.*

With a shake of my head, I try to make myself remember why I'm here. For Tobias to buy this property.

It would be a great investment piece.

It's on the water. Right now, the location is a teardown in Brickell, but the surrounding buildings are perfect. Beautiful high-rises.

While we walk outside, I can't help but stop and admire the view. The Atlantic Ocean stretches into the horizon. Taking a deep inhale, I allow the salty air to calm my sexual frustration. A dip in the Atlantic might help. Doubtful though. Not unless it were thirty-three degrees and I'm doing a polar bear plunge.

"It's beautiful," Tobias says as he comes up behind me.

He's standing close. Close enough that I can smell the faint smell of his cologne. It's woodsy and fresh, and a complete contrast to the ocean air competing for my attention.

My heart starts to beat rapidly. I don't want to look at him. I don't want him to see the lust in my eyes.

"Yeah," I whisper, turning my head to look at him because as much as I will myself to not, I can't stop it.

He wins.

I regret the movement immediately.

He looks at me as if he's always known me, and I feel unnerved.

"I grew up here."

"Here?"

He gestures around us. "On the property, actually. In this very structure."

"So, this is personal?"

He nods. "It's very personal. This is where I learned everything. Where I became the man you see before you now."

"Tell me your story," I hear myself say. "Please."

"Where did I leave off?" He lifts his hand and runs it through his hair, tugging lightly on the unruly strands that have grown wild due to the wind billowing off the ocean.

"It was going to be the best day of my life." Tobias's voice is calm as he says this, his gaze steady. "Yet as so many tragic stories go, it ended up being the worst."

This time it's me who steps closer. There is an invisible magnet connecting us, and I can't pull away.

"This is the building where I learned about the business. Where I met with the cartel. Here, I learned the way to separate distributors from suppliers. For years, our businesses weren't run that way, but then it changed."

"Why?"

"Well, that's a different story. That's the story of how the man who raised me died, but you didn't ask for that one. We were talking about my worst day."

My heart beats frantically in my chest. How can anything be worse than that? But I don't even need to know the answer to know anything is possible.

Evil exists. I have seen it. Lived it. The horror I lived through . . . well, I would never wish that on anyone. It feels as if my stomach is being ripped apart as I remember my own worst day. My hand reaches out to rub my wrist. To rub the tattoo. And then I remember the boy. The boy . . . who died. I shake my head and drop my hand, pushing the image of the paper airplane away.

"Please."

"Okay."

"I think I mentioned it was my birthday; I didn't celebrate it. Often, we moved around, trying to expand the business. I didn't have friends, so why have a party. This year would be the same. My father, however, had other plans."

He had mentioned before that it was just his father and him, but where was his mother? I'm not sure if it's my place to ask, but I do anyway.

"Where was your mom?"

"She died in childbirth."

A part of my heart broke. He lost his mother and his father. He is an orphan. Like me.

"That day, my father woke me, and it was so different. That day, he wanted to celebrate me. I always thought that since my mother died on my birthday . . ."

Tears form in my eyes, and I feel myself hyperventilating. I'm choking from the emotions clogging my soul. It's as if I'm being ripped apart. The pain I see in his eyes is, I'm sure, in mine as well.

"Tobias, I—"

"It's time. They're here." Gideon's voice rings out through the open air.

I have so much to say. So much to tell him. There are words stuck on my tongue, and I can't say them now, not in front of Gideon.

I feel devastated because I want to know his story, and I want to tell him mine. There is something about Tobias. He's familiar to me. He is me. My pain knows his pain.

"We'll continue this later," he says, and I nod, but I know we will.

Never before have I wanted to open myself up, but now I want to.

I reach my hand out and touch his. An electric current of emotion tingles when our hands touch. Our gazes are locked, and time stands still as we stare into each other's eyes.

A million words are spoken. Words that say that everything is about to change between us. I don't know what this means, but I can no longer pretend that I don't want to know him.

I don't hate him. Not even a little. No. Instead, I want to learn everything. I want to see the man he became, and most of all, I want to know how he became that man.

Something tells me there is so much more to this story. My own pain seeps to the surface. My trauma and loss. I take a deep breath, and so does he, then he nods.

"It's time to go."

"Okay."

He drops my hand, and then the look in his eyes change. The moment of vulnerability is gone. The hard façade of the walls he built drops down, and I am no longer the woman he almost confided in. Nope, now I'm a stranger.

I feel cold. It's a feeling I don't want to have. He starts to walk, and I hurry to catch up. A part of me wishes there was such a thing as a time machine, or maybe even a way to stop time. I would have frozen the moment for longer. Basked in his trust.

But now, seeing his icy façade, a part of me is afraid he'll never finish. That he will think twice of what he tells me. Because I know why he stopped talking, but I don't understand the look he's giving me.

He looks angry, maybe he hates me again, and I don't understand what I did. For a second, he must have forgotten himself and let me in, but now he remembers.

I hope that's not the case because something tells me he needs me to hear his story. And the scariest part . . .

I think I need to as well.

CHAPTER TWENTY-SEVEN

Skye

IT'S INTERESTING. FOR WEEKS, I WANTED TOBIAS TO GIVE ME space, and now that he is, I don't like it. Since we got back from Florida two days ago, he has told me not to come into his office.

It's weird.

Almost all the paperwork is done for the purchase of the building, and we are only waiting on a few more things, but I still never anticipated our working together would be ending so fast.

But I guess it's official. Or it will be official soon: Tobias Kosta, a legitimate businessman. Owning property all over the world. Investing money and living off the fruits of those investments, but it still seems weird. Why retire?

That question still lingers in the air. The answer feels unattainable, always out of reach. He's dangling a piece of fruit in front of me but won't let me take a bite. Thinking about it makes me think of how wrong about him I was. Yes, he's not warm and fuzzy, but deep down, I know he has a good heart. Take what he did for me . . .

Had he not looked into my father's health, I would never have known that my father is sick.

Speaking of which, I need to try to get him to talk to me again.

An hour later, I'm walking through his front door.

"Dad?" I call out, making my way through the foyer. I don't have to go far before I find him.

He's in the living room, and as per usual, he's sitting in his favorite chair. Reclined back, clicker in hand.

A woman is talking loudly from the TV. It sounds like she's bickering with someone. My head turns to see what he's watching.

The news.

Local.

A brunette in her mid-forties seems to be arguing with some older man.

About what? Who knows?

But it's obviously entertaining my dad because he has barely glanced my way.

"I brought dinner," I tell him, lifting the bag up to show that I'm holding food from his favorite Italian restaurant in my hand.

He shuts off the TV and then is pivoting the recliner to face me. "Chicken parmigiana?"

I roll my eyes. "Of course, I bought chicken parmigiana. Dad, who do you take me for?"

A flash of humor crosses his features. "Just making sure." Standing from his chair, he inclines his head. "How did you know I hadn't eaten?"

My shoulders lift. "I took a guess."

Dark brown eyes meet mine, and I can tell right away he's happy I'm here. They almost sparkle with amusement. "That was rather presumptuous of you," he jokes.

"Dad . . ." I place my free hand on my hip and cock it. "It's six o'clock. There was a very good chance you hadn't eaten."

He walks over to me, places his hand on my shoulder, and gives me a squeeze. "Am I that predictable?"

I laugh at that. "Yes, you are."

His lips spread into a smile. I use the opportunity to look at him. He looks happy. However, it doesn't diminish the lines on his face and the yellow tint of his skin. "Let's go eat."

Together, we walk to the kitchen. I place the bags on the table and then grab paper plates and plastic cutlery.

Once we are both served, we sit in silence, eating and enjoying every bite.

"Are you still working for Felix Bernard?" my father asks as he places his fork down and moves to grab his water. That was a nice surprise, him not reaching for the booze. But I have to assume it's because he's ill.

My stomach muscles tighten; I wonder if he will tell me tonight.

"Actually, I'm working on something else."

He places the glass down and looks at me. The lines on his forehead are more pronounced now—he's curious. "Care to enlighten me?"

"You know I really can't do that." My mouth curves up into a smile.

"Fine. I am happy." His words are confusing.

What is he happy about? Me not telling him or . . . "Happy about what?"

"I don't like Felix Bernard. I never liked you working with him."

His comment has me dropping my fork. "What? Really? But you never said anything."

He lifts his shoulders. "You never asked."

"You don't need to be asked for you to tell me something." This time, I'm leveling him with my fiercest stare because I know that I'm talking about something else completely.

I wonder if he will catch on to my motives.

His lips thin. Lines form between his brows that resemble the number eleven.

His mouth opens and shuts, but it's his eyes that tell me everything I need to know, he's not ready to talk.

"Are you planning on letting me in on why you don't like Mr. Bernard?" This is my opportunity to press, and I'm not going to miss it. Hopefully Dad plays along.

"I don't really know him." Yet there's a file in his office with a question mark next to his name.

My father is lying.

There is a lot more he's not being open about.

There are two choices for me right now, I can ask him point-blank, or I can play dumb.

I choose the latter as I cut into my chicken parmigiana. "I didn't even realize you knew him at all."

"He does own property in Reddington." His voice is so nonchalant, it pisses me off. After everything we've been through, why is he still holding back? *Maybe he's protecting you.*

"He does?"

This is something I didn't know. How did I not know this? It wasn't in any of the paperwork. I make a mental note to see what I can find out.

"Really? What property?"

"He owns the shopping mall."

His words hit me in the chest. The shopping mall? The shopping mall that was built around the time my parents died? If I remember correctly, it was built in a part of town that was once warehouses. An area my parents would never take me. An area the city cleaned up and developed and is now thriving.

Was this the legitimate business he had in town? Did he kill his competition and then build a business to cover up his presence? It sounds plausible, but I would need proof.

What sort of proof, though?

We continue to eat, and when I'm no longer hungry, I start to push my food around my plate.

"Everything okay?" my father asks me, and I stop my

movements and look up at him. His plate is cleared, fork down, and he is staring intently at me.

"I'm just thinking . . . "

"About?"

I want to tell you.

I want to come right out and tell him the truth. But I can't say that. I have to say something else.

"My new client." *Is that the best you can come up with, Skye?* It always goes back to Tobias. That man is never far from my thoughts. I'm addicted to him.

I need help.

An exorcism.

"Who's this new client? Anyone I know?"

"Tobias Kosta."

His hand slams down on the table. I'm not sure if it's shock or anger, but when I meet his gaze, the answer is obvious. Anger. "Are you serious?"

I play dumb again. Everyone knows Tobias Kosta. "Oh, do you know him?"

He shakes his head. "Not personally, only by reputation. Not a good one at that."

My shoulder muscles tighten. Instantly on edge. The need to defend him pumps through my veins.

"Well, that's not your place to judge. He's not what people think," I snap back. My brain tells me to drop it, but my irrational side that has gotten to know that there is more than meets the eye with Tobias overpowers me.

He's the type of man who holds you when you cry, my brain screams at me to say, but instead, I bite back that comment, sucking in my cheeks to stop my mouth from speaking things I can't take back.

"What exactly do you know about what type of man he is?"

Shit. I walked right into that.

"I've been working with him for a few weeks now, and I just—"

"Stop. I didn't make the sacrifices I made, and do the things I needed to do to get you into law school, just so that you could work with the dregs of the earth. That was not what I had in mind when I—" he stops himself.

"What is that supposed to mean? What did you do, Dad?" I lean forward in my chair, my elbows resting on the table.

"That's not your concern."

"Of course, it's my concern. This has to do with me."

"What I did to pay for your school is not your concern. I worked hard, I busted my ass, and in the end, you got the best education that I could provide you. I thought you'd make the world a better place, but instead, all you're doing is cleaning it up from the criminals who—" Again, he stops talking.

"The criminals who what?"

"Forget it. There's no talking to you."

"Dad?"

He stands from his chair, and I follow suit. "I don't want to fight with you." My voice is low, sober.

"We aren't fighting."

"Then why are you leaving?"

"Because I'm disappointed in you, Skye." And then he turns and starts to walk out of the room.

My heart feels heavy. This is not what I wanted when I came here. I don't know how much time we have, and I don't want it to end this way.

"Dad," I call out to him as he takes another step, this time to leave the room. He stops and turns around to look at me. "I'm sorry. I love you." My words have him pivoting to look at me.

His chest rises and falls. His serious face softens. "I'm sorry, too, sweetheart." Then he's hugging me. "I'm so sorry I got cross."

"It's okay, I understand."

"No, you don't. You didn't deserve it. I am proud of you every day. I'm so damn proud. I remember the girl you were, and I just—" A tear leaks from his eye. "I just wanted to give you everything."

"You did." My own eyes mist.

"I tried. I tried the best I could."

"Dad, there was nothing I ever wanted for," I tell him, and one lone drop of water trails down my cheek.

"You were and are my world, Skye."

I pull back and look at him. My lips spread into a large, genuine smile. A playful one. "No other father would do half the stuff you did for me."

"I didn't do much."

"I remember you taking me every day to the mall once it opened," I remind him.

"You liked to shop." He shrugs.

"But you couldn't afford it."

His cheeks redden. "I made do."

"And then there were all the movies I dragged you to."

His hand bats the air. "That was nothing."

"And every day, you made me toast with strawberry jam because you knew I loved it." At my words, his arms encircle me, one hand in the small of my back, the other rubbing comforting circles.

"You did love that." He leans down and places a kiss on the top of my head. Like he used to when I was a little girl. When I needed him to make me feel safe.

"I did. I still do." I hold my father tighter. I don't know why he won't tell me the truth about what he's going through, and I don't know if he ever will. But at this moment, protected in his arms, it doesn't matter. Time isn't something we have much of. We could have months, or we could have weeks. I refuse to waste the moments we have.

It's been three days since I have seen my father, and the way he looked and talked still haunts my mind. I wish I would come out and ask him point-blank about everything, but truth be told, I'm scared. As much as I need to know from him that he's dying, I'm petrified for him to confirm it.

I'm not usually this timid. Hell, I'm about to throw myself into the lion's den tonight. But with my father, I will always be the lost little six-year-old who needed a home.

Looking at myself in the mirror, I stare at my reflection. My long black gown looks modest from the front. It's the back that will stun, dipping lower than the small of my back.

Like Tobias, I have one goal, and tonight is when I set it in motion. It's finally here. Tonight is the gala with Felix.

I'm not at all prepared. The first thing I want to do is ask him questions, but I don't feel like he will answer any of them, not unless his guard is down. Maybe I can get him drunk.

The next thing is I need access to his computer. Not just his files. No, I need access to his apartment, which is risky, but seeing how he stares at me makes it even more so.

I won't get access tonight, but if I play my cards right, it could be soon. With my lipstick in hand, I pace the foyer of my apartment, waiting for him to buzz that he's here. I don't like that he knows where I live, but it's a necessary evil. I'm starting to fidget when the buzzer goes off.

It's him.

It's time.

The only time I have been with Felix before tonight has been at the office or court, so I'm not sure what security he has. That's another reason I'm going out with him, to size up whether there is even a shot in hell that I'll be able to find out anything this way. There is also the chance that I'll need to come up with yet another plan.

I head down the stairs, and I'm not surprised to find one of Felix's men standing there by the door.

He wouldn't get out to greet me.

What I have realized by working with him this year, and most recently, the work I have done with Tobias, is men like this are never alone. Even when you think they are, someone is there watching. I wonder if that will change now that Tobias has retired? Or if, in fact, it won't change until he does whatever else his ominous warning means.

I follow Felix's man to the car, and after he opens the door for me, I step inside and take a seat beside him.

"Don't you look gorgeous tonight," Felix coos as he traces my body with his creepy eyes. I'm happy my front is covered because this man gives me the serious creeps.

It's not often I feel like this—unsafe—but I do. This is not something I feel around Tobias. He might also undress me with his eyes, yet it doesn't feel like this.

It's not that Felix is ugly. He's older than me, probably by at least twenty-five years, and he's obviously aging well and in amazing shape, but something in his eyes is off. A disconnect. He looks like the type of man who would kill innocent bystanders simply because he doesn't like how they stand.

"Thank you." I try my best to smile and appear unaffected. But the faster I get to the gala and the faster I get home, the better.

There is a sinking feeling inside my gut that I'm being set up as bait or as payment by my boss to this man, and I don't like it at all.

Luckily, the gala is held relatively close to my apartment, and we pull up after only a few minutes. I'm also lucky Felix didn't try to make small talk. Although I'm supposed to make him feel comfortable, I realize I'll have to devise another plan. I don't know how I'll ever be able to access his apartment unless I spread my legs for him.

Not something I'm willing to do.

When the car rolls to a stop, I wait for his security team to clear the area and then open the door for us. When I step out, I realize the problem with my dress. Felix didn't see the back when

I stepped into the car, but now that I'm exiting, my back is on full display. Standing on the sidewalk, I feel the error of my ways.

His hand rests on the small of my back, but it's his fingers that bother me. With a flared hand, his thumb is rubbing circles on my skin. And with every step I take, it gets lower and lower, until when we walk inside and stop, his finger touches the top of my ass.

I step away from him, breaking the connection. He's not having it, though. He steps up to me, his smile cocked, and in challenge, he offers me his arm instead. He dares me to object with his eyes. I hate this man.

Now on his arm, he introduces me to everyone. I'm his arm candy for the night. Not once does he introduce me as his lawyer or reference the firm I work for. To anyone looking, they must think I'm the younger woman he's sleeping with and worse, by his age, power, and business connections, must assume I'm using him. It's degrading.

And he is one hundred percent playing it off.

"And who is this divine creature?" I hear from behind me. Yet again, I am introduced to a middle-aged man I have no interest in speaking to.

We make a few turns around the room. On the next pass, Felix has an objective. We are headed toward a crowd forming around a man.

"Come on." He leads me with him, hand on my exposed skin.

The crowd in front of me parts, and I see everyone is talking to the attorney general of New York. Rumor has it, he's going to be nominated by the president to be the attorney general of the United States. He sure did come a long way.

The attorney general is a local hero where I grew up. But back then, he was the district attorney. Young and eager to make more of himself, and *he sure did.* As I walk up to him, I don't expect him to recognize me. But he smiles warmly at me when Felix and I stand in front of him. I'm not, however, surprised when he scowls at Felix.

Despite Felix's wealth and power, Attorney General Fitzpatrick has made a name for himself by trying to clean the streets of crime, especially drugs.

Like me, I'm sure he has no desire to associate with men like Bernard, despite the campaign contribution I have no doubt he has probably made over the years.

"Ms. Matthews, it's been too long." He extends his hand.

"Sir, it has."

"How is your father?"

"He's good." I decide to lie. Dad wouldn't want him to know. They used to work together in our small town. That was before, but the fact he still remembers Dad warms my heart.

"That is so wonderful to hear. Please send him my best."

"I will, sir."

"Felix," Attorney General Fitzpatrick says.

"Jack," Felix says, and I'm shocked that he refers to the attorney general by his first name. I'm not the only one shocked—Jack obviously is as well.

I wonder if it is meant as a taunt. Fitzpatrick's lips form a thin line before he shakes his head and steps to the side to greet someone else.

When it's only the two of us, Felix looks at me. "I didn't know you knew him."

"I didn't know you did," I fire back.

He wants to ask more, I can tell by the way he narrows his eyes, but then another man is standing before us. Yet again, I've gone back to being eye candy. When Felix is deep in conversation, I discreetly take a step back until the distance between us grows far enough that I can make my escape. I'm almost by the wall when I feel a presence behind me, then I hear him.

"You shouldn't be here with him," his gravelly voice whispers in my ear.

"Don't tell me who I can be with," I snap back. I am sick of men telling me what to do.

"You forget yourself. But more importantly, you forget who owns you."

"No one owns me."

"Mr. Williams would have a difference of opinion."

"He's the one who sent me here with Felix. And it doesn't matter. I thought you were done with . . . us."

"Is that what this is? You upset because I haven't called?"

"Shut up," I hiss.

"Ohh. That's what has this kitten so angry."

"I'm done with this conversation, and don't you ever call me a pet name."

"Just look at me, Skye. Admit it to yourself. It will be easier. We're inevitable. You want me. I sure as hell want you. Give in. I'll make it worth your while."

He's goading me. I know he is. The fucking asshole. But it's working. I want to touch him. No, I need to.

So instead, I step away and put distance between us. I start to make my way toward Felix, but I'm not ready to deal with his leering, so I head in the opposite direction from both men.

To the bar.

A server with a glass of champagne walks past me at exactly the right time, and I politely accept the bubbly drink. From where I'm standing, I see Tobias. I chose a bad location because now he's front and center, and I have no choice but to watch him.

Even if there was somewhere else to look, I can't make myself turn away. Not even when a beautiful tall and lithe blonde makes her way over to him. My hand tightens on my glass. I can't see his face clearly from where I am, but I don't need to see it to know exactly what's happening.

She's moving close. Whispering in his ear. Her hand is on his arm. She moves again, and now I see his face. I see his eyes. It's too far away to make out his feelings, but he must like the attention because she becomes more brazen as the seconds go on.

It feels like an eternity as I watch, frozen in time. I need to look away before he sees me.

But I'm too late.

His dark gaze meets mine. I'm off. The idea of him seeing my feelings is too much. I head across the room, find Felix, and tell him I'm going to the restroom. Exiting the ballroom, I don't make it far before I feel someone's hands bracket my arms and pull me from behind.

Before I can speak or even scream, I'm thrust into a dark closet. My heart hammers, transporting me into my mind. Just as I'm about to go back there—just as I'm about to panic—I smell his scent. His hands come next, encompassing both sides of my face. He's in front of me, around me, all over me. His breath fans my forehead, and his voice follows like a weighted blanket, soothing and warm.

"Only for you."

CHAPTER TWENTY-EIGHT

Tobias

A T MY WORDS, THE TENSION IN SKYE'S BODY LOOSENS. Neither of us likes the enclosed space, but I can tell that with me here, she feels safe.

I'm not surprised that when she's around, I'm not bothered, either. There is something between us, and as much as my emotions regarding Skye Matthews have ping-ponged over the past month, one thing is certain: I want her.

The need to seal her mouth with mine is all I think about. It consumes me. What will she taste like? Minty? Or maybe like strawberries? When she turns ever so slightly, my lips graze hers. Neither of my guesses were correct. She tastes like redemption.

I want to grab her and pull her into me, but I don't. Not yet. I can wait. I won't be greedy. I won't take something not freely offered.

In the bathroom on the plane, it was clear she wanted me, but now I need her to make the first move.

She tilts her body closer, her lips touching mine, and that's enough invitation. I wrap my arms around her and pull her close until our bodies touch. The tiny space between us is gone. We are fused like magnets. A groan escapes my lips at how small she feels next to me.

"We shouldn't."

Her words tickle my lips.

"Wrong answer," I growl.

"Yes," she whispers, and I finally take what I want.

"Right answer." Our lips fuse.

Her lips are pliable under mine, opening of their own accord. My tongue swipes against hers, and she purrs in my arms.

Tongues tangling.

Hands roaming.

It's hungry.

Desperate.

She's kissing me as if she will never kiss me again. Which is not okay, so I kiss her harder. Implore with my mouth that this is happening. We are happening. I devour her until her small hands rest on my chest, and I move to pull away, resting my head on her forehead. I let her catch her breath.

"We shouldn't have done that."

"Do I need to kiss you again to show you why we did?"

"Maybe?"

"Maybe isn't a yes. I want your yes."

"You didn't get one the last time . . ." she trails off.

I level her with my stare. "Yes. I did."

"I don't think—" Her words are interrupted by a scuffle somewhere near the door. The noise is loud and jarring against the quiet and isolation in the closet. Skye's body tenses beside me. I can feel the rigid edges of her spine where I hold her. I pull my lips away.

"What's going on?"

"I don't know, but I am going to find out."

"Do you think it's safe?"

I would laugh, but something tells me that wouldn't be the

appropriate way to respond to her. Instead, I lean down and place a kiss on her forehead.

"I'll be okay. You don't have to worry about me. Now, stay put and be quiet. I'll be back."

"Okay."

"Wait for me."

"Okay." Skye draws in a deep breath as I crack the door open before leaving.

She probably doesn't want to stay in the closet, and I probably shouldn't leave her in there, but I'm not sure what's happening out there, and she wouldn't want to be seen with me if there is a big commotion going on. The thought annoys me.

I understand she is here in a professional manner, and sneaking out of a closet with your client while out with another one won't bode well for her career, let alone her reputation.

Luckily, there is no one outside the door, but I hear loud voices, and one sounds like Felix. I move toward the noise, careful not to be seen. The commotion is going on in the room adjacent to the back entrance. The exit sign brightly illuminates the space.

"You need to escort Mr. Bernard out of here," the attorney general says to a few members of the security team.

"I have a ticket," Felix retorts.

"I'm not sure how you managed that—"

"I happen to be a well-respected man in this community," Felix cuts him off.

"Enough. I cannot have men like you seen in my presence. Leave." The anger in the attorney general's voice is palpable.

"Men like me? Men who donated to your campaign?"

"I don't want your dirty money," Attorney General Fitzpatrick hisses.

"That's not what you said when I was handing over a check during your last election. My 'legitimate money'"—he air quotes—"was good enough for you then."

"Escort him out." He turns away from Bernard.

I know that Felix brought Skye here, so I also know he will go looking for her.

Turning back around, I make my way back to the closet as quietly as possible, but as I swing the door open, I'm met with nothing.

Skye is gone.

CHAPTER TWENTY-NINE

Skye

THE INTENSITY OF THE KISS SHAKES ME TO THE CORE. IT FELT like my body was moving of its own accord. As if I was hovering from above, watching myself get lost in Tobias but had no way to stop it.

The moment his lips touched mine, I was gone.

I shake my head to rid myself of the memory, but when I do, I remember where I am. Alone. In a dark closet.

My breathing grows frantic and choppy. I can't be here. The familiar feeling of panic and claustrophobia weaves its way through my blood and phantom pain.

He told me to stay, but I can't. I need to leave. The memories pound in my brain. My stomach muscles tighten, and a chill runs over my body. It's like a knife is stabbing me . . . or a bullet is lodged in my gut. My right hand brackets my left, thumb rubbing.

It's okay. You aren't there.

You aren't hurt.

In the darkness, I reach for the knob, and like Tobias only a few seconds ago, I crack the door and make sure I don't see anyone. The coast is clear. No one is around. Stepping into the hall, I take a few steps, and then I spot the door to the ladies' room. That's where I'll go.

It's not the need to use it that has me opening the door. It's the need to calm myself. Once inside, I walk straight to the vanity and look at myself in the mirror. I swear my lips are swollen. Thoroughly kissed.

Yep, that's me.

What the hell did I do? How can I have kissed Tobias?

Because you want him.

I shake my head, nope. Don't think those thoughts. It happened once but can never happen again. He's my client. But also, and more importantly, it doesn't matter that he's going legit. He's a bad man. He's the villain. He's the person you warn your kids about. There is no happily ever after with a man like that. Nope. There is a trail of blood, and that's all.

No matter how hard I try, I can't calm my racing heart. I shouldn't have done that. Regret sits heavy on my chest. Reaching my hand out, I turn the water on, rinse my hands, and then wet my lips.

As if water will rinse away my sin.

Nothing will. I can't do it again.

Time passes as I stand in front of the mirror, hating my reflection. Finally, when my lips are back to normal, I head out. I don't make it two steps before I see Felix's man looking for me.

I am led to the car. The temperature has dropped. The one warm night has turned chilly. I wrap my arms around my chest, hoping to cocoon the warmth of my body. It doesn't help.

The familiar car is parked close by. I'm walked to it, and then the security reaches his hand out and opens the door. Felix is already waiting for me, and I shiver at the thought that it's not the cold making me shiver. It's the end of the night and what he expects of me. He won't get anything. And not merely because I can still feel Tobias's lips on mine.

I scoot into the seat, careful to keep the widest distance I can between us. I notice the center divider is up between the seats. I shut the door, and as we pull away, Felix doesn't speak. The tension in the air is so thick I can taste it, and it has my back going ramrod straight, ready for anything.

It doesn't feel like we are moving. The car crawls forward, and every bump and every inch we take, every mile we make . . . I wait for him to strike.

My stomach is in knots. My hands rest on my thighs, balled in the excess material of my dress. I'm wound so tight emotionally, but I fear I might snap if he says something. Even worse, I'm afraid of what those words would be.

I finally break the silence.

"Everything okay?" I ask.

"It will be." That's not an answer. It's cryptic. I don't know what happened, and I don't know what's wrong, and if this were Tobias, I might press. But I really don't want to talk to Felix. I turn to look out the window.

"It's a beautiful night," I say more to myself than to him.

"Enjoy it while it lasts." More cryptic words. I hate cryptic words because, again, his comment makes no sense and has set me on edge.

"What does that even mean?" I ask, my voice barely a whisper.

"You'll see soon enough. You all will see soon fucking enough." It sounds like a threat.

Harboring a glance at him, I see that his dark eyes seem to twinkle with the moonlight. They make him look like the villain he is.

If I had more fight in me, I would ask what he means. But to be honest, he's in such a bad mood I don't want to know. I just want out of this car unscathed.

A few minutes later, I get what I want. The car pulls to a halt, and from the window, I can see the familiar façade of my building. As soon as the car stops, I don't wait for anyone to open the door, and I don't wait for him to say anything. I just mutter good-bye under my breath and step out, closing the door behind me and rushing to the door to my building. A part of me expects him to follow, but I am happily rewarded with nothing. I grab my keys from my bag as I walk by the doorman. By the time I'm up the stairs and at my apartment door, my breathing is ragged. As I swing it open and then close it behind me, I let out a large giant breath. Thank God, this night is over. I don't even bother going to the bathroom. I don't bother taking off my dress. Nope. I do none of those things. Instead, I fling myself on my bed and close my eyes.

I'm not sure how much time goes by, but when my eyes open, they feel glued together. My lips are dry. My mouth is chalky. Lifting my hand, I rub the sleep from my eyes. That's when I realize I fell asleep with my dress on. I didn't even wash off my makeup.

Throwing my leg over the side of the bed, I stand. At least I took off my shoes. My bare feet hit the wood floor, and I make my way to the bathroom. On my walk, I unzip my dress and step out of it. Then I head into the bathroom, turn on the sink, and splash water over my face. I'm not sure what time it is, probably the middle of the night. I look like I got hit with a bat.

There is no way I'll be up to go to the office. I duck my head and put my mouth under the faucet and drink. I feel like a sorority girl after a frat party. Once I'm done, I head back into my room, slip under the covers, and grab my phone. Before I fall asleep, I shoot one text.

Me: Calling in sick.

Then I turn my phone off and fall asleep.

A pounding on the door wakes me.

What the hell is going on?

Bang.

Bang.

Again, the sound.

It feels loud enough to shake the whole apartment, probably even loud enough to wake the neighbors. My hand lifts and scrubs at my eyes.

"Who the hell is banging this early in the morning?" I mumble to myself before standing from the bed and grabbing my robe. Tying the sash to keep it from gaping, I head to the door. I regret the decision to get out of bed the moment I look through the peephole. There, standing behind the door, is the imposing body of Tobias.

Why the hell is he here?

Then it comes back to me.

A late-night text message, one where I told him I was going to take the day off.

"Skye, open the door," his voice commands through the thick wood of the door. My neighbor will probably call the police if he doesn't stop shouting at me.

Maybe I should do what he asks before there is a problem. I don't, though. Nor do I say anything. Maybe if I'm quiet, he won't know I'm home.

As if he can hear my thoughts, he speaks. "Skye, I know you're in there. I can see your shadow through the door."

I huff as I turn the lock and swing open the door. Tobias stands tall and commanding right outside the doorframe.

"What do you want?"

"Good morning to you, too."

I cross my arms over my chest. I'm in a robe in my foyer, and he's looking at me like a starving man, and I'm dinner.

My legs wobble beneath me, but I somehow manage to keep my face neutral. At least, I think I do. For all I know, he can see through all my walls. I hope not, or he will know that despite my straight face, I'm a mess.

It takes everything inside me not to stare at his lips. Not to look at the way his mouth moves when he talks. I stare into his eyes, but that's not much better. What I see inside them makes butterflies explode in my stomach. Wings flutter. Nervous energy courses through me, but I don't break my eye contact.

"Why are you here?" I say through clenched teeth, annoyed that this man has this big effect on me.

Leave before I do something stupid.

"Let's go."

"I'm not going anywhere with you."

"Get dressed. We have stuff to go over." His voice is no longer flirty. It's commanding, and I know I don't have a choice.

Without another word, I turn, leaving him on my doorstep.

Making quick work of getting dressed, I throw on a dress, heels, and then head to the bathroom to straighten up. Five minutes don't pass before I'm as ready as I'll ever be.

"That didn't take long," Tobias says, now standing in my foyer.

"Who said you can come into my apartment?" At my words, or maybe my attitude, he grins. He's having fun with this. I am not. All I can think about is the damn kiss and all the reasons I can never kiss him again. Yet my damn brain refuses to stop replaying it.

It's like a movie on repeat you can't turn off.

"I didn't think you'd want me waiting out in the hallway so your neighbors could see me."

"So instead, you wait in my foyer with the door open, and they can still see you."

He does something I don't expect. He laughs.

This man who doesn't smile or laugh with his closest friends has managed to do both for me. A strange feeling of electricity courses through my body. It feels like pins and needles, and my heart batters my breastbone at the thought.

I can't feel this way. It's not good. I can't think of a reason he does these things in front of me and not in front of anyone else. If I do, I might want to kiss him again. Hell, I might want to do more.

A round two in the bathroom, but this time, I won't let him leave.

Nope.

Neither can happen. First off, he's my client, and second—and more importantly—he's a distraction. I can't afford any distractions right now.

It's bad enough that I screwed up my big opportunity last night with Mr. Bernard.

Today is a new day, and I will not make the same mistake twice.

CHAPTER THIRTY

Tobias

S HE'S CUTE WHEN SHE TRIES TO ACT MAD AT ME, BUT I SEE right through her. She's scolding herself for being affected by me. Well, take a number. So am I. But I'm done caring about that shit. Now that I had a taste of Skye Matthews, I need another.

"Let's go. The car is waiting." I turn my back on her and walk toward the stairs.

Something tells me she never takes the elevator in this building. It has disaster written all over it. There is no way this elevator isn't stopping midway between floors and then crashing to the ground level.

Behind me, I can hear her shoes hitting the carpet. A part of me expects her to make a reference to last night.

She doesn't, though. No words are uttered as we walk down the stairs, and then once in the car, she's silent as well.

"Today, we need to go over the final papers on the Miami deal."

"Fine."

Her one-word answer pisses me off. I'd rather she scream that it was a mistake than stay silent.

Maybe it was a mistake, but it's one I plan to do again. Now she needs to get with the program. A part of me, the nice part, thinks I need to tell her the rest of my story. Another part doesn't want to.

"You know, I could have looked at the papers at home. You didn't have to drag me into your office to do this."

"Are you going to have this attitude all day?"

"Yep."

"Good to know."

She shrugs. "You asked."

"I did."

"I'm just tired."

"Tired?" I ask. She left earlier than me. "Why are you so tired?"

"I went to bed late." She's not looking at me. She's staring at the window.

"Why didn't you sleep?"

"I was busy." She turns to look at me. Her head is tilted down, and she has an angry scowl on her face. It seems she is daring me to press, and knowing her, she is.

"Doing what?" This time when I speak, my voice is rough. I want to know what the fuck she was doing with Bernard that made her so damn tired today.

"It's not your business." Just as I'm about to demand she answer, the car rolls to a stop in my garage, and Skye is throwing the door open and jumping out of the car.

This only pisses me off more. If I find out she did anything with Bernard, I'll kill him. I was always planning on killing him, but this will be different. This will be slow.

Who am I kidding? It was always going to be torture.

Stepping out of the car, I also head up to my office. Skye has a head start, but I'm quickly on pace. We are almost to the second

floor when I catch up with her. If she thinks I'm letting this attitude go on another minute, she's wrong. I step past her and use
my frame to block her.

"Not so fast."

Skye takes a step to the left to maneuver out of my path, but
I cut her off. She moves to the right, and again, no go.

"Not happening."

"Move out of the way."

"No." I step in. This time, she steps back. The stairs might be
open, but there is still a railing. A railing she is now pushed up
against with my arms bracketing her in place.

"What are you doing?"

"What I should have done the moment I saw you."

I move in a step until my body presses against her. The space
between us is almost gone.

"We can't." She breathes out.

"We can," I respond.

"I'm your lawyer."

Flimsy answer. "That can be fixed."

"So, you drag me around for a month, and now you want to
fuck me, so you fire me? That's a sexual harassment lawsuit in
the making."

"See, there I go doing something illegal. That's why I need
you with me all the time."

"Tobias . . ." she trails off as I move my hand and run my finger over her jaw until it rests on the hollow of her neck. Her eyes
are wide, her pupils dilated. Despite what she says, desire is clear
on her face. I close the distance, lowering my head, and I'm about
to kiss her when Gideon's voice rings through the air.

"T—"

I pull back and look toward him as he sprints across the room
to the stairwell where we are.

"What's going on?" I can tell right away something is wrong.

"Problem with the shipment." While, technically, Gideon is taking over, the transition isn't final. I need to go.

Turning back to Skye, I say, "We'll finish this later." I don't wait for her to respond and instead head toward Gideon to sort out whatever the fuck happened.

My temper flares to an inferno. "Talk."

"It never made it to Lorenzo."

"What the fuck!"

Someone will die for this. Now the question is who. The shipment came in from Holland, five thousand pounds of MDMA, packaged as pencils.

"It landed, got in the trucks, but before Lorenzo received it, it was lifted."

"I want to know what happened, now!" My voice bellows through the space. "Who was behind this attack?"

It seems targeted, happening before I transition out. This feels personal, and I can think of only one person who would benefit from me losing that many pills.

Felix.

This is fucking war.

I'm done waiting for confirmation of my father's death. Regardless of that, Felix needs to disappear, and I'm going to make that happen. It's time to put this to rest already. Time to end the war that started twenty years ago.

There is one more thing I need to do. I need to talk to Skye. She needs to know everything, and it's time I tell her. First, I need to talk to my boys.

An hour later, I'm at Lorenzo's, but I'm not alone. Gideon is with me. The next two people who show up are Cyrus Reed and Jaxson Price.

Jaxson Price is a renowned billionaire, but most don't know

he is also a hacker. And not just any hacker, but the best in the country. This man can bring down a country for fun and make it look so easy you'd think he was shopping online.

"Lorenzo said your shipment was hijacked," Jaxson says.

War was here, and I was happy to have this man by my side. I step forward.

"It was, and I need to know how."

I take great precautions to make sure this never happens, which means this is somehow tied to Emil.

"What the fuck happened?" Lorenzo steps forward to shake my hand. Regardless of the gesture, I can tell he is pissed by the way his nostrils flare.

"I'm going to find out," I answer.

His lips thin with anger. "Tobias—"

"Lorenzo, you will have your merchandise."

If I were anyone else, there would already be blood on the floor. He's a kick the crap out of you first, ask questions later type of guy. Lorenzo is hotheaded on a good day, but the reason he isn't now is because he trusts me. Despite my efforts to keep my distance and walls up, this man is my friend and would die for me. Plus, he knows I will get him the pills he needs. No matter what. No matter the consequences.

Gideon, however, is a different story. Whether Lorenzo can trust Gideon or not is a different question.

"This will be handled," Gideon responds. Stepping forward, back straight, he exudes power, and it's the right move. Lorenzo needs to see this side of him.

"Guess you haven't retired yet," Lorenzo jokes, back to his normal self. That's the crazy thing about Lorenzo. He can go from serial killer to boy next door at the drop of a hat.

"I was so damn close."

That's the truth. I knew I wouldn't hand over the reins until the Felix business was over, but still, I'm not happy that this happened. However, this incident speeds up the final step.

"How do we handle this?" Lorenzo's right-hand man, Roberto, asks.

"We strike and hit hard," I say before Lorenzo cuts in, voice stern and forceful.

"We gut the little bitch."

Given the opportunity, that's exactly what he would do, but as hungry as I am for blood, we need more intel before we strike.

We need to figure out where it was hit, and for that, I turn to Jaxson.

"What do you need from us?" I ask him.

"I need to know everything about the shipment. What is your objective here, other than to"—he looks at Lorenzo—"gut the little bitch."

"I want my drugs back." I have enough money and pills to get Lorenzo his shipment on time, but it will set me back, so I prefer to recover the original one.

Jaxson nods at my request. "Let's work backward. Find the interception point. I can track the shipment from there, and hopefully, we are in time to make sure they aren't distributed again from your opponent's side. Sound like a good plan?"

"Yes."

"Okay. Good. Tell me the flight number and send me the tracker for the truck you were using for transport, and I'll figure out who took it."

"This shipment was five thousand pounds of ecstasy, packaged as pencils. It made it to the trucks."

"I'm going to hack the airport surveillance as well, then. Maybe the leak originated there."

"That makes sense."

"Who knew about the shipment?" Jaxson's question has me looking around the room and then back at him.

I clench my teeth. "Other than Gideon and me, no one on our end. No one knows who I get the pills from." All my hard work to keep things separate, not let anyone in, and for what? Shit got taken anyway.

"That means it's probably your contact at the airport or even from the Holland side."

What Jaxson says makes sense, and it pisses me the fuck off. I like Emil and have done business with him and his father before him for years. I would hate to kill the motherfucker.

"And we think the original call for the attack came from Felix?"

"Who else?"

Jaxson shrugs. Lorenzo shakes his head. Gideon is the one to speak. "There is no one else. It's Felix."

He's right. This is an attack on me, and I don't have many other enemies. Sure, it could be an up-and-coming rival, but Felix fits better. Felix has been gunning for my uncle's business—and my father's for years before that. It doesn't matter that I'm on my way out. The man wants me gone.

"Then we don't wait for Jaxson's intel before we strike." Pivoting to talk to Jaxson, I say, "You send all the intel to Gideon. Once you find Lorenzo's drugs, Gideon will get a team together to intercept."

"I'm going to take care of that." Lorenzo has an evil smile on his face. "You worry about Felix. I want to find the men who thought they could hijack a truck en route to me."

Poor fucks won't know what hit them. I'm more than prepared to deal with both the truck and Felix, but I'm happy to only have to concentrate on one matter.

This truce has gone on long enough. Felix made a mistake thinking Gideon was already in charge, and even if he was, I'd still go to war for him.

"If that's all, I have my work cut out for me."

"Yep, let me know where the fuckers are." Lorenzo claps Jax on the back before Jax turns to me and nods, and then he's striding out the door.

"I'll talk to you soon," I say to Lorenzo before Gideon and I are heading out the door as well. When we are finally back in the car, Gideon lets out a breath.

"That was fun. I wouldn't want to be the poor schmuck who decided to rob from him."

I'm quiet for a second and then face him. He looks how I feel, fucking exhausted and sick of this shit. Dark circles edge his eyes, his hair is unruly, and his jaw is stiff enough to cut glass. "This is going to get ugly."

"It was bound to happen. We both knew Felix might go after the business."

"We did."

"Thanks for not—"

"Stop. You're like my fucking brother, man. I don't care if I'm one step out the motherfucking door or that door is long shut . . . you need me, I'm there. I know you can handle this alone, but this wasn't an attack on you. It was on me."

At this, Gideon goes quiet.

It's true. This has nothing to do with him. It's all me. And I'll take care of it.

CHAPTER THIRTY-ONE

Skye

I HAVE NEVER SEEN TOBIAS ACT THE WAY HE JUST DID. MY HEAD is still spinning.

I'm left standing on the stairs when he walked away. I'm not even sure what I'm supposed to do.

I take the stairs leading up and then the stairs leading down. Just as I'm about to make a decision, the decision is made for me.

One of his men is walking toward me.

I've never met the guy, but he looks like he's part of his security team. Dressed in all black, an earpiece visible, and I bet a gun is under his suit jacket. He's one scary dude, though. I wouldn't want to be his enemy.

"Mr. Kosta extends his apologies, but something came up. He won't be needing you today. He also mentioned he's not sure when he will in the near future, and he will be in contact with you."

The answer is cold and formal, and I'm not sure what it means.

The man flipped a switch. He went from wanting to kiss me to leaving me and telling his messenger boy his excuse for leaving me in a damn stairwell.

My cheeks feel warm as I head back down the staircase. Warm isn't the right word to describe it. My cheeks feel like someone took a flamethrower to them.

I've been rejected, and I'm walking with my tail tucked between my legs as I sneak out.

Nope.

This isn't me.

I'm not going to be embarrassed at my dismissal. Pulling my back muscles straight, I walk with my head high until I hit the street. Then I lift my hand and hail a cab. Once inside, I let my shoulders slump. As much as I don't want to admit it, I wanted him to kiss me again, and now I'm berating myself over the fact.

Some time away will hopefully rid me of this crap.

Instead of going home, I go to my office. I plan on calling Felix and seeing about spending some time with him. I can do it under the guise of work, but if I can get into his apartment . . .

I just need a reason, and I'm sure if I go through his caseload, I'll find something.

The office is quiet when I arrive but louder when I get to Mr. Williams's office.

"I have to advise you not to do this." I hear him say, but I don't know what he's talking about or with whom. I make my presence known, and he signals for me to take a seat in the chair in front of his desk.

"Very well, Felix. I'll send her over." Mr. Williams hangs up the phone and raises his chin to look at me. "Bernard wants you in his office. There are papers for a transfer of property he wants you to look over, and he figures it'd be better for you to do it at his office, in case you find something that might be useful to him."

"No problem. What file?"

"He has it. Just go to his office, and he will set you up."

"No problem. Now?"

"Yes."

I stand from my chair and move to leave the room. Once back

in the hallway, I decide there is no point in heading to my office. All my files are on my laptop at home if I need to work later.

It's only a few blocks, so I walk to Felix's office building.

His "office" houses his legitimate business. He's a real estate developer—shopping malls, to be exact.

When I arrive, I notice it's a lot like my office building, a typical high-rise with security. It appears to be an upstanding office building from the outside, but I know better than that. Felix Bernard is not a good man. And now that I'm where I need to be, I'm hoping to get some sort of hint of where he might have evidence of his crimes against my family. I won't turn him in, but if a file accidentally arrives at a local detective's desk, I won't be disappointed.

"How can I help you?" the security man says as I approach the desk.

"I'm here for a meeting with Mr. Bernard. Skye Matthews."

He looks down at his desk, picks up the phone, and dials. I can hear him say my name and then nod. "You can go up to the tenth floor. The direct elevator is over there."

Shit.

I take a deep breath and head toward the elevator bank. It's no big deal.

Recently, since I've been working with Tobias, my hatred of elevators has escalated. It's like all my deep buried feelings from my parents' death are back and rearing their ugly heads.

I have no idea why it escalated. It didn't start until I met him, but now, it's almost like I can still smell death in the air.

Shaking off the feeling, I step into the elevator and practice the breathing exercise I was taught as a child. Inhale deeply and then exhale slowly.

The ride is much faster than I expect, and before long, I'm stepping off and being greeted.

"Ms. Matthews, Mr. Bernard wants you to go right in," a pretty woman behind a large Lucite desk says.

The space is modern, and I realize this is the first time I have ever been here. I'm not surprised by the décor. Everything is glass and Lucite. Very sparse, unfeeling, and modern. Perfect.

I'm almost afraid to touch the door, which again, is all glass. Who knows what this man will do if I leave a fingerprint? I do it anyway, and as soon as I do, my stomach flutters from nerves.

The last time I saw Felix, he was cold, but he made no secret that he wanted me. I'm not sure what this is. Am I here for a file? Or am I here for something more?

When he looks up from his desk, I let out a sigh of relief. If he wants me, he's not thinking about that now. He is hyperfocused on something else, and whatever it is, it's stressing him out.

"Skye. I need you to go through these files." He's lifting up a manila envelope for me to take.

"Oh, okay," I say as I remove the folder from his hand. "What am I looking for?"

"Anything that can help me." Something about his words sounds evil.

I narrow my eyes. "What do you mean, *help me*?"

"I want to develop on this land, but the land is protected. Find me a loophole."

Looking down at the folder and back at him, I nod. "If there is something, I'll find it."

"I want you to find me a loophole, even if there isn't one, and make sure it happens."

My eyes go wide at his words. I know how corrupt he is, but this? I didn't realize his corruption spread even into his "legitimate business." Isn't the point of a legitimate business to be clean? He's already implying he will break the rules.

"I'll see what I can do."

Then I'm being shown to a spare office to work.

CHAPTER THIRTY-TWO

Tobias

TWO DAYS.

That's how long it takes Jaxson Price to find the location of the stolen shipment. Actually, it only took him two hours. The rest of the time is what it took us to come up with a foolproof plan to rid the assholes who stole from me. That's why I'm glad Jaxson is on my side of the war.

Lorenzo said he wanted to handle it, but that shit didn't fly for me.

They didn't steal from him. This isn't an attack on him. This is my war.

My men are all with me. We are rolling in twenty men deep, ready to show these fools exactly why you don't fuck with me.

The ride goes by in a flash, adrenaline running through my blood. When the cars roll to a halt, we are up half a block, parking in front of a different warehouse. We fall out, fanning in four directions to cover the whole building. Gideon moves in, attaching a bomb to the door, and moves back before it blows. One of his specialties. He might come across as pretty laid-back, but he's deviant. He loves blowing shit up.

We all have our gear on. Then we are running into the building, guns raised. Shoot first. Ask questions later. But keep one alive.

My men know I want to leave someone alive.

By the time we stop shooting, no one stands but my team. Gideon, however, has someone by the throat.

"This one is not dead."

"Good. Take him with us."

"Back to the building?" Gideon drops the man to the ground and kicks him in the stomach before grabbing the zip tie in his back pocket and securing our new captive's hands.

"Yep."

"Found the stash," I hear Chaz, one of my security guards, say.

"Grab it. Fast."

My men pack up the drugs, and I head back to the car. We leave the bodies for the authorities to find. They won't find anything that will tie it to us.

Forty minutes later, the scumbag is tied up in a chair in my warehouse by the dock. I wouldn't bring him back to the city because I don't need that shit where I live. He's not talking yet. *Yet* being the operative word. He will soon.

Gideon is already starting. I roll up my sleeves, grab a knife, and make my way over.

"Who do you work for?" I ask, not even looking at him, bored of this shit already.

But I need confirmation before I blow Felix out of the water. So far, there has been no connection to him. My men scoured the warehouse where they found my drugs but found no evidence to pin him to the theft. Not that I thought there would be.

Hence my desire to keep one alive.

"Ahh, you're playing hard to get?" I place the blade over his cheek, trailing it down to his jaw.

The pressure isn't hard, but it's enough. A crimson line follows in my wake.

"We can do this the easy way or the hard way. You can choose."

"What's the point? You're going to kill me anyway," he spits.

"This is true. But what happens between now and then will be worlds of difference. It's really up to you. I'm good either way." I shrug.

He still doesn't speak, so I shrug again.

"I'll take it that's your answer." I turn to Gideon. "Get the tequila?"

"Salt?"

"Yep."

"A lime as well." He laughs, knowing full well what I'm about to do. I nod at his comment. "Seems like a good time for a drink."

Before long, Gideon is stepping up, tequila in his hand. As soon as he's standing beside me, I take the knife and draw a deep slash on the exposed skin of our captive's chest.

The man in the chair is biting his cheeks to stop himself from screaming, but Gideon pours booze over the wound, and that's all it takes. The man can no longer refrain. The scream echoes through the air, fueling my sadistic need to hurt him. I cut again. Gideon pours. We continue for ten minutes. He still doesn't budge.

Got to hand it to him, he's tougher than I thought. I'm not sure why he keeps quiet. Felix won't have his back.

"You don't need to stay quiet for him. It won't help you, and no one is coming to rescue you."

For a second, I think I see something pass over his face, but when he doesn't open his mouth, I turn to Gideon. "Remove his pants."

That makes the man's eyes go wide.

"Ready to talk?" I smirk.

"I don't know anything," he mutters.

"That might be true, but maybe you saw something." I lift my knife in show as I step closer to him.

"A rich guy. Mid-fifties. Nice suit."

Leaning over, I trail the blade up his thigh. My intentions for where it will strike next clear. "Go on."

"A Bentley."

I look at Gideon, who knows the confirmation we need. It's Felix.

"Kill him. Make it fast."

The man doesn't fight. He knows he's going to die and is ready. But at least it will be fast. The gun goes off within seconds, and his head slumps forward.

"Clean up the mess," I say to Chaz. "Let's go."

With that done, we go about getting Felix.

CHAPTER THIRTY-THREE

Skye

IT'S BEEN FOUR DAYS. EACH DAY, I EXPECT TOBIAS TO SEND ME a message, yet each day, there is nothing. I continue to scour every law to figure out a legal loophole to get the easement for the property in Upstate New York lifted.

They are claiming the land should be protected for wildlife, and as far as I can see, the easement will pass. Which means the land won't be able to be developed.

Something tells me there's nothing I can do to make Felix not do something horrid that will make me cringe.

But I really have no choice but to tell him. A part of me wonders if this happens more than I care to know. *Is this how he amassed his fortune?*

Maybe this is important. I mentally note to look into all his business dealings in Reddington. I know he developed the mall there. Maybe I haven't been looking in the right place. Maybe this is about the land. I'll need to look into everything that happened that day.

Not now, though. The one good thing about all of this is I

have access to his real estate dealings, and although there are not going to be any giant red flags, I'm sure if I find the purchase information on his properties, I can work backward.

At least, that's my hope.

Today, however, is not that day. I'll need to go back to Reddington to cross-reference.

Before heading to speak to Felix, I open the filing cabinet. Most of the business dealings are on the computer, but I noticed that his earlier files are also in the cabinets.

I thumb my way through them, looking for anything that stands out. I hit the jackpot when I see a file called Cypress Bay. That's one of the strip malls developed in my hometown.

Grabbing the file, I throw it in my bag, close my computer, and place it in as well. I take the file and papers I printed for the current project, and then I'm off down the hall, ready to talk to Felix. Outside the cracked door, I stop. Hearing voices, I'm not sure whether I should go in.

Felix's voice booms through the tiny space left open, and I know I should go. Instead, I listen.

"I don't care what you say!" he screams before the room goes quiet. Someone must stop him from speaking, but I don't hear the same voice from before.

"No! I don't give a shit!"

Silence again.

He must be on the phone. Whoever he's speaking to is probably trying to calm him down.

But who?

"Listen to me, you fuck. You wouldn't be where you are today without me." I hear the slam of the phone.

I take a step back. This is not the time. He sounds pissed.

"I don't care what that fucker says. He's a cocky, arrogant ass, and he can't control me."

"What do you want to do, boss?"

"I want to kill the bastard."

"Which one?"

Felix laughs. It sounds deranged.

"Both. But let's start with Kosta. He thinks he can hit my warehouse. He wants a war, and I'll give him a war."

"But—"

"No buts. I don't want to answer to anyone. Hit the building. Kill everyone."

My heart pounds in my chest. He's going to kill Tobias. I have to do something. Tobias needs to know. He needs to prepare. A wave of nausea hits me. What if I don't get to him in time? What if I'm too late?

Slowly, I move away from the door, being very careful not to signal I'm here. I make it look like I'm heading toward his office, not retreating.

When I'm a safe distance away, I turn and walk in the opposite direction, toward my office so that I can head to reception without anyone being tipped off.

Once I'm at reception, I turn to the pretty receptionist. "I have an appointment I have to go to." I make sure to give an embarrassed smile, one that implies I'm probably going to a doctor or something. "If you happen to see Mr. Bernard, will you tell him I'll call him with an update on his file?"

"Of course, Ms. Matthews."

"Thank you." I smile, trying desperately not to show any emotions that give my real feelings away.

With my spine straight, I walk toward the elevator, my heels clicking against the marble with every step I take. It sounds like war drums in my ear, making my heart pound to the rhythm. Once I'm inside the elevator and the door shuts, a puff of oxygen escapes my mouth.

The coast isn't clear yet, so I stand perfectly still until I'm away from the watchful eyes of the camera in the corner. But once it's stopping and I'm jetting out of the building, I pull out my phone.

I dial Tobias, praying he answers. When he doesn't, I swear my heart might explode from fear.

I try again, but nothing.

This is the moment I wish I had his sidekick's number. Gideon. But I don't. And I can't even leave a message because his phone could be tapped. I don't know what to do. A feeling I haven't had in a long time clings to my skin.

Helplessness.

I'm utterly hopeless. And now I'm back in the storage closet. Bathed in darkness. Waiting for death. No.

I didn't die then. And Tobias won't die now. That's when I start to run down the block, arm in the air, to hail a cab. If he doesn't answer, I'll go to him.

I just pray I'm not too late.

CHAPTER THIRTY-FOUR

Tobias

"ANY WORD FROM FELIX? DID HE RECEIVE THE PRESENT?"

The present being his soldier's head in a box . . . Courtesy of Gideon. I didn't give two shits what we did with his body but seeing as Gideon wants to establish a name for himself once I'm out, I understand the move. It's clear and decisive. *You don't fuck with me.* And once I'm gone, you certainly don't fuck with Gideon.

For the first year after this transition, Gideon will have to be extra lethal. That way, no one tries to steal the reins from him.

Now back in the office, I'm waiting for the other shoe to drop. We are preparing for Felix to get the package. It's being sent as we speak. By tonight, we should be at war.

"It hasn't been delivered yet."

"What's taking so long?" I ask.

"Not sure."

"Find out."

He nods and then pulls out his phone and fires off a text.

"Boss?"

Patrick walks into my office.

"Yeah."

"Ms. Matthews is outside the building."

"And?"

"Should we let her in?"

I had forgotten about Skye. I haven't seen her since the day I left her. Knowing Skye, she's probably pissed off.

Things are pretty crazy in here. My men are everywhere, preparing and sorting shit. It is not a good time for her.

"Show her in." I'll meet her in the lobby.

Walking down the stairs, I'm rounding the bend when she comes into focus. She sees me and runs toward me, and my men jump into action. Guns raised. Grabbing her.

"Let me go," she hollers.

"Get your hands off her." I step up. Chaz drops his hand but not his weapon. It's still pointed at her.

I walk up to Skye. Her chest is heaving as she tries to catch her breath, but that's not the thing that has me worried. What has me worried is the way her hands are shaking and the way she rubs frantically at the inside of her wrist.

"Calm down, Skye." I reach out, pull her hand away, and rub at her wrist. "Take a deep breath." I hold her gaze steady. "Inhale. Now exhale."

Her eyes go wide. She looks down at her wrist, and her face pales. I'm about to ask her what's wrong, but then she's snapping out of her trance, pulling away and facing off on me.

"You have to leave."

"What?"

"You have to leave now. Everyone!" Her voice is loud, and it has me reaching out my arms and bracketing her shoulders with them to stop her from doing anything rash.

"You need to calm down and speak."

Her chest rises and falls. "He's coming," she rasps out between pants.

"Who's coming?"

"Felix," she whispers.

"Speak. Now." My fingers come to her chin, cradling it a moment before forcing her eyes to meet mine. "Speak, Skye." The command comes out firm but soft. It gets the job done, because she leans into my touch, exhaling.

"We don't have time. He's coming. He's going to hit the building."

"This building is locked down. Guards are at every post." Despite saying this, I turn to my men, signaling them to prepare. But it's too late. Skye is screaming as a large Mack truck comes barreling up the street, over the sidewalk, and rams through the glass and into the lobby.

The sound of tires screeching and glass shattering is followed by an explosion that rocks the building.

Smoke descends upon us. Billowing until I can no longer see. From that moment, it's anarchy.

We were hit.

Despite every precaution we took, they drove a Mack truck into my lobby.

Gunfire rings out. I should be fighting, but all I can think about is where's Skye? I move through the smoke. My lungs burn. The smell of burning flesh permeates the air.

Some of my men are probably dead, but right now, I don't care about that. I need to find her and get her out of here.

It's hard to see anything. The visibility isn't even a foot in any direction. I can't hear, either; the blast took care of that. But I have to move anyway. I squint my eyes, hold my breath, and move in search of her.

The thick air loosens, and a clearing forms. Then I see her. But if I can see her, so can everyone, and the thought of that has me springing into action, lifting my gun, and firing.

A never-ending army pours into the building. One after one, they pile in, guns raised, bullets flying. I take aim, hitting them as they enter. At this angle, I'm like a sniper, picking them off one by one.

Chaos ensues as another bomb explodes and cuts off the air again. Taking cover behind a fallen desk, I use the metal as a barrier and aim.

"Watch out!" I hear her voice before I see her, and then she's running toward me, pushing my body, and throwing me to the floor. Biting pain radiates through my side as I hit the ground, and the spot I was just in blows up. Then Skye is on top of me.

Her hair fans my face.

The room around me is spinning, but I know we have to get up.

"Skye." *She winces.* "Are you okay?"

"Yes. Are you?" she asks.

"Yeah. We have to get out of here," I say through gritted teeth. I move to stand and pull her up and behind me, then I lead her out toward the basement. Gideon is behind us, right on our heels, Chaz, too, and Benedict.

"Make sure all the men are out. Kill everyone left behind. Clean up the mess as best you can. The cops will be here."

"They should have already been here," Gideon mumbles under his breath.

"I'm sure Felix rigged that." I open the car door and push Skye in. I don't have time to be gentle. We need to get out of here. Now. Usually, I would stay back to fight, but I have Skye to think about.

"Take down the whole building if you have to." Gideon's eyes go wide, but he knows it's the only way.

The cops will be here. If they find the computers, my early retirement will not happen in the way I want.

It will happen with me behind bars.

CHAPTER THIRTY-FIVE

Skye

E VERYTHING HAPPENS SO FAST.
First, I'm screaming for Tobias to move, and the next thing I know, the air is thick with smoke. At first, I stumble, then I freeze in place, taken back in time.

The noise around me becomes a soft hum. Sharp pain. Rocking in the corner. The gentle pressure of my wrist as I inhale to calm the frantic beating of my heart.

Suddenly, the hum turns into a ringing, and I shake my head back and forth. I'm not there. I'm not hiding in a closet. No. I'm in the middle of a war.

The sound around me rushes back, and then I'm back, and I remember why I'm here and what is happening. I hear the gunshots and try to look through the smoke. It's a mess. I hear a voice. It's Tobias, and he's looking for me. He doesn't see me, but I see him, and I also see the man rushing toward him, pulling his arm up and lifting a gun.

I move before I can think better of it and throw my body over his, trying my best to protect him from being shot. Before I know it, I'm being pulled through the haze, down the steps, and thrown into a car. Then Tobias is taking off, firing orders into his phone.

We are going somewhere, and we are going fast. I don't bother asking where, because I doubt he will tell me. From beside me, I hear him wince as he makes a sharp right turn.

"Are you hurt?" I ask him.

"Just a scratch." He hisses, but from the tone in his voice, he is lying.

"Are we almost there?" I ask.

"Why, you have other plans?" he jokes, but it comes out flat. It's when the car hits a bump and swerves that I know for a fact he is hurt.

"You are not okay," I state, unbuckling my seat belt and leaning forward. I pull his shirt up, and he grimaces. That's when I see it, blood. I move the material, and it oozes.

"Fuck. Tobias! You're hurt."

"I'm fine."

"You aren't fine. You're bleeding. We need to stop the bleeding."

"It's just a scratch."

"Then why is your face pale? I need to stop the bleeding." I look around, but there is nothing in the car. What the hell am I going to do?

Then it hits me, and I'm pulling off my blazer, balling it up, and placing it over the wound. He squirms at the pressure but continues to drive, weaving in and out of traffic. Once we are over the bridge, I'm completely lost, but that is probably the goal. If anyone is following us, they would never be able to find us.

If he's trying to keep us safe, does that mean someone can track my phone?

"Should I turn off my cell?"

"No one knows you're here."

"But someone back at your office—"

"Skye." He turns briefly to look at me and then turns back to the road. "There is no one alive back in the office who can tell Felix."

My mouth drops open, his meaning coming in crystal clear. His men killed everyone.

"How?"

"How did they die?" he asks.

"Yeah." I don't even know why I am asking this. It's sick. I shouldn't want to hear, but there is some sick need to know.

"Skye."

"Just tell me."

"I blew up the building."

At this point, my eyes must pop out of my head, and my heart is pounding so hard I swear I can hear it.

"I—don't—I didn't—Are they dead because of me?" I don't even know what to say. I'm stuttering and speechless and shaking all over.

"Stop." One of his hands drops off the steering wheel and touches my hand. "This isn't on you. You saved us." His finger caresses my tattoo. At the movement, the air in my lungs rushes out of my mouth. It feels intimate and familiar. Like he's done this before. I feel safe all of a sudden.

As he strokes my skin, my breathing regulates. I'm grounded. He grounds me. This man is able to calm me.

No one calms me.

Well, that's not true. No one has calmed me in a long time. Not for years. Not since—

"Skye." I turn to face him, ripped from my thoughts. "We're here."

The car rolls to a stop, and then he's opening the door and pulling away his hand.

"I need you to follow me."

"Can you walk?" I ask him, still not sure how hurt he is.

"Of course, I can walk." He smirks, and the way his lip tips up makes me think everything will be okay.

I nod and open my own door, then walk around the front of the car and head off with him.

The house we pulled up to is massive. It's not at all what I suspected. It looks like an old estate, and in the distance, I can hear the water crashing against the beach.

"Is this yours?"

"It is."

"Is it safe?"

"Are you asking if Felix will try to blow this place up?"

"I am."

"He won't. No one knows about this place. They don't know the location. The only people who know I own this estate are Gideon and Cyrus Reed."

"The banker."

"The banker," he confirms.

"Is that safe for him to know?"

"I can trust Cyrus with my life." There is conviction in his words, and I drop it.

As soon as we are walking up to the house, another car pulls up, and instantly, I step beside Tobias.

"It's fine. Cyrus sent his doctor."

And then he falls.

CHAPTER THIRTY-SIX

Tobias

I LOSE MY BALANCE, BUT I'M QUICK TO CATCH MYSELF. I DON'T like showing weakness, but it seems only fitting that this woman sees it again. How many years had passed since I'd met her? Since I was so insignificant in her life that she never recognized me. But now, with the blood loss, I no longer care. This whole time I've been angry. But now, with the world spinning around me, I turn to her.

"You don't even know me. Why bother to care if I live or die? Why are you even helping me when you don't remember?"

"What are you talking about?" she asks, confusion on her face.

In my state of delusion, I let something come out of my mouth that I didn't want to share. I need to be better, or I need to just tell her. I think I'll go with the latter.

Although I'm weakened, I still manage to walk into my house with no assistance. Skye hovers, but she knows me well enough to know I don't want her help. Once we are inside, I lead the doctor into the living room.

"Are you sure you want me to look at you here?"

"Yes," I grunt as I look down and see why he asks. There is a trail of blood in the foyer.

Someone will eventually clean it up, and to be honest, I don't have the strength to walk farther into the house. I'm stubborn, but I've also lost a shit ton of blood.

When my shirt is lifted, I see Skye grimace. Unlike me, she is not used to seeing blood. Over the years, I have grown tolerant of the sight. I don't even notice it. The smell no longer affects me. For a time it did, though. There was a time twenty years ago when the smell would bring me to my knees. But as time passed, the memory faded. Take Skye, for example. It's obvious her memory has dulled.

Any resentment I might have had over that notion has also disappeared. A part of me thinks that's the easier way of coping, better than the vengeance that lingers in my heart. Maybe once this is all said and done, I'll be able to move on; maybe I'll even find peace. But is there absolution for a person like me?

Doubtful.

"Please remove your shirt completely," the doctor says.

This time when I do, and when the doctor pulls away Skye's blazer that has been pressed into the wound to stop the blood, I watch her face. It has gone pale, and her skin has a sheen of sweat beading on her temples.

"Skye, look at me." She's staring at the wound.

I reach out, grab her wrist. I start to circle . . . "Inhale." Her eyes shoot up at that word. They are wide. Shocked. *Why?* I rub a circle again. "Exhale."

"How?" she whispers to herself, and I'm not sure what she's talking about, but her skin is pale like she saw a ghost.

"Did I ever finish my story?" I say as the doctor injects me with a syringe and then is pouring a disinfectant over the wound.

Her gaze lifts up from where she was watching me touch her. "You didn't."

As the liquid cleans me, I let out a hiss, looking up at the doctor.

"You were very lucky," he says to me. "It's a through and through. The bullet mainly caught external tissue. You will be fine. However, you need time to regain the blood loss."

I turn back to Skye. It's time for her to know everything.

"Please tell me." She places her other hand where I'm rubbing her tattoo. "The best and worst day."

"The best and worst day," I agree before I close my eyes and remember the way the sunlight beamed in through the window that morning. The way I jumped up when my father said he had a surprise for me. "It was my birthday," I tell her. "March second." Her mouth opens in shock. "I know. Let me continue." She nods her head. "My father and I had just recently moved to New York. He was working on a deal, a big one. One that would change everything."

Skye is now holding my hand. Her breath is coming out heavy. The doctor is stitching my ribs, and a burning feeling shoots up my chest.

"He told me that day, he wanted to take me out. The whole day was my choice. I didn't know what to do first. A new town. A new beginning, another birthday, but this time it would be different."

"Where did you go?"

"The first place he took me was a trail. We walked and talked. It was a bit chilly, but I didn't care. I just liked to spend time with him. He told me that we would be here for a while. That this would be our new home. That the job he had been working on was becoming very lucrative. I was young. I didn't know what that meant. He said he had basically taken out the competition. But again, at that age, I didn't know. I thought my dad owned a business, and he did. It just wasn't the business I assumed."

"What business was it?" she whispers, eyes still wide, chin trembling.

"What business do you think?" I answer. Her mouth opens and closes, trying desperately to make sense of the crumbs I am leaving for her to pick up. Only then will she truly understand.

"I thought it was your uncle who got you into the business?" she asks.

"My uncle got me into it, but only because my father was dead." Her hand reaches out and holds mine.

"When did your father die?"

I trace my thumb over her wrist. "Patience. Don't you want to hear the rest of the story?"

"When did he die?" Her throat bobs, and I lift my hand to touch her jaw, caressing it lightly.

I don't answer her question. Instead, I continue to relive that day. Smell the trees, taste the ice cream, remember the way my cheeks burned from smiling so wide.

"When I think back, I should have known it would all go to shit. I should have known I didn't deserve the happiness. I was the son of a monster after all. After the walk. I wanted to go eat ice cream for breakfast, and we did. The next place we went was to a local ice cream shop. It was the old-fashioned kind, where you sat down, and they had milkshakes and servers in a little apron."

"We had one of those where I grew up . . ." she trails off, but I continue.

"I ordered a waffle cone with two scoops of vanilla ice cream, extra whipped cream. If I think really hard, I can still taste it." Skye smiles, our hands still joined. She squeezes. "After the ice cream, my dad made a call. I expected the day to end, but I was wrong. It was only just beginning."

The whole time I speak, she never breaks our stare. "What happened that day?"

"A massacre. My father died. And a girl saved me." Lifting her hand, I turn it over until the small paper airplane tattoo faces me, and I place a kiss on it.

She sucks in a gulp of air. "I don't understand." Her face is pale like she's seen a ghost.

"What don't you understand?" I ask. Then she speaks, and my breath leaves my body.

"But-but you're dead."

CHAPTER THIRTY-SEVEN

Skye

I LOOK INTO TOBIAS'S DEEP BLUE EYES, AND NOTHING MAKES sense. I was told he was dead. His gaze is unwavering as his mouth opens.

"I'm the plane. You're the sky."

My eyes close at his words, and then I'm back there, Twenty years ago, seeing it all as if it's happening now.

"Wake up, darling," I hear from beside me. My arms stretch out and wipe away the sleep.

My mom is standing beside my bed, cupcake in hand, a candle lit and waiting for me to blow. This is her tradition. Every March second, on my birthday, she wakes me up with a cupcake. And from here, I get to be a princess for the day.

No matter what I want, I can do it. It's a yes day. I know exactly what I want to do. I want to go to Marvelous Michael's, so I close my eyes and make a wish. I wish for a birthday like no other. Full of excitement and adventure. Not that anything interesting happens in Reddington. I live in the most boring place on earth.

Mommy and Daddy don't like it, either. They mention mean men, but I don't know what they are talking about. I have never seen a bad guy.

I have never seen anything. Hence the wish. I wish something exciting would happen. Something you only see in the movies.

"What's the pout for, sunshine?"

"I'm not pouting."

Her soft finger reaches up and pats my lips. I smile. She's right, I was.

"Only smiles on your birthday."

Then she reaches her hand out. "Come on, big plans today!"

I allow my mom to pull me up and out of bed, then head into the bathroom. Mom says I have to brush my teeth and get showered. Now that I'm six years old, Mom trusts me to do this on my own.

I'm not sure how long I shower, but at some point, my mom knocks on the door, and I have to assume I've been in here for a long time. I throw on the clothes I put on the floor, and then I head out to meet my parents in the kitchen, where they have breakfast waiting for me.

"What are we gonna do today?" I ask.

"Anything you want," my dad answers.

"Anything I want, you say?" My mother nods at my question. "Well, then, I want to go get milkshakes then to Marvelous Michael's," I tell her.

"Good choice," they say in unison.

We spend the morning being lazy. We eat breakfast. We watch TV. I open presents. They give me a sun necklace. It's a small sun made up of little sparkles. Daddy said it's diamonds.

From what I heard, diamonds are very expensive. I proudly put it on, beaming up at them.

"Time to go."

Together, we all head to the car, and then we are off.

Al's Diner. It's in town, and all the kids love it for their birthday because of the freshly baked cakes, fried funnel cake, and best of all, milkshakes.

I heard Mom and Dad say they hope it stays open. I'm not sure what that means. Why wouldn't it stay open? But they mention a mall being built. I have no clue what they are talking about, but I'm happy to be going there.

Once inside, I head straight to the booth we always go to.

There is even a jukebox in the corner. That's one of my favorite parts, getting quarters from my parents and playing all the old music.

My parents sit at a table, and I ask if I can have quarters and walk around alone. I'm six now, after all.

I check out all the tables as I walk. Every one of them, hoping to see anyone I know from school. I don't recognize anyone. There aren't even any kids here today. Lots of old people. But I do see the small door behind the jukebox. I have always wondered what's in there. I'm not supposed to open it, but still, I'm curious. It's hidden, after all, and no one will know.

I peek inside, but it's nothing. It feels like a major disappointment. I thought maybe it would lead to a secret pathway.

Shrugging it off, I fill the machine with quarters and pick my songs. I place my last coin in the slot, and I turn around to see my parents ordering. They have a goofy smile on their face, and I know without any doubt they didn't just order me the milkshake; they ordered me the birthday special. It's a giant sundae with a million scoops of ice cream, and they even have sparklers on it. I didn't tell them I wanted it, but I did.

I'm surprised how empty the restaurant is. Typically, there are more kids here. But today, there are only a few tables full. Maybe ten. No kids. Wait, that's not true. There is a boy at one of the tables. He looks a few years older than me. Like that age where he's almost a teen but not quite. I watch as he stands, and then he's looking in my direction.

He's all by himself. He seems happy, and when he turns away,

I see him waving at a man at the table directly next to the one he just stood from. It's probably his dad.

His dad is surrounded by a bunch of other men, and they seem to be in deep conversation. The boy's lips thin like he's annoyed that his dad isn't paying attention to him, but then he goes back to walking in my direction. I step away and start back to my table. As he puts a coin in the jukebox and flips through the music selection, I stop and watch him, wondering what type of song he will pick.

A song can tell you a lot about a person.

Still staring at him, I want to walk over and peek, but as I look from him to my parents, deciding what to do, I hear a strange sound. It sounds like a pop.

Pop. Pop. Pop.

A weird odor pours in around me, and then I hear screaming. "Run!"

The place erupts into chaos. I look at where my parents are, but my mom is shaking her head, screaming at me to run.

Run? Where will I go? I move toward the bathroom, but there's a loud explosion, and I can't see anything. I can't see anyone. The only person I see is that boy. He's still standing by the jukebox, looking around.

He starts to where his dad was, and that's when I see the man. A mean-looking man with a gun in his hands. It's pointed at the boy. I dash toward him, pushing him out of the way, throwing my weight over his.

We both hit the ground with a thud.

The side of my body burns, but I don't have time to worry about it. Instead, I'm looking down at the boy. He goes to speak, but I lift my head and place my fingers over his lips to silence him.

I think he said something about his dad, but now more men are shooting. It's like a war. We need to move; I grab the older boy's hand and use all my strength to pull him with me through the chaos. I don't know where my parents are, but they would want me to hide, so that's what I do. I lead us behind the jukebox to the small closet. Once inside, I close the door.

My heart pounds. There is barely any light. Only a small sliver that creeps in from the door that won't fully shut. Hopefully, no one sees it.

My heart pounds as we wait.

Pop. Pop. Pop.

I can't control the way my body shakes. A scream is lodged in my throat, but I don't dare let it out. That's when the boy turns to me. His hand reaches for mine.

"We're going to be okay."

I shake my head, back and forth.

He narrows his dark eyes. "Yes. We are. I promise we will be okay."

"We are going to die . . ."

"We won't. Because of you. You saved my life," he whispers.
"Why?"

I don't answer his question. What can I say? I shrug, and pain cuts through my side. I wince at the movement. "Are you hurt?"

"I think so."

He opens the door a tiny bit. More light penetrates the space but not enough that anyone can see in. It's enough for me to see him, though. His large blue eyes stare back at me.

"We're going to be okay," he says, but I don't believe him. My breath is shallow. My head spins.

"Take a deep breath."

I can't. I try, but I can't. He reaches across the space and takes my hand in his. Then his finger draws a circle on the pulse of my left wrist.

"Look at me. Inhale," I don't know how old he is, but he's so strong. "We are going to be okay, I promise. Now exhale." His fingers continue the pattern as he prompts me to breathe.

As he whispers soft promises, I can't help but become transfixed on the front of his shirt. On the design of a paper airplane.

"You're the plane, and I'm the sky," I say, my voice wobbling

228

from blood loss. I don't want him to see my pain, so I let my lips spread wide and give him a wink.

He smiles down at me, and for a moment, I forget all about the pain. "I'm the plane, and you're the sky," he repeats.

My head shakes back and forth. My eyes open and meet his gaze. His hand reaches out and swipes the tear away.

"You're alive," I whisper.

"I am."

I don't understand what's happening. How this is happening. After I got out of the closet, my life changed. Everything I loved was gone. And I thought I had him, but then I—

"I was told you were dead."

"Sometimes I wish I were," he says as he flips my hand over and traces the little paper airplane tattoo I had placed on the same spot where he calmed me so many years ago. "You got this for me."

"I did."

"Why?"

"Because you saved me."

He leans forward, his hand leaving my wrist and lifting the side of my shirt. I feel his fingers tracing the scar that day left. I lift my own hand and place it over his heart and shake my head. "I didn't save you. You saved me."

"We saved each other," Tobias answers as he moves closer. Our faces are a mere inch apart. "Why did you think I was dead?"

"He told me you were."

"Who told you?"

"My dad—" Then I'm shaking my head. "My adoptive dad."

Tobias's eyes are wide, and they look deep and endless. "What exactly—?"

"Stop."

He does.

"I don't want to talk about him. I don't want to think about him."

"What do you want, then?" He leans in closer. So close, my chest heaves into his.

"To see you. To touch you. To understand how you are here. Are you here?" I move closer, tracing my fingers over his skin and down his jaw. I trace the lines of his face. Trace his face as if I'm remembering. And I am.

I remember the boy in the closet with me. The older boy who kept me safe. Kept me calm. He might think I saved him, and in a way, I did. I stopped him from falling to the same fate as my parents, as his dad, but he saved me. His presence has been with me since that day. He's guided me.

I reach up and touch his cheek, feeling the stubble there. He's so handsome with his dark hair and light eyes. I can't stop touching him, and I don't want to. He lets me. He lets my hands roam. My fingers remember, and then as I do, he barely breathes. He doesn't move; he just stares, and then he's touching me back. His hand wraps around my back and pulls me close.

"I was so mad," he says as his lips hover over mine. "I thought you forgot me. I thought I spent my whole life looking for you, and you forgot me." Something in his eyes makes me think he wants me to apologize.

"I'm sorry," I say, the words falling out of my mouth before I can sort them out. Tobias pulls back, his eyes wide.

"Don't be," he says.

"I never forgot you. You were always with me." He lifts my wrist to his mouth. "And still are."

He kisses my skin, pulling back to look at me. His gaze lights a blaze inside me. My heart races. It feels like a moment on pause as I wait for him to do something. His tongue moves across the tattoo, sending shivers to run over my body. Then he pulls back, removing his lips from my wrist and pressing his mouth to mine. I kiss him back. The kiss becomes heated, and soon we are both breathing hard. I am lost, and if I'm never found, that's a fate I would take just to be in his arms.

CHAPTER THIRTY-EIGHT

Tobias

I HEAR THE SOUND BEFORE I SEE HER. BLINKING MY EYE, SHE comes into focus. Skye is walking in.

Lifting my hand, I scrub at my face. What happened? The last thing I remember was kissing Skye. Now, I'm lying down in my bedroom. The shot the doctor gave me must have knocked me the fuck out.

"You're up." Skye smiles at me as she crosses the space and stands beside my bed.

"How long was I sleeping?" I ask her before a yawn escapes my mouth. She laughs.

"A while," she responds.

"That's not an answer, Skye."

"You're right. It's not." This time she smirks. "It's not important. You needed your rest," she answers.

"I'm fine."

"You most certainly are not fine. You were shot."

"I've had worse."

"Good to know.

"What happened last night? How did I end up here?"

Her cheeks color a bright shade of red. "Are you hungry?" she asks, trying to change the topic. It's cute, but I'm not having it.

"I'm not an idiot. I know I kissed you. I mean, how did I end up in this bed, asleep? Alone?" I raise my brow.

"The doctor gave you something to relax you. I'm sure you remember that?" I nod at her question. "Then you kissed me . . ." she leads, and of course, I remember that, too. How could I forget that? I could be out of my mind on psychedelics, and I wouldn't ever forget that.

"Still following." I grin. "But that doesn't put me in this bed."

"That's it. Nothing else happened. You walked us back to this room. Got in bed and fell asleep." She shrugs before her eyes narrow in a sexy yet mischievous way. "You were a real letdown."

"Ouch."

"Just keeping it real."

I laugh at that, but the movement makes me groan. I might not have sustained any serious injuries, but it will take a day or two for me to feel like myself again.

"Stop moving. You're going to hurt yourself." Skye moves closer to me, her hand reaching out to adjust my pillow. "So, are you hungry?" she asks again.

"I can eat."

"Good. Then I'll be right back." She adjusts my blanket, pulling it up a bit higher from where it dropped. I follow her gaze as she does and enjoy the sight of her cheeks reddening even further.

My chest is exposed, and she is enjoying the view.

"I can get up," I tell her, and she shakes her head forcefully.

"Are you kidding? No! You cannot get up," she mockingly scolds, all while smiling. "You know you were shot, right?"

"Me? I don't know what you're talking about. I'm perfect." I laugh.

"You are the worst patient ever. That's what you are. Just sit, and I'll get you something to eat." With that, she walks out of the room.

I'm alone briefly before Gideon walks in. The first thing I notice is that his hair is disheveled. The next is he has dark circles under his eyes.

"How's the patient?" he asks before crossing the space.

"Fine. Fuck. Why does everyone keep asking me?"

"Well—" He looks me up and down with a bemused look on his face.

"Yep. Got it. I'm in bed, shot. I know. I know. But fuck, I'm fine."

"If I were you, I'd milk it." He waggles his brows suggestively.

"Milk what?"

"You know what? If I had Skye Matthews wanting to play nursemaid—"

"For fuck's sake, Gideon. Shut the fuck up before I have to get out of this bed, stitches or not, and kick your ass."

He laughs. The fucker laughs.

Just as I'm about to respond with another threat to rip his throat out for even thinking about Skye in that way, there's a knock on the door, which then squeaks open an inch.

"Can I come in?"

"I'll be getting out of your hair." Gideon waggles his damn eyebrows at me. "Word of advice. Let her take care of you and then fu—"

"Get out, now." Gideon once again chuckles, but at least he leaves.

Skye smiles at him, clearly having no idea what he just said. She walks back toward me, but this time, she's carrying a bowl in one hand and a spoon in the other.

She places the bowl on the side table before sitting on the edge of my bed, right next to me. Then she's dipping the spoon in the oatmeal.

"What are you doing?" I ask. Please tell me she's not trying to feed me.

She looks at me, her expression serious, and then rolls her eyes. "Isn't it obvious?"

I reach my hand out and touch hers, trailing my fingers down her forearm that holds the spoon still dipped in the bowl. I squeeze lightly. "Not to me."

"Were you hit in the head or something?" Her tone is mocking, but I can see how her lip tips up. She wants to smile.

"Nope, just shot."

With her other hand, she removes my fingers from where they are wrapped around her wrist. I drop my hand. "I'm feeding you," she playfully orders.

"I'm not a child, Skye."

Placing the spoon back in the bowl, she lets out a sigh before looking at me. Her gaze is fierce. Protective. "I need to take care of you." Her voice even more so.

"I don't—" I start to say, but then I see something that makes my breath hitch in my chest. Her eyes appear misted like she's holding back tears.

"Let me take care of you." Her voice has changed. This tone tells me she's scared, and this is something she has to do. She needs this. I understand. I felt the same way about her. After all this time, being near her was something I had to do, and now that she knows, I won't let her go. I nod my head, hating it but giving it to her anyway.

She resumes her task, and I silently pray Gideon doesn't return. Although knowing that bastard, he would be all for it if it got me laid.

I let her feed me.

Even though I don't want to. We are both quiet as she does. The moment settles upon us, but it's not uncomfortable.

"Do you hurt?" she finally asks, breaking the silence.

"No."

She places the spoon down in the bowl. "Are you sure?"

"Skye, trust me when I say this. After everything I've been through, this is merely a scratch."

Her blue eyes look huge right now, but it's the way her mouth forms an O that has me laughing.

"You were shot." She scoffs.

"I was clipped." I shrug.

"It went through you!"

"Again"—I take her free hand in mine, raise it to my mouth, and place a kiss on her palm—"I promise this isn't the worst of what I've been through."

"With your uncle?" I nod. "Want to talk about it?"

"Not particularly." The last thing I want to do is talk about the past when I have Skye sitting beside me.

"We have nothing else to talk about right now." She has a point, but I don't want to burden her with my past. While she was raised in a loving household with an adoptive dad who clearly cared for her, I was raised by my uncle, who wanted to mold me into a villain.

"I grew up in a very different time. In a very different reality than you did."

"Drugs?"

"And then some."

"You can trust me."

"I know I can, Skye." I take a breath. "He was the man who brought the majority of cocaine through America in the early 2000s. Anyone doing coke at that time was probably doing coke that passed through our hands."

"Was it very dangerous? Growing up with him?"

I want to laugh, but I don't. "It makes what happened to us look like a walk in the park," I answer truthfully without details.

"H-How did you ever survive?" Skye's voice cracks, and her expression is tight. She's trying her hardest not to fall apart but is failing.

I lean forward and place my lips on hers. "Where there is a will, there is a way."

"And you had the will." I can feel her smile against my lips.

"I did." Pulling back, I let out a yawn.

"You need to rest."

"I rested all night."

"Rest some more." Usually, I would call her bossy, but she's right. I need rest, especially with everything coming next with Felix.

With that, I feel Skye take my hand, and my eyes close.

CHAPTER THIRTY-NINE

Skye

TOBIAS FELL BACK ASLEEP. AS MUCH AS HE THINKS HE'S ABOVE needing to recoup from a gunshot, he's not. His body is obviously exhausted, and he's too much of a tough guy to admit it, but alas, it didn't matter.

He's now lying in bed, breathing softly with a peaceful look on his face. His usually hard and focused features look rested and relaxed for the first time since I've met him for the second time. Even when we were kids and he held me in that storage closet.

My brain is on overload, trying to remember everything that has passed between us since we've been reacquainted.

At any point did I know? A part of me thinks I did, even if it was subconsciously. There was always a gravitational pull to him. And ever since he re-entered my life, my thoughts of the older boy from the closet were always close by.

Somewhere inside me, I knew.

Standing from where I'm perched on the bed, I peer around the room.

What am I supposed to do now? Do I just sit here, or am I supposed to be doing something?

With the quiet of the room, I can't help how my mind wanders. There is so much we don't know. The first thing is Felix. We know he's involved, that much is clear, but the whys are still out there, hovering above us where we can't see.

Then there is the matter of Tobias. Glancing back at the bed, I part my mouth into a smile. He's resting peacefully, his chest rising and falling with every inhale and exhale, but then my lips thin.

I was told a lie, and I need to find out why.

Why didn't you tell me the truth, Dad?

About anything.

It's not just that he lied about Tobias, but he still hasn't told me that he's ill.

No matter how often I call to check in, and I call often, he doesn't utter anything about his health.

At first, I felt disappointed that he wouldn't confide in me, then hurt, but now, I'm just plain angry with him.

I don't know what to think. I need to ask him why he lied. Why he told me that Tobias died.

I start to pace the room, but finally, I can't handle it anymore. I need to call him. But first, I need to make sure I can. I don't know the protocol.

Where's Gideon when I need him?

I check on Tobias one more time before I leave, and yep, he's still out for the count. Then I'm opening the door slowly so as not to wake him, and I slip outside to go in search of Gideon.

Despite the fact that it's early in the morning, the halls are dark. This place is also confusing as all hell.

If this were a children's book, I'd find a piece of bread and leave crumbs for myself. This place is huge. It reminds me of a British manor. I bet the security is intense.

Not that it matters in the long run.

The security in his building was crazy, yet Felix could still hit him. I shudder at the thought, at how lucky we were, because many of his men were not.

Hell, we were almost killed. I almost lost Tobias before I found him.

It takes me over five minutes before I see a light a few feet up the long dark hall, and when I make my approach, it looks like an office.

Gideon must hear me because he's speaking before I even step inside. "Can I help you, or are you just sulking out there?"

Taking a step to enter, I lift my gaze to see Gideon staring right at me. I'm at the threshold of the room. "Can I come in? Am I disturbing you?"

"You don't need to ask, Skye."

With that settled, I step inside despite the anxious feeling that's beginning to work its way inside me.

The first thing I notice is that this room is not at all like the office building where Tobias resides. Although I have never been in his residence, from what I gathered from the rest of the building, this is the opposite.

Where the building was cold and modern, this home feels warm and lived in.

It's not traditional as one would think when they look at the façade of the manor, but it's not sterile.

It's the perfect transitional home. Wood paneling that's been painted gray.

A black suede couch sits on the opposite wall of the Lucite desk. A clear swivel chair behind the desk.

Spotting a couch, I head over to it and then sit. My hands rest on the soft material.

"Am I allowed to call someone?" I ask him.

"It depends. Who will you be calling?"

"I wanted to call my office and—" I sigh. "I need to speak to my father."

"About?"

My first instinct is to glare at Gideon, but then I realize that he's just being careful, and after what we've just been through, I realize he has no choice but to ask this question. I temper my attitude and answer his question, regardless of if I want to.

"My father told me—" I stop. How much does Gideon know about Tobias's and my shared past?

I narrow my eyes. "Do you know?" I keep it vague.

"That Tobias and you met before?" he answers.

"Yeah, but do you know how and when?" His eyes soften as he nods at my question. Compassion and pain are there.

"I know."

"See, the thing is . . . I didn't know Tobias was alive. My father told me he had died. I asked about the kid in the closet. What had happened to him? He told me." I bite my lip, trying to stop myself from getting emotional.

Gideon lets out a giant breath, and I know his answer before he even speaks.

I can't call.

It's written all over his features. From the way his brows furrowed, forming elevens to age his face, to the way his body has stiffened. Shoulders tight.

"Skye," he starts, and I lift my hand up to stop him.

"I know. I can't contact him. Not after what just happened."

"It isn't safe. Not for you. Not for him and not for Tobias. Give it a few days."

"Okay."

With that out of the way, I stand from the couch and head back out the door.

For the next thirty minutes, I walk around the house aimlessly, eventually finding my way back to Tobias's room. I crack the door open and let myself in. He's still asleep. Still peaceful. I sit beside him and watch him breathe.

Thankful for the opportunity.

***

Hours pass. I kept myself busy after I was told I couldn't call my father yet by reading a book next to Tobias while he rested. Eventually, my stomach told me it was time to eat with an angry growl, which brings me to the here and now. I'm going to make myself lunch. I'm not much of a chef, but I'll have to do.

Maybe I'll find more oatmeal in the fridge that I can heat.

"Is the patient sleeping?" Gideon asks me as I enter the kitchen.

"He is."

"In all the years I have known him, I have never known him to sleep this much."

"To be honest, before this, I would have thought him an evil vampire who never slept."

"He just feeds off the blood of innocents."

"More like feeds off the blood of his enemies."

"That sounds more like him."

We both laugh.

"What's to eat around this place?"

"I can have someone make you food. We're pretty short on staff right now as we had everyone go on vacation and are operating with merely a skeleton crew for safety reasons, but I'm sure someone can cook."

"Don't be ridiculous. I can cook. I'll just make myself at home."

"You do that."

Gideon stands from the table and makes his way out the door. I walk over to the stainless-steel fridge, open it, and start to rummage through all the food in an attempt to figure out what I'm going to eat. I settle on eggs. Those are easy, and I can't possibly screw it up and burn down the house.

Pulling out the carton and a stick of butter, I then search for a pan.

This kitchen is huge. It could hold five of my kitchens within it. It takes me a full five minutes to find the pan and figure out how to turn the stove on. Apparently, the panel is hidden.

High-maintenance much?

Luckily, no one was here to see me fussing about. Although I am quite positive there are security cameras, something tells me they are probably not watching me cook. Or at least one can hope.

I crack the eggs and get to work.

I'm lost in my thoughts when I feel a presence behind me.

At first, my breath catches in my chest, but when his cologne wafts in the air, I relax as he steps up behind me.

This whole time he's been sleeping, I wasn't sure if he'd still remember what happened before he crashed or if it would be forgotten as just something that happened under the pressure and pain of being shot. But as his lips find my neck and he places a kiss there, I know he didn't. Tiny goose bumps break out across my skin, and I turn my head to look over my shoulder. He takes that opportunity to move back and look down at me.

"Thank you for yesterday and this morning."

"Of course."

"Are they almost done?" He gestures to the stove.

"Yeah, only a few more seconds."

"I'll get you a plate." From behind me, I hear him moving around, and when the eggs are ready, there is a fork and plate beside me.

"Thank you." I place the food on the plate and head toward the table.

"Now eat your eggs," he orders playfully, sitting down in the chair beside me.

"Aren't you hungry?"

"Yes."

"Do you want me to make you some?" I move to stand, but he places his hand on mine and shakes his head.

"No."

"But you just said . . . ?" I trail off, eyebrows lifted in confusion.

"I know what I said, Skye, but that's not at all what I'm hungry for."

My lips form an O.

"Eat. I'm not a patient man. And I have been waiting over twenty-four hours to finish what I started."

"It's not my fault you fell asleep."

"Skye . . ." he warns. "Eat."

I take one bite, but as I swallow, I find that I don't want eggs, either. "I'm no longer hungry."

"Good answer."

Then his lips are on mine.

CHAPTER FORTY

Tobias

PULLING AWAY, I LOOK DOWN AT HER, SILENTLY ASKING A question. She nods at my unspoken words. I take her hand in mine and lead her toward my room. Once inside, I pull her toward me once again.

"I need you," she says, her voice merely a whisper. I lift her shirt off. She kicks her pants down desperately. Once she's fully naked, she stands before me, beautiful and proud and absolutely fucking delicious.

"Fuck."

She's gorgeous.

My cock jumps to attention as I trail a path up her body with my gaze.

Looking at her should be illegal. Then again, I do have a passion for playing on the wrong side of the law.

She's the type of woman that wars are started for. Men would kill to protect her.

I already have.

I'd do anything for Skye, including die.

"You have too many clothes on," she grins, and I move to remove my pants. My shirt is already gone.

Now naked, I reach over to my side table and pull out a condom.

Skye watches my every move. She swallows, then licks her lips as I run my hand up my cock, then slide the condom on.

Sliding my hand up her bare leg, I part her and rub circles on her clit.

Knowing what she needs, I push one finger inside her. She's warm and wet, and I can't wait to fuck her.

She whimpers.

"You like that?"

She doesn't answer, but her hips lift.

"Words, Skye." With each deep thrust of my finger, her breathing becomes heavier.

"Do you want to come on my hand . . . or my cock?"

A desperate plea escapes her lips at my question, and I capture the sound with my mouth, sliding my tongue across hers as she whimpers. She is close, her muscles squeezing the shit out of my finger, and I don't know how someone so tight can take my entire cock. Then before she does, I remove my hand, lift it to my mouth, and lick it clean.

"Bed. Now."

Stepping forward, I push Skye back with my body until she hits the bed and falls backward. Her lips part. I climb on top of her and rub the head of my cock against her slit.

She answers by lifting her hips, trying to get me inside her.

With one sudden thrust, I'm fully engulfed in her heat. I push all the way inside her to the hilt. Her grip tightens around me as I retract and then push back in. I keep up a slow, leisurely pace, pleasure rippling through my body. Fuck, she feels good. She tightens her arms around me, her nails biting into my skin with each thrust.

Time has no meaning. I don't know how much has passed, but I'm lost to the sensation of being inside her. Our bodies are so tightly entwined, I don't know where she ends, and I begin. She claws at my back each time I retract from her, and each time I drive back in, she gasps.

She begs and pants. Pleading me with her sighs to fuck her harder.

I pick up my pace. I pull out, then slam back in.

Hard. Fast. I give her exactly what she needs and wants. My pace is brutal. The slapping of our bodies is primal. I feel desperate, as if I waited my whole fucking life for this. It's as if I'm lost. I'm the goddamn paper airplane, flying, and she's the fucking sky.

That's when it happens, the telltale clenching of her inner walls, and sensation takes root inside me. I try to hold back and wait for her to find release.

"Let it go, baby. Come on my cock."

And when she does, I let go at the same time.

"So good," I rasp.

I lose myself completely, finishing inside her. We both lie back, breathing heavily as we catch our breaths, fully satisfied, and sated. Together, entwined in each other's arms, neither of us moves.

"Next time." I bite on her earlobe. "You're going to ride me bare until I become a part of your fucking DNA."

We just enjoy the moment, basking in it a little longer. But it doesn't last long before there is a knock on the door. I jump out of bed and stand, pull on my pants, and crack it open. Gideon is standing on the other side.

"Not a good time." I groan, doing my best job not to kill him right now for ruining the moment.

"Sorry," he responds. "When you didn't answer . . ." he trails off. I shake my head at him, leveling him with a stare. One that says *leave*, but since he's already here, I have one question.

"Update? All good?"

"Building is down."

"Good."

With that done and settled, I close the door and head back to bed, where Skye is waiting for me.

"Everything okay?" she asks as she rolls over to look at me.

"Yes," I say, my voice soothing, not wanting to bring that shit into the bed. "Yes, it's all good." I kiss her, then lie down next to her.

I look at her and see the sadness creep into her eyes. "You know you can talk to me, right?"

"Of course, I do," I say, sitting on the bed and reaching out to touch her face. "But I don't want to talk about that now."

"And what do you want to talk about?" she asks.

I grin, drawing her closer. "How I'll never get my fill of you."

"Is that so?" she asks, her voice rising playfully.

"It is." I move until my face is nestled in her neck, making her giggle.

I stay pressed against her soft skin, allowing myself to breathe her in. We lie there for a few minutes before I feel her stir.

"What are we going to do?" she finally asks, running her hand through my hair. I pull back and look into her eyes. Her gaze penetrates me. So many unspoken words. So many questions.

"What do you want to do?" I ask her.

"I don't know," she says, shrugging. "I just don't want you to get hurt." I lean in and place my lips on hers.

"And for that, I am thankful. But for now, I want you to trust me."

"Okay. I can do that . . . for now."

"Good." I nod. "Okay. Enough talk. Time to rest."

I lean back onto the pillow and open my arm for her to get closer. She snuggles into my chest as my arm drops around her small shoulders to hold her.

On my back, staring at the ceiling, I focus on her breathing, listening to the moment she falls asleep. When it levels out, I allow my own breath to calm, letting me drift off as well.

CHAPTER FORTY-ONE

Skye

I STRETCH MY ARMS OVER MY HEAD AND LET OUT A LONG, drawn-out yawn. For a moment, I forget where I am, blinking my lids to remember.

Then, with a jolt, it all comes back to me.

The car. The fighting. The bomb. The rushing to get to the safehouse.

I still can't wrap my brain around everything.

It's been crazy. Surreal. I always knew that something didn't make sense with my father's story, and now I know why.

He wasn't dead.

Tobias, *the boy, wasn't dead.*

But despite the revelation, my brain and my heart are having a hard time grasping it.

I've spent years mourning him. And now one night of loving him has changed me. But how long will it take for me to feel safe and grounded again?

I roll over to see that Tobias is still sleeping next to me. He has a peaceful look on his face and I just want to keep this momentary calm, regardless of the mountain of unknowns awaiting us.

We still need to figure everything out and talk about what happened. Talk about Felix, talk about what Dad could know, and where we go from here. There has to be a *we* now. I cannot go back to a time without him again. No one has found us yet, but our time is running out.

"Morning." Tobias stretches his arms above his head. The blanket lowers with the movement, giving me a view of the V of his abs.

"Morning." I bite my lip, not exactly knowing where we stand today or even what we are going to face. "So . . . ?" Looking away from him, I focus my attention on the window. The rolling hills have a whimsical quality that makes me want to escape here forever.

"So?" he quips, and I know if I turn to face him, he'll be smiling. Something I'm still not used to seeing but can't help but crave.

"What're you up to today?" I ask lamely.

"I should call a meeting with my men."

"Okay." I'm waiting for the *but*.

A hand lands on my shoulder. My pulse accelerates. Tobias's touch is enough to have my heart catapulting into overdrive.

"But I'm not going to do that just yet . . ."

Thud. Thud.

"What are you going to do, then?"

His fingers start to work their way down my back. "Spend time with you."

"Is that what you want to do?"

And then, without warning, he grabs hold of me, flips me over, and pounces.

"You really have to ask?" He smirks. "But first, breakfast."

Tobias crawls down my body. Teeth and tongue nipping and licking as he makes his way down to where I'm desperate for him.

A moan escapes my mouth as his hands land on my thighs and opens them.

Then his mouth is on me.

Fuck. I love breakfast.

———————

I sit at the table while Tobias pours us both coffees.

"I feel like we need to talk about what happened," I blurt out.

"Negative," Tobias replies. "After breakfast, we can talk." He returns to the table with two mugs. I lift mine and take a sip.

"Fine."

Tobias smiles at me. A few minutes later, there is also a plate of eggs and a piece of toast in front of me. I could get used to this, *I think.* Except this isn't what life would be like. This is us avoiding the truth.

I eat silently, waiting for Tobias to finish his food so we can talk. He gulps down the last of his breakfast, and then he sighs.

"Fine."

"Fine?"

"You want to talk? Let's talk," he mutters.

"Well, when you say it that way . . ." I deadpan.

Tobias smiles, then leans forward and takes my hand in his. "It's not that I don't want to talk. I just want to enjoy you. I've looked for you for years, then I found you, and you didn't remember me. Now that I have you, I don't want to ruin it. Give me a few days with you. Let me live in this bubble for more than a second, please."

"Can you do that?" I ask. "Can you put everything aside and enjoy yourself?"

"Yes, I can. And I'm going to start now."

I have no idea what he means, but then I understand when he pushes the plates out of the way, and I'm lifted by my ass and placed on the kitchen table.

"What are you doing?"

"What does it look like I'm doing? I'm going for a walk," he deadpans before he places his hands on my chest, pushing me until my back hits the table. Next goes the thong. Once they are gone, he's pulling my legs apart.

"Again?"

"Once will never be enough, Skye. I'll never get my fill of you."

The cold air hits my exposed skin, but I don't have time to catch a breath before my body shivers from excitement. He leans in, nuzzling his nose in the apex of my thighs. Then he's moving his mouth over my heated skin, pressing kisses to my mound, swiping his tongue across my core.

He's torturing me.

Teasing me.

Trying to drive me crazy.

It works.

I'm past the point of madness.

When he pulls away, I whimper in protest, but his mouth slams against mine, shutting me up, as I taste myself on his tongue.

A heady aphrodisiac. It drives me wild.

"I'm going to fuck you," he growls.

Tobias pushes up from where he's kneeling in front of me.

His eyes meet mine, gaze hazy with lust, as he pulls down his gray sweats and grabs his cock in his hand.

"Don't move."

My breathing is erratic, my chest heaving as I wait.

Tobias steps forward, tugging from root to tip, and aligning himself with my core.

"Please," I beg, and then he's pushing forward, filling me completely in one forceful move.

He holds steady.

"More." I lift my hips, plunging him in deeper.

"I thought you wanted to take a walk?"

"Tobias . . ." My back arches. "Fuck the walk. I can find a better use for my legs right now."

He chuckles, pulling all the way out, then plunging back in.

A primal moan pours from my mouth. Tobias leans forward, lifts my pajama top and takes my nipple in his mouth.

Biting.

Sucking.

Our hips rotate together. Driving in and out, he picks up speed, thrusting at a punishing clip.

The sound of a plate hitting the ground doesn't stop us. He continues to move inside me.

I wrap my arms around his back, pulling him tighter. Then he pulls out slowly. So damn slow. But it feels like heaven.

He answers my moans by slamming inside me. His pace and movements are frenzied as though he's in a rush. Reaching his hand out, he places his finger where our bodies meet and strokes me. I quiver and shake at his touch.

It isn't long before I feel the impending release, my body tightening around him. I throw my head back, my eyes shutting, and fall over the edge. Into the abyss. Into heaven.

CHAPTER FORTY-TWO

Tobias

I TRY TO GIVE HER NORMAL.

Soon our lives will be anything but, which is why I lead her away from the kitchen and toward the bathroom.

It's a calculated risk to shower together. I'll want to have my way with her again, and I take the chance of never leaving the bathroom again. Once the water is warm, I pull us under the relaxing spray and then wash us both, rubbing the shampoo in her hair, taking care of her.

She keeps looking at me, looking at my bandaged wound. But I'm not weak.

"Stop looking at me like that," I say.

"Like what?"

"Like you want to take care of me."

"Maybe I do." I think about her words, and as much as I want to argue them, I feel the same way. An invisible thread tethers us, a bond no one will ever understand.

We lived.

We both lived through the terror, and for the rest of our lives, we will have the scars and memories to remind us. I pull her close to me and hold her wet body to mine. Her heart beats against my chest.

All those years ago, there was a moment when she stared into my eyes, panicked, and I fell in love with that girl. That fighter. The girl who saved me. I might have been angry, but that feeling never left.

I rinse the soap out of her hair, and once we are done, I wrap us in towels. Leading her into the bedroom, I grab her a pair of my sweats and a T-shirt. Tomorrow, Gideon will be wanting to speak. Tomorrow, everyone will. But we have tonight.

"What do you want to do?" I ask her.

"Go back in time," she answers honestly.

"To when?"

"To the day we first met."

"Would you change it?"

She nods. "I would. The only thing I wouldn't change is meeting you. But instead of what happened, I would cross the room and ask you to play with me."

"Let's do that."

"Do what?"

"Play a game." I take her hand in mine and lead her out of the room and down the hall.

"Where are we going?"

"Patience, Skye."

"Says the man who gets everything he wants every time he wants it."

"That's not true. I had to wait for you."

"You could have just told me."

"Where would the fun in that be?"

She stops walking, her head scrunching. "Why didn't you tell me?"

"You didn't remember me, Skye." That should make her understand.

"You were angry." Her voice is a whisper.

She's trying to understand what I felt this past month. I shrug it off like it's no big deal, but to me, it was. To me, it was devastating.

"I told you this already."

She shakes her head back and forth, a line forming between her brows. "All this time. All this time you wasted, and for what? You really are an idiot."

"I never said I was smart," I say with a chuckle. Only this woman can make me laugh at an insult.

I pull her arm and make her walk, and I'm surprised when she drops it. Maybe, like me, she knows the past is approaching. Soon, we won't be able to hide from it.

"I'll take the floor. You take the couch," I say as we walk into the library.

"Um, okay. Why?"

"As I said, I'm giving you that wish."

She smiles broadly. "Deal." She sits and then looks up at me as I move about the room. I grab the first game I see from the shelf and place the old board game on the ottoman in front of her, then take a seat on the rug. Skye squints her eyes at what I brought with a confused look on her face.

"What game is this?"

"It was my mother's. My nanny taught me, but don't worry, I'll teach you," I assure her with a smile.

"This game looks ancient."

"Well, I did grow up playing it." I shrug.

"Exactly . . . ancient."

"I'm not much older than you." I level her with my stare.

"Old enough that I have no idea how to play this," she teases.

"Four years older. That's nothing."

"How do you know so much about me? I never told you my age."

"Don't you know by now, I learned everything about you the moment I saw you in the courtroom."

"Was that planned?"

"No."

"How did you know it was me?"

"I could never forget your eyes."

She looks down at her hands, and I follow her stare. She's looking at the tattoo; the one she placed on her skin to honor me. My chest tightens. Looking back up, I see that her eyes are filled with tears.

"Don't."

"I believed him," she whispers.

"I don't want to do this now."

"Maybe we should."

"No, Skye. I want one goddamn normal day. I want one day when we don't have to talk of death and murder and revenge. For twenty years, those thoughts have occupied my brain. Give me one day, and I will give you one. Please. Please give this to me, even if it sucks."

Her hand reaches up and swipes at the tear, and then she nods. "You think it will suck? You don't like board games?"

"Not particularly," I admit.

She cocks her head to the side. "Then why are we playing?"

"Because you asked."

Her big blue eyes go wide. "And you would do anything I asked?"

"Within reason."

"Interesting." At that, her lips tip up into a mischievous smirk.

"I'd love to know what you are thinking," I state, though I have a pretty good idea exactly what she is thinking.

"I bet you would." She laughs while shaking her head. "Doesn't matter. We aren't doing it."

"Shame."

"Stop. Head out of the gutter. We are playing this game." She looks down at the old board game. "Okay, since you pulled it out, how do we play?"

"You roll the dice and move your pieces," I deadpan, and she rolls her eyes but laughs.

"Real helpful, Sherlock."

I smile at her as she takes a turn. She has no idea what she's doing. I can't stop laughing as Skye thinks about her next move. She plays with her tongue sticking out one side of her mouth, concentrating on not moving any of the pieces. It takes a while for her to get the grasp of the strange old game, but not long after, she's laughing and joking, and her smile lights up the room.

A part of me feels light and happy for the first time in a long time. I can't remember the last time I haven't had the weight of the world on my shoulders. But here, sitting beside Skye, I feel the calm that only she can bring.

CHAPTER FORTY-THREE

Skye

REALITY HAS A WAY OF CATCHING UP TO US.

We spent the night in each other's arms, but this morning, I woke alone. It was the most perfect twenty-four hours, but time doesn't stop for anyone, and before it slips by some more, we must face the aftermath of the war.

My arms stretch over my head, and my eyes blink at the morning rays streaming in from the large window in the bedroom.

I spent yesterday entwined in Tobias's arms, making up for lost time, but now, in the early morning sunshine, I step out of bed and walk over to the large window to look at the view. The property is beautiful. I wasn't paying attention when we first drove here, nor when I was nursing Tobias back to health, but I am now, and even though I don't know where here is, it's gorgeous.

It reminds me of the town I grew up in, Reddington.

The trees are dense, and I wonder if that's why he picked this location. No one would be able to breach it and find us in this little stretch of paradise.

Staring out into the horizon, I watch the trees sway slightly with the wind. It looks beautiful, like a perfect summer day. Something tells me today won't be that.

Moving away from the window, I walk across the room to enter the bathroom and go about making myself presentable. I don't know what is in store for me today, but I need to be ready.

It's not long before I'm showered and dressed. I throw on a pair of leggings and a T-shirt Tobias left on the counter for me, then I walk out of the bedroom and go in search of him.

I hear their voices before I see them, but Gideon and Tobias are already sitting at the table when I enter the kitchen.

"Morning." Tobias moves to stand, but I shake my head. He's still healing, and we didn't rest much yesterday.

He said he wasn't hurt, but last night before bed, I noticed the grimace. We weren't gentle. My cheeks feel warm as I remember the night before. And the day. And the morning.

I put my back to them so they don't notice the blush I'm sure is creeping up my cheeks. Grabbing a mug, I fill my own cup with coffee and then sit beside Tobias at the table. He leans over and places his lips on mine.

I'm surprised by his show of affection. I assumed he would be hands-off, but it seems clear by the way he pulls back and looks at me that he's more the "marking my territory" type of guy.

"Morning." My mouth splits into what I am sure looks like a silly grin on my face as I look over at Gideon, who sits across the table from me.

"Morning, Skye."

"Am I interrupting anything?" I lift the coffee to my mouth and take a sip.

"Nothing you can't hear," Tobias responds.

"Because I'm your legal counsel?" I ask.

He shakes his head, takes my hand back in his, and runs his finger across my tattoo. "No. Not because you're my lawyer." The way he looks at me makes me shiver, and I know without words,

I'm here because I mean something to him. Because he wants me around.

Because he needs me.

This whole time, since Tobias has been back in my life, I couldn't pinpoint the feeling I have when he's around. It's only now, now that I remember, now that I can understand our shared past, that I know why I've felt a connection to him from the moment I looked into his eyes. His words from all those years ago are still crisp in my ear. *I'm the plane, and you're the sky.*

"What time will the guys be here?" Gideon reaches for the water in the middle of the table and pours himself a glass.

"Soon." Tobias turns to face him while reaching his hand out to place it on my lap.

I wish I wasn't wearing leggings. The feeling of his skin on mine is the best feeling in the world.

"Who's coming?" I place my hand over his, needing the connection. I always want to touch him. It's the only thing that brings me calm.

"Just a few of my most trusted confidants."

"Do you need me to—?" His hand moves, and then his fingers are pressing down a little on my tattoo as if he's telling me to stay.

"You aren't going anywhere, Skye. Where I go, you go." When I don't say anything, he drills me with his stare. "Do you understand?"

"Kind of," I squeak.

"Room," he says to Gideon, who is quick to stand and vacate the space.

Then my chair is being dragged closer to him. The scratching sound echoes through the air. We are face-to-face, only a breath away.

"You are the only thing that matters to me. You are everything. Do you understand?"

"Yes."

"If you told me to drop this—"

I shake my head. "I won't."

"I know, but I would."

Leaning forward, I place my lips on his and say all the things I'm too scared to say with a kiss. I'm not afraid of much but losing him petrifies me. I already lost him once.

"What's wrong?"

I ponder whether I should say what is bothering me, but it pours out when I finally open my mouth.

"I can't lose you again."

Tobias moves fast, and the next thing I know, he's pulling me from the chair and placing me in his lap.

Touching might bring peace, but this, being cradled in his arms, feels like home.

"You won't."

"You can't promise me that." I tuck my head against his chest.

"No, I can't."

We have both lost so much. We know reality is not always sunshine and roses.

"We need to speak to your father." Tobias's hand tightens around me, preventing me from moving away. Instead, I tip my head up to look at him. "We need to know why he lied to you."

"Maybe it wasn't a lie? Maybe he thought it—"

"No, Skye. He knew. He was the policeman on duty that day, and he adopted you. There is more to this story than we know."

I nod my head in agreement.

"It's time we find out everything." He bends his head and places a kiss on my mouth. Silencing any objections.

He's right.

I spent my life fearing the dark, but it's time I swing the door open and see everything. It's time the past is brought out into the light. Only then can we move on. That's when we will see the truth.

CHAPTER FORTY-FOUR

Tobias

E VERYBODY IS HERE.

All of us sit around a large table as if we are about to play poker. But we aren't. We are not at Cyrus's house.

This is not a Friday night, and the hundred-thousand-dollar buy-in is not on the table. It's not a friendly game with zero money. No, this is something quite the opposite, and unfortunately, it keeps happening. It's not easy to leave the underworld, and it's even more difficult to leave when you have unfinished business.

"What's the plan?" Lorenzo asks before he lifts his scotch to his mouth, and I look over at where he sits. He's beside Matteo, who's his cousin and former boss. *So much for retiring.* It's not just him who has come out from his self-proclaimed exile from this life. Alaric Prince is also at the table, as is Cristian, who took over for Alaric when he retired from arms dealing.

On the far side are Cyrus and Trent.

"We need to lure Felix out of hiding." It's Trent who speaks, and everyone in the room agrees.

"It's not that easy." All eyes turn to Cyrus. "From what I've heard, no one has seen him since the attack. Jax, anything to add?" Jaxson Price is not physically here, but his voice rings through the air via the state-of-the-art surveillance system that Jaxson and his security company installed.

Jaxson has been tasked with finding Felix, which means he probably already has. "He hasn't been seen, but that doesn't mean we don't know where he is," he says.

"Where is he, then, Jax?" I lift my own glass and take a swig.

"His building." With the surround sound in the room, Jax's voice booms through the air.

"His apartment building?"

"Yep."

"Ballsy." Placing my glass down. "He's not even pretending to hide."

"Nope. According to his staff, he has a cold, but he's been conducting business from home. He's even been Zooming about a new mall he wants to build."

"Are you fucking kidding?" This pisses me the fuck off.

"Nope." And I can tell by Jaxson's voice that he's serious.

"I'm here—" I begin before Lorenzo cuts me off.

"Getting laid," Lorenzo jokes, and I narrow my eyes at him.

"Careful." My voice rings through the air with a clear warning.

Lorenzo holds his hands up in apology. "My bad." He looks at me and cocks his head. "Speaking of that, care to explain how you went from annoying your lawyer to—"

"Lorenzo," I warn.

"Not annoying her."

"How much do you know about my past?" I say, and that's when I hear the sound of soft footsteps.

"Our past," Skye cuts in, walking across the room and taking the seat next to me.

"Not a hell of a lot," Cyrus's rough voice answers.

"Because the asshole keeps us all in the dark." Lorenzo has

always given me shit for being closed off, so it's no surprise when he says this. "The time for silence is over. Tell us everything."

I let out a long sigh and feel Skye's hand under the table, holding my hand.

"This story is twenty years in the making. Some pieces are missing." I leave out the little details not relevant to the story. I don't tell them it was my birthday. Nor do I mention Skye's being the same day. "My father and I had just moved to Reddington a few months earlier. The cartel sent my father to distribute cocaine through New York. The plan was to create a foothold through the Tri-State and Upstate areas. Reddington's proximity to both gives him not only access to the docks but also the safety of hiding under the radar in a small town."

Skye squeezes my hand.

"The plan wasn't well thought out; there was already a distribution pipeline. A war started. Far enough from town that it didn't touch it, but we had enemies, and the enemy wanted to make an example of us for the cartel.

There was a mom-and-pop diner in the town, one that was famous for its shakes. It's all I wanted, and, well, there was a hit. It was a massacre. My father was killed, and Skye's parents were caught in the crossfire."

"Felix?" Cyrus leans forward, and I nod at him.

"Yeah."

"This vendetta you've had for him stems from this?" From here, I can practically see the wheels turning in Cyrus's brain. His face is stern, jaw locked.

"Yes."

"And does he know?" Cyrus looks to be working out all the loose ends in his head, but until I tell him everything, there will still be pieces of the puzzle he won't be able to connect.

"No."

Cyrus lifts his brow.

"My father's name was Tobias. I changed my name to his after he died and changed my last name to my uncle's."

"Felix thinks he's fighting over control for New York, not some past blood on his hands?"

"Yes."

"And you?"

"I have been looking for confirmation that it was ~~him~~."

"And did you find that?"

"On paper, no one has ever been able to put the gun in his hand. He wasn't there. He didn't go down for the crime. No one who was captured afterward could ever say that Felix was involved. The local drug runners were all rounded up and arrested. It was the biggest drug bust and takedown in New York's history."

Lorenzo nods. "It was all over the papers. It made careers. I didn't realize it was you. I knew you were a Kosta, but I assumed you were the son of George Kosta. He was a legend."

"George was my uncle. My mother's sister's husband. He raised me."

"How did you keep this from us?" I can tell by his tone that Cyrus is pissed.

"Not easily."

"And you never fucking thought we should know?" He stands from the table, his chair flipping over. I get it. We have gone to war with each other. Keeping this from them is a huge breach of trust.

"Cyrus." He's gone.

"Give him a minute," Matteo says. "Listen, man, I get it. I know why you didn't let us in, but see it from our point of view. We let you into our home. You met our kids."

This is an unwritten rule amongst men like us, and I broke it. Standing from the chair, I head out the door Cyrus left from.

"Tell me why I shouldn't kill you." I hear as soon as I'm in the hall.

He's pissed.

"You came to my house and lied to my fucking face. I put Ivy's life in your hands. I trusted you with my fucking family." Although I never lied outright, an omission of truth is the same thing in our circles. "I knew you wanted out. I knew you hated Felix. I don't even care about that shit. But your fucking name . . . Like. Hell."

"That boy died the day his father did."

It's not untrue. A part of me did die that day. That's why hearing that Skye thought I was dead shocked me to the core. It wasn't really far from the truth.

"That's not enough of a reason." The hurt is clear in his eyes. He treated me like family. Unconventional family, but family, nonetheless.

I step forward and place my hand on his shoulder. "I fucked up." I drop my arm and step back. Giving a moment to collect his thoughts. "I won't do it again."

"Yeah. You fucking did." He lifts his arm and then tugs at the root of his hair. "Is there anything else you haven't told me?"

"No."

He nods, not to me but to himself, and then he locks eyes with me, lifting his pointer finger. "One. You get one."

There is no need to clarify the threat. He will kill me. And to be honest, I would deserve it. I have killed for less. Without another word, he strides back in and heads toward the table.

"What makes you think it's Felix?" He's back to business, and I'm happy for it.

"When he rose to power in New York after that incident, it made the most sense."

"But you have no proof. Nothing that connects him to the massacre." I shake my head at Cyrus.

"No."

"So . . . this could be completely separate."

"It could, but I don't think it is."

"And you?" Cyrus turns to Skye. "You work for him. That's not a coincidence."

"No," she answers.

"Why do you work for Felix?"

"Well, I don't work for him as much as I work for a law firm that happens to represent him." Cyrus shoots her a look that tells her to cut the crap. "But since we are opening up, yes, I had reason to believe Felix was involved."

"Why?"

"I had evidence that placed him in Reddington at the time . . . doing business. I thought it seemed a bit too convenient."

"What evidence?" Cyrus is a dog with a bone. Until she tells him everything. He won't stop.

"My father . . ." She shakes her head. "My adoptive father has a file on the massacre."

"Why does your dad have a file on the crime?"

"He was the cop on duty."

"Explain."

"My adoptive father was the cop who found us in the closet. When I woke up in the hospital, my parents had died. I was shot. Things were confusing, and I had no one. At first, he fostered me, then he adopted me."

"He also told you I died," I mumble under my breath.

"He did, and I'm going to find out why. But first, we need a plan." She narrows her eyes at me, and I can't help but laugh. Everyone at the table turns to me at the sound. It's not something they hear often, so I can understand the surprise.

"Tell us about the file you found." Cyrus says.

"Ironically, it had nothing to do with our parents' case," she explains. "It concerned other crimes that year."

"Go on . . ."

"It involved properties that my client, Felix Bernard, financed. It didn't say much, but it got me thinking. What were Felix's ties to that town, and what would he have to gain? Since I now know his shopping malls are a front for his other enterprises, it made me wonder if he was the puppet master behind everything."

I nod. "This was the smoking gun for me as well. I connected

Felix to a building permit in Reddington. He purchased the property prior to the massacre."

Skye's eyes narrow, and her nose scrunches. "What was the purpose of the war?"

"For him to control the narrative. He owns the land and the supply chain of drugs, so he used the property to traffic the drugs through the state. The location is prime real estate."

Skye clenches her jaw for a second before nodding her head. It seems we both came to the same conclusion.

"My father's business put a damper on his plan," I add, and she lets out a sigh.

"And my family was a casualty," she says in a broken whisper.

Skye stirs in her chair, moving her body so her face is no longer visible. I know what she's doing. She doesn't want anyone to see the emotions playing out on her features. It's a habit I know all too well. For years, I have been keeping everyone in my life at arm's length.

Seeing the pain so clearly on Skye and knowing how much I wish to take the pain away makes me see I was wrong. You can't do everything alone. Sometimes you need support and people to lean on. I look around the room. Those people are here.

"I've been a dick," I say to everyone and no one in particular. "To all of you." I pivot my body and look at where Skye's back faces me. Lifting my hand, I place it on her lap, and she turns back. "Despite everything, you're all still here. Thanks."

"Shit's boring. Nothing better to do," Lorenzo teases, but I know he's full of shit. The room is quiet for a second before Cyrus leans forward and places his elbows on the table. He looks fucking exhausted.

I feel it. The past few years have been hell. Probably the next after this, too.

"We need a plan. One to lure Felix out of hiding."

Again, silence descends as everyone considers ideas that'll get Felix to expose himself.

It's Skye who speaks first. "Use me."

What the fuck! There is no way anyone would ever contemplate doing that, but as my gaze lands on Lorenzo, I see the wheels already turning.

"No!" I tell anyone in the room who would dare even consider it.

"Hear me out—" she starts, but I don't let her continue.

"I said no. Absolutely not." I glare at her as I reply sharply.

In typical Skye Matthews form, she squares her shoulders, doesn't look at me, and addresses the other men in the room. Her defensive nature and tough exterior piss me off and turn me on in equal measures. I push down the latter and welcome the anger.

"Where does Williams think I am?" She's looking at Cyrus when she speaks as if he's running the show. Spoiler alert: he's not.

I glare at him. "Do not answer her."

She spins her attention back to me. "It's a logical question. Does he know I'm here?"

"No," Cyrus answers her, not me.

"I made it look like you were shaken by the fact you think your client is missing." It's Jax who speaks this time through the speakers in the wall.

Skye has a dazed expression on her face. "And how did you do that?" she asks. There is a bite in her voice that she reserves for when she is annoyed. She's pissed. Rightfully so.

She stands from the chair and paces around the room. She moves back and forth, and I wonder what she's thinking. Knowing her, it pisses her off that Jaxson Price most definitely hacked her email and pretended to be her. This doesn't shock me, but then again, I have seen him do worse.

It's fascinating to watch the emotions play out on her face as she decides what to say. Her mouth opens and shuts, and lines form around her eyes. When she finally speaks, it's not what I expect. "This plan works. Also, Jaxson . . ."

"Yeah, Skye?"

"Don't hack me again, or I will kill you."

He laughs. "Duly noted."

"What are you thinking about over there, Lawyer Lady?" Trent teases, amusement present in his voice.

"Use me. If he doesn't know I'm with you, I can be bait." Skye speaks so matter-of-fact it's almost hard to object. However, it's not going to happen.

"As I said before, no." I drill her with a look to shut her up and stop this insanity. My eyes narrow, and my jaw clenches because, to make matters worse, she isn't looking at me when I do.

Nope. She's looking at Cyrus and then Lorenzo. While I'm biting back my anger, she's imploring these men, my men, to agree with her. To let us sacrifice her.

"No. Fucking. Way." I abruptly stand from my chair, causing it to fall to the floor with a crash.

"Tobias!" Everyone turns toward Matteo. "She has a right to this fight." I narrow my eyes at him.

"Careful, cousin, you're treading into dangerous territory. Tobias looks like he might skin you alive."

"He might, but trust me when I say she's right. Sometimes you have to put away your fears."

"Priceless, coming from you, Matteo," I snap. "If this were you . . . Oh wait, this *was* you, and you lost your shit."

"You can't always protect her. Sometimes, she has to protect you back."

"Don't I fucking know it? She and I have the bullet wounds to remember the two times she did." Pulling my shirt up for emphasis, I dare anyone at this table to object.

That's when I feel the soft touch of her hand. It's on my shoulder, trying to get my attention and calm me. It's working. Having her close is enough to calm the beast inside of me. The next thing I know, she steps up to me and wraps her arms around my middle.

"I need to do this, Tobias." She's not asking permission, nor should she. She is telling me, but she still wants my support.

"Tobias . . ." Her lips touch mine, pleading with me to see her side. "My parents died, too."

I know she's right, and I also know this is the best option for us. Reluctantly, I nod, and she kisses me again before pulling away.

"Fine. We do this, but we need a foolproof plan. One where there is no way Skye can get hurt. You hear me, Jax? No matter the plan, and I don't care how you do it, we need eyes and ears everywhere."

"Got it."

"Now, everyone, grab a drink. It's time to figure this shit out."

One way or another, we are getting Felix. I only pray there are no complications.

CHAPTER FORTY-FIVE

Skye

THE GUYS ARE ALL GONE. IT'S JUST US. THE PLAN IS THAT tomorrow, I will resurface, and despite Tobias's objections and my annoyance over being hacked, I'll play the part I need to play of the concerned lawyer.

At this moment, rumors are circulating that Tobias Kosta died in the explosion. This is the narrative we want. Under this false story, we have time to move about and draw Felix out. Which also means I need to step up, go into the office, and set myself up to get Felix out of hiding.

It's too much to think about right now. Instead of spending my night wondering and worrying, I intend to spend the little time I have with Tobias.

When we are back in the bedroom, I notice Tobias appears distant. He doesn't look at me. Instead, his face is pointed in the opposite direction, and he's locked in a stare. But there is nothing there. Knowing him, he's looking off at a speck on the carpet and lost in his thoughts.

"What are you thinking about?" I ask.

He doesn't answer. Instead, he tugs me closer to him, wrapping his arm around me as I rest my head on his shoulder.

"I'm thinking about how if he touches you, Skye—"

"He won't," I interject, moving to pull away. But Tobias won't let me.

"You don't know that. You can't." His voice sounds velvety smooth, yet it's still laced with steel. "What if we're out, and someone tries to hurt you?"

"That's not going to happen. I can take care of myself."

"But what if it does?"

"Tobias, I can handle myself. You don't need to worry about me."

"I have worried about you for twenty years." It feels as if my heart has broken open.

I'm briefly transported back to the past, when I'm still in the closet.

My eyes close of their own accord, and I can see it like it was yesterday. I want to reach out and touch the boy sitting across from me.

His movement from beside me has me returning to the present, but I wish I could go back in time and be there for him.

I can't go back. I can only move forward. Live in the present.

Take care of him now. I want to heal him, calm him like he calmed me all those years ago.

"You can't protect me all the time," I say into his hair. "I'll die of boredom if you try. I need you to let me live my own life and help you. We need to do this together. It's the only way, Tobias. The present isn't much different from the past. We lived through hell because we had each other."

My words hang in the air. The room goes quiet around us. Neither of us speaks, probably because neither knows what to say. I look down at my hands, wringing my fingers together.

"Why do you think he lied to me?" I break the silence.

"That's a question only he can answer." The edge to his tone worries me.

"I need to speak to him."

"You will, but not tonight."

He moves from beside me and drops down to kneel in front of me. Taking my hands, he holds my wrist, swiping his finger over the sensitive spot.

"Skye, once this is over, we can get to the bottom of everything." He tilts his head back and closes his eyes, then he opens them and looks at me. "I promise, but please, not before Felix is taken care of. I need to know you're safe."

I understand where he's coming from. The same thoughts ran through my brain when I heard Felix was going to go after him. Even before I knew who he was and our connection, I couldn't lose him. I didn't want to live in a world without him.

Not then. Not now. Not ever. A sharp pain tears through me at the thought, and I realize . . . I love him.

I love Tobias Kosta.

I have loved him probably since the day I met him. The day in the closet when I found peace in the most horrific moment. The revelation takes my breath away. I'm too scared to love him and lose him. I can't bear the thought of watching him die.

"What's wrong?" His fingers have moved, and they are now tilting my chin up. In the reflection of his eyes, I see it. He doesn't need to say anything because he loves me, too.

"You love me," I whisper. Not a question but a statement. He nods.

"And you love me?" The look he gives me takes my breath away. Like he was lost, and now he's found.

"Yes." I smile, feeling my heart flutter. "I love you, too. But—"

"Talk to me."

"I don't want to love you and lose you." That's my biggest fear. "I'm so scared."

"I know," Tobias says. "But you don't need to be. Don't be

scared. Everything will work out. It always does." His eyes soften. "You won't ever lose me. I will always be here, Skye."

With that, he's stands up from the floor, taking my hands in his and leading us farther into the room until my legs hit the bed.

I'm pushed back until I'm lying down, and then he's removing our clothes. Once we are both fully naked, he crawls up my body. I feel him poking at my entrance, already hard and engorged.

Even though I know it's coming, he takes my breath away with one quick thrust that has me letting out a gasp at the sudden movement.

For a moment, nothing happens. He's allowing me to adjust.

Together, we lie there for a brief second, the feel of us connected almost too much to handle.

I wish I could stay this way forever, but as I look up at Tobias, his jaw locked, I see the restraint he's using to keep still.

I tilt my hips up, telling him with my body what I want.

He lowers his mouth to mine and starts to fuck me.

He gives me exactly what I need. Moving at an addicting pace, he drags himself in and out.

But soon, it's not enough, and I need to feel more. Wrapping my arms around his neck, I kiss him harder at a frantic, desperate pace. He answers my pleas, telling me with the way his body moves inside of me how much he wants me.

"Faster," I pant. "Harder." I wrap my legs around him to urge him on, trying to make him speed up his movements. He lets out a hearty laugh. The sound doesn't happen often. I love that laugh as much as I love the man it belongs to.

Despite his amusement, he gives me what I need and pumps faster.

He thrusts harder.

My breathing becomes frantic as he tries to push me over the edge.

I'm so close but not there yet.

"More. I need more."

Snaking his hand between us, he pushes his thumb over my clit, massaging it in delicious, slow circles.

He picks up his pace. My heart beats faster, and a heady feeling spreads through my body. I'm close, so close, and by the way his movements become more erratic, I think he's close, too.

Together, we find what we need. Together, we fall over the edge.

We stay entwined in each other's arms for a few more minutes, allowing our breathing to regulate. When we both calm, he pushes off me, and I immediately miss his weight. My eyes drift shut. I shift on the mattress, resting my head on his chest. His arms wrap around me and pull me closer.

"I never want this moment to end," I say into his neck, muffling my voice, but I know he heard me.

I wait for him to reply. One second passes. Two. Three. He presses a kiss to my forehead, silent for a few minutes before he does.

"It won't."

———————•———————

The next day, however, does come. The moment is broken, and I'm scared we will never get it back. I only have one more day here with Tobias before I have no choice but to go back home and back to my life.

I wonder how we will spend the day.

It's the last one for a while.

As if Tobias can read my mind, he crosses the distance of the kitchen and stands in front of where I am sitting at the table.

"Come on. I want to take you somewhere."

I place my mug back down on the table and tilt my head up to him. He looks so peaceful today. Not like the man I have seen in the office. No, this is a different Tobias. A lighter one. I wish he would always be like this. This Tobias is like the sun, and I want to bask in it. Tomorrow, this look will be gone, and I'm not sure when it will be back.

"Where are we going?"

"It's a surprise." The playfulness of his smile echoes in his voice.

He's devastating when he smiles. If I weren't already in love with him, I would be after today.

Standing up, I step forward and throw my arms around his neck. Tucking myself into him, I inhale. His subtle fragrance of cinnamon and wood tickles my nostrils.

He places a kiss on the top of my head before pulling back and taking my hand in his.

Then we are heading out the back door of the house.

"A walk?"

"I wanted to show you the property."

We continue to walk until we reach a path in the woods, then follow that. It's darker in this part of the woods, and the sun barely peeks in through the branches of the trees.

It reminds me of a fairy tale. The dark woods and a long path . . . I almost expect a cottage at the end.

But instead of a cottage, in reality, there is a tree house.

"What is this?"

"Come on up, and I'll show you."

On the side of the tree is an old, rickety wooden ladder.

Tobias stops suddenly, slowly moving to face me, then motions to the ladder.

I cock my head, then laugh. "Hell to the no."

His gaze lowers to mine. "I promise it's perfectly safe."

"It looks like a death trap."

"Would I ever let anything happen to you?"

"No."

"Then up you go."

With Tobias standing beside me, I make my way up.

It's larger and much safer than I thought it would be from the outside. This wasn't built by kids. This looks professional.

"How did you know about this?"

"I built it."

"Why?"

I move into the tree house and take a seat on the floor. Tobias, who looks too large for the space, surprisingly doesn't.

"I built it one day for my children."

"Your children?" My heart drums in my chest.

"The ones I will eventually have."

A nervous giggle bubbles up from my mouth.

"Oh."

"Don't worry, I'm in no rush."

"Good to know." I playfully swat his hand, and he captures my wrist. His fingers spread over my skin, his thumb on my tattoo.

"What do you remember of your parents?" he asks.

I bite my lip. "Not a lot. Not as much as I hoped." My head tilts up, and I try to remember.

My mom's blue eyes come into focus, her smile and her laughter. My dad sits beside her. His hazel-green eyes look at her with love. The way he smiles is contagious.

"I remember how he looked at her."

"How was that?"

"He looked at her the way you look at me." With love.

The way he's looking at me now. Like I am the moon, sun, and the *sky*. His sky.

"Do you remember a good place?"

"Our place was taken from us. Our place was Al's."

"When this is all said and done, we'll fix that. We'll make new memories."

"I don't know if I can."

"You're the strongest person I know . . . you can."

"And you?"

"I remember this tree house."

My eyes go wide. "This exact one?"

He laughs. "Yes."

"But how . . . ?"

"This was my first home. The home I should have lived in. And for a while, I did. But then my father uprooted us. Wanting to grow the business, he moved from town to town to make sure he had the connections he needed and eventually moved us to Reddington. Years later, I bought it back."

"But you said you built this."

"Well, technically, I rebuilt it. The one I used to sit in as a small child was long gone, but it sat here in this tree. I remember hiding here the day we left. I didn't want to go."

"What happened?"

"He eventually found me. He said that we would be back. That we were off on a grand adventure."

"Grand adventure all right. More like a Greek tragedy," I mumble.

"It was an adventure. He was right. Though it was not the adventure he had envisioned, it still was one. And now you're by my side."

"I'm happy I am."

"Me too, Skye. Me too."

After that, we sit in silence.

Feeling the enormity of the last part of the adventure before this story ends.

———————•———————

Hours later, we sit together in his bed, but no matter how much I try, I can't stop thinking about my father.

This afternoon was about my parents, but there is no end to this story without my adoptive dad.

All the lies and mistruths were piling up. A mountain has

grown of all the things he hasn't told me, and I don't know how to climb to the top and see the big picture.

My hand slams down on my lap, and Tobias snaps his head in my direction from where he is sitting on the bed next to me.

"Everything okay over there?" He chuckles.

A burning sensation spreads in my mouth as I realize I've bitten my lip so forcefully that I have torn the skin. The taste of copper touches my tongue as I swipe it out to soothe the wound.

"I need to talk to him tonight."

"Who do you need to talk to?"

Cocking my head, I give Tobias my best *are you fucking kidding me* look.

He chuckles again, a sound I will never grow tired of. It's my favorite sound, like music to my ears, especially since I know that it doesn't happen often.

"My father, Tobias. Duh." I roll my eyes.

"Duh? Really? Did I miss the memo? Are you in high school?"

"Har. Har. Har. But seriously"—I sigh overdramatically, playing right into Tobias's previous comment—"what do I even say? I feel like there is so much I want to say to him. About his health. About the lie. But I don't know where to start."

From beside me, Tobias reaches his hand out and takes mine in his. He lightly rubs my hand, then he trails his fingers over my tattoo.

I think my tattoo is his favorite part about me, and as much as I like to touch it to calm myself, Tobias might like to do it even more than I do.

"I wish I had an answer for you. I wish I knew what to say. The thing is, as much as you don't want to hear this, you don't have much time with him. I don't think you should waste the moments you have fighting. So maybe don't tell him you know and wait for him to come to you. How about you just ask him about me? Ask him where he got the information."

"Okay, so you don't think I should tell him I know he's sick?"

"No. Skye. You can't, and not just because you violated a lot of laws to do it. Which is technically a problem since you're a lawyer but mainly because he's gotta tell you. You know that, right?"

"I do."

"Just be calm. Remember, if he hasn't told you, it's because he's not ready for you to know you're losing him. Maybe he doesn't want it to be real."

"Yeah," I groan. "I know you're right. But I feel like I don't know him at all."

Tobias drops my hand, and I almost protest, but then he's wrapping his arm around me and tucking me into his chest. My favorite place to be. The only place I feel completely safe. The only place I feel completely at home.

"He's the man who raised you. The man who loved you." I nod against him, my nose tickling from the tears lodged in my eyes that I refuse to shed. I stay curled up in his arms for a few more minutes, soaking in the strength he gives me. Then when I feel I can, I reach for my cell phone.

Before I can think twice, I dial.

It takes a few seconds for him to answer, but then he does.

"Skye?" His voice sounds older and even more tired than the last time, if that's even possible.

"Hey, Dad."

"Hey, sweet girl. How are you? I've missed you." Hearing him say that, I almost want to abandon this whole plan. I don't want to upset him. Tobias is right. We might not have that much more time.

"I'm sorry I haven't visited in a few weeks, Dad."

"Too busy running the city." His chuckle warms my heart. I will cherish that sound.

I try not to let my voice crack. "Hardly."

"Don't sell yourself short. You're incredible."

My heart aches as unshed tears pool. Tobias must know it, too, because his lips touch my forehead.

"Dad—"

"Yeah."

"I've been thinking . . ." I stop, trying to decide how best to broach the topic.

"Never a good pastime."

"I know. I know. Damn brain." I laugh. "But recently, I've been thinking a lot about my life. About my past."

"My dear, sweet girl." It's almost said as a warning, and I know he wants to change the topic. Been there done this conversation, I know the next line already, "Leave the past where it is."

"No, Dad, please. I need to say this."

"Okay." He sounds hesitant. Maybe even nervous.

"I know you told me that boy died," I mutter, not making any sense.

"What boy?"

"You know what boy," I say, harder than I mean to. How can he forget or be confused? There has only ever been one boy.

From where I'm sitting in Tobias's arms, I can feel his body tense. It no longer feels like I'm cradled into a warm chest. Now it feels like rocks are my backrest. This isn't just about me.

I move into him, wrapping my free arm around his torso. I'm not sure how I'll be able to talk with my head in his neck, but I can't let him go right now.

"The boy in the storage closet with me."

"Oh."

I take a deep breath and will myself to calm down and not yell at him.

"How did you know he died?"

"That was a long time ago—" I know what he is going to say. He's going to try to change the subject, but I'm not going to let him.

"Dad." My tone is a warning.

He lets out a deep breath, followed by a rattly cough.

Stay the course, Skye.

"You kept asking about him, but the thing was, I couldn't find anything on him after he went to the hospital. It was the strangest thing. It was like his presence disappeared."

"And that was enough for you to tell me he was dead?"

"It was so long ago I can't remember."

"Please, think," I practically beg.

He's silent for a minute, then he coughs again. "I asked around. I even called the DA."

"And . . . ?"

"Eventually, I was told that the boy had gone missing and that he was most likely dead. The hit was for his father . . . so everyone assumed they got to him, too."

"And you didn't look into it?"

"Things were crazy then. I had more important things to do than look for a criminal's kid."

"Dad." I stop him because I don't want to hear any more about how everyone failed Tobias.

"I had you, Skye. You needed me."

"Maybe he needed someone," I whisper, and I'm not sure my dad hears, but I know Tobias does.

I pull back and look up into Tobias's blue eyes. They are endless ocean and forever skies; they are home. "I'm sorry," I mouth to him, and he gives me a small smile.

"I have to go, but I'm going to come visit soon." I feel defeated, and my heart is breaking. "I love you," I say.

"I love you, too."

Once off the phone, I can't help the tears that fall. "I'm sorry."

"You have nothing to be sorry for. At least we know now." Tobias is trying to hold it together, but when I look at him, I see the real him. I see beyond the façade he portrays. I see a man who's hurting and needs closure.

That he still doesn't have.

"Come here." He moves away from me, then stands from the

bed. I stand as well before he is taking my hand in his and pulling me with him.

"What are we doing?" I ask as I follow by his side.

"We're going where I go to think."

"The tree house again?" My cheeks feel warm about the way he kissed me, the way he touched me there.

He halts his steps and looks down at me, and I can't help but marvel at the twinkle in his blue eyes. "Nope," he responds. "We're going on the roof."

"You go to think on the roof?"

Tobias's expression stills and grows more serious. "I do."

"Why?"

"Let me show you." The deep timbre of his voice has butterflies fluttering in my stomach.

"Okay," I respond.

Holding my hand, he leads me toward a door and then up a flight of stairs. Like the ones in his office, they are wide and open. But now that I have found Tobias again, I don't think I'm claustrophobic anymore. Having him with me anchors me.

He throws open another door at the top of the stairs, and this one leads outside.

The fresh air smells different than in the city. It smells of salty water and trees.

It smells like freedom, and I can understand why he needs the air.

We take a step farther onto the deck, and that's when I see Tobias tip his head back to look up. I follow suit.

Stars illuminate the night sky. Like little tea lights, they flutter and flicker from above.

Once on top, my mouth hangs open.

"I have never seen anything so beautiful," I say in awe.

"I have." He's not talking about the stars.

"Why do you come here?"

"I like to look at the sky," he says, but I know there is a double meaning there.

Flashes of the last month flutter through my mind of all the times I have caught him looking up. "It's because of me?" I whisper.

"Yes."

Like a freight train, it hits. My knees buckle beneath me, but Tobias's arms bracket around me and catch me.

"I'm what calms you?"

"Like I'm what calms you." He motions toward my tattoo. Taking my wrist, he places his lips over it. Then he lays me under the canopy of stars and kisses every inch of my body. Telling me with each press of his lips what I mean to him.

How he's always loved me from the beginning.

How our souls were always entwined.

And then, underneath our sky, our mouths touch. Our tongues collide. His arms wrap around my back until there is no space separating us.

He kisses me, and I kiss him. This kiss tells of promises and futures of a shared past and love.

Beneath the canopy above, he tells me over and over again that we were fated. That we are whole.

That we are the other part of each other's soul.

He kisses my lips.

Spreads my thighs.

Then he makes love to me.

And with each thrust of his hips, I'm lost.

But then, most importantly, I'm found.

CHAPTER FORTY-SIX

Skye

THE NEXT MORNING, I WAKE WITH A NEED TO SHOW TOBIAS the spot where I go to think. He showed me a part of himself, and I want to do the same.

I look over at him. He's still asleep on his stomach. His back muscles are exposed as the sheet has crept down to only cover his lower body.

Leaning in, I place a kiss on his cheek, and he stirs at the contact.

"Morning," he groans. "What time is it?"

"It's still early."

"You leave today."

I feel those words in my bones.

Today I leave.

Today I'll be separated from Tobias.

"I do." I nestle into him, wrapping my arms around his waist. "I'm not ready to go."

"I know." He places a kiss on my head. "But it will be over soon."

He's not wrong. It will be over soon, but who knows what the outcome will be.

There are so many things to say, but I don't know where to start. I can't think. All I can do is listen to the thumping of his heart as we both grow silent.

I don't know how long I hold him, but I eventually feel restless of the unknown. "When do I have to head home? Do we have time to make a stop?"

"I wasn't going to take you."

It feels like I'm punched in the gut. I go to move, but Tobias's arms won't let me.

"I can't be seen, Skye."

He's right. The whole plan rides on him not being found.

"I know. You can't. That being said, are you able to sneak away from here for a bit?"

Please say yes.

"I think we can work that out."

"Good. Get up." A smile breaks across my face, and I place my hands on his chest and push up.

"You're not the boss."

"No?" My lips spread wide and then I wink at him.

His own smile plays on his face. "You know, that's how I knew."

My eyes widen. "Knew what?"

"That it was you."

His comment shocks me and makes no sense. I shake my head in confusion.

"I don't understand. I thought you did some crazy background check and that's how."

"I did." Tobias's hand reaches out and swipes the stray piece of hair that has fallen in front of my face. "I searched for you for years, but I didn't know you changed your name or that you were adopted. It wasn't until I got Jaxson Price to look into you that I saw the closed adoption papers."

"Then how did you know?"

The tips of his fingers move from my hair, trace my jaw, and then settle on my lips.

"You looked at me in the courtroom; you smirked at me with a mischievous smile, and then you winked."

"I'm not following."

"You did that as a child. That day." He drops his finger from my mouth but replaces it with his lips.

We stay entwined in each other arms until it's finally time to leave. Once we are in his car, he asks me where we are going, and I tell him Reddington.

Thirty minutes later, we are pulling up to the cemetery. I don't have us park near my parents' grave, instead, we park beside the tree. The old oak that I have been visiting for twenty years.

Silently, we get out of the car and walk up the small hill. When I stop at the small cross, Tobias moves to stand beside me.

We both look down at the makeshift grave site.

"Who's buried here?" he asks, and I can't help but laugh, and he places his hand on my shoulder to turn me to face him.

"You."

His blue eyes widen. "Me?"

He looks at me like I'm nuts, but I guess from his point of view, I am.

"Yeah, so—This is awkward."

"I'm *dying* to hear this story, apparently." And at least he's not disturbed to be looking at his own grave.

"After my parents died, and I was adopted, you know how I looked for you and was told . . ." I can't say it. It still hurts too much. To repeat the lie. "I wanted—I used to come here and talk to you. This was the only place I could think. Where I felt calm. Every day I came here. Eventually, I decided to make a cross because it didn't feel right to just talk to the air."

"As opposed to the sky," he deadpans playfully.

"Exactly, talking to the sky is weird," I tease back.

"So . . ." He looks around the cemetery, his gaze settling back on the white cross. "This is where I was buried?"

"Yep."

"And the penitents roses? Were those for me?"

"They were. They were my way to apologize for living when you didn't."

From beside me, I see Tobias grin, and then he starts to shake his head with a chuckle. "I stole from my own grave."

"You what?"

"Nothing."

I move until I'm standing in front of him and place my hand on my hip.

"Tobias Kosta," I playfully scold. "Did you steal the flowers I placed for you on 'your grave'?" I air quote. "Holy crap, you did." My mouth drops open and then slams shut. "You decorated your office with them to mess with me?"

"Guilty."

"You're lucky I love you because you are one sick man."

"I've been told that a time or two."

"But you're mine."

It's surreal to be back in my apartment. It's been a few days since I camped out at Tobias's, but it feels like that's where I belong. Back in my own space, everything feels off.

From the limited information I have, Jaxson Price has taken the last day to fit my apartment with listening devices. Creepy? Yes. Necessary? Also, yes.

With the plan in motion, I need Felix to come to me. It's the best way to lure him in. The problem is, since the truce was broken between him and Tobias, he hasn't been seen in public. If we can convince him that Tobias is dead, missing, or on the run, we think he will resurface.

There isn't much time to get ready. Taking a quick shower feels wrong. It's like I'm washing off the memory of Tobias, but I do have to go to work, so I have no choice. With my hair wet and clinging to my skin, I stare at myself in the mirror. My reflection is blurry because of the condensation in the room. Will Felix be able to see through my act? Do I look different from the girl who went to the gala with him?

Do I look like a girl who found out the boy she missed was right in front of her face? That the man she was falling for was the same person?

I hope not because our lives are at stake. My ability to fool the snake is imperative to the plan. By the time I'm dressed, it's eight o'clock. Monday morning sucks on a good day, but when you are doing what I am, it's unbearable.

I walk into the office an hour later. Nervous energy courses through me. It feels like my stomach is empty, and my heart is beating so fast it might explode. My hands shake at my sides, but one touch to the spot on my wrist is enough to calm me. I stride through the lobby and into the elevator.

The whole time I ascend, my eyes are focused on my wrist. On the little airplane. I'm not sure what will happen today, but I know from the bottom of my heart that Tobias won't let anything happen to me.

I called in sick last week. Then the weekend came, and now I need to show my face and pretend I'm scared for Tobias. I walk through the office, head held high, but I thin my lips to show no emotion. It's exactly how I would have looked before, not allowing anyone to see past my icy façade.

When I get to my desk, I see a note from Mr. Williams's assistant on my desk, saying he needs to see me in his office right away. I don't bother placing my stuff down before I head in his direction. By the time I'm standing outside his door, it feels like I might pass out, but I take a deep breath and pull myself together.

Standing in the entrance, I see that Mr. Williams is waiting for me.

"Skye, come in here and take a seat," my boss calls out to me.

I walk into his office, and Mr. Williams is standing with his arms crossed. He gestures for me to sit.

"Have you heard from Mr. Kosta?" he asks.

I school my features before I sit down and let out a sigh. "No."

Acting has never been a problem for me, and right now, my life depends on it.

He moves to pull out his chair, and then he is sitting in front of me. "From what the police told me, the building came down."

"D-Do they know what happened?" I drop my voice, making myself sound sad and concerned. He looks up from his desk and shakes his head.

Hook, line, and sinker. I can tell by the way his eyes soften that he's buying my act.

"I know this will be hard on you, seeing as you have been working with Mr. Kosta, but I need you to get back into the swing of things."

I'm torn on how to feel right now. On the one hand, I need this, but I still wish there was another way. Felix Bernard is the last person I want to work with.

"I'll do what I have to," I tell him.

Mr. Williams pulls open a drawer and grabs a folder. "I need you to work on this file."

"No problem. I can get started right now." Taking the file from his hand, I give him one last small smile before I turn and walk back to my desk. Once there, I place the papers down, put on my headphones, and open the file. The plan is coming into play.

Now, I just have to wait. Draw him in and make him think everything is safe. Tobias is impatient, so I hope we don't have to wait long. If my assessment of Felix is correct, the cocky son of a bitch will take the bait.

The plan is simple. Go in to work and lure Felix out. But after the initial part is over is where it gets tricky.

Time.

How long will it take for the snake to leave its hole? The police announced they haven't found the body of billionaire Tobias Kosta, so that doesn't mean he's dead. As of right now, it's still a search for his body. Eventually, it will either become a recovery or a manhunt.

Tobias has enough political sway that the latter wouldn't happen, but we can't act yet because Felix hasn't left his penthouse. However, I will reach out to him.

One of the things I have figured out from his file is that I can't find a loophole for him to obtain the land. Everything is perfect; everything is legal and meets the criteria needed to be protected. There is no way to legally fix this mess, but that doesn't mean I have to tell Felix.

I plan to tell him I found a mistake when I pulled the paperwork, and I figured out that the land was not filed correctly. That I have found a loophole, and because of this, the land is not, in fact, protected.

This is how I will lure him out.

When we meet, I will suggest celebrating our success. This will be the tricky part, convincing him to come to me. If I can't, I'll have to figure out a way to get Tobias and company into his penthouse. I don't want to think about that, though, because something tells me that's the riskier undertaking.

The hardest part about this week is seeing Tobias. Despite the danger, he insists on seeing me every day and sleeping over. It's risky as all hell.

But ever since words of love were spoken, neither one of us was willing to be without the other for too long.

At night, I find him touching me, almost like he's afraid I'll disappear. I find myself doing the same thing, almost pinching myself every time I'm with him to make sure it isn't some dream.

Tonight, he doesn't try to sneak in while I sleep, nor does he wait to wake me from a dream. No, tonight, he's barging through my door. Then his lips are on mine. The way he kisses me is like he's in a frenzy.

It's desperate and passionate.

Something tells me he's scared of what the future will bring. Of what tomorrow will bring.

Now, with the plan in action, anything could happen.

He kisses me like it's the last time.

His fear tastes like possession.

A primal need to never let me go.

My arms wrap around his neck as his soft tongue delves inside my mouth.

The kiss doesn't end. Instead, I tug at his disheveled hair and pull him closer, desperate not to let him go.

He laughs against my lips. "I love you."

"I love you," I repeat through heavy pants. "It's always been you."

Tobias is my air. My breath. My soul.

And I'm his sky.

My fingers trail across his shirt, and one by one, I unfasten each small button.

"You kiss me like it's our last kiss," I mutter against his mouth.

"I will never let anyone hurt you." A promise. "I will die for you."

I slide my hand down to the belt of his pants. He steps out of them, and the material hits the floor.

Then he's moving toward me. His hands lift the hem of my dress above my head.

Once I'm standing in front of him in only a bra and panties, he removes those, too.

Standing naked before him, he reaches out his hand and works his way down the hollow of my neck, over my breasts and down my stomach until his finger swipes against my core. Teasing.

"I need you." He lifts me, carrying me toward my bedroom. "I couldn't stay away now if I tried. I need to be inside you."

He throws me on the bed.

Crawling back up my body, he aligns himself with my core and then slowly sinks inside me. Once he's all the way seated, his hips begin to circle, and then he rocks in and out.

It feels amazing.

He thrusts in and out of my body. He slams in over and over again, moving his hips at a faster clip. My nails scratch at his back.

Our movements become frantic. I brace for each thrust of his hips. He fucks me like a dying man, a desperate man, a starved man. Like I'm what will save him. Like I'm his salvation.

I'm what keeps him alive.

My body shivers and quakes as he pulls out and then enters me again. He thrusts, going deeper and deeper.

My body pulses around him, and his own climax follows quickly after. "Fuck!" he shouts out his release. "You belong to me. You're mine. And I will protect you to my dying breath."

CHAPTER FORTY-SEVEN

Skye

THE TIME TO PUT THE PLAN IN MOTION HAS FINALLY COME. I grab my phone from the table, pressing the call button when I find Felix Bernard's name. My pulse thumps in my neck as I wait for him to answer.

"Bernard speaking." Hearing his voice makes my back go ramrod straight. My words dry up in my brain as I try to remember the plan.

"I have good news, sir," I finally spit out, trying desperately to keep my voice calm. Hopefully, it's convincing. Everything rides on there being no doubt or reason to question me.

"Ms. Matthews?" he asks.

"Oh, sorry. Yes, it's me. I have been working all night and forgot to introduce myself." I give a little embarrassed laugh, laying it on thick.

Really, Skye? Is that the best you can come up with?

"Is that so?" he leads as if I will say more. I don't. Instead, I lift my free hand and bang it against my head. How in the world am I supposed to do this? I hate this plan. The worst part . . . it's my plan.

"Yes. Sorry," I mutter back.

The line goes silent, and I look down to see if the call was dropped. It hasn't been. Holding my breath, I wait for him to speak.

"Ms. Matthews, what can I do for you?"

He sounds unamused by my call, and I wonder if maybe this isn't a good plan. Maybe he's on to me? It's a risk I'm not sure I should be taking. Inhaling, I push down my doubts.

"I found the loophole you were looking for." I hope to lure him in by not saying too much.

"Really?" He sounds unconvinced, and I wonder if this has all been a farce. Did he send me on a wild goose chase, and now he's stumped about how I solved the problem?

"Yep. Took me a while, but I cracked it," I say lightly, hoping he buys it.

"Extraordinary."

Here it goes. "Can you meet me at my office—"

"No." His blatant dismissal doesn't bode well for me.

Now what?

"Would you like me to come to you?" I offer up, knowing this isn't the plan. Tobias will never go for it. It will be awful when I have to tell him. Inside Felix's fortress would be the last thing Tobias wants. But what Tobias doesn't know won't hurt him.

"That would be perfect." After Felix tells me when and where to go, I hang up the phone, and then I dial again, this time to call Jaxson Price.

"Skye," Jax answers.

"Jax. I need you to help me with a few things . . ." I trail off before biting my lower lip and waiting for him to answer.

"Why does this sound like a bad idea?"

"It's the only idea. The only one that will work."

And then I tell him my plan.

This is the sketchiest thing I have ever done. Getting out of the cab one block from the destination screams red flag, but according to Jaxson, this is what needs to be done.

I had heard Jax was odd, but this is next level.

My steps are hesitant as I walk down the abandoned cobblestone street. The area doesn't look like the kind of place where a billionaire would keep his office, but I guess in his line of work, it makes sense.

This isn't a normal building; this is a superhero lair. Like Batman minus the bats. Rats, however, might be a part of this equation. A shiver runs up my spine at the thought.

The street is dilapidated. The building as well. I'm only a few steps from the address when I hear a creaking sound, and a door that blends in perfectly to the façade of the building opens. Tentatively, I pop my head in. No one is there.

"In here," Jax hollers from somewhere deep inside the building.

The door is electronic, I realize. What can't this man do? Taking a step inside, I glance around at my surroundings. It's exactly what I would imagine for a lair.

Dark concrete floors, high ceilings, and state-of-the-art electronics. All he needs is an older British butler to complete the picture.

"Let me show you what you need to bring Felix down."

Something tells me whatever he has to tell me will be above my pay grade. I'm nervous to find out.

CHAPTER FORTY-EIGHT

Tobias

"WAS THAT JAX?" I ASK CYRUS, WHO IS SITTING ACROSS from me in my library having a glass of cognac with me.

"It was." His voice is flat, but I can tell by the way the right side of his lip is tilted, he is amused by the turn of events.

"So . . . she didn't listen?" I'm not at all surprised.

"Nope." Now he's fully grinning. Not something he normally does, so he must really be enjoying this. I can't help but shake my head. Skye Matthews is unbelievable.

When she came to me with the plan, I said no. A full stop—no. The thing is, I always knew she wouldn't listen; it's one of the things I love about her. How could I have thought she would? She's the girl who stepped in front of a bullet for a boy she didn't even know. Also, the woman who ran into a war to save my life.

"Well, I guess we proceed with the plan," I say to Cyrus, lifting my glass to my mouth and taking a swig. After I place my drink down, I pull up my phone, dial, and place it on speaker so Cyrus can hear.

"Good thing we made a plan." Jaxson laughs through the phone line.

"I don't care what you have to do. Jax, you make sure Skye is safe. You hear me?" My voice is firm and final.

He chuckles over the line.

"I'm glad you find this funny."

"She'll be safe. She will get into the apartment, and the whole time, I'll have eyes and ears on her." He tries to sound reassuring.

"And if she gets caught?"

"She's using the bathroom—"

"You know as well as I do that anything can go wrong."

Jax is silent for a second, but it's Cyrus who speaks. "We will be there. All of us, ready to strike."

"I just need the alarm off. The device I gave her will interfere with the cameras, a portable EMP. It will knock down the image, and they will just think it's a bad connection. In the meantime, she will find the computer connected to the mainframe, insert the zip drive I gave her, and then we'll be able to download all the files from his computer and take down the whole system, all at the same time. Storm the castle and whatnot." He acts like this is no big deal. For him, it's not, for us either, but for Skye . . . It could be the difference between life and death.

My teeth grind together. I hate this plan.

"How do you know where the computer is and that she will be looking in the right place?" There is no confusing the angry tremor in my voice. A lot is riding on this plan. Skye is riding on this plan. We can't afford mistakes.

"Eyes and ears, dude. I have the blueprints, too." His words bring me no comfort.

"You better," I seethe.

"Tobias." Cyrus interjects a hint of warning in his voice. Fuck that. He wouldn't be this calm if it was his girl.

"Yes, Cyrus?"

"Leave Jax alone. We are all doing everything we can to keep her safe."

I let out a sigh. He's right. I'm being fucking crazy. But I'm pissed. I told her to drop it, and here she is, going about her business like I didn't.

It's what I love about her, but still.

"When do we leave?"

"As soon as we get the call to get in place."

Great. Just fucking great. All I can do is wait. Wait, as if I have nothing better to do. Which apparently, I don't.

CHAPTER FORTY-NINE

Skye

I'M HERE EARLY. MY HEART IS POUNDING THROUGH MY CHEST as I'm shown into Felix's building and then led to the elevator that takes me to his penthouse apartment.

Despite my hatred of enclosed spaces, that's not even the worst part. I'm scared the plan will backfire.

When I suggested it, Tobias said no. Maybe he was right. Maybe I was wrong to go through with it without his support. There is no question that Jaxson has told him everything by now, and Tobias will be part of the cavalry sent in to capture Felix. I wonder how pissed with me he will be.

"Skye." I hear Jaxson's voice through the earpiece I'm wearing.

"*Hmm?*" is the only answer he will get. I'm not sure if this elevator has cameras.

"You need to calm down. I can hear you breathing all the way from here."

"*Mmm.*"

"Once you get inside, I'm not going to turn the EMP on right away. It will be too obvious. I want you to sit down with him. Ask for a drink. Play it cool. Maybe flirt."

"No."

"Good, because Tobias will probably kill me for that idea."

"Once he gets the call that something is wrong with his security cameras, I anticipate that he will tell you to wait and make yourself comfortable. That's when you go looking for his office."

"How will I know where it is?" I mutter, trying to make sure my mouth doesn't move when I speak.

"I have the blueprints." When I don't say anything back, he continues, "I got you. Trust me."

As soon as the elevator opens, I'm met by Felix.

He looks every bit the villain. Dressed in all black, he has his hair slicked back and wears a lecherous smile on his face.

There is no hiding the way he leers at me. His gaze lingers on the exposed skin at my neck.

I wore a rather seductive outfit.

Probably a bad idea now that I think about it. But if the plan goes awry, at least I can pretend to seduce him and then pounce.

"Ms. Matthews, I was surprised by your call, but I can't say I'm not thrilled as well."

"I'm happy to please." With a coy smile, I move farther into the foyer.

"Is there anything I can get for you before we get down to business?" He means work, but by the way he looks at me, one would think I'm about to perform sexual favors on him.

"Something to drink would be lovely."

"Come. Follow me." He leads us into the living room, then walks over to the beverage cart in the corner that hosts an array of decanters. "Scotch?" His brow lifts in challenge. I rise to the occasion.

"That will be perfect."

His smile spreads. It was a test, and he likes the way I responded. The EMP can't go off soon enough.

Felix makes work of pouring us both a finger's worth, then we are sitting across from each other. Taking a sip, I allow the liquid to calm my nerves. Then I make a grand show of opening my bag and pulling out the file he gave me. As I'm about to open my mouth, a man I have never seen before walks into the room.

"Mr. Bernard, I need to speak with you for a moment," the man says.

"I'll be right back," Felix says as he stands and follows the man out of the room.

I give them ten seconds before I'm standing as well and creeping through the door, heart racing. The security system is off, but that just makes me more nervous. I need to be more careful.

"Jax," I whisper. "Are you there? Can you hear me?"

"I'm here," he responds, and I'm thankful because I don't have much time. I need to find his home office before Felix notices I've walked off.

"Where do I go?"

"According to the blueprints of the building, you need to go past the kitchen."

I do as he says, quickly checking the kitchen. Once I see that the coast is clear, I make my way down the hall, all the while listening for Felix. He's likely still trying to figure out the glitch.

Making my way down the dark hallway, I feel my heart racing. My fingers are sticky with sweat. I check each room I pass until I find what I'm looking for. It's the office.

"Found it."

"Okay, look for the computer."

I can't believe I'm doing this. My fists are gripped tightly as I look around the room. It's dark and empty. I have to find it, but when I don't, I let out a groan.

"Keep looking," Jaxson says through the earpiece. "We have sixty seconds before the cameras are live again, and in that time you have to disconnect the alarm."

I walk past the desk, and that's when I see it.

"Found the computer, but I can't do this." I groan.

"Well, now that you're there, you don't have a choice. We have thirty seconds. I'll talk you through it."

Jaxson's voice is calm and playful. I know he's trying to keep me calm, but it doesn't help. Reaching out with trembling hands, I look at the monitor.

"This is super simple, Skye. You just need to download the data, and then bring the system down."

"Wow. Seriously. And how am I going to do that?"

You are way over your pay grade here. This is James Bond shit. If I make it out of here unscathed, it will be a modern miracle.

"Well, that's the easy part." His voice is playful, and I swear if Jaxson Price was here right now, he would be beaming at me with a shit-eating grin, and I . . . well, I would smack it off his face.

"Really? You don't say. You're not the one standing in his office—"

"Just insert the zip drive I gave you."

"Oh, that's it?" I say sarcastically.

"Yep." Easy for him to tell me what to do while safely far away. I'm the one standing in front of the computer with the zip drive clutched in my hand, waiting for someone to catch me.

I have never done something like this before, but I've also never been this desperate. It's worth the risk. I take a deep breath before inserting the flash drive into the computer. Nothing happens at first, and I feel it mocking me with the silence.

I want to scream at Jax and ask him what's happening. But I don't. I can't risk being heard. I've already spoken too much. As if he can hear me, he speaks. "Files are downloaded. It's uploading the virus. The whole system will be down in less than ten seconds."

"And the cameras?" My heart batters against my breastbone, threatening to explode.

"You have fifteen seconds to get out of that room."

Great. Just great. Fifteen seconds. By the time I remember

how to get back to where I came from, fifteen seconds will have already passed.

Stop. Put your big girl panties on and get the fuck out of here. I drop the drive back in my pocket and turn around.

Peeking my head out the door, I look left and then right. Thankfully, the hall is clear.

But who knows for how long?

Slowly, I make my way back into the long corridor that brought me here and try to retrace my steps to the living room.

My heart thunders in my chest.

It's only a few more feet until I'm free.

You can do this.

One foot in front of the other.

"Look what we have here," I hear from behind me. There's no need to turn around, I know Felix has caught me.

I won't let him scare me, though. Straightening my spine, I turn around, head held high.

He's too close, and when he steps in, I try to sidestep, but it's the wrong move because now I'm backed against a wall. Cornered.

"I'll have fun breaking Tobias's little toy."

CHAPTER FIFTY

Tobias

Pacing back and forth. This is what hell feels like. Knowing the woman you love is in a building with a monster, and there is nothing you can do about it. I signal for the team to breach the apartment. It takes one second for the door to open, and then we are off.

"Go!" I whisper-shout, and then I run in with my gun drawn.

I check the hallway before I signal my team to go in after her. From across the room, I see that Felix has Skye pushed against the wall. He doesn't hear us or see us. We have the element of surprise working in our favor.

Skye's eyes catch mine, but Felix is still ignorant of our presence.

"I'll have fun breaking Tobias's little toy."

"I'm not his toy." Skye takes a step forward but not before she winks at me. Her hands lift to his shoulders seductively. I want to shoot him, but by the weapon in Felix's hand and his close proximity to Skye, it's not a good idea. "I'm no one's toy."

Felix's weapon isn't lifted, and despite my reservations, Skye moves into action, lifting her knee.

She shouts back something I can't make out. I don't wait for an invitation before I storm the room, throwing my body into Felix's. The gun drops from his hand, and my fists lift to connect with his face.

He swings back.

Sidestepping, I block his punch, lunge forward, and throw us both to the ground.

The silver metal of his gun gleams, but he's not fast enough. I grab it first.

Lift and point.

———————— • ————————

Time to have fun. Now that Skye is back at my compound and tucked away in my bed, I'm ready to see what Felix has to say. She wasn't happy that I made her leave, but she doesn't need eyes on this part of the plan.

All the guys are already there, probably chipping away at what little soul he has left. That is, if he even had one to begin with. Knowing he's responsible for making Skye and me orphans, I doubt he does, but still.

They kept Felix dressed in the room where he's being held, but this will be short-lived. No better way to torture him than to strip him of his dignity. And other than a few welts and bruises, he seems untouched. Tied to the chair and with his arms locked behind his back, he's ready.

I don't speak before I punch him square in the nose. His head thrusts back as a loud crunch echoes through the air. Next comes the blood. It pours down his face.

I turn to see Lorenzo looking at my handiwork with a sick smile on his face. He loves this shit. Sick fuck. For me, it's the means to an end.

I step back up to him, and this time when I punch him, I aim for his eye. Let's see how he feels when he can no longer see. I watch as his eye starts to become red. It will be swollen soon when the cut from where my knuckle hit begins to bleed. Felix smiles up at me, eye closed, blood seeping out of his mouth.

"You like this shit?"

He fucking nods.

I walk up to the table and grab a knife.

"You like killing innocent people?" I say as I stab the knife in his thigh.

Felix doesn't speak. He just smiles. He's trying to appear strong.

Lorenzo steps up.

"Let me." He flashes a sinister grin. "I do like to make myself useful."

It's a slight movement, but I see how Felix's arm shakes.

Lorenzo's reputation precedes him. He will kill him. And it will be the most painful death ever.

Again . . . sick fuck.

Lorenzo takes the knife out of my hand and then moves closer.

"Consider Lorenzo Skye's representative." Then he stabs him in the gut, twisting the blade to the hilt and leaving it lodged inside him.

"W-What does Skye have to do with this?" Felix's eyes roll back, but then Lorenzo strikes him with his palm across the face to rouse him.

"Oh, you didn't know. Skye's birth parents were killed in the massacre at Al's." Lorenzo pulls the knife out, and blood oozes from the wound.

"What fucking massacre?" Despite the crimson stain growing on Felix's shirt, he grins at me.

My blood starts to boil at his words. It feels like hot, molten lava is pumping through me.

"The one you ordered that killed my family."

He spits to the ground, and bright red rivulets drip down his chin. "I don't know what you're talking about. You think I remember the casualties?" He chuckles, and it sets me off.

My revenge pours out of me into fists. In blood and sweat and tears. I'm a man possessed. Transported back to a time before taking out my anger and pain on his body.

"You killed my family. You came to Reddington and killed my family."

"You think you know," he mutters.

"What did you say?" I punch him again.

His face is so swollen I can barely make out his features. "You think this ends with me." He spits. "You haven't even scratched the surface."

"What the fuck are you talking about?" He doesn't respond. I punch him again and again and again. "Talk!"

"F-Fu—"

"Tell me!"

"Ask R-Ralph—"

I shake him, trying to get him to open his eyes, but they won't open. "Don't let him die." I slap Felix's face, trying to get him to wake up. I shake his shoulders, and his head slumps forward.

Lorenzo steps up and places his hand at his throat. "Too late."

"Fuck."

———•———

"Tobias?" Skye asks sleepily.

Tucked in my bed is my favorite place for her. Skye looks so small, blankets and pillows overpowering her presence in the bed. Her hair fans across my pillow, the dark locks a stark contrast to the crisp white sheets.

"Yeah," I reply. She sits up at my voice and looks at me, wiping the sleep from her eyes. "Sorry to wake you."

"What's going on?"

I don't know how to say this to her. How to tell her that Felix is dead, but there might be someone else involved. I don't know how to tell her it could be her father.

I haven't already gone to Reddington out of respect for Skye, but by tomorrow, I need to find out what Felix meant.

"I think there is something you need to know," I say simply.

Now she looks more awake. "About what?"

I pace, and while I do, I see the familiar, concerned look on her face as her brows knit together.

I move to sit next to Skye on the bed.

"What's wrong?" she asks, her voice so small and frightened, so unlike the girl I know. She looks at me, and for a moment, all I can see is the little girl in the closet, fighting back her fear. But as soon as I see it, it fades away, replaced by the amazingly strong and beautiful woman she has become. "You can talk to me, Tobias."

"I spoke with Felix," I say, keeping to the truth but not telling her anything that can be used against her in the future.

Her eyes widen, and I know she understands.

"Earlier, he mentioned that someone else was involved. That we only touched the tip of the iceberg."

"What do you mean? Like another gang?"

I shake my head.

"Why do you look like that? What aren't you saying?"

"He said we didn't scratch the surface," I say, my voice falling to a whisper.

"And that means what?"

I reach out and take her hand. "I don't know, but someone else is pulling the strings." I pause, not knowing how to say this. "He told me to ask Ralph. That's your father's name, right?" And also, the cop on duty that day, but I don't mention that.

"No." She shakes her head back and forth. "No, that makes no sense. He doesn't know anything." Skye is obviously distressed.

"It might not be what we think."

Her head moves back and forth.

"He might not be involved, but—"

"He never wants to talk," she mutters to herself.

"We need to talk to him."

"No."

"No? Skye, this isn't about something dumb. Felix mentioned him by name."

"It's not that," she says. "I'm just worried he won't talk." She looks down at her hands, and I can see a tear slip down her cheek. "And what if he does? What if he . . . ? No. He couldn't have been involved. Could he?"

"You need to talk to him," I tell her.

"I'm not sure what to say," Skye confesses, her voice cracking. "I mean, I know what I should say, but I also want to make sure . . . I want him to know I love him, but—"

"I know."

"He raised me. He adopted me. What if he's . . . ? He's still my dad." She wipes a tear from her cheek. "I can't do this."

"I know." I pull her in close. "But we will never feel settled until we figure out what Felix meant."

Her head bobs up and down. "I'm scared of what my father will say." She looks up at me for a moment, then buries her head into my chest. I put my arm around her.

"Everything will be okay."

"And if it's not?"

"Then we will cross that bridge. We will get through it together."

I can feel the way she trembles. Whether from the cold or my words, I'm not sure.

"You really need to talk to your father."

"I will," she promises. "I know. I'll talk to him tomorrow."

"Promise?"

"I promise."

CHAPTER FIFTY-ONE

Skye

THE NEXT MORNING COMES BEFORE I'M READY. I DON'T WANT to face my father. I don't want to know the truth. I'm not ready to deal with the consequences of that truth. What if everything I know about this man is a lie?

I didn't sleep last night; I tossed and turned the whole time, wondering what he would say. Is he a crooked cop? Did he take bribes? Did he murder my parents? Or is this a case of mistaken identity? Maybe when Felix said Ralph, he didn't mean my father—my adoptive father.

I shake my head back and forth. Whatever the truth may be, it won't change the fact he raised me and took care of me. That he adopted me after the massacre.

From beside me in the bed, Tobias moves. My tossing and turning probably woke him.

"Are you okay over there?" he asks me. I turn to face him. He looks beautiful in the early morning light. His eyes seem bottomless, full of so many feelings and emotions. The man next to me in bed is not the man he is anywhere else. With everyone else, he's closed off, but with me, he's different. It's like I have my own private version of him.

He is the boy before the crime. He is the boy I fell in love with when he soothed me.

"I'm not," I admit.

"Talk to me, Skye."

"Why bother? You already know what's bothering me." I sound like a petulant child, but I don't want to do this.

"I wish I could tell you that you didn't have to do this, but—"

I let out a sigh. "I know. Fine. I'll drive up there today." This time I'm fully huffing. I'm certainly not acting like the lawyer Tobias originally hired.

When it comes to my father, I'm still the scared little girl who had no one.

"No. I'll drive you up there."

"Absolutely not."

"There is no way I'm letting you go by yourself."

"You really aren't going to have much choice."

Tobias takes my hand and turns over my palm until my tattoo faces us. "See this?" I nod.

"This shows you are mine. I fucking own you, Skye Matthews. I have owned your soul from the very first moment we met. And you know what? You have owned mine as well. Where you go, I go."

My mouth opens and shuts. I have no idea how to respond.

My heart pounds in my chest. He's not wrong. Every word he says is the truth, and in his tone, I can hear his conviction.

"We are going. And we are going today."

His hair is disheveled. His eyes narrowed. He looks like a man possessed.

"I don't know if he will talk if you're around."

"He'll talk," he deadpans.

"Tobias . . ." I draw out his name in a warning.

"What?" He's acting clueless, but he knows exactly what I'm saying. But I clarify anyway.

"There is no threatening my father. I don't care what role he played in everything."

"No promises." He goes to move away from me, and my hand shoots up to stop him.

"Tobias!"

He lifts his arms out in surrender. "Fine. Fuck, Skye. I don't know how you do it . . ."

"Do what?"

"Undo me." His arms envelop me, pulling me close until his nose is buried in the crook of my neck. "You make me do things I would never do. You make me think of a world where maybe I can be something different, something more."

"You can."

"When you say that, I believe it." He holds me close, placing soft kisses on my neck, but then he pulls away.

I groan at the movement.

"As much as I want to do that, and I do, we have to go. If your father is involved—"

I reach my hand out and grab his. "You can't hurt him."

"Skye."

"No, Tobias. You cannot hurt him. You can come, but I will never forgive you if you hurt him."

Tobias looks at me, but he doesn't speak. His jaw is set, lips a thin line. But I can see it in his eyes. He doesn't have to say anything; I know him. I know the way he looks at me, and I know the promises behind them. No matter what we hear today, he will never hurt him.

Not because he doesn't deserve it, but because I asked.

Tobias Kosta loves me.

My hands shake as I reach for the front doorknob and insert my key in the lock. I take a deep breath and push through, trying my best to ignore the way my stomach churns with nerves. When I step inside, I go in search of my father.

It feels as if my heart might beat out of my chest, but there is one saving grace. Tobias is waiting in the car.

I asked for that, and he agreed.

So now, I'm making my way through the foyer, each step slower than the next. There is no one in the kitchen, and as I make my way down the hallway, I'm shocked to see my father sitting on the couch.

His face tilts up, and it looks like he's been crying, his nose red and his eyes watery.

"Hi," he says quietly.

"Hi," I reply, trying to keep my voice cool and calm. "I need to talk to you."

He shifts awkwardly but nods for me to take a seat.

"No. I'll stand." But instead of standing, I pace. My feet cross the distance of the room, only to walk back. I don't even know how to start this conversation. Pain radiates through me like I'm being stabbed in the chest.

"I wasn't expecting you today, was I?" he asks, confused. His nose scrunches as if he's trying to remember whether I told him of my visit prior to showing up.

I hadn't.

"No. I didn't call."

"Is everything okay?" He moves to sit up straight, but he lets out a groan. The veins on the side of his neck pulse.

He's in pain, and it breaks my heart. No matter what I hear, I will always love him for taking me in.

"What are you doing here?" He rubs at his face, he looks tired. Maybe he was sleeping? Seeing him like this has me wanting to turn around and tell Tobias that there is nothing here. No story. That Felix was wrong. But as much as I want to do that, I can't.

I wring my fingers as I pace. *Why is this so hard?* "I came to ask about the day my parents died."

"What about it?"

I come to a complete stop before turning to my father. "Felix Bernard."

His face goes pale, and the mug in his hand slips, crashing against the wood floors. I scramble to pick up the pieces of ceramic splattered around the couch.

Carefully lifting the broken shards, I place the pieces on the coffee table. The mug was empty, and other than the small drop here or there, the floor is clean. I'll wipe it up later.

"Dad?"

My father rubs his forehead. His eyes are wet. He's trying not to cry.

"Talk to me. Tell me the truth."

A tear falls from his eye, and I can feel my heart break. I put my hand on his shoulder and squeeze gently. He looks up at me. "I've been trying to protect you." He shakes his head. "I've been trying to protect myself. I never wanted you to hate me."

"What did you do, Dad? Why won't you tell me about the past?"

He takes a deep breath. "This is going to be hard for you to hear, so please don't interrupt."

"Okay."

"It was my fault. Everything was my fault."

The sobs that rip through my mouth can't be controlled. Anger follows next. "You killed my family!" I shout, my anger palpable.

"Skye—" His Adam's apple bobs, but I don't let him deter me.

"No! You killed my family." I close my eyes. Trying desperately to calm down. To swallow down the despair lodging in my throat. The grief I feel is raw and primitive. It feels like I'm being abandoned all over again. "Why"—I swipe away a stray tear that is drifting down my cheek—"did you adopt me?"

"Look at me, Skye." Opening my lids, my gaze meets his.

Then I'm moving to stand in front of him. "You were innocent. You had no—"

"I had no one because of you." Another wave of tears pours down my cheeks. Then another thought hits me. "You only adopted me because you thought you owed me something, didn't you?"

"It wasn't—"

"Yes or no! Were you planning to adopt before me?"

"No, but—" His voice cracks. "Please—"

"There are no buts!" I cut him off.

His face is pale, his cheeks ashen. "Please let me explain. Please, it's not what you think," he begs.

"Did you or did you not have something to do with their deaths?" I'm pacing now, my anger needing an outlet.

"It's not that simple."

"It is that simple to me." My feet are probably making marks from the way they stomp down in anger. My whole body is shaking.

"Skye, plea—" His words cut off, followed by a thump. The sound has my heart stopping.

It feels like I can't breathe as I turn to see my father slumped over the coffee table. I'm moving across the room and checking his pulse a moment later.

"Skye—"

"Shh, it's okay." He's alive, but something is wrong.

"I-It w-wasn't me," he stutters out before his eyes flutter shut. His pulse is still there. Beating faintly but still there. Grabbing my phone from my pocket, I call 911, then Tobias. It's only a second later when Tobias is in the room, then a few minutes pass before the EMS team wheels him away. I try to ride with him, but I can't.

I pray he's okay.

He can't die.

He can't leave me.

Hospitals are the worst. The sterile scent of bleach and the over-whelming sense of death and sickness are always present. It's been a long time since I've been to a hospital—twenty years, to be exact. Not since the day I woke from surgery and learned my whole life had changed.

When I still lived in town, my father was never sick, so I never needed to come back here. But now, walking with Tobias, no time has passed. My feet halt as I walk toward the reception, the ghosts of my past still here and present.

I stand breathless for a moment. I never expected to feel this way. My soul is crushing under the weight of my past. Tobias is here to help me. But even the feel of his skin on mine as he holds me isn't enough to push me on.

I'm so angry. So fucking angry.

This might have been the last time with my father, and I spent it yelling at him.

I could lose him.

"He can't die."

Tobias doesn't say anything. What can he say? We both know it's inevitable.

My fists ball at my side, and Tobias stops walking and grabs my arm, pulling me with him in the direction opposite the re-ception desk.

"What are you doing?" I whisper shout.

Then he's opening the first door he sees, a closet.

"Are you fucking kidding? My dad is dying, and you—"

"Stop. You need to calm down." He places his hand on my shoulder. "You're going to see your dad, and you need to be calm."

"I am calm."

His head shakes. "No, Skye. You're not."

"I'm not." My body shakes with an unsuppressed sob. "I'm so confused."

Tobias reaches his arm up, his fingers lifting my chin to meet his stare. "Talking to me."

"I'm so angry. But how can I be angry? But I am. I'm furious. Furious at myself for being in the dark. Furious at my dad for lying. Furious at the world for making him sick. And mostly, I'm furious that I'm helpless. He is sick, and none of the other things matter, but it still hurts." The sob pours out of my mouth, body shaking, tears falling.

Tobias wraps me in his arms and holds me. I cry and sob and curse the world, and then a calm falls over me. "Thank you for being here with me, despite everything."

"Where you go, I go. Remember what you said . . ."

"You're the plane."

"And you are my *sky*," he finishes for me.

"That's not exactly what I said." I smile softly at him. "I'm ready."

Together, hand in hand, we leave the closet and make our way to the reception desk.

The woman who sits behind it is middle-aged and looks up as if she's annoyed that I'm asking her questions.

"I'm looking for Ralph Matthews."

"I'm sorry, we can't give out information about patients."

"But I'm his daughter." My tone is more abrasive than I mean it to be, but my emotions are all over the place today.

"I'm sorry, but we still can't give out information."

I stare at the woman at the desk, pleading until she finally relents.

"He's in triage. Room 202." Before she can say anything else, I'm running down the hallway, Tobias trailing me.

I still don't understand how I ended up here. How I ended up where it all began. The memory, like the familiar smell, tickles my nostrils, begging me to remember. It feels like only yesterday when I was waking up in the hospital bed. When Ralph Matthews was placing his hand over mine, his head downcast, as he told me about my parents. Now I'm back, and the most painful thought of all is that this all happened because of me.

I walk into my father's room and stand next to his bed. I put a hand on his arm, and he moves a little. "Dad?" I ask quietly. "I'm here, Dad."

"Skye?" he asks, barely audible.

"Yeah, Dad, it's me."

"You're here?" There is confusion in his voice. "After everything that happened?"

"I am."

"Skye?"

"No. Don't. Not now. I'm sorry I did this to you, Dad, but I want to say I love you, and I know you've always been there for me. I never took the time to appreciate it. I love you, Dad, and I'm sorry for everything."

The nurse comes in and smiles at me. "It's great to see your father awake."

"Hi," he says in a hoarse voice.

I get up and pour water from the pitcher on the bedside table into a glass for him. I hand it to him, then help him drink.

"What happened?" he asks, his voice hoarse.

"You passed out, Dad. You're at the hospital."

"I'm sorry for bothering you, honey," he says.

"I'm here for you, Dad. Just tell me what you need. I know you're sick."

The sadness in his eyes is overwhelming. It makes a sob bubble up from my mouth, but then his gaze grows serious. "To tell you the truth."

I sit next to my father's bed with his hands in mine. His breathing is erratic, and he's sweating profusely.

"I-I need you to know before I start that I love you," he says weakly.

"I love you, too, Dad." I kiss him on the forehead.

"I'll understand if you never want to see me again after what

I tell you, but I need you to know I love you. I never wanted to hurt you. I never wanted to hurt your family."

It feels like I can't swallow, but I push the word out of my mouth, regardless.

"Okay."

"At the time . . . Reddington was a different place. When I grew up here, it was safe. But around the time when you were a small child, things were changing. Our location made us ideal. The proximity to the highway and the ports made us ripe for the picking. Elements moved into town. Dark elements. I didn't know anyone would get hurt. I was asked to help. I monitored this man. He was a bad man. He was bringing drugs into the city. I was told to watch his every move. No matter where he went, I had to report back his exact location—"

"Who did you report to?"

"The district attorney."

Fitzpatrick.

CHAPTER FIFTY-TWO

Tobias

THE WAITING ROOM IS QUIET. I'M HERE DESPITE THE FACT I don't want to be. I don't give a shit what happens to that man; I'm here for Skye. Only for her. Always for her.

From across the room, I see Skye entering the space. She looks broken, and just like that, I spring into action. Moving toward her, I take her in my arms.

She's crying.

"The doctor said he doesn't have long. His organs are no longer functioning."

"Is he—?" I start to ask, but she shakes her head against my chest.

"No. But soon." She holds me closer. "I need to speak with you."

"Okay." I move back and take her hand in mine, pulling her with me until I find an empty room. Once we are standing inside the room, she starts to shake.

This isn't good. Whatever he told her isn't good.

"It wasn't my dad."

"Bullshit."

"He told me everything. It wasn't him."

I pace. I can't seem to stand still. Energy courses through me, angry, confused, but I don't want to take it out on Skye, so I walk back and forth across the hall. "Please." I inhale, schooling my features, trying my best to not let her see the other side of me. "Talk."

"At the time, one of the things my father was tasked to do was watch your father's movements."

"I'm listening."

"He had to report his whereabouts."

"To who?" I bark harsher than necessary, considering where we're at and why.

"The DA. To Fitzpatrick."

Before I know what I'm doing, my fist hits the wall. "Fuck," I yell, balling my hand into a fist, to stave off the pain.

It all makes sense. All the pieces I hadn't connected now come together. DA Fitzpatrick had high aspirations and, over the years, has risen in rank. His final goal: Attorney General of the United States. That's what he's hoping for now, only months from a nomination.

He used the information to take out my father, then cleaned up the city and leveraged the win to further his political agenda.

"Fuck."

"Yeah," she mutters, rocking back on her heels.

"We need to take him down. Take them all down."

Her eyes widen and she takes one big step toward me. "Not my father. Please, Tobias. Let him pass in peace."

I take a step back, needing the space. This is all a lot and I need to think without the distraction of her hands on me.

"I can't believe you're going to let him get away with it. All these years, he's been living a lie."

Her hands drop to her side and her head dips to the floor. "It's not that I'm going to let him get away with it. I just don't know what to do."

"He needs to pay," I growl, curling my hands into fists.

"It's not that easy."

Her tone takes on a hard edge and I know I'm pushing, but I can't stop. We were both put through too much and I want retribution.

"Yes, it is."

"You need to calm down. He's dying, Tobias." When her voice cracks on the last part, some of the fight bleeds out of me.

"Fuck. I'm so fucking angry," I say, grabbing a fistful of hair and pulling to feel something other than anger. It doesn't help. "He killed my father. He might not have pulled the trigger, but he was complacent."

Skye's mouth opens and shuts as if she doesn't know how to respond. The search to find the person who killed our parents is supposed to finally be settled, but still, it's not done. There is one more person we need to take down.

This is bigger than Felix. Bigger than Skye's father. I look around the room for a few seconds.

"I wanted to know who killed them. But now—" My hands are shaking by my side.

Skye drops her eyes to the ground. "I understand." And she does. If anyone does, it's her. "What now?"

"Now I need time to think. Please give me time."

Then I'm striding out of the room, leaving her alone. Walking out of the building, I need air to breathe.

CHAPTER FIFTY-THREE

Skye

AFTER TOBIAS STORMS OFF, I'M LEFT STANDING IN THE ROOM by myself. I'm not sure where he goes, but one thing I do know is that he'll be back.

It's not even fifteen minutes that I'm waiting before he strides back in, pulling me toward him and planting his mouth on mine.

"I'm sorry."

"I know."

He doesn't need to say anything when he starts to move us out of the room. I know him, and I know where he's taking us.

Together we walk into the hospital room, Tobias holding my hand. The room is stale, the smell of bleach and death overpowering any comforting scents I always associated with hospitals. I sit next to my father, holding his hand. He's awake but barely. He's weak. His eyes don't open when we stand beside his bed.

"Dad?"

They flutter. "Skye?"

"Yes, it's me."

"I thought . . . left." His voice is so weak, I can barely understand him.

I shake my head back and forth, words failing me.

"She would never leave you," Tobias says from beside me, and my father opens his eyes a little wider, looking for the voice.

"W-Who—?"

"Hello, Mr. Matthews. I'm Tobias Kosta, but you know me as Nick Baros."

The sound that rips from my father's mouth is painful. Not the type of pain that comes from a scrape or bruise; this pain comes from his soul. He knows exactly who Tobias is. He's the boy who he said died all those years ago. I'm sure it's a name that haunts him.

"I-I'm so sorry," he stutters, broken. "I . . . I"

Tobias shakes his head, stopping my father's next words. I momentarily stop breathing, knowing how devastating it will be for my dad to have Tobias refuse his apology. The lack of closure as his life ends will haunt him in the life after this.

But what Tobias does next is a shock to my entire body. He moves closer to my father's bed, takes his hand in his, and whispers, "I know. And I forgive you."

A choked sob rushes from my mouth. The doubt and fear washed away with that acceptance. The weight of what happened to Tobias will always be there, but I know that this is a giant step in letting go of the anger. The gift he's given my father is one I'll never forget. My heart is breaking knowing his time is almost up, but a sense of peace fills me at knowing he'll pass without those heavy burdens he's carried for years. Forgiveness has allowed him peace too.

My father takes a deep, labored breath, and when he speaks, the words are barely audible. "Th-Thank you."

A second later, my father reaches for me, and Tobias moves out of the way, letting me sit on the edge of the bed.

"I-I l-love y-you," my dad mumbles. "Not r-ready."

"Please don't speak, Dad. You need your strength."

His head moves. It's a small movement, but I know what he is trying to say. *No. There is no more strength to be had.*

"Be-Before I—"

"Shh."

"L-Listen. J-Journal. Bed. Fitz—" He starts to say, but then his words go quiet. His eyes widen, and he takes one more breath. "I-I'm sorry," he tells me.

"It's not your fault," I say. My voice is small.

"I-d-don't want to d-die now. Not read—I-I don't w-want to l-leave yo—"

"I'll be okay." I place a kiss on his hand. "Dad." A tear slips down his cheek. "You can go. I'll be okay." I sniffle quietly, my vision blurring as my eyes mist.

The machines hooked up to him go off. I watch as he takes his last breath. For all those years, he was there for me, and now he's gone. The room goes quiet. We sit beside him.

"He—" A sob breaks through my lips. "He died. My father died."

Once embraced in Tobias's arms, I begin to sob. Tears stream from my eyes. He holds me.

He tells me with no words that he loves me. That he has me. That I will never be alone.

———————————•———————————

The sky above us is painted with clouds. Tiny raindrops trickle down as we make our way from the car to the small church in town. It feels fitting for the day. Dark and ominous. The heavens crying from the loss of such a selfless man. A man that had secrets only because he tried to protect us after trusting the wrong people. Tobias walks beside me, his arm tightly wrapped around my waist as if he's trying to hold me up. I welcome his strength right now and lean into it.

Together, we walk into the church, and he leads me to the front.

We sit down.

The pastor starts to speak, his words like a soft hymn above the beating of my heart.

He tells stories about how my father impacted the world and how he would be missed.

Before long, it's my time to speak. I'm not prepared to stand, nor am I ready to talk, to say my goodbyes, but I know I have to. I owe it to him and myself. I need closure.

I stand from my seat and make my way to the podium, my hands shaking so hard I can't control them.

From where Tobias stands, I can tell he wants to come to my side, but I shake my head. I need to do this on my own.

Looking out into the room, I see the men and women from this beautiful town. The people who helped raise me when my family tragically died that day not so long ago. Then I see him. Attorney General Fitzpatrick. Sitting amongst my father's friends, playing the part he has decided to play.

Taking a deep breath, I try to calm myself.

Today is about my father.

About the man who loved me enough to make sure I was always okay. To make sure I smiled. To make sure I was cared for. I will not let anyone take that away, especially not today.

Pulling my gaze away, I lock eyes with Tobias, who looks as if to say, "I love you, and you can do this." I smile at him and then pull the paper out.

I look around the room and feel the tightness in my throat as I realize that this is my father's last day before he's buried. I try to smile. "I want to thank you all for coming out and for showing my dad so much love and support all these years." I pause, clearing my throat to continue. "My dad was an amazing man, a hard worker, and a man of integrity." The tears begin to fall down my cheeks.

"It is with a heavy heart that I am here to honor my father.

He served as a soldier, then a police officer, and later, a detective. For over twenty years, he has been a pillar of the community. He was my father, not by blood but by love. He had a great sense of humor and always had a smile on his face. His death is tragic. It is hard to describe how much he will be missed. When I was six years old, my dad saved me. Like the hero he was, he found me and saved me.

"He was the only family I had from that time on . . . When I was sixteen, my dad took me for my first driving lesson. He made sure I always had toast and jam before bed, and he always did my math with me. When things were tough, he still managed to put me through college, and most importantly, he gave me a home. He always tried to do the right thing and help others. I can't say that he always succeeded, but he did his best.

"My father's death came too soon. I wasn't ready. But even if I had years to prepare, I'd never be prepared to lose him. He was the most important person in the world to me. His love and support got me through difficult times. We shared many memories together. He was the only person who knew how to make me feel better when I was upset. Dad, you will always be with me. Thank you. Thank you for saving me."

When I'm done speaking, I turn behind me and look at his face in the casket. I place a kiss on my finger and then touch the center of his shirt over his heart. Tears stream down my face, and then I feel his presence as if it was that day when he pulled me from the darkness and showed me the light. *I love you, Dad.* I turn back and make my way back down the steps. One by one, his friends and colleagues come to me. They hug me and tell me their own stories about what a wonderful man he was and about how he touched all their lives. And I know without a measure of a doubt, his presence will never leave. He will always be with me.

CHAPTER FIFTY-FOUR

Skye

I SIT ON THE COUCH. I CAN'T CRY ANYMORE, BUT EVERY TIME I think I'm done, the tears start again. Despite everything my dad did wrong, he did right by me.

From across the room, Tobias whispers to Gideon, but I'm not prepared to think about my father's last words. I need to grieve still. Feel the pain. Yet again, I'm alone in this world.

No. That's not true. I have Tobias. He has always been with me. Our gazes meet from across the space, and before I know it, his mouth stops moving, and he is walking over to me and sitting down. It's like he can hear my every thought.

"It's okay," he says as his arm wraps around my shoulders.

"How did you know?"

Tobias inclines his head, then raises his brow at me. I lean into him.

"I miss him so much." I try to stop the tears, but they just keep coming. "He might not have been perfect, but he was my dad, and I loved him."

Tobias lets me cry. Holding me close, he strokes my back and places kisses on my temple. "He was, and he loved you, too. He's always with you, Skye."

"He was my whole life. He was all I had."

He pulls away and looks at my face.

"Always," he says softly. "I'll be here for you."

We spend the rest of the day in Tobias's house. He takes care of me. Holds me. He is everything I need.

I toss and turn all night, barely able to get more than a few minutes of sleep at a time. My brain is constantly trying to understand what happened all those years ago.

Finally, I can't take it any longer and decide to call it, and just get up for the day. I don't want to face the world, but I know I need to.

"What are we missing?" I say out loud to myself, but I must wake Tobias up because I see his hand lift, and he starts to rub the sleep from his eyes. I'm not sure what, though. "Did I wake you?"

"Kind of, no biggie."

"Sorry," I say squeamishly.

He moves to sit up. "You look exhausted. Did you sleep?"

"I couldn't sleep. I can't believe the asshole had the nerve to show up at his funeral."

"The fucker sure has a lot of fucking nerve, that's for sure. Is that what kept you up?"

"Not just that. I've been thinking about it, and I haven't found a connection to Felix."

We need to figure out the last piece of the puzzle.

Dad's journal.

"Where's the journal Gideon grabbed from my dad's house?"

Tobias stands from the bed and rifles through a box in the corner.

"Here."

I collect the journal from him and get comfortable. It's thick. Riddled with Dad's messy script, tiny and slanted.

An hour later, my eyes are tired from deciphering his

handwriting, but I have a better understanding of his role in all of this.

From what I read, the attorney general put everything into place. Dad included records of payments from Fitzpatrick, in exchange for detailed accounts on Baros.

The ledger and phone logs won't be enough to prove murder, but Dad left me a parting gift.

A confession.

A statement of the role he played in the massacre.

I skim the words again, rereading it over and over. There's a boulder lodged in my throat. Tobias slides the journal from my fingers, sets it on the mattress, and takes my hands in his, simply being here for me.

I turn to face him. "Fitzpatrick had Dad on his payroll."

We knew this, but it's different reading about it from my dad's own journal. Surreal, even.

"We already knew as much."

"I know, but . . ."

"But he's your dad," Tobias finishes, and I slide my hand out of his, press my knees to my chest, and wrap my arms around them. "It's okay to be sad about it."

"Dad thought he was helping Fitzpatrick clean the city. In the journal, he says he didn't know anyone would die when he provided Fitzpatrick with Baros' location that day." I pick up the journal again, turning it over in my hands. "We need to do something."

"Yeah. I got nothing." His dark brows slant with his frown.

"As of right now, all I have is that the attorney general was Reddington's district attorney, and he paid Dad to keep the city clean. Somehow, the information Dad gave led him to a massacre. What's the connection with Felix—"

"Wait!" Tobias stills. "Remember the gala?"

"Yeah. What about it?"

"Remember when we were in the closet?"

"Of course, I remember that." That was when he first kissed me. I feel my cheeks starting to warm.

"Not that part." Tobias chuckles, the sound making me smile. It's a sound I will never grow tired of. But now is not the time for these thoughts.

"Which part?"

"The commotion. The fighting. That was Felix and Fitzpatrick."

"There's a connection between the two?"

"It was pretty heated, so I'd have to say yes."

"What were they fighting about?"

"The attorney general wanted Felix gone."

"What else happened?"

"Felix bitched about the contribution. That Fitzpatrick didn't care that it was dirty money when it got him the attorney general position."

"Interesting." I close my eyes, trying to connect the pieces of the puzzle. "Do you think Felix—" My mouth opens.

"What?"

"I just had a thought. It might be nothing."

"Or it might be everything." Tobias's brow raises.

"Give me that." I point to the printouts of the files Jaxson provided for us. They are from the zip drive I downloaded from Felix's computer.

Tobias jumps up from the bed, moves to the table in the corner to the makeshift office we've made to look at files, and tosses it to me. Then I'm settling into all the documents, desperately trying to find the connection that will bury him.

An hour passes before it hits me. I'm looking at this from the wrong angle.

"I think I know what we need to be looking for," I tell him.

"Really? What?"

"Okay. So recently, Felix wanted me to find a loophole so he could build on a property he owns."

"I'm not following."

"When I was working for Felix, he asked me to look, he implied if I couldn't find something legal, he would find another means to get the land and build on it."

"Okay."

"Which makes me think maybe he's done this before. Maybe in the past, he's done shady things to get land. What if... What if Fitzpatrick is tied to another property? What if this is over property Felix owns in Reddington?"

Tobias throws a file to me, and I look down at it. "What is this?"

"I don't know. It looks like a list of some sort."

"Interesting. Let's see what it says."

Together, we look over the list to decipher its meaning. There are a few names on the list. The next page has lists of court cases. Fitzpatrick's name is all over it.

Tobias looks over the page. "It looks like someone threw out a case and tried another one . . . over land."

"Do you think this is the proof?

"It's hard to say." He is staring off into space. "But I think we are on to something."

I lean back in my chair and toss my pencil on the table.

"I found it!" I scream a moment later.

"What is it?"

"Look."

"Fitzpatrick had the original owner, a man by the name of Michael Laundry, arrested and tried for embezzlement. When the land went up for auction, Felix scooped it up. I wouldn't put it past them if the case was bogus and completely fabricated."

"We got him. That's the connection. Felix couldn't get the land without Fitzpatrick, but Fitzpatrick couldn't clean up the city without Felix. He leverages that arrangement straight to the New York Attorney General's office and then straight to the top."

"Holy shit!"

"What?"

"Look at this." Tobias passes me another folder. "It seems Felix kept evidence. Lots and lots of evidence."

My fingers flip through pages, transcripts of phone calls. Screen shots of texts. It's everything.

"He was probably blackmailing him."

I'm still in shock. "We got him."

I knew the encrypted files had to be important, but this is more than I expected

"We do."

"Now what?" I ask.

"We need to come up with a plan. It's not enough for us to know. We need to take him down."

CHAPTER FIFTY-FIVE

Skye

DESPITE HOW HARD I TRY, I CAN'T HELP BUT FEEL NERVOUS. I know I will be safe here, but I can't help but feel that something might go wrong. What if I never have a chance to confront him? What if the computer doesn't work? What if Jaxson didn't set up the feed right?

It might be over the top to have all the evidence we've gathered playing during this celebration of the attorney general's accomplishments, but Tobias thought this would hit him where it hurts the most.

His ego.

To me, it feels like my heart will burst out of my chest.

This isn't like the last gala I attended. Yes, I'm dressed to the nines, wearing a long purple dress with a slit up the side that exposes my leg, my hair is done up, and long diamond earrings dangle down my neck. But this time, instead of searching for the person who killed my family, I'm about to take him down.

Tonight, the party is being held in a grand ballroom with a beautiful chandelier. It has floor-to-ceiling windows that look out into the city. It should take my breath away, and it usually does, but tonight, I can't breathe enough to enjoy the sweeping views.

People are everywhere, some on the dance floor and some at tables. My gaze moves throughout the space, looking for my target. He's standing at the far wall, talking to a group of people. Attorney General Fitzpatrick.

Walking into the crowded room, I head in his direction. As I walk, my skin pricks with awareness. My eyes dart around to find Tobias, and when I do, I almost falter. Our gazes lock. He looks at me so intently. The blue of his irises is not visible from this distance, but still, it would be easy to get lost in them.

He nods his head, a silent sign that he is here. Yet again, he's making sure I'm okay. I nod back and continue toward the devil himself.

Making my approach, the attorney general sees me. He's quick to smile and hold out his hand. Every part of me screams to pull away, but another part of me doesn't want to give any hints. I want to see this bastard's face as I serve the damning blow. So, I extend my hand and shake his, squeezing as hard as I can.

He eyes my hand curiously, pulling out of my death grip.

"How are you, Skye? I can't imagine how hard it is to be here tonight after just losing your father."

Inhale. Exhale.

"I'm okay," I say with a fake smile. "It is very hard."

"He was far too young to die," he says in a concerned tone, shaking his head as though he gives a damn.

"Yes. He was. But there is one thing that came out of this . . ." I lead, and his forehead scrunches. "There is nothing like a dying man's confession." His face freezes at my words. "When you have nothing left, you want to absolve yourself of sin. Do you have anything to absolve?"

Fitzpatrick's face turns a dark and angry shade of red. "This is highly unprofessional, dear."

"I am not your *dear*. But now it's your turn to pay." I narrow my eyes and glare at him.

"I don't know what you are going on about, but if you will excuse me—"

He's about to step away when the monitors set up around the space turn on, all the evidence of his treachery and bribery playing for everyone to see. Then pandemonium erupts. Police enter the building and surround him. He tries to step back, but there is no place to go.

His head snaps to me. "You ungrateful little bitch. Everything you have is because of me."

"No, everything I have is despite you. You will die in prison when I'm done with you."

He lunges for me, but an officer storms him, pinning him against the wall.

"You are under arrest for the murder of Tobias Baros, Matthew and Stacey Gilbert—" One of the officers starts to run down the list of everyone in Al's that day.

And another one steps up with handcuffs in his hand. "Please come with us," he orders.

"I will have your badge." I watch as Fitzpatrick turns to another officer. "This is all a misunderstanding."

No one listens, and as he's pulled back, his screams become more desperate and more pleading.

When the police officers shuffle him away, familiar arms wrap around my stomach. The smell of his cologne infiltrates my senses.

"Time to go." His words tickle my neck.

"Where?" I ask.

"Anywhere. As long as I'm with you."

CHAPTER FIFTY-SIX

Skye

THE FIRST PLACE WE GO IS HOME. NOT TO TOBIAS'S HOUSE but to Reddington. To my father's grave. A few days have passed since the gala and since Fitzpatrick was arrested, and the world knows what he did to rise so high. His political aspirations are now dead.

He's going to jail for a very long time.

Hand in hand, we're here to say our goodbyes. To tell my father how we did right by him, how he will be proud.

Standing in front of my father's grave, Tobias drops my hand and steps up. He speaks for a while, but I don't hear the words. All I hear is his promise to always take care of me.

From where I'm standing, I see the way he looks up at the sky as he talks, and seeing that move makes my heart fill with so much love. He's found peace in the sky, and I hope I can give him the same.

When he's done, he moves closer to me, places a kiss on my lips, and then steps away to give me my space.

It's my time now. But I'm not ready to say goodbye. My throat burns from the sobs lodged inside me. A raw, primitive grief works its way through me as my teeth chatter. Closing my eyes, I will myself to remember the good times, and I do. They come back to me with laughter and smiles, and most of all, love.

I can see him grin at me when I would get an answer right. His eyes when he was proud. I can smell the jam in the air when he made the snack that my mom used to make for me when I was sad.

Tears roll down my cheeks. Swiping them away, I take a deep breath, and then I kiss my finger and place it on the tombstone. "I have so much to tell you. I hope you aren't angry, but I stole your files." I can't help but laugh because I know him, and he wouldn't be mad. He would tell me how proud he was of me. How smart I was to put everything together. "I figured it out. Tobias and I got them. We got them. I just want you to know I don't blame you. I never did. I know you felt it was your fault, but it wasn't. It was never your fault. Thank you for taking me in. I love you for giving me the love I needed, always."

After we say our goodbyes, we walk over to another set of graves. The ones I always visit because it brings me peace to be here.

"I love you, Mom. I love you, Dad," I whisper to the tombstones. More tears flow down my cheeks as I kneel to touch the cold surface. "I want you to meet someone very important to me. Mom, Dad, this is Tobias. He was with me that day. The day you left, he saved me." I continue to tell them everything, and then when I have no more words in my lungs, I stand.

Tobias is next to me, and his one arm wraps around my waist. Together, we walk into the future, leaving the past behind us.

Ready to live and love forever.

EPILOGUE

Skye
Two years later . . .

TURNS OUT, PUSHING A NINE-POUND HUMAN BEING OUT OF your body is not pleasant. My hand reaches out blindly, searching for my husband's.

Tobias latches onto it, lacing our fingers together.

"I need a distraction." I'm practically begging.

I turn away from the team of doctors and nurses, giving Tobias my full attention. It helps. As soon as our eyes lock, the idea that I am about to have another piece of the man I love—that our child will look like him, act like him (God, help me), and sound like him—hits me.

Adrenaline rushes through me.

And the drugs.

Which, in hindsight, is my husband's most brilliant idea to date.

I love the drugs.

If I weren't already married, I'd have proposed to the anesthesiologist.

Who am I kidding? I did.

Tobias snarled at the poor man and reminded me it was his idea.

Leave it to the drug dealer to suggest drugs.

I thank the epidural gods and squeeze Tobias's hand, repeating, "I need a distraction!"

"I never jerked off in the bathroom after I got off the elevator." He says it so casually, I almost miss the meaning.

But then it slams into me, and my cheeks turn a bright shade of pink. Around us, the doctors and nurses are stunned silent. I'm about to yell at my husband when I feel it.

The last push. And I hear the most beautiful sound. Our son.

Tobias
Three more years later. . .

We don't come to Reddington often, but when we do, there is one place we always go. It's the one place most people would think we wouldn't go, but it's important to us to make peace with what happened all those years ago and make new memories.

It looks exactly the same all these years later. Still decorated in 1950s style with black-and-white-checkered floors and blue leather booths. Al's Diner. The smell of chocolate infiltrates the air.

It used to make me sad to come here. It used to break Skye as well, but now, as we sit at the booth with the cold, refreshing taste of the milkshake in front of us, all feels right in the world.

The taste of the sweet concoction is enough to make me smile every time we come, but it's my son's laughter as he wipes whipped cream off his nose that makes my heart soar.

Across the table, Skye holds Mason.

I never thought I could love anyone as much as I love Skye, but then she gave me a son. He is everything right in this world.

Life hasn't been simple since the day we took down the people who killed our family. Walking away from my business wasn't as easy as I thought, but it was worth it. Every hardship we went through was worth it to get to this place. Gideon took over and he's been ruling with an iron fist. As for Fitzpatrick . . .

He got what he deserved.

He was found guilty. He was sentenced to life in prison with no possibility of parole.

Good fucking riddance.

After the gala and after we said goodbye to Skye's family, we went to Miami and said goodbye to mine.

I proposed on the roof of our home.

Yes, the moment we got back from Miami, I forced Skye to move it with me, and since that day, she has never left my side.

Then I made her marry me.

Again, in our house.

And the honeymoon, well, let's just say the tree house got round two.

As for the days, well, she's still my attorney, but now she only works for me, and let me tell you, I keep her too busy to object.

Now legitimate, my empire has grown even more. But instead of drugs, I have expanded my real estate portfolio. Building high-rise apartment buildings is what keeps me busy these days.

But the most important thing in my life is my family.

From across the table, I watch them while they drink from their milkshakes. She tells our son funny stories.

He loves everything that she says. Right now, she's talking about planes. At three years old, he dreams of building planes and flying them.

That's our favorite thing to do together: make them from paper and watch them take off. After leaving here, we will go to the park next door and do just that.

Sometimes, I wonder if I'm dreaming, or maybe I died here all those years ago.

Maybe I was the one who was shot, and Skye was just the angel sent down to show me the way. A man like me doesn't deserve this life. Or, at least, that's what I felt like for a long time. Day by day, Skye has helped me see that everyone deserves a second chance. It took me a long time to agree, but then, like she always does, she made me see it.

That despite my sins, I'm worthy of happiness.

Mason and Skye are my second chance. This time, I'll do it right.

"I think we should get milkshakes tomorrow, Daddy," Mason says as they finish their milkshake. I can't help but laugh. If it were up to him, he'd get one every day. My son. A son who will not live in the darkness as I had to. A son who will only be touched by light.

"I have to agree. We should get milkshakes every day." Skye laughs, and I lift my brow.

"Really?"

"Yep . . . I have that craving."

I place my cup down and cock my head. "You have a craving?"

Her lips spread into a giant smile, the same smile she gave me four years ago when she told me she was pregnant.

"Are you sure?" My heart thumps in my chest as I wait for her to answer.

"Yeah."

"Sure, about what, Mommy?" Mason asks.

"That you're going to be a big brother." Skye's eyes are filled with tears.

Standing, I grab my wife in my arms.

"Thank you," I whisper against her lips.

"For what?"

"For giving me a family. For giving me a home. For being my past and my future."

ACKNOWLEDGMENTS

I want to thank my entire family. I love you all so much.

THANK YOU to my husband. Thanks for cooking dinner while I was in the cave!

Thank you to my kids. I love you guys!

Thank you to the amazing professionals that helped with Broken Reign.

Suzi Vanderham

Jenny Sims

Marla Esposito

Jaime Ryter

Champagne Formats

Hang Le

Jill Glass

Kelly Allenby

Grey's Promotions

Thank you to Jacob Morgan, Savannah Peachwood, Sebastian York, Kim Gilmour, and Lyric for bringing Broken Reign to life on audio.

Thank you to Kimberly Whalen.

Thank you to my AMAZING ARC TEAM! You guys rock!

Thank you to my beta/test team.

Special thanks to Libra and Not Gemma for always being there for me.

I want to thank ALL my friends for putting up with me while I wrote this book. Thank you!

To the ladies in the Ava Harrison Support Group, I couldn't have done this without your support!

Please consider joining my Facebook reader group, Ava Harrison Support Group

Thanks to all the bloggers! Thanks for your excitement and love of books!

Last but certainly not least . . .

Thank you to the readers!

Thank you so much for taking this journey with me.

CPSIA information can be obtained
at www.ICGtesting.com
Printed in the USA
LVHW042230090522
718327LV00027B/550